Dear Claire,
Never stop wishing
on stars! Big l
Amelia

EverWish

By Amelia Oz

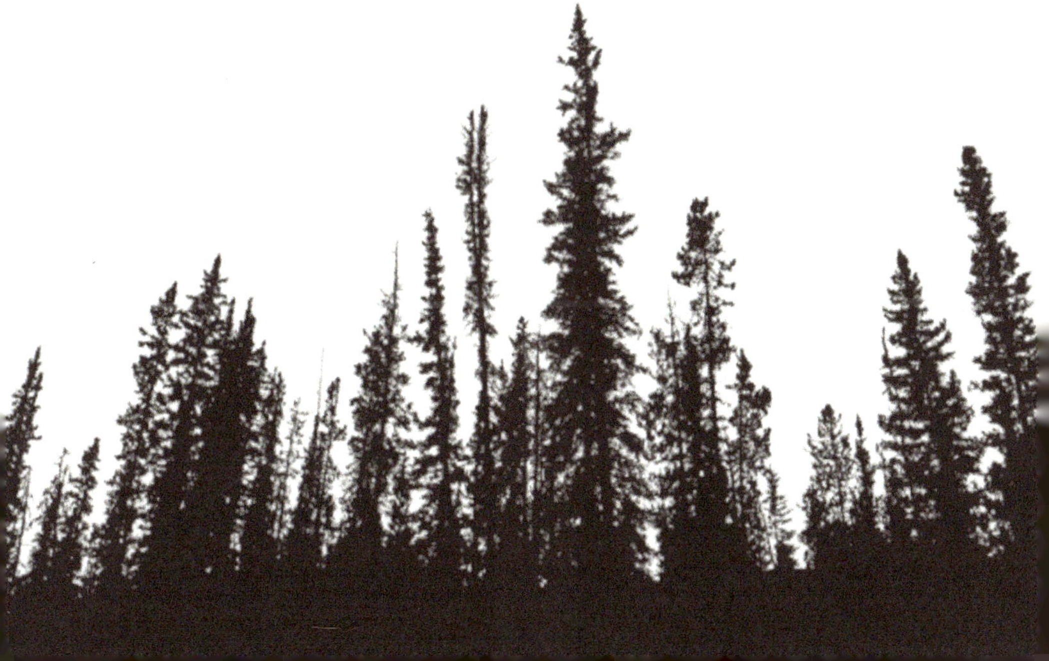

Amazon Edition
First Edition 2020
Published in United States of America

ISBN print book: 978-1-7353940-2-2
ISBN ebook: 978-1-7353940-1-5

Cover & Interior design by: Platform House Publishing
Utkamandarinka/Adobe Images
Zacarias da Mata/Adobe Images
Edited by Rebecca Carpenter

For my husband, who is my wish granted.

For my son, who knows love infinity.

"I want to die while you love me,
While yet you hold me fair,
While laughter lies upon my lips
And lights are in my hair.

I want to die while you love me
And bear to that still bed
Your kisses turbulent, unspent
To warm me when I'm dead..."

Georgia Douglas Johnson

Table of Contents

Prologue
Birthdays

Vivian

Dying on my twentieth birthday was not something I planned to do. Not when there was so much to live for, here in this car. My wrist trembled, making it difficult for him to cut through the medical band with the tiny manicure scissors he'd acquired from the nurse's station.

The baby made tiny snuffling sounds. Could she sense my terror? The books we'd read together mentioned how babies felt their mother's emotions. Maybe that had only been true when she'd been curled beneath my ribs. Had that only been yesterday? He captured my hand gently and made quick work of his task. We needed to hurry.

"Maybe she's hungry?" my husband asked softly. The dark corners of the parking lot surrounding us were quiet, the hospital on the hill above us still but for a man hobbling towards its emergency room doors. It wasn't safe here.

"Anything?" I asked again.

He checked his phone and shook his head.

"No. It'll come soon."

How could he be so calm? But I knew the answer. He was calm because I was not. The rock to my storm.

Lasho's dark eyes shone as he stroked the curve of Stella's head with a tentative fingertip. "Do you think she'll grow hair? It will probably be like yours." Behind this was another question. My own "gifts" hadn't appeared until six years old. His voice shifted to a husky whisper as he leaned close to our daughter. "You're going to be brave and fierce like your Mamma." Her soft sounds quieted.

"She knows your voice," I murmured, swallowing past the lump in my throat. He flashed me a shy grin and his eyes were so full of love it was almost enough to distract from the terrible choice we were making. I'd ruined his life.

"I would do it all again. No matter what," he said, reading my mind as if it were his own. His words cut deep, undeserved as they were, but I smiled to reassure him. He looked so young, so exhausted.

"Let's go. I'll feed her as you drive," I urged, my soul bleeding. She looked too tiny for the newborn car seat Lasho had installed in the backseat—and I selfishly couldn't let go of her. His fingers threaded through my hair and cupped the back of my head, drawing me close until our lips touched.

"We agreed to wait for the signal. We can trust him. They'll protect us."

I nodded but inside I screamed *hurry, hurry*. He snapped my seatbelt in place just as the soft chime of a text message filled the car. He scanned the screen, winked and started the engine.

Lasho navigated the car to the road and when no one came running from the hospital I released a pent-up breath. It was two in the morning on a weeknight, which meant the highway was mostly quiet but for the big trucks carrying goods through California. As the baby settled against me, I stared through the window at the dark evergreen trees and big leaf maples, their orange and gold hues subdued in the moonlight. Their shapes whipped past, and I strained to see some sign of our protectors.

A mysterious pattern of shadows emerged, a racing form that kept pace with the car. I blinked, my heart stuttering and then thudding hard. The apparition was dense, weaving several yards behind the tree line, dipping to the shoulder of the road in taunting swoops before skimming between the blurring branches. A face formed within those shadows, its eyes ghastly, hungry and locked on mine, while its body remained a thick mass of streaming grey matter. Black lips formed into a mocking, nightmarish grin.

"Drive faster." My voice, hoarse and low, conveyed everything important. The engine roared and we leapt forward. The wraith matched our speed as the moon trailed from above. Lasho shifted gears and the scent of something burning drifted through the vents.

"Go faster. Please." My lips pressed the tender flesh of our daughter's forehead. I wished she'd waited a little longer to be born. I wished for her to be courageous and to be loved and to live a very long life. I wished we'd known about the curse much sooner. I wanted a lot of things. The wraith grew in size as another form merged with it so that it blanketed the side of the car. I turned from it, staring at the dark ribbon of road ahead.

"Should I stop?" I shook my head, too weak from her birth to help him make a stand.

We reached the top of a hill and the lights of a truck appeared in our lane approaching from the opposite direction. His arm crossed my body protectively as the massive shadow suddenly covered the windshield, blocking our view of the danger ahead. A scream ripped from my already raw throat, a denial from the deepest recesses of my soul. "No!" I clutched my little family, the three of us one for a last moment before there were no more moments left.

Chapter 1
The Tower

Stella

"**S**top wasting time and just *jump*!" my cousin shouted over the waterfall's roar.

I glared at Silvan, who posed bare chested at a much safer distance from the cliff's edge. He leaned against the mossy rock wall, watchful as I smoothed my damp hair into a haphazard topknot. His poetic good looks, with tanned features and tousled brown curls to his shoulders, were a bold-faced lie. Right now, he was evil as fuck.

"You could just lose the dare," he suggested with a sneer. "Maybe you really *want* an eighteenth birthday party. Balloons at the Portland Beer Garden and all the Vano boys asking you to dance."

I finished securing my hair and flipped him off. He wanted me to beg off or negotiate, so I kept my mouth shut. Although at least a foot shorter than my cousin, I was also a year older, which should have entitled me to a little more respect. He leaned towards me. *Tsk-tsk*. I fought dirty when cornered, a fact he seemed to remember when he paused mid-step.

"Steellaa! Nooo…". I peered over the edge and located Amanda along the opposite side of the river. My best friend hopped and waved as a growing group of men with backpacks surrounded her. I bit my lip. We'd left her alone—but to be fair we usually never saw others this far off the trails.

"She's gonna kill you," Silvan noted with interest, leaning back once more.

"She'll kill you first when I tell her you dared me." I taunted, breaking my silence.

The dare *had* been Silvan's idea, but the race to the top of the cliff had been all mine. We'd left her pulling up plants and mumbling to herself about blah, blah herb collecting blah, blah Oregon soil blah, blah when we'd sneaked away. The water below cast an iridescent shimmer and I dragged in a deep breath of pine and rain scented air.

"Hey, does this remind you of that thing you were painting with two people falling off a cliff?" I rolled my eyes at his description of the Tower card. The Major Arcana tarot card was often positive—symbolic of change and adventure—definitely not a harbinger of death. At least I didn't think so. Could death be considered an adventure?

"Bok, bok," teased Silvan. I glared and he threw his palms up with a laugh. "Okay! I take back the dare. I won't suggest a birthday party to Baba—and I don't have to play Fortnite with you. You trash talk and you're a terrible team player." Geez. I'd shot his avatar in the face once, and it had been an accident. Sort of.

"Besides, I knew you wouldn't jump sixty feet. There's a reason they call this the Devil's Prayer—and that water is spring-fed." Allowing Silvan to gain the upper hand would be...galling. *Never show weakness.* The world drinks the tears of the weak. I tucked my white t-shirt into black yoga shorts.

"Game marathon this weekend, snacks on you—and no crying."

His smirk collapsed into a cautious frown just before I launched myself off the ledge. The fall was both endless and swift. A quick slice through the surface and then the world became a violent vortex of bubbles. Small stones shifted beneath my feet before I launched upwards, the waterfall's pounding spray masking my squeals of victory. Breathless, I kicked backward but there was no sign of Silvan above.

Amanda waited on the riverbank with a faded beach towel draped over folded arms. I dogpaddled slowly towards her, taking my time. When my palms scraped bottom, I looked up and grinned, flashing my signature dimples. Her face remained stony. *Oh boy.* The hike back to the car was going to be very, very long. I sighed and rose to pick my way over slippery stones to where she stood on a flat rock, her own sneakers submerged to their laces. Amanda often tried to overcompensate for my motherless state—something I didn't need.

"Did you see Sil push me?" I asked between chattering teeth. She exploded.

"Don't even start with me, Stella! I *saw* you leap off that ledge! When are you going to *stop* being so impulsive? That was easily a six-story drop and there could have been downed trees beneath the water..." Her voice ended in a low hiss, as she darted a glance at our audience. The strangers were speaking to one another in hushed tones, and Amanda returned her attention to me.

Now that we were within arm's reach, I noticed her sweaty and pale face, her ponytail half undone. A true beauty, with dark brown hair and hazel-green eyes, she resembled her hero, Audrey Hepburn. She gripped the towel with white knuckled fists. My smile dissolved. Amanda was not someone who flustered easily.

"Hey, I'm sorry. I didn't mean to scare you this much. Really—I'm fine. We checked the depth first and everything," I lied. That actually would have been a good idea. Her lips trembled as her gaze slipped over her shoulder. She stepped close and leaned towards my ear.

"Do you trust me, Stella?"

"Yes." It was true. I'd known her since we were seven years old, more like sisters than the only children we were.

"Go back into the water until these men leave."

What? I looked down at my sleeveless t-shirt. Sports bra firmly in place, no boobs visible. I scanned the guys behind her.

"Don't look!" She dug her short nails into my forearm. I yelped and rubbed the tender spot.

"This water is glacial," I protested with a shiver.

"I'll explain later. Just keep standing in the water. Please!" Her imploring expression bordered on desperate. Amanda was the most rational person I knew. She was responsible, helping her mom run a successful mystical shop that sold things like crystals and incense for spiritual seekers and yoga moms. She was not a drama queen. I frowned.

"Scarlet."

She said it. The word we'd made up stories about. The word we agreed meant that a serial killer was behind the door or an earthquake was about to swallow us if we didn't *run* right that second. With rounded eyes, she mouthed it once more as I stared in disbelief.

Scarlet.

I stepped backwards until my ankles submerged in the clear current. My elastic band had snapped in the fall, leaving me with a heavy mass of dripping hair down my back. A sudden breeze rustled the treetops and raised gooseflesh upon my chilled skin.

Her brow furrowed as her hand twisted the necklace at her throat.

"Whatever you do, don't leave the water," she warned. I snapped my teeth together, throwing up my hands. She acknowledged my compliance with a slight nod.

"Why can't she leave the water?" asked a deep voice.

Amanda's face flashed alabaster-pale as I leaned sideways to better see the stranger who spoke. The ends of his russet hair shone gold in the sunlight, and with his gunmetal eyes he would have been classically handsome had his face not been marred by a scar over his left eyebrow. His clothes were too new and expensive for a local, seasoned outdoorsman. Too aw-shucks ma'am looking to be a rapist-murderer— although that might just make him a successful one.

Amanda floundered, her lips parting a few times without sound. I cut in, my natural sarcasm taking over. "We're doing an experiment on hypothermia."

He smiled ruefully and gave me a once over. Few people ventured this deeply into the forest outside of deer season, as there were only ancient, overgrown wagon trails and most people preferred the neater, public park trails. The other men in the clearing remained silent, their unsmiling faces fixed on me. The man with a scar studied the tree line of subalpine firs on the opposite shore. I squeezed the ends of my wet t-shirt, tugging it away from my skin.

"That jump was very impressive."

"Thanks." At least *someone* appreciated my bad-assery. Amanda's slender nostrils flared, and my smirk faded. *Scarlet.* He shrugged and turned away, only to return with a wagging finger.

"It's just that…I've never seen anyone fall so slowly before. You drifted down like a snowflake. Maybe because you're so small…" He trailed off as his eyes scanned my wet legs.

Amanda jerked towards him, flinging the towel over her shoulder. "Haven't you heard of Galileo? The acceleration and velocity of objects falling near the earth's surface fall with the same speed—9.8 meters per second squared. Petite or not, she fell at a normal rate." Amanda, ever the science nerd, tended to spew random facts when she was nervous. The guy was a serious crackhead, though. No one fell "slowly" without hitting something on the way down or a parachute attached. Maybe she'd said the safe word because she'd seen them do drugs? Still didn't fit. The safe word was the equivalent of a house on fire.

I forced a laugh and gave the stranger a wink. "It felt like only seconds to me."

"Right. Hey, what's wrong with me? Two girls alone, so far off the main trails—we must be making you nervous." My arms crossed but Amanda made a warning grunt before I could snark back at the arrogance of his question.

"You're shaking. Would you like my jacket?" He unzipped the fabric, revealing a taut physique—and a handgun nestled in a shoulder harness. His bashful smile never wavered. *I'm just a harmless fella with a Glock.*

Orphaned since my first week of life, my maternal, overprotective grandfather had raised me to respect "stranger danger" and the importance of self-defense. That included teaching me about guns and making sure I could handle them with confidence. This was the Pacific Northwest after all, an area the FBI nicknamed the "killing fields" for a reason. Bodies were easy to hide and evidence quick to decompose in the moist climate of the Cascade and Olympic Mountain ranges.

"That's a decent weapon." It wasn't completely irrational that someone afraid of apex predators would bring a gun through denser, more isolated areas of these forests. The thing was, most bear and cougar hunters would've packed rifles, not pistols. Not unless they wanted to become a meal.

The stranger's smile was friendly as he ignored my comment and shrugged out of his jacket. When he held it out to me, I noticed he stayed well back from the water's edge. I would have to step out of the water to accept the jacket.

Amanda said nothing, her gaze burning so effectively into my forehead that I rubbed the space between my eyes. Although my ankles and feet were numb, I shook my head.

He drew a hand across his brow and his smile faded. A tattoo of twisting roses and vines encircled his thumb, the ink so vivid it appeared alive.

"It's cool here in the mountain's shadow and that water must be freezing. Wouldn't you rather come out and dry off?"

"Nope. I'm-I'm-all-g-g-good-here."

"Suit yourself. What are your names? My name is Marcus."

Amanda turned and pressed me further into the water. With wind-milling arms, I splashed backward until the water flowed around my knees. The current grew stronger, and I ground my feet into the rock-strewn bottom to keep my balance. Why was she doing this? It wasn't like the men couldn't jump in after us if they wanted to.

With a huff of air, Amanda twisted back to Marcus.

"Just *go*." There was a resonance to her voice that she rarely used. One of the men turned towards the forest before his companion stopped him. The back of my tongue suddenly tasted of sea salt. Was that a symptom of hypothermia?

"Your ink is...*interesting*," he said, ignoring her order.

I knew that he meant the small tattoo on the inside of Amanda's wrist. She'd gotten it with her parents to celebrate her own eighteenth birthday in April. The color was a gorgeous azure blue she'd said was made from rare beetles. The tattoo itself represented the element of water, matching her mother's.

Marcus straightened. His face seemed more angular, his mouth and eyes hard.

"My, my. Aren't you the brave little snack?" The corner of his lip curled. Amanda remained silent and his focus returned to me.

"Come closer," he commanded. The taste of wood ash exploded

across my tongue, making me splutter. It tasted of evening campfires and wildfire residue.

"Stay," Amanda said harshly over her shoulder. The wood ash flavor instantly faded, mingled with the sudden briny taste of saltwater. Alarmed, I tried to touch my lips but my arms and legs refused to cooperate. I tried again to speak, yet my tongue felt too heavy, my lips disobedient. Marcus moved down the bank, giving him an unobstructed view of me. A tattooed thumb rose to rub his bottom lip. "Tell me your name."

My lips parted to tell him to go to hell. I tried again and again, yet my mouth refused to shape words. My vocal cords failed. Thankfully, I *could* control my breathing and inhaled slow and deep. *Stay calm, stay calm, think...*

"Hey! It looks like a party! Amanda, did you see Stella jump?" Silvan yelled as he jogged out of the woods. I struggled harder.

Marcus' companions shifted and formed a semi-circle around their leader, but Silvan charged forward, oblivious. My eyes widened in warning, but Silvan had his sights on Amanda as he paused at the water's edge. Amanda crooked her finger and Silvan stepped towards her with a lopsided grin, wincing as ice water filled his sneakers. Within range, Amanda struck, pinching the skin over his flat stomach. He yelped and danced back in confusion, but she grabbed his wrist, pulling him close to her.

"Ow! Why'd you do that? What'd I miss?" He rubbed his belly with a hurt frown. The men laughed and my vision went red.

I growled in frustration, furious. No one assaulted Silvan but me. I *willed* myself to move and after a long moment my arms became unstuck from their rigid pose. Pushing past the lethargic sensation, I drew in another breath, feeling control return with each inhalation.

"*Damn* it," I shouted, relieved that I had command over my voice again. The weighted sensation dissipated. A swift breeze kicked up, causing water to lap the shore.

"Stella! What a beautiful name. And what unusual eyes you have, Stella," he mused aloud. His gaze roamed my bare arms and hands as he frowned in confusion. "What clan do you belong to?" he asked. Amanda cleared her throat.

"It's so important to make sure people have the right *permissions* to avoid misunderstandings. Consequences can be so painful," she said in a steel-edged voice.

Amanda had lost her mind. Was she worried about them having proper hunting permits now? Hadn't she noticed my paralyzed state? Marcus rotated his palm in a sharp gesture. The other three men moved to line the shoreline with military synchronization. One of them was missing a hand.

Marcus grinned. "There would have to be witnesses—"

A violent boom rent the air and the world pitched. The ground shook with a powerful vibration that echoed around the river. I shot forward just as Amanda splashed deeper into the water, pulling both Silvan and me to her with surprising strength. The strangers, however, all looked in the same direction—to a spot located deep in the woods to the right of our little clearing.

It was eerie how they all stood at rapt attention. Like prairie dogs I'd seen at the zoo once. The tremendous blast still ricocheted. Hundreds of miles of nothing but sequoia and evergreen trees surrounded us, absorbing the sound. Marcus focused sharply on me as I struggled to pull from Amanda's grasping hands.

"Who *are* you?" he spat.

"No one," I whispered. I rubbed at my chest as a strange warmth buzzed at my center, tingling along my spine.

"The Lion roars," one of the men said in a voice that clearly conveyed, *Oh shit*. I followed their line of vision to the solitary figure of a man at the edge of the forest.

He was tall, with muscular shoulders and arms that narrowed into lean hips. Larger than the other men, he flexed his long fingers yet remained preternaturally still. Dark sable hair framed a face any artist would pay to paint, myself included. The perfect angles of his face framed eyes so dark they could be black. I trembled, my limbs shaking uncontrollably. A deep growl split the air, and Amanda dropped my arm abruptly, stepping away from me. So much for one-for-all.

I was suddenly glad for the chilled water encasing my calves. My skin heated as I continued to stare at the newcomer. There was something familiar in the way he stood...Pain shot through my temple, and I gasped, touching my head. Between blinks, the stranger was across the clearing. The world tilted as he plucked me from the water and carried me to the dry bank. The sharp pain faded as quickly as it had arrived, enough that I noted the man who cradled me wore a soft grey t-shirt and dark jeans. Dumbly, I noticed the cotton darken as it wicked water from my drenched clothing and skin.

When he brought us to a standstill, his face turned to mine—and any protest gathering in my throat died as I took him in. Inches apart, his tiger-like eyes were not black after all, but swirls of cognac brown and gold, framed by thick, sooty eyelashes. His nose was aquiline, and his lips had the most exquisitely shaped cupid's bow.

Dear Lord. He was big, with muscles that resembled stone, hard and unyielding where my hands grasped his back and shoulder. Self-awareness flooded, and I released him to fold my arms awkwardly against my chest.

The world went from silent to bursting with sound in a second. Amanda was speaking, and I heard Silvan protest the stranger picking me up, but neither of us paid them any notice. Emotion swirled beneath his beauty, a pained contradiction behind his eyes that only made his perfection more poignant.

"Your lips...," he murmured. My brain stuttered and blanked. He was staring at my mouth. "...your lips are blue." *Huh?* His gaze, stormy and bottomless, swallowed mine.

"Where do you think you're going?" He hitched me higher in his arms as if I weighed nothing.

"Hmm? Nowhere." My voice came out a croak and my cheeks warmed. His lips twitched before his gaze tore from mine to where Marcus and his friends were skulking from the clearing. Nearly to the edge of the trail that headed upland, all four froze in various poses of flight when the stranger directed his attention to them.

"Did they touch you?" His gaze remained upon the other men. He seemed otherworldly in his physical beauty, making the heavy sense of brutality and power he exuded even more potent. Thick, shiny locks swept from his forehead, and I drifted closer to his jaw. He even smelled amazing. Like sandalwood, frankincense and mint mixed with something elusive.

His face tilted towards mine and he raised an eyebrow. I swallowed hard. *Oh.*

"N-no. No t-touching." He scanned my body, lingering over my collarbone, and bare arms. My cheeks burned, and his hands seared into me as hot as branding irons against my chilled flesh. I scowled and a corner of his lips curled slightly before his scrutiny shifted to Amanda and Silvan. Amanda stared at the ground; hands clasped tightly before her. Her meek silence was unsettling. The stranger gave a single nod and the men disappeared down the trailhead.

"How far is it to your car?" Even his voice was mesmerizing. It was what I imagined whiskey would taste like. Dark and forbidden...*Seriously pull it together idiot.* I struggled half-heartedly and cleared my throat. He released my legs but kept one strong arm across my back as I slid to a standing position. He leaned forward, and I could have sworn something brushed the curve of my neck as my feet met the ground. I felt his deep inhalation near my skin and shivered when he exhaled, his breath warm across my skin. I stumbled and his arm returned, tightened.

"Wow," I mumbled. The stranger arched a brow, and I flushed, looking down at my wet shoes in mortification.

"Where is your vehicle?" he repeated in a harder tone, and Amanda's head whipped up.

"Not far. We have to walk that way about two miles." She pointed down the mountain trail, directly opposite from the path Marcus and his friends had taken.

Shaking his head, he contemplated me once more.

"Farewell, *petite etoile*." The heat of his gaze caused my breath to shallow and my legs weaken. *Stop looking at him. Stop looking at him. Oh gosh, stop looking at him.* He blinked, and a shadow of a frown crossed his features. Why was he frowning?

He glanced back at Amanda. "Can I trust you to get her home?" he asked, his tone frigid. Amanda nodded. Before I could take offence at his assumption that I needed a babysitter, he turned and strode back to the tree line where he'd come from. Silvan grabbed my shoulders. "Whoa, Stella! Your eyes!"

"My eyes?" I rubbed them with the back of my hands. Shaking Silvan off, I walked to the trailhead and searched fruitlessly for movement within the evergreen fronds that grew around the great Sitka spruce trees and nurse logs. He'd vanished. Dense clusters of tree trunks stood with moss-covered branches amidst a lush carpet of sword ferns. No movement. No sound. Not even birdsong.

"Your irises are like—shining. What's wrong with you?" Silvan asked next to me. I looked away and touched my eyelids, confused.

"No offense, but you can be one of the meanest girls I know, Stella."

"Stop with the sweet talk, already," I muttered.

"I just meant that, if I tried to pick you up like that, I'd wish I were dead in three seconds," Silvan said in amazement. "You don't know that guy, do—"

"We need to get out of here," Amanda interrupted in a shaky voice.

"What the hell happened, Amanda? I couldn't move and you said the safe…" My eyes widened in shock when her hand slapped across my lips. The rage I felt must have shown in my eyes because she whipped her hand back.

"Shh!" she pleaded. "Stella, everything has changed. I hope you'll forgive me one day. No talking or freaking out until we're in the car, preferably with the locks engaged." I stared at her until Silvan groused about having to walk home in the dark if we didn't get a move on.

As we descended the mountain, my mind raced in furious cycles. Amanda's stricken face when she'd said our sacred safe word, the lingering taste of ash that still coated my tongue, the stranger who felt like gravity and his burning eyes as he'd called me *little star*. Most of all, I wondered what Amanda needed forgiveness for.

Chapter 2
The Sword

Alaric

It had taken all of my formidable willpower to leave her. I prowled into the hotel, but then stomped back out, needing to walk the night-kissed streets and work off the frustration reverberating through my bones.

The young woman I'd been tasked to protect at all costs haunted me. Her lovely face was heart shaped, with a delicate bone structure and a softness to her cheeks. Her eyes were extraordinary; large, cobalt blue and full of innocence. I'd felt a ripple of her aura under stress and gone charging to her side. One moment I was in New York, and the next I was standing in a forest. It was foolish, and I was not a fool.

My cloaking ability helped to disguise my appearance and prevented humans from seeing me when I didn't wish it. I could even become shadow when necessary. Yet today I'd appeared as a human—in Oregon of all places. The Primati community would be burning up the channels, wondering why. In the forest, I'd assumed the visage of the young man I'd once been while still mortal. In the end, very few remained alive that would remember this face.

Still, I'd been recognized by the sorcerer leading that group of young novices. My aura was too intense and distinctive to be anyone else. Especially when enraged. Not just reckless, I'd *wanted* them to see me as the lethal threat I was. Fortunately, I'd taken care of that loose end as soon as Stella had safely reached the carpark. Because she'd gone untouched, I'd simply threatened the young men with dismemberment, showing them the beast to make sure they heeded my warning. It had been a mistake.

Rumors would fly. I was the Primati Enforcer, responsible for ensuring the laws were adhered to and that the Ancilla, or humans, were not interfered with against their will. I'd just drawn attention to the very place I wanted to keep secret.

I punched the hood of a parked Audi in the darkened alley. My fist touched pavement before I pulled my arm out and repeated the action again and again. The alarm silenced when I jerked the wires from beneath the ignition. Disgusted and still furious, I watched as my bloody arm healed, the liquid drying and flaking to dust.

Darkness rippled nearby, and I knew that one of my elite guard would take care of my indiscretion. They would have the automobile towed, a likely story created, and the driver recompensed. Even now they likely had the entire area locked down from pedestrians who might stray too close.

"Grayson," I whispered.

A nearby shadow coalesced into a middle-aged man in a dark suit. "Yes, sir."

"Return to her house and keep watch over her tonight. Track any activity—I want to know everything."

"Yes, sir."

Satisfied that Grayson would do exactly as I ordered, I exited the alley and walked to the custom Ecosse Titanium motorcycle waiting for me on the street. I pulled away, blazing down the alley and onto the rain-darkened cobblestone lanes of Portland. The streets were quiet, and I kept my speed down out of respect for humans and their cameras, as well as the rain-slick roads. Not that a good spill would kill me.

Nothing could.

But an accident would be more work for my team, and I didn't feel like adding to the whispers. My reputation, bolstered by the occasional bloody beheading, had been enough to maintain the respect and allegiance required of my position for centuries. But how much longer? How long before Murad's weakness finally led to all our downfalls?

At a traffic light I caught the sulfur of magick. An ordinary human would not have noticed, yet it irritated the back of my throat. A very sensitive human might detect something as *off*, yet they would not understand why. Stiffening, I glanced to my flank, but noted only an electric bus in the distance.

Seconds ticked without a green light, and I realized it was magick that kept the light red. Control over the electrical was usually the gift of a sky or water witch. The SUV next to me made a right turn, and I spied the source of the trick.

She appeared sixteen and wore a tank top emblazoned with a picture of the Ramones. A black crinoline skirt, ripped stockings, and combat boots completed her look. Her inky hair was pulled into two pigtails reminiscent of bicycle handles, and she stared at me with lips pulled back in a frozen grimace of fright, her heavily made up eyes wide.

Grabbing the lion by its tail, are you? I made a move as if to get off the bike and she ran. Ran like hell was after her. And I would have been had I not had better things to do.

Damn Portland. Its eclectic weirdness was one of the reasons I'd selected this area to hide Samuel and his granddaughter Stella these past years. That and the perpetually wet weather repulsed the more dangerous creatures unknown to man. Only born water witches liked wet and damp, a fact they'd twisted through history to shield their most protective element so humans would think it their weakness.

As the cycle purred along the quiet streets, an image of Stella's father came to mind, a slender poet with gentle manners. Lasho had been killed in a car crash in San Francisco with his wife, Vivian, just a day after Stella's birth. Stella was the last of her mother's bloodline, a fragile human without anything special about her other than who she descended from. Except I'd seen flashes of silver in her eyes today, a hallmark of her ancestors that should not be possible.

Stella would remain here during her lifetime, surrounded by the mercenary water witches I kept on retainer and where the rain and wet forests provided a natural repellant to all but my allies. I hoped the little witch at the stoplight, who with the power I'd felt was more likely a century old, belonged to the coven I paid to protect Stella. Too many teenagers resided in Portland; humans were unaware this overgrown population was simply due to the large number of powerful water witches and warlocks who disliked aging. As long as no human was harmed, their numbers violated no Council Law.

The air grew cooler as I slipped past the lights of Portland and onto dark streets and highways I remembered when they'd been muddy trails. I reveled in the biting wind, my speed only decelerating as I approached the enormous house overlooking the Columbia River. Dark twists of trees stood sentry several hundred yards from the sprawling, two-story complex. I parked at the end of the long driveway and paused a moment to gather my power, careful to keep my aura tapped down.

As expected, protection spells surrounded the property. They layered the land and trees, encircling the house in spherical patterns I would have admired if I hadn't also been aware they would be exceedingly unpleasant. *Damn, this is going to hurt.*

The fog arrived upon my first steps, so thick a mortal would not have been able to see a hand before a face. I marched unerringly towards my target, closing my eyes and ignoring the phantom fingers sliding across exposed skin. Once they had a taste of me they drew back quickly enough.

There would also be a directional spell to distract the average visitor from interest in the house. It was a common trick in the witches' arsenal. The spell clouded the intentions of the person, sending them wandering in another direction. It was once described to me as the feeling of walking into a room for something and then forgetting what it was you were there to find. I was immune to such mind tricks.

The sounds began. Vicious howls and low growls rose from the fog in every direction, raising the hair on my skin and recalling the bite of dagger sized fangs. Crunchy, squirmy things writhed beneath my boots as I continued, smiling in admiration.

The cold came next, frigid frost that would have thickened the blood in my veins and hindered my steps if I hadn't been me. Fire Witches and Sorcerers would be slowed significantly by this type of cold, yet my unique warmth prevented such an effect.

The heat ensued, blazing warmth that singed my eyebrows and dried my throat as effectively as a mature forest fire. Comfortable in the roasting temperature, I nevertheless frowned at feeling my hair char away. As I neared the full-length veranda, I felt the piece de resistance as stinging electric lines whipped from the air and sliced into my arms and legs. They came whistling from above and below, charged heat that would have cut me in two had I not regenerated as fast as they made me bleed.

"Damn it, Clara! Cut this shit out!"

Laughter rang from the open doorway. A heartbreakingly lovely woman stood framed in porch light. Long red hair swirled as she bent in half with laughter, slapping her thighs. She wore jean shorts and a white t-shirt that read, "Don't make me call the Flying Monkeys." Barefoot, she stomped on the wide-planked porch as if hearing the funniest joke ever uttered.

"Oh, Alaric, don't be such a spoilsport. I've been dying to try this stuff out. It's been years since I've had so much as a stray bunny this close without an invitation."

I reached the porch and shook my arms until they regained feeling. "I'd have to say they work fine. You might want to tinker on that heat cycle. I barely felt it. It was more of a tepid baby's bath."

She stopped giggling and glowered. "*What?* That heat spell is one of my best sellers. Silicon Valley and Wall Street asshats pay top dollar for that add on."

I offered a conciliatory grin and she bit off her next comment. Smiling hugely, she jumped into my arms, laughing when I swung her around.

"It was actually pretty vicious," I conceded. "Glad I left the bike, or it would've been a hunk of smoldering metal by now."

She pulled from my arms and tilted her chin.

"I would've used it as an incense tray, darling," she boasted with a toss of her strawberry curls.

I chuckled darkly. "Vicious, Clara, vicious."

"I'm just glad that gorgeous hair of yours is growing back already." Her smile faded as she stepped back and searched my face. "Hmm. I haven't seen you in this form for many years." Clara was one of a handful who could recall my true appearance before the wars.

"The better to blend in, Clara."

"Hmm. I always thought you avoided this form because it reminded you of your human life."

"You're very astute and your memory long," I said simply.

"As you pay me to be, Alaric," she responded sadly.

I nodded, knowing she would be here even without payment. A very big deal considering how acquisitive witches could be. And Clara was Queen of all water witches west of the Atlantic Ocean, her borders reaching into the Pacific where they touched those of her right hand or First Sister, who led Australasia.

"I saw her," I said.

"I heard." Clara had spies everywhere.

"Your novice is too weak to adequately act as a companion. There was an earth sorcerer there, loyal to Daria, claiming he and his novices were just seeking a stroll."

Her lips tightened. "I heard about this and will find out why I wasn't informed of their visit in advance, per our treaty."

Her dislike for Daria Demir, the Earth Witch Queen, was evident in her avoidance of her name. I shared her dislike, but for different reasons. Daria and I had nearly been betrothed as humans. My refusal of her hand had created a great deal of trouble over the years. Daria's right hand, or First Sister, was Marcella, a woman with a great deal more wisdom and self-control. She was able to temper most of Daria's worse impulses—but not always.

Leaning against an elegant porch column with crossed arms, I studied the distant ribbon that was the Columbia River.

"I think I'll stick around to watch over the girl for a while."

Clara twirled the same lock of hair over and over. I felt her apprehension and it mingled with...relief?

"To prevent anyone from recognizing me, I'm going to seal off my aura, and I need your help to make sure it works for an extended period." I uncrossed my arms and straightened.

"Where will you stay?"

I knew she would not offer her house. Witches were very territorial and Clara, in particular, enjoyed her solitude. I shared her preference.

"I can help you find a suitable place if you want." She clasped her hands in a prayer pose and peered up at me over her fingertips.

"That won't be necessary," I said with a shake of my head, "Grayson has accompanied me and will make arrangements." She nodded, her face relaxing.

"You do know Stella is eighteen in two months? She's already halfway through online college courses for an Art History degree. Before that she was homeschooled," she said in an abrupt change of subject. "How will you get close to her when she spends all her free time in the woods or inside that claptrap her grandfather, Sam, insists they live in? If you read my reports, you would know that she's not exactly a social butterfly." I frowned, only now recalling from reports that Stella had indeed been homeschooled.

Clara held up a slender hand. "The report I sent last month would have told you that Stella and her friend decided to complete their final year in a real high school," she said with rolled eyes. "It begins in two weeks and I already have coven members prepared to enroll as new students and most of the teachers for her selected classes." I watched with hooded eyes as Clara examined her fingernails before buffing them on her shoulder.

"I know and hear all. In this case, I hear she wants the "full experience" before graduating, including prom." Clara pretended to gag.

"You will also learn the pleasure of dealing with her father's people," she reminded me with a sour expression. The full-blood Romany were not well liked in the Primati, or supernatural, community. Mainly because they did not *care* about the Primati community, or our rules. If the Romany were an animal, it would be the Honey Badger— resourceful, determined and causing mischief just because they could.

They were also skilled as keeping just under the radar. I held them in great admiration.

I grunted in acknowledgment. "That's right. There's a grandmother, correct?"

Clara made a *pfft* sound and waved a hand. "That harridan is absolutely uncooperative. Her family call her "Baba" but she is no sweet grandmother. And it's not just her. There's an entire village of their family in the area, most involved with scamming tourists with palm reading or small businesses. Thankfully, the girl doesn't spend much time with them."

I quirked a brow, distracted as a heavy wind arrived, blowing rain sideways onto the porch. Clara was quite put off by them. I would have to make the grandmother's acquaintance in person.

Clara moved to her front door and I straightened to follow.

"She has family and that matters. In truth, seeing her today made me realize how delicate and fearful she is. She needs all the protection she can get."

Clara drew up short, her pretty face stunned.

"Fearful? Are we still talking about *Stella*?"

I nodded, recalling how she trembled in my arms.

"Um. Petite blonde?" she continued to quiz.

"Of course," I growled.

Clara drew closer and patted my shoulder, her touch turning into lingering strokes that stopped when I scowled.

"Girl's gotta try, big boy," she said with a mischievous grin before pivoting to enter the house. I heard her mutter the word "delicate" under her breath. Her shoulders shook as she walked away.

"Better come inside. We've loads to talk about. You also need to put some clothes on. My worthless heat spell seems to have burned off all your clothing." I looked down and confirmed she was telling the truth. Shrugging, I strolled in after her.

The house was all warm wood and curves. Its interior was surprisingly devoid of excess furniture or bric-a-brac. I smirked at the absence of any reflective surfaces. Especially mirrors. Clara would ensure any portal was kept under lock and key within her personal domain. She was crazy as hell but never dropped the ball on defense.

She led me to a modern upstairs bathroom. Waving at a wardrobe bag hanging from a hook, she shot me a playful grin. Without doubt, I knew I would find clothing in my size.

"Prepared to have a naked monster visiting, were you?"

Laughing, she danced towards a door at the end of the large bathroom.

Shaking my head, I grabbed a fluffy towel and wrapped it around my hips.

"Are you kidding? I've had about a dozen calls on my bat line in the last hour reporting your whereabouts. Your aura lit up the sky this evening."

Framed in the opposing doorway, she did a slow pirouette before landing in a graceful position.

"By the way, please try not to terrify my coven members, Alaric. They are petrified of *The Lion*, many of them growing up with tales of your terrifying ways. They see you, they expect to die. You nearly gave Bromely a heart attack earlier."

I grunted, glad to see the shower stocked with soap and shampoo. "She the Goth from the traffic light?" She nodded.

"I never kill the innocent, Clara." I rebuked her with a frown. Truly, I'd enjoyed frightening the little witch, and it served her right for messing with the traffic lights.

She said nothing, just tapped her front teeth with cherry tipped nails. I raised a newly regenerated eyebrow until she sighed and continued.

"I know. Just as I know you will do as you please. Just putting in a request in case you were interested in retaining top talent. Recruiting is a bitch these days, and she's been a solid performer. In fact, she's been my right hand and very loyal. We minions are not easily come by," she said. Very few dared to use that tone in conversation with me. Yet Clara had earned an explanation.

"She was reckless to stay me at the traffic light. Once my aura is sealed, no one should recognize me. If they can't recognize me then they can't fall apart and come crying to you," I responded coldly. She wisely dropped the subject and moved to the mirror-less sink area to refold a stack of washcloths.

"You know, she has up to the age of twenty-one for the curse to strike. You can't mean to personally guard her until then? Three years is a long time."

My expression was implacable.

"Who will manage the Council while you're here?" she continued, pressing the small squares of cloth into perfect folds. "Murad still disappears for months on end—"

"Don't," I ground out and she fell silent, her hands stilling on the counter as she turned to meet my eyes. Gritting my teeth, I forced myself to be tolerant. I was not in the habit of explaining myself, even for old friends. I turned the water on and adjusted the temperature until it was scalding before I trusted myself to respond.

"Don't question me on this."

She nodded but failed to show any sign of fear. Clara the Brave. I softened.

She saw my change of expression and relaxed somewhat. "I suppose I just want to know how Murad is," she admitted. "He's still far from the charming conversationalist he once was."

Clara had more latitude than most to speak so familiarly of my brother, yet I knew to trust no one with all things. Especially in regard to the King and his affliction.

"My brother continues to improve. As you must know, he has attended more Council meetings and will take his place at the Samhain celebration in France."

Of course, she would know this—Clara was on the Council.

"Okay. Subject dropped. While you clean up, I'll see what I can do to strengthen the deterrent spell around the city," she offered.

I dropped the towel and entered the shower. Shutting the glass door, I adjusted the spray until it hit the back of my neck. Steaming water sluiced for long minutes, but I felt her presence still. It afforded the opportunity to offer a reminder.

"And don't forget to increase the number of your coven keeping eyes on her. Grayson will be coordinating with you, and we should try to keep them at a distance to avoid crowding her, especially as she seems a bit shy. She's very...sweet. Amenable."

I heard choked laughter and wiped at the condensation. I was alone. Reaching out with my senses, I felt her drifting farther away into the house.

Folding my arms, I lowered my head and allowed the water's spray to batter my skin. Clara was not herself. *Neither am I.* I turned, banging my head lightly against the tiles before resting my forehead against the cool surface. *Damn minions.*

Chapter 3

Moon Reversed

Stella

"**I** asked for coffee."

Amanda shrugged and took another mouthful of her own mint tea. I pretended to take another sip of the green, frothy juice in my glass and immediately gagged to further my point. She smoothed the frayed edges of her yellow cloth placemat as if it were fascinating. Her homemade lattes were legendary, with ground bourbon beans her father sourced from local, artisan coffee roasters. They kept cow's milk on hand just for my lattes. Sighing, I pushed the glass away.

"Mom made that for you before she and Dad left for the market this morning. It will hurt her feelings if you don't drink it." Amanda guilt-tripped me. She still wore her Hello Kitty pajamas and the horned-rimmed eyeglasses she used when not wearing contacts.

I eyed the glass with distaste. "I love your mom, but I'm not her test bunny. What is this anyway? It tastes like what pond algae looks like."

"I saw kale stems in the compost, but she may have added spirulina.

I thought you liked her goddess juice?" Marion was always experimenting with new juice concoctions and making us try them.

"Normally. This is not the usual."

"I loved mine. Maybe she didn't put in enough green apple. Want me to add some?"

"No. What I would *like* is for us to talk about what happened in the woods yesterday," I reminded her for the umpteenth time. "Stop trying to distract me with juice."

Amanda wiggled her nose to nudge her eyeglasses up. "You know, doesn't Sam's favorite nurse come on Saturday mornings? I bet she brought you Voodoo donuts or something. You can always have breakfast at your house."

"First off, Carol is a health nut. It's unfortunate. Secondly—and I cannot believe I am actually saying this—I'm not leaving your side until you agree to talk." I began ticking off my fingers. "One, what happened that you use our secret safe word? Two, why couldn't I move or speak? Three, why did you act all meek when hot guy showed up and manhandled me..." That wasn't *exactly* what had happened but I was on a roll. "...And most importantly, what did you ask me to forgive you for?"

She arched a brow and stared out the window, blowing on her tea. Although early morning, it was overcast. Even with the skylight centered above Amanda's kitchen, the room was gloomy without the overhead lights turned on. Amanda's kitchen was unique for the fact they had no stove. Electronic gadgets, yes. Smoke detectors in every room, yes. But nothing with a flame.

Her mom had been traumatized as a child and her pyrophobia had rubbed off on Amanda, despite my attempt to desensitize her to it. One can only jump out at a screaming friend with a lit candle so many times before it just gets sad. I'd had to stop after the ninth "therapy" lesson because Amanda's hair started falling out and Marion had called Sam.

I waited in stony silence until Amanda leaned forward, placing her cup on its matching saucer.

"Do you remember when we learned about Occam's razor?"

"The monk who liked a close shave?" I offered her a bland smile. Occam's razer was a problem-solving principle, but I forgot the guy's first name. It basically meant that when forming a hypothesis about something, the simple and known solution is usually the best.

"Ha-ha. He was a friar. I'm serious, Stella. You're making this into something bigger than it needs to be. I'm sorry. I don't mean to be so mysterious, but I just really need to talk to my mom about what happened first. She and Dad left to set up for the market before I woke you this morning. If I promise to ask them tonight, will you *please* just drop it for now?"

I shook my head, incredulous, and checked the clock ticking above her refrigerator. Amanda normally loved to talk. About everything. Even if you weren't interested in what she had to say. *Especially* if you weren't interested.

"Since when do you need to talk to your mom before discussing something with me? And why didn't she wake us before they left? You usually help them on Saturdays," I argued, leaning back in my chair.

"You've just asked me more questions in five minutes than the last five years." She shook her head, exasperated. "Mom probably saw you crashed in my bed when they got home last night and figured we could use the chance to sleep in. I'll talk to her tonight." She averted her eyes as she took another sip. I frowned but she was right. After showering and eating Amanda's microwaved macaroni and cheese, I'd fallen asleep early. Normally a night owl, I put it down to the excitement of yesterday.

Nostrils flaring, I crossed my arms and tried not to lose my temper. We were walking on the edge of a massive fight but holding back.

Amanda most likely because she hated confrontation. Me, because storming out of her house at this moment meant a possible run in with Scott, her next-door neighbor and my ex-pseudo boyfriend, who, if he still kept the same Saturday shift at the glassblowing shop, would be walking out his door in five minutes. Seeing him face-to-face would be a masochistic experience I could do without this morning.

Needing to act, I jumped up and carefully poured the green gunk down her garbage disposal. Whatever happened in the woods was a mystery I needed to understand. I'd felt helpless. Why couldn't she get this? I put the glass in the dishwasher and marched down the hall to her family room. I would have stomped, but I was barefoot and too lazy to make the effort.

The family room was a plaid meets floral explosion, the result of her parents' compromise on decor. Family photos filled most surfaces, and it was cozy in a way that my own home was not. We didn't have photos for one thing. My grandfather despised nostalgia.

I sidled up to the corner window and peeked through the cream silk curtains towards the house next door. Scott's jeep still sat in front of his house. I watched the portion of his front yard that I could see while my fingers played with the ends of my French braid. Waiting for Scott, I thought about the young man who plucked me out of the river yesterday. His scent had been amazing—warm and intoxicating. Sandalwood, pine and spearmint...

Hearing a sigh, I turned to find Amanda sinking into a nearby sofa. She normally joined me at the window, my partner in all things stalkery.

I peeked between the curtains again and was rewarded by the sight of Scott walking across his yard to his jeep. A white thermal shirt clung to his defined arms and his sandy hair was messy, as if he'd just woken up. He climbed in and looked down at something I couldn't see. Probably searching for music. Maybe even the Doors album we'd listened to over and over last summer when he wanted to educate me on his favorite 70's music. I'd pretended to be unaware of the classics to make him feel good. As I was a poor actress and often hummed along to the songs, that just made him dumb.

After a month of seeing each other nearly every day, Scott, my first and only boyfriend, had dumped me, accomplishing it spectacularly when he'd made out with a Portland Timber cheerleader on the hood of his car—after he'd locked eyes with Amanda and I sitting twenty-five yards away on Amanda's front porch. No words were exchanged. His message was loud and clear. If I didn't put out, he would replace me with someone who would. Proving spectacularly that he wasn't worth it.

In turn, I stored a dozen eggs in our very warm garage for a month, waiting for the right moonless night, and egged the inside of his mailbox. I'd felt bad about it when his dad had given up trying to clean the stench and bought a new mailbox. I should hate him but oddly didn't. I definitely hated that I still found him attractive. That I still remembered what a great kisser he was. Someday he would beg for my forgiveness and confess his undying love. My response would be to tell him he'd missed his chance. At least, that was the most common scenario.

"I thought we agreed to save the boy drama until after college? Careers and then hot love lives, remember?" Amanda reminded me.

Scott's car rolled past my car, braked and then backed up. His head turned towards Amanda's house. I ducked, flinging myself to the floor. Holding my breath, I only dared another look once the rumble of his car engine faded. Satisfied he'd gone, I joined Amanda on the couch.

"I don't know why you're still hung up on him. He's a class A douche bag." In Amanda's world there were three levels of douche-baggery. Scott won the jackpot and top honors.

"I am *not* still hung up on him."

She lifted an eyebrow. "Did you know he had sex with Mrs.

Hopkin's niece right after she returned home from a mission in Brazil? She's like, twenty-four and has a fiancé."

Mrs. Hopkin's was her Mormon neighbor across the street. Her niece led bible studies. I was impressed despite myself. He did seem to enjoy a challenge, and I was very glad I hadn't succumbed to become another notch on his bedpost. Save that honor for the next idiot girl. I wanted spectacular or nothing.

"At least he already graduated so we won't run into him when school starts," she commented. I snorted and curled my legs beneath me. It'd been Amanda's idea to matriculate into public school for our final year.

"Tell me again why we're doing this?"

"Because with early credits, we won't be losing time with college—and you need to socialize with people your own age," she said firmly, "normal people, not those feral relatives of yours, and I want to have an actual report card with straight A's to put in my scrapbook. We'll be creating memories." My eyes twitched with the effort not to roll them.

"I don't like people. People don't like me," I stated for the hundredth time while nudging her leg with my toes. Amanda sighed and pushed my cold feet away.

"People like you just fine. You just need to remember to smile and cut down on the sarcasm." I plastered a toothy smile on my face. "Me? I'm a ray of sunshine." She gave me a pointed look and I shrugged.

"I can't help it if people are annoying. Anyway, I need to go home and check on Sam. Then I'm going to visit your mom at the market today and ask her advice on why I couldn't speak or move and had to stand in freezing water while you Jedi-mind tricked some freaky guy. If I didn't know better, I'd say it was paranormal." Amanda stiffened.

It felt silly to say out loud. I mean, magical stuff didn't *actually* exist. In fact, I wasn't even sure that's what really happened. For all I knew it could have been dehydration or maybe even hypothermia playing tricks on my mind.

Amanda bit her lip and refused to meet my eyes.

"I'll have to tell her that I jumped from the cliff, but what will she do? Tell Sam on me?" I wondered aloud. My grandfather was nearing his ninety-seventh birthday and recovering from hip surgery. It was doubtful that Amanda's mom would want to upset him. But then, neither did I.

"I'm also wearing your clothes home. I may or may not return them." As I'd put on her favorite pink t-shirt and navy sweats after showering at her house last night, she narrowed her eyes but said nothing. Fine then.

I made it to the foyer before she caught up to me.

"Wait for me."

Surprised, I shook off her hand. "I thought you were trying to get rid of me?"

I didn't want her to come home with me. I had no idea what state Sam would be in. We had Carol to help us during the day, and a night nurse about to start, yet his moods were unpredictable.

"Stella, we both know that if I ask you *not* to go to the Market to see my mom, you'll go straight there. I might as well go with you." She smiled grimly. "Give me five minutes to change."

"Fine." I waited until she walked upstairs to her room. As soon as I heard footsteps cross the floorboards above, I scooped up my backpack and wet sneakers by the door and hurried outside.

My heart sang at the sight of my baby—a 1995 Volkswagen beetle. It was ancient, but what I could afford. Sam surprised me by having it re-painted in vintage gulf-blue the week I brought it home. He'd wanted me in a "safer" car with all-wheel drive, but I'd adamantly refused to allow him to buy me one. We always had what we needed but I had no idea what our finances were and he'd been retired for a long time.

Plus, I loved my VW and was proud of making a modest amount of money from my artwork and the occasional dance class. Having wheels and the freedom to go places without anyone's help was satisfying. One day I'd have to take care of myself and every penny counted.

After tossing my burgundy backpack and shoes in a backseat crowded with canvases and crates of old oil paint intended for the town's recycling center, I started the engine just as rain began to polka-dot my dusty windshield. At the stop sign I spotted Scott's jeep idling next to the curb a block away. My face burned, imagining his regard as I rolled past. Glancing into the rearview mirror I released my pent-up breath when his jeep remained in place, his windshield wipers flicking the rain in slow sweeps.

My VW left Troutdale behind as it purred noisily along the twisting roads of the Historic Columbia River Highway. Emerald green trees and foliage surrounded me as hawks and eagles dipped and circled the cliffs above the river. Rolling down my window, I breathed in the fresh moist air that carried the lingering, acrid odor of smoke from last year's wild fires. It'd been a miracle when the fires had stopped just short of leaping towards our house. The scent reminded me of the interaction with Marcus in the forest and I rolled up my window. Amanda's refusal to talk about what happened with the strangers hurt more than I cared to admit. We never kept secrets from each other.

The rain began to pelt down in earnest as I made the turn onto our long driveway. Passing our neighbor's fence, I nodded at the grumpy goats and lazy cows that always seemed to congregate near the wooden railing, no matter the weather. The dirt road snaked through a half mile of maple saplings, white oak trees, and wild blueberry bushes before the house came into view.

The rare visitor who called on us was always taken aback by the sight of the massive oak trees shading our front yard. The trees were remarkable, but their decorations dropped jaws. My heart warmed to see the hundreds of hollow eggs that swayed from tattered silk ribbons in the trees. Most had been hand-painted by Sam or me over the course of our years together. Although sealed in a protective glaze, it was a miracle we'd only lost a few to windstorms and curious squirrels.

The house itself was a three-story, Queen Anne Victorian, built by a wealthy banker for his family when the current city of Portland was still a frontier village they nicknamed "Stumptown." It was a large, wood framed house but old and certainly not a fancy one. I liked the creaking floorboards and peeling butter-yellow paint we never got around to repainting.

Stepping barefoot out of my car, my toes sunk into the wet moss that blanketed the edge of our driveway. I glanced up at my attic bedroom window. At thirteen, a phase of wandering in my sleep and waking up in our backyard had freaked Sam out. He'd hired a tree service to cut down the thick limb that once rested near my window, and alarms were placed on the glass panes to keep me from plunging to my death while sleepwalking. Another branch had grown since then, and on windy days it nearly reached the base of my windowsill, a fact I carefully avoided pointing out to Sam.

I spied our handyman raking leaves to the side of the house and met Roger's gloved wave with a peace sign. Rain slicked the painted front steps, but I managed to leap them two at a time. The front door opened, spilling light onto the graying porch boards.

"Come in, come in!" beckoned Carol. She tsked as I passed her into the house.

"Where are your shoes?" It was a frequent question from Sam's nurse, as I would walk barefoot twenty-four hours a day if I could. I flicked the rain from my arms and tossed my backpack into the hall closet.

"In the car."

Carol scrunched her round face in disbelief. A youthful fifty-something woman, with a pleasing face and brunette bob, her jeans and green top revealed the figure of a woman who liked to run and ski. Or wrangle grumpy old men into physical therapy.

"How's Sam?" I asked, reaching my hand out to touch the gnarled handle of his walking stick where it rested forlornly in our umbrella stand. An avid hiker, Sam's slow recovery was affecting his moods.

"Your Granddad is sleeping soundly after a breakfast of biscuits and gravy. He said I made them just like his "Mamma did back in Virginia" and I told him he was just being nice." I grinned. Sam was such a charmer.

"He told me you spent the night at Amanda's house and seemed glad you were off having fun. You have about an hour before he wakes up."

"Cool. I'm dying for coffee—want some?" Nodding, she followed me down the hall to our dated kitchen. "I'll grind the beans," she offered. I smiled in gratitude and pulled mugs from the cabinets.

"So, how's Thomas?" Carol was proud of her youngest son and a former member of our homeschool group. A little shy and on the scrawny side with glasses, homeschool had been a way for Thomas to avoid the painful teasing he received from his former classmates.

"Oh, he's coding all kinds of programming now as a consultant. He starts his sophomore year of college next month." Her face beamed with pride. "He's working part time for the Maryhill Museum," she said just before the loud burr of the coffee grinder kicked up. I waited until the grinder was silent and the scent of fresh ground beans filled the air.

"Maryhill? Isn't that the park with the Stonehenge replica?"

"The very one. He's been giving tours of it." She pulled a pink box from a bag resting on a chair. My mouth watered at the scent of fresh donuts and she smiled knowingly. I grabbed plates and napkins.

"I know how much you love these. I'm just glad Thomas is happy." She laughed. "He's happy, which makes me happy." Carol was an eternal optimist and loved her son. We sank into chairs at the round wooden table and I prepared my cup with milk and a sprinkle of cinnamon.

"How's your school work?" she asked. She used a napkin to hand me my favorite donut, its surface decorated with a cute vanilla icing mustache.

"Still taking online classes but I have no idea what I want to do besides art. I start senior year of high school in two weeks." It was kind of fun saying that out loud. Like a girl saying typical teenage stuff when on the inside that experience felt so unrelatable. I stuffed down my feelings with a huge bite of yeasty sweet dough. The several minutes were spent in blessed silence as we enjoyed the rich, velvety brew and I finished my treat.

"I'm glad you'll get that experience. I found my love of nursing in high school. I was a volunteer candy striper." she recalled fondly.

"You're lucky. I just want Sam to get better." Loneliness and uncertainty caught me off guard and lodged in my throat. I pushed the plate away.

"You'll be okay, Stella. Sam's had a very long life and has more to live. But when the time comes, plenty of young people forge their way through life without family. You still have your friends." Right. Like my best friend who was keeping secrets from me.

I took my empty cup to the sink and Carol followed, setting her mug gently next to mine. She bumped my elbow and slipped away. I sighed and made my way through the foyer and down the hall to check on Sam. He snored softly beneath his favorite orange and red Pendleton blanket, his thick, white hair combed neatly, even when lying down. I tiptoed out, leaving him to dream of catching largemouth bass. My legs ate up the wide stairs to my attic bedroom, passing doors of small storage rooms that held holiday decorations and Sam's old books and papers from when he'd been a country doctor back east.

My bedroom faced the front yard, its large space a welcome sight with its exposed wood beams and wide plank floors. I stood for a moment and drank in the sight of familiar sloped ceilings and the bed frame crafted from twisted juniper branches. I flicked a wall switch and a web of fairy lights sparked overhead, crisscrossing my ceiling. We didn't have air conditioning, so two fans near my windows provided ventilation when I painted. They also helped me sleep, the cool brush of air across my face and steady hum better than any lullaby.

I hurried to the long wooden table covered with paint projects and inspected my latest work. The tower card had dried beautifully and I sighed in relief. This would be the eighth set commissioned through Amanda's mom for her customers. Each deck was unique and stamped with my personal signature—a golden star in the right lower corner of each card. The completed works for this particular project were lined up in a neat row, their jewel-like colors gleaming. Marion reprinted my original fifty-six Minor Arcana cards, then included the unique twenty-two Major Arcana cards that I painstakingly created for each new deck.

There'd been an extra set, one I'd gifted my paternal grandmother last year. She'd shrugged upon unwrapping its box and tossed it into a drawer, unimpressed.

I moved to a standing rack of clothes and, in a red mood, selected a short, crimson summer dress with cap sleeves and buttons down the front that I'd purchased at a vintage store for fifty cents. Once my teeth were brushed in the tiny bathroom crowded with paint cleaning supplies, I stared at my pale but determined face in the acrylic mirror above my stained sink and resolved to find out exactly what secrets Amanda was keeping from me. There had to be a logical explanation for how my will had been stolen for those brief moments. I couldn't live without knowing the answer.

Chapter 4
The Fool

Stella

A lthough late afternoon, vendors, visitors, and street performers were enjoying the vibe of Portland's Saturday market. A steel drum tinkled a gorgeous African melody as the trembling voice of an indie singer wove in and out of a tune with ukulele accompaniment from another. Wet children ran from the sprinklers at the Legacy fountain, one nearly clipping the stool I sat cross-legged upon.

I shook my fist in their direction, to the horror of the parents chasing them. My perch allowed me to lean against the door frame of the manga shop, where Silvan was currently working. It was a great spot to people watch. The narrow lane was filled with shop stalls and a mix of people, with storefronts facing one another on either side.

Kicking off my sandals, I pinched my lips in thought. Marion's Mystical was diagonally across from me, its window display filled with rocks, Buddha statues, and a whole host of crap that made the new age crowd go nuts. A closed sign gleamed against the darkened windows.

Absently, I unwrapped a stick of gum and stuck it between my teeth.

The spot where Marion usually set up her booth had been replaced with a crepe seller. In all the years I'd known Amanda's family, this was the first time they'd been closed on a Saturday without a planned vacation or holiday. I checked my cell again. No response to the dozen texts I'd sent Amanda.

Mrs. Withers, the old lady who owned the map/bookstore next door to Marion's Mystical, was sweeping outside her storefront. She caught my eye, scowled, and abruptly went inside her store.

I'd questioned her earlier about whether she'd seen Amanda's parents and my attitude may have been a trifle aggressive. Sighing, I twisted the mala bracelet tied to my ankle that read "Fuck off" in Morse code and glanced down at the sketchpad in my lap. I'd intended to draw ideas for the Sun card from the Major Arcana, yet the page was filled with different versions of the Knight of Cups, his fingers gently cupping a golden chalice. The margins were filled with eyes. Eyes with intense, glowing irises and fringed by lush eyelashes.

"Why are you loitering and blocking my doorway?" a sharp female voice asked.

I carefully closed my pad. Tucking a pencil in the spiral binding, I glanced at the young woman who stood nearby with pursed lips.

Silvan's boss, Jing San, loved nothing more than to find fault and complain. She looked my age, but Silvan had seen her passport once and confirmed she was twenty-six. Slight of build, she had a narrow face and dark hair past her shoulders with a wide streak of red that ran diagonal from her crown. Today she wore overalls over a bandeau top, her hair twisted in a knot and held in place with a silver letter opener.

"I told her she could, Jing!" Silvan called from a corner of the store where he was manning the cash register next to Jing's only other worker, Ford.

Jing crossed her arms, ignoring Silvan.

"See? Silvan said I could. Besides, how am I blocking the doorway if you're standing in it?" I countered.

"You are in the corner of the door. A nuisance!" she jeered.

I may have been loitering, but people had been flowing easily around my spot and into the busy store since I'd moved the stool outside—the better to watch for Amanda or her parents. The manga shop was actually pretty cool. It wasn't my thing, but the manga and anime drawings in most of the books were true art. Jing, however, was uptight in the extreme. Which is why I enjoyed irritating her every chance I got. Maybe not a wise choice given her hobby of collecting samurai swords. I eyed the letter opener in her hair with wary respect.

I had every confidence she could use those swords with skill. During last year's Comic-Con she'd surprisingly gone along with Silvan's plea to cosplay with us.

Jing had arrived as an anime vampire with sharp-looking Tanto daggers strapped to each arm and leg. When people had pressed to take photos with her, she'd left. But not before throwing a dagger across a room to land between the eyes of Hugh Jackman on a Wolverine poster. Jing was not a people person either.

"Are you chewing gum?" she asked suddenly, her eyes locked on my mouth.

"Pssh. No." Her lips tightened. Jing hated chewing gum with an unreasonable passion, and I wasn't looking to make a scene right now. I shifted to offense.

"Come on, Jing. I'm not blocking the doorway. Your nerdy manga customers can get around me just fine."

"Nerds? My customers are business people. They are lawyers, teachers..." she trailed off, her eyes locking on something over my shoulder. Her arms uncrossed, and she stood straight, lips parting before they pressed together.

Curious, I followed her gaze and saw nothing special. When I turned, Jing was standing with her feet planted shoulder length apart, her pupils dilated so that hardly any brown remained. I half tumbled off the stool, adrenaline immediately pumping. My first thought, as irrational as it might be, was that Marcus had found me. Jing stepped back; her slim arms swung behind her. *Thanks for the help.* I tried to land with one foot caught in the wooden stool.

A strong hand grasped my elbow and helped me steady into a standing position. Alarmed, I glanced at Jing, but she stood with several feet between us.

I stopped breathing when a trace of woodsy sandalwood and pine caught my attention. A subtle layer of frankincense and spearmint completed a scent that belonged to only one person I'd ever met. I felt him, although we no longer touched. His proximity vibrated awareness from the crown of my head to my bare feet.

I blinked to see Jing give a tiny nod before melting back into her store. "Don't forget to bring my chair back inside," she called over her shoulder. My mouth was suddenly too dry to give my usual mocking reply.

"You should be more careful," a deep voice murmured. The hand released my arm with a lingering brush of fingertips that triggered an involuntary shiver.

Turning slowly, I looked up. My first impression was of soulful brown eyes and tousled sable hair. I drank in the stranger from the forest. I'd half convinced myself that I'd imagined his good looks but here he was, just exactly as I remembered except today his t-shirt was black. He tucked his hands into the pockets of dark denim jeans, and I recognized the Omega chronograph watch he wore as a version my Romany cousins sold counterfeits of.

His face—all of him really—belonged in magazines or film, and I couldn't look away from the intensity of his gaze or the impure curve of his beautiful lips. He was drinking me in as well. I came to my senses and realized I was just standing there, gaping, and closed my teeth with a snap. The music of the market had faded while late afternoon sunlight dappled across the lane in mellow peach shades.

"Hi," I croaked. Clearing my throat, I tried again. "You're real."

"Yes. So are you." His lips twitched.

"How did you find me?" I asked.

His brow furrowed. "Find you? Couldn't this just be a coincidence?"

I considered his words. The odds of meeting the same stranger from the forest in the shopping district would be an incredible fluke.

"Actually, I was about to ask you the same thing. First you appear in the forest and now right in my path."

I played with my pursed lips, unsure of whether he was serious or not. His perfection drew attention and both women and men did a double take as they passed. I couldn't blame them. It was like seeing the Queen of England buy paper towels at Target—he didn't blend well with the normals.

As I considered what to say, his expression shifted. His nostrils flared, eyes darkening as they dropped to my lips. He resembled a wolf suddenly, staring at prey. Instinctively, I let my arm drop and straightened.

The sketchpad fell from my nerveless fingers to the sidewalk. I scrambled to scoop it up, making sure the pages remained closed. He removed a hand from his pocket and slowly rubbed the shadow along his jaw. He didn't just look at me. He observed every detail and it made me feel...devoured. I shook my head at the strange notion.

"I apologize for not introducing myself yesterday. My party was waiting for me deeper in the forest. My name is Alaric."

His voice was a deep, accented river of honey. I blinked, recalling Amanda's challenge to be more social. I squared my shoulders and extended my hand.

"Hi, Alaric. Nice to meet you. My name is Stella. Thank you for running interference with those guys yesterday. I was afraid they would never leave."

He eyed my hand and I nearly pulled it back, annoyed that he seemed to actually be considering whether to take it or not. Just as I began to rethink my offer, his large hand engulfed my own. His hand was warm and strong, his palm dry and lightly calloused as he gently clasped mine in a firm press of skin.

My thumb settled over the muscle between his thumb and forefinger, and I felt his blood pulse. Did *his* thumb brush across the top of my hand? Just as I was sure he could feel my heartbeat speed up he withdrew from my grasp. The air buzzed and I struggled not to stare.

"Hello, Stella. Very nice to meet you. Are you shopping for—" he glanced at the store sign "—comic books?"

I gasped with a delighted smile, hoping Jing was close enough to hear Alaric refer to her precious manga as comic books. As no letter opener pierced his body, I assumed she was too far away to have heard him.

"No. My cousin works here part-time. It's my day off and I was just stopping by to visit." Partial truth.

"Ah. Who's your cousin?" He peered through the window into the store.

I squinted through the doorway, following his line of sight. "He's the tall skinny kid speaking with the woman staring at you right now." It was true—Jing was watching us. I couldn't blame her. Alaric was stare-worthy.

"His name is Silvan."

He nodded, eyes lingering on my fingers as I played with the end of my braid. I cleared my throat and tried to stop fidgeting.

"So, are *you* shopping?"

"Just enjoying the sunshine and doing some sightseeing," he said with an easy smile.

My heart stuttered. "You don't live here?"

"No. I'm staying at the Regis Arms for the week. My work is in security, so it takes me all over. I travel quite a bit but live mostly in New York City."

He didn't look old enough to have a career that took him all over the place, but then I remembered there were many twenty-two-year-old CEOs in the tech field. The accent I'd heard yesterday had the melodic quality of French, yet today it had disappeared into a non-descript American. I mentally flagged the inconsistency, wondering where he was really from.

"Must be nice. I've never been anywhere, but someday I want to travel." It was true. I wanted to stand in distant countries and paint landscapes, test the light in different parts of the world.

"Really? Where would you like to go?" His voice was compelling, his expression slightly pained. Before I could answer, the world's most annoying sound erupted behind me.

"Stell!"

Dear Lord, please not now.

Chapter 5

The Emperor

Stella

Alaric scanned the Portland Market over my head and my scalp tingled with dread. My fingers clenched the sketchpad, prepared to use it in self-defense.

"Stell!" repeated my cousin, Midora. Sharp, pointy nails dug into my shoulder, and I winced. This was about to get very embarrassing. Why did they have to show up *now*?

Alaric's hand shot out so fast it left just an impression of movement, and Midora's claw disappeared within his grasp. I noted two things. His eyes had flared from chocolate to onyx. An impossible thing. And that he still gripped Midora's hand, keeping her from hurting me.

I twisted around to find three young women. My cousins Midora, Mira, and Medea stood in a semi-circle, all in similar outfits of bohemian dresses with boots and beachy brunette hair—and matching expressions of astonishment.

Alaric still gripped Midora's hand, although that black gaze had lightened once more to brown. I blinked hard. No way had Alaric just grabbed one of the twisted sisters.

Alaric's other arm had hardened into an iron barrier, preventing me from thrusting forward as a wedge between them. I watched, eyes wide and with churning stomach, as he gently turned her wrist in a practiced move and bowed, lowering his lips to hover the barest breath above her skin. He blinked up at her with liquid intensity. *W.T.F.*

I expected talons to strike those soulful eyes. At minimum, a hard slap across his face. At worst, a UFC style attack with Mira on his back and Medea holding his scalp.

But, incredibly, her outrage morphed into a feminine smile. Stunned, I observed her arm grow noodle limp, her hand curling into his like a Disney princess.

What. The. Actual. Fuck.

Her smile must have been approval, because he closed the hair-breadth distance, pressing firm lips to the back of her hand. It was fast, lasting the barest second, but the image burned into my retinas. I laughed lightly in shock.

"Forgive my impudence. I supposed you must know the lovely Stella here and couldn't resist." Alaric lay his free hand across his breastbone, sincerity and limpid remorse in every line of his expressive face. I noticed he kept her hand in his. The man had turned into a freaking BBC character from the eighteenth century.

His pose brought attention to the molded planes of his chest, the fine hair dusting his muscular forearms mesmerizing. His beauty stunned as I tried to remember to breathe properly. Medea and Mira must have agreed with my assessment because I heard their sighs. The girls were four to eight years my senior. You would think they could control themselves.

"Not at all." Midora assured him as she thrust out her chest and batted her stupid spikey eyelashes with not so much as a glance in my direction. This was the same crazy woman I'd once seen shatter the kneecap of a three-hundred-pound cat-caller using a flying kick. She'd been wearing a skirt and high heeled boots at the time.

"We're her cousins. Her father was our uncle. The better part of the family."

I rolled my eyes. He released her hand, yet it remained curled in the air for a few seconds. Scowling, I imagined breaking those nail extensions to the quick. Midora whipped her hand back, rubbing it. She looked at me, one thick eyebrow raised.

Mulishly, I blinked, refusing to make formal introductions.

I felt Alaric's warm hand against the center of my spine and started. We stood so close I didn't think my cousins could see his touch. I should have pulled away. I didn't like to be touched, let alone by someone I didn't know. But the contact was electric, causing my cheeks to flame. I didn't pull away. Surprised with my own acceptance at the casual touch, I nevertheless focused on the distracting sensation, letting it anchor me. Perhaps Alaric wasn't the gentleman he seemed. But his hand was warm and it remained in a respectable location.

Midora introduced herself and her sisters and then cooed over what an interesting name he had when he politely responded. The sweet, musky perfume they preferred curtained the area. Medea agreed about his name while smoothing a dark lock of hair across her breast. Mira's lips were still parted like a fish. I listened to them chat about the weather while my short nails pressed half-moons so deep into my palms I expected to feel blood drip. I disliked them so much.

"Stell, you never mentioned Alaric before." Midora deigned to acknowledge me.

"We just met. And I told you not to call me that. My name is Stell-ah," I demonstrated it for her. "Maybe you should talk your hus-*a*-band into springing for vocab lessons," I suggested in the saccharine voice that drove her crazy.

Midora grimaced and took a step in my direction. My brows rose as my chin dropped in mock surprise. *Come on, then.* I knew she was bluffing because the tiny gold hoop looped through her left nostril was in place. Ever since I'd ripped out her nose ring for locking me in a closet when I was eleven, she was careful to remove it before tangling with me. My cousins were spiteful, but there was nothing wrong with their memory.

"M&Ms!" came Silvan's loud greeting. "What are you doing here? Why don't you come inside? We have cookies for customers." Silvan had taken to calling the three sisters after the chocolate candy since he was a child. I had no idea why the nickname stuck. There was nothing sweet about them.

Silvan was trying to divert a scene. I knew *he* knew better than to intercede on my behalf. The nervous glances he flicked towards Jing's figure in the window made me realize that his timely distraction was for her benefit. Jing had fired him twice already, and he might not survive a third time if we started a street fight in front of her store.

If it were anyone else, Midora would have exploded with a tirade at the interruption. Yet the family adored Silvan for his musical talent and usually left him alone. Silvan was our neutral territory, even with his penchant for mischief.

"No, thanks, Sil," Midora grumbled. "We just stopped by to ask *you* to tell *that* one—her sharp purple nail came way too close to my face as I silently dared her to try while I didn't have my back turned— "that Baba wants her to spend the night at the compound Monday night. Stella's blocked all of our cell phone numbers again or we would have called."

I glared at Midora. "You can tell Mahari to shove it up her—"

"Don't even think about it," Medea hissed.

"—ass," I continued, drawing the word out. They hated that I used her name and not Baba, their nickname for our shared grandmother.

They clasped their bony sternums as if I'd blasphemed in front of a priest, except for Mira, who wore a slight smile. I flushed when I felt Alaric's gaze on me. I'd probably never see him again and his opinion shouldn't even register on my radar, yet I imagined I was making a pretty poor impression.

"There's a solar eclipse on Monday. She just wants the family together—you know how superstitious she is," Medea said in a flat voice. As if the moon had anything to do with me.

"*And* she wants you to sleep over at her house. You can't stay with Silvan or Aunt Lemontina," Medea groused, tossing her chestnut hair over a shoulder.

"Nope."

"You can't say no, Stella," Mira warned.

"Nope," I repeated, my lips popping on the *p*.

Mira stomped her foot. "You—"

Midora flung an arm out, as if holding her sisters back, and I rolled my eyes. Always so dramatic. I was too old to be bullied and ordered around by the old tyrant and her lackeys. Mahari could stick it.

They eyeballed one other, communicating silently between quick glances at Alaric. Even in modern America, in the Romany culture, young women were "well behaved" in the presence of men. They'd tried to explain to me once how this deception actually made them feminists but the logic seemed convoluted to me.

Nearly six inches taller, Midora stared down her nose at me while speaking to the others as if I were dirt beneath her heel. "She's as stubborn as a cat. You know she won't come. Let's just tell Baba that she agreed. When she doesn't show up, she can be someone else's problem."

"Yeah. That's a great idea," I agreed. They were practiced liars, but Mahari would see through them, as always. They lied about everything, regardless of whether there was a need. Almost always for their own amusement. When I was twelve, as an April Fool's prank, they convinced me that Sam had died. They'd found my tears hysterical. It was the last time I cried in front of them.

Alaric continued to hang out throughout our exchange, surprising me when he could've marched off to a thousand more interesting ways to spend his time. They took turns kissing Silvan on both cheeks and moved eagerly in Alaric's direction, but I stepped in front of him on impulse. My movement was abrupt, causing me to trip over the stool again. From behind, warm hands steadied my waist before they dropped away.

It was a mistake. Speculation lit their hazel eyes and Midora's gleamed with satisfaction. I could only imagine the mileage they would get from teasing me about this. I'd just waved a red flag in front of bulls. Stella was acting jealous over a man. They completed fawning goodbyes over my head to Alaric, and he responded with that molasses voice.

"Alaric, did Stella tell you she sometimes does dance demonstrations at our studio? We're having a party there next Saturday. It's fun. You should come," Midora suggested with a sly smirk in my direction.

Silvan jumped in. "Hey, yeah. I'll be there, too."

I almost failed to hear his response over the roar of blood in my ears.

They didn't acknowledge *me* with a farewell, just turned to go in a cloud of spice-filled, musky perfume. *Good riddance.* Silvan returned to work.

Self-conscious, I tucked my sketchpad under an arm, grabbed the stool, and entered the store. Alaric moved out of my way without comment.

I placed the wooden seat near the counter and rested my sketchpad upon it. Inexplicably cold, I hugged my waist and studied the artwork hung on the wall. Typical of the bright colored posters in the manga store, this one featured a girl in a sailor suit with blond pigtails.

I snapped my gum, imagining Alaric walking down the lane, probably shaking his head at the odd exchange. It may have been impolite to walk away without saying goodbye, but I couldn't bear the look of disdain in his eyes and it was better to avoid an awkward end to our second meeting. Better that he just remember me as some strange girl he bumped into twice—or likely not at all.

Silvan appeared in my peripheral vision, talking to a young woman. "No, way. That work was done by Osama Tezuka himself..." His palm appeared beneath my chin and I spit my gum into it. He withdrew to wrap it in a piece of paper, never losing track of his conversation. I was glad he noticed before Jing, but it cost me my last piece of Big Red.

"Why don't you want to see your grandmother?" a deep voice murmured near my ear.

Relief weakened my knees just as nerves pulled me taut. I turned and gazed at his profile. He examined the same poster I'd been staring at. His jaw was defined, his profile commanding. What would he think if I opened my pad and began to sketch? He looked in his early twenties, but the confident way he carried himself made him seem much older.

"You're still here?" My voice sounded thin, even to me.

He appraised me coolly. "Do you want me to leave?"

Confused, I shrugged. "I figured after meeting my cousins and witnessing our usual fireworks that you'd find better things to do."

He parted his lips, closed them and then started again, a questioning look in his eyes. "You don't like your family?"

This was a difficult question. The correct answer was that I didn't feel I had one outside of Sam and Silvan. Silvan was the younger brother I wished I'd had—but without having to actually live with him. Maybe Alaric came from one of those big, close-knit families and couldn't understand how a person could be completely satisfied with just a few but very important people in your life.

"Well. Long story short, my parents were killed in a car accident when I was a baby. Placed into adoption until my mom's dad found me." I found it hard to meet his eyes, the exposure too much.

"Mahari and her extended family, including Silvan, are from my dad's side. They're Romany and kicked my dad out of the family when he ran away with my mom, who was a gadji, or non-Roma. I heard they had big plans for him, and he just threw them away for my Mom." Alaric's intense interest as I spoke threw me off. Nervous, I rambled on.

"We're not close. They've never come to my house, for example. They *do* try to make me come to them all the time. Just to punish me for my mom. I don't trust them."

For the love of all that is holy, stop talking!

Alaric tilted his head, hanging on every word. Was he just being polite?

"So, it's just my grandfather and me, outside of Silvan. I wish Mahari and the others would just leave me alone."

His silence was drawn out, and I began to think desperately of other things to talk about. "I'm sorry, *petite etoile*." I recognized the phrase—little star—from French lessons. His voice sounded hurt. *For me?*

"Family is everything," he said simply.

"Family is who you choose," I countered.

"You think DNA is all that connects you?" His question was sincere, as if he were trying to understand. Much better than being judged or pitied.

"Obviously. We have nothing in common. I didn't know my dad.

I've never even seen a photograph of him, because my grandmother had them all burned when he ran away with my mom."

This was a far deeper conversation than I wanted to have with a practical stranger. I had no idea what was compelling me to share such deep family secrets.

"You're bleeding," a sharp, feminine voice accused.

Startled, I discovered Jing standing at the counter.

She stared at my shoulder—at a small darkened spot that could have been anything. My dress buttoned from a V neckline to the hem above my knees, which made slipping the cotton fabric from my shoulder easy to do. A small wound appeared, blood still bright within a short, deep scratch I recognized as the work of Midora's pointed nails.

Alaric's hand was suddenly there, holding the cloth from my skin, his face so close I could feel his breath against my exposed clavicle. *Whoa.* Taking advantage of the proximity, I inhaled the scent of his hair. Sandalwood and frankincense. My head swam and I started to lean into him.

"It doesn't hurt," I murmured. Actually, Jing making a big deal about it made me realize that it did sting a little. Alaric took a step back, his face devoid of expression as he stared at the bloody scratch.

"Is this normal? That your family hurts you?"

"Isn't that what family does?" The muscle tic along his jaw was fascinating.

"Don't worry, it was probably for something I did to her first, but can't remember." Actually, I remembered very well. I was lucky the beeotch hadn't taken my arm off.

"It needs to be cleaned," Jing said. "Follow me." She marched away without waiting for agreement, leading the way to the back of the store. We followed. When a man stumbled into her path, she twisted quickly to avoid him, causing him to turn in a circle.

"What happened?" Ford asked, Jing's other employee.

Ford was a native Ohioan and resembled a young farmer with his ruddy complexion and ready smile. Pleasant looking, with russet hair and khaki pants, Ford was the polar opposite of the efficient, edgy Jing at whom he was now looking with eager, puppy dog eyes.

"Watch the front," Jing responded shortly. *She could've at least said please.* Ford smiled warmly, not appearing offended in the least. Jing entered the code into the keypad on her office door as Ford moved away to speak with a huddled group of boys.

The lights automatically switched on, her collection of swords and daggers gleaming against a stark white wall. She gestured to the only seat in the room; a swivel chair that rested before a freakishly neat desk. I took the seat as she opened a mini refrigerator and retrieved a first aid bag. She sighed at my raised eyebrow.

"I don't have a lot of room, so I keep the first aid in the fridge. Plus, your cousin is always getting paper cuts, and he likes when the ointment is cold." Her tone was wry, but a tiny smile appeared; rare evidence of her grudging affection for Silvan.

"If you like him so much, why not give him a raise? He's the reason you have so many return customers." My suggestion caused her eyebrows to shoot into her hairline.

"Who says I like him? Silvan already earns too much. He wastes time talking to people about the products and he can't…"

Alaric made a coughing noise but I was already very, very aware of his presence.

"Oh, Alaric this is Jing. She owns this place. Jing meet Alaric."

"It's a pleasure to meet you. Jing is a lovely name. Is it Chinese?" Alaric asked, an odd mischievous smile on his lips that made my palms sweat. Jing peeked up at him. "My mother was Chinese. My father was Japanese. And before you can ask, Jing is a maternal family name that means gentle."

I snorted in disbelief. Putting aside the irony of her name, Jing had never shared this personal information with me and I'd known her for years. As she opened a packet of antibacterial ointment, Alaric touched one of the sheathed swords. Jing had threatened us all with certain death if we so much as breathed on her precious collection. He turned and met her eyes with a challenging smile, one eyebrow raised. My jaw dropped.

She would kick us out. Perhaps grab another sword and start swinging. Instead, her lips curved in a small smile and she gave an imperceptible nod. This man had mad powers over womankind. Perhaps humankind.

Alaric unsheathed the samurai sword from its black wood and leather casing, examining its oiled blade and intricate hilt. He expertly tested the weight with both hands as Jing pushed the dress from my shoulder and applied salve with a gloved fingertip. Did she just sniff my shoulder? I glanced over to see her press a bandage to my skin. Alaric grunted in appreciation and I returned my attention to him. His movements with the weapon were mesmerizing. The blade flashed in quick, controlled movements, as he kept the edge close to his own body within the small space.

His expression relaxed into a happy grin as he admired the steel. "So itsu, me o ake tama ma neru nda."

She snorted. "Fuminshou."

He knew Japanese? It was a difficult language. I'd tried to teach myself some profanity, for Jing's sake, and could never get the hang of writing the characters.

"You speak Japanese?" I asked Alaric. They exchanged a fond look, and I wondered at how quickly he seemed to put people at ease. He flashed me a smile, forcing my lungs to momentarily seize. "Are you impressed?"

"Don't be," interrupted Jing as she tossed the bandage wrapper in the wastebasket. "His accent is terrible, and he speaks like a baby."

Alaric said something else in Japanese and Jing laughed. I'd never seen her so relaxed. Jing was a pretty girl, but when she laughed, she became beautiful.

I stood abruptly. "I should go."

They shot me odd looks, but Alaric slid the sword back into its sheath and returned it to the wall. He snapped his feet together, hands placed on the sides of his legs as he bowed low and swift before the curved sword. Jing watched him with a wistful smile. The turnabout in her personality was creepy.

My attempt to leave turned awkward when I had to wait for Jing to enter the door code. Why would you lock yourself inside your own office? Alaric surveyed the television monitors above the desk as he followed. Jing was nuts about security for sure.

When the door opened Silvan appeared, his knuckles lifted to knock. "I saw Amanda. Only her back, and she was at her mom's store." Silvan shared my worry. He cared about Amanda, and it wasn't like her parents to change their routine without telling someone.

I checked my phone and found a new text from Amanda. It was brief, consisting of two words. "The door." He jumped out of my way as I hustled to the entrance.

Outside, weary peddlers were packing up, and the crowds had thinned considerably.

I pushed past a group of young men in beanies smoking herbal cigarettes and ran the short distance to Marion's Mystical. The store front was dark, without movement inside. The lane in both directions revealed only thinning crowds, no sign of Amanda's dark hair or shape. The blue door remained locked, its "closed" sign mocking.

"There," Alaric said softly. He bent and teased the edge of a white envelope from beneath the door. I crouched and pushed his fingers aside. He allowed it and I tugged the paper free with pinched fingertips.

I ripped at the envelope and Alaric leaned over my shoulder as I scanned the torn magazine page again and again.

It was a glossy image of ancient Stonehenge.

"She's gone to England?" Alaric asked.

I flipped the page over and scanned the beginning of an article about the prehistoric monument. Frustrated, I checked the envelope.

"There." Alaric pointed to four tiny pencil marks.

They were numbers. 0200. *A flight number?*

I knew her cell lock code and it was 6714—the number otherwise known as Kaprekar's constant, after a renowned Indian mathematician. My dearest friend was such a geek. A flight number would also be unlikely. Amanda hated to fly. When they'd gone to Alaska, they'd gone by car and then ship.

I folded the page, unbuttoned my dress a few inches and slipped it beneath a bra strap.

"I don't know what it means," I said honestly. Amanda usually gave too *much* information. She'd behaved like a completely different person in the last twenty-four hours. What would make someone so solid flake out like this?

"Do you think she could have been forced to leave this message by someone else?" I glanced at Alaric when he didn't respond.

Hands in pockets, he stared at the neckline of my dress. I touched my throat and he shook his head, refocusing his eyes on a point down the lane.

Had I accidentally flashed too much when I put the note away? My cheeks warmed. It was getting late and I needed to go home to think more on the strange message from Amanda. Which meant parting ways with Alaric. I would never see him again.

My stomach sank at the thought. *Get a grip. You've known him one day! Remember how you mooned over Scott?* One thing I'd learned was to let go of the impossible. My pride couldn't handle another rejection and Alaric was so far out of my natural orbit he qualified as another stratosphere. But wasn't life about reaching for the stars?

"It was nice to see you again. But I should get home and check on my grandfather." I don't know what I expected. Maybe that he would ask to see me another time. Perhaps ask to exchange phone numbers. Disappointment blossomed, dark and glacial, when he did neither.

He wasn't even paying attention to me, just standing there with eyes narrowed at the front of Mrs. Wither's map store. I cleared my throat, but he didn't so much as offer a handshake. Unaccountably offended, I didn't linger. I had no time for mysterious men, no matter how handsome. I had to know what was going on with Amanda, and whatever happened in the woods yesterday had to be part of it. I needed to get somewhere private and study the photo again. It didn't sting at all that he let me walk away without a word. Not at all.

Chapter 6
The Hanged Man

Alaric

My fingers flexed as I fought the urge to sling her over my shoulder and take her to one of my many strongholds. This was turning into more than duty, and this could never *be* more than duty. If the plan worked, she would be claimed by another, if only in name. My brother.

And yet I could not stay away. Her loyalty towards those close to her was apparent. Despite what she claimed about trust, she'd forfeit her gum into the hand of the boy and tried to get him a raise. She'd lost so much in her young life, yet she still met the world with a raised chin. She was brave. She was anything but the docile girl I'd imagined her to be. Her female cousins, cunning and sharp, had all been wary of her.

Even with the potions Clara and her coven used to mask Stella's natural beauty and scent, she was hauntingly lovely. Even her hands were beautiful, with artistic, elegant fingers I imagined twisting in my hair while I ravaged her mouth...

Fury at my lack of self-discipline arose once more. She was a rose to be plucked by another. My role was clearly defined as her protector until she turned twenty-one or until the curse took her life. Her future might as well have been written in blood upon a page.

The growing distance between us left me feeling oddly empty. I'd sensed her confusion, but it was best—safer—that she leave the area. I needed the distance to clear my head. More importantly, I needed to assess the threat that lurked within the map store. The unique stench of magick emanated from beneath the closed shop door, and I needed to know if the witch was friend or foe. I stood before the door, considering.

How easily I'd nearly destroyed the barrier that masked my aura from the world, losing control for an instant when Stella's cousin assaulted her. The sight of Stella curling away from Midori's claws had very nearly brought out the beast. In a crowded human market, I'd nearly severed the stupid woman's hand, leaving her a stump as a reminder to keep her hands to herself. Only Stella's proximity to the beast and fear for her safety had kept my temper in check.

The First Law: Do no harm to the women and men of the Creator. Of course, unsanctioned violence happened. Humans disappeared or were injured by rogue demons and Primati all the time. But I was there to bring justice. Usually. There were years here and there when I'd been distracted with Murad's business or too busy with other realms to pay attention.

Within those gaps, my elite guard, led by Jing San, had kept the balance. I respected her too much to be entertained by the sight of the famous Samurai general operating a comic bookstore. She was my most loyal captain and I trusted her with my life—and Stella's.

For four years Jing had been embedded here as a personal favor, with almost no contact with me so that her location, and Stella's, was protected. This was the first I'd seen her in her new environment, and I was glad that she still had Ford, her blood companion, to keep her company. She might not have agreed.

It had been an honor to hold Dojigiri again. Made of steel so fine it could cut through demon flesh as easily as gossamer threads of sea silk, Jing had killed hundreds with the notorious katana blade since becoming an immortal Chishioni vampire.

Seeing Dojigiri on a wall like a common collectable in the manga shop had been startling. The infamous weapon had originally been crafted for her father, a powerful Shogun, by the great sword smith, and part fey, Muramasa. I possessed one of his swords myself yet kept it in a vault. Jing always did have a sense of irony.

She'd lived for two things since I'd found her covered in blood beneath a weeping wisteria tree: revenge on the Chishioni vampires who'd turned her and murdered her family; and serving the loftier purpose of the High Council by my side.

One thing was clear—we would not be able to hide Stella for much longer. Her eyes flashed silver when angered. I'd siphoned some of her energy by touching her back before her cousins noticed, yet it was something to discuss later with Clara. I ground my teeth with the knowledge that I would also have to speak with my brother about this turn of events. He was going to insist that we move to Plan B. The only allies we had here outside the water witches were the elusive TirieFliuch.

The fey were unbothered by moist climates, yet their shrinking numbers mostly remained in the Scottish Hills. A distant cousin of their clans, the TirieFliuch, existed in the Olympic forests of Washington. Too small and quick to be seen, their numbers were unknown. My brother, the Noble King, paid the Fey Queen well with Ottoman jewels to ensure the TirieFliuch kept their silence about our activities in the Pacific Northwest these last several years. Her influence and fear of retribution had kept our secrets safe thus far, but there was no guarantee when loyalty could be bought.

A stronger trace of sulfur rose again, confirming it originated from the map store. Clara aside, I had good reasons to detest the mischief of witches. I nudged the door open.

A brass bell clanged above my head. Shutting the door behind me, I sent my senses out. Confirming no human hearts beat within the room, I engaged the lock and flipped the door sign to "closed." Silence and dust motes met my perusal as I scanned the shelves and low tables. Poster tubes and map making tools lay near the register, but nothing living hid behind the scarred wooden counter.

I stalked to the back of the store and kicked open the door that held a sign that read "Office", too impatient to wait for an ambush.

The room was larger than expected, filled with filing cabinets and additional shelves of books. Oversized maps lined every surface of exposed wall. One in particular was interesting, as there was a girl standing immobile in front of it. I recognized her as Clara's right hand, Bromely, even though she looked very different from last evening. Her pigtails were gone, for one thing.

I tried not to laugh at her attempts to become invisible. The spell was camouflaging her against the ancient world map and wainscoted wall behind her. Of course, I could see her, but her stillness told me that she didn't know that—yet.

I wandered the room, keeping an eye on her shimmering outline as I did so. I picked up a book here...inspected a page there. When I circled to where she stood, hands at her sides and eyes closed, I paused. She was really very skilled. Her pulse and heat were masked so that another witch or Primati would've likely not been aware of her presence. The entire surface of her was an exact replica of the wall behind her. A perfect facsimile—as long as she kept her eyes closed. Only very great power could mask the eyes, as they were the windows of the soul.

Sorcerers, evil and soulless, would have been able to utterly mask themselves.

I leaned forward, as if interested in the southern plains of the African continent. I placed my face just above the left side of her head. This close, I could feel her living essence through the spell's tightly woven concealment. Her heart was now detectable and thrummed as quick as a hummingbird.

"Marco..." I murmured.

Bromely's shape quivered.

Not being able to help myself, I gave a low growl.

Her spell imploded with a tiny sonic pop, revealing the witch.

"Polo!" she cried.

Witches found it difficult not to finish spoken phrases or sounds. A half-finished secret knock, a partially complete saying such as "a bird in the hand..." the list was endless, and their compulsion drove them crazy. Only the most seasoned witch had the self-discipline to resist, and Bromely must have been at her limits with holding the camouflage spell.

I grinned as she slid down the wall, holding her face in terror.

"Please don't kill me. I'm with the First Order," she wheezed. The witch thrust a thin wrist over her head, revealing Clara's mark. Three blue waves.

I stepped back. She trembled and cried in the most boring way. I watched, impatient, as she wiped her nose on the sleeve of a green army jacket. She hugged her legs, covered with leggings and dirty boots, and began to rock.

"Stop sniveling or I *will* kill you," I finally snapped.

"Yes, sir," she cried. Sighing in disgust, I slouched into a leather chair and waited. I had to give her credit when she finally lifted her puffy face. She blinked through her tears like the most experienced of actresses. I had no doubt her fright was real. But she was no silly child.

"Laying it on a bit thick, aren't you?" I observed.

Her hands stilled where they wiped her cheeks.

"Aren't you a little old to be so dramatic?" Although she appeared very young, her aura was much, much older.

Her gaze hardened, and her tears dried. She rested her wrists on her knees, looking at me.

"Clara said you were her right hand. I find that hard to believe. First the traffic light and now spying on me."

"I wasn't spying. I was looking for one of our coven members, Susan Withers. She owns this store. I know she was here earlier because of a locator spell and there were signs…but I'm sorry about the traffic light. I was just so surprised to see you…"

I waved away her explanation. Witches were notoriously good liars.

"Do you know anything about the people who operate the mystic shop next door?"

She nodded grudgingly.

"And?" I barked.

She jumped. "I don't know. You'll have to speak with Clara. Something's been happening. A number of our people have disappeared."

I sank even further into the chair, pondering her words. Tapping my knee, I eyed her hunched form.

"Grayson," I said. Bromely's eyes widened, the blackened smears around them highlighting the white of her eyeballs. She began to shake.

The air pulsed.

"Please. You can't trust anyone," she hissed, desperation clear in her voice.

The shadow grew and solidified into my personal guard. Grayson preferred the appearance of a gentleman and wore an expensively tailored Dior suit, his silver hair combed elegantly back from his gentle countenance. Looks were deceiving. Grayson held his position due to his intelligence and loyalty, yet I'd also seen him garrote a demon with just a silk tie. His reputation as the Lion's left hand was legendary. Based on her reaction, it seems Bromely had heard of him.

Grayson glanced about the room, a meat cleaver in one hand. The effect was ruined somewhat by the pink and green apron tied about his waist.

Satisfied there was no immediate danger in the room, Grayson turned and offered me a short bow.

"Apologies, Alaric, I was just preparing dinner. The hotel chef has no idea how to prepare a proper braised paleron." He whipped the bloody cleaver behind his back, which placed it directly in front of Bromley's face.

A shriek rent the air, and Grayson whipped around and frowned at her, cleaver at the ready.

I hid a grin. "It's just one of Clara's witches, Grayson," I explained.

A former military man for England, Grayson had even less patience for hysterical witches than I did. He stepped away from Bromley but kept her in his sightline, the cleaver now arcing in figure eights at his side.

"Grayson, I want you to arrange a meeting tonight at the hotel. Let Clara and Jing San know that I will expect them at midnight. You should also be there."

"Yes, sir. It will be a pleasure to see Jing San again, sir. Will she require anything...special?"

I had no doubt that Grayson would have a lineup of blood donors at the ready if Jing requested one.

"No. She still has Ford with her." As her Blood Companion, Ford was the primary source of the blood Jing required to survive.

He nodded, but I detected a small slump to his shoulders.

"I also need you to research everything you can on the owners of the mystic shop next door to this one."

"Yes, sir." Grayson was already removing the bloody apron.

"...and I want to know what you can find about Lasho's family."

Grayson's brow furrowed before he realized who I spoke of. "Ms. Stella's father," he confirmed.

"Yes."

"I can tell you," Bromely cried out. "I know the gypsies. Or at least I know one of them."

We both ignored her.

I nodded at Grayson, and he disappeared.

When the room cleared of his presence, I turned my attention back to the witch at my feet. "How do you know what I speak of?"

Something in my expression put her off as she gulped and lowered her chin before answering.

"Clara has had me watch Stella for several years. I've never been allowed to make direct contact. But I take dance lessons from her cousin's studio so I can keep watch. It's one of the few places she goes. I've made friends with one of them. A boy."

A corner of my lips curled. "You know who Lasho is?" I queried.

"Yes. Stella's father. The beloved youngest son of their matriarch. He eloped with Stella's mother and they died together." She was well-informed.

"Have you witnessed any abuse of Stella by her father's family?" I asked casually. She paused, and I had my answer. My fingers gripped the armrests as I prepared to stand.

She crossed her arms over her chin, cowering. "Wait! Did you ask if Stella abuses them or if they abuse Stella?" she asked. I paused. Considered.

"Either," I clarified, curious.

"Uh. It's pretty equal. They used to bully her quite a bit, but now it's more Stella. It's smart. She keeps them on the defensive before they can start anything," she explained quickly.

My girl is strategic. Wait. She was not my girl. Could never be my girl.

"What about the grandmother...Mahari?"

She frowned. "I hardly see her. She doesn't hang out with the younger people in the family outside their homes, and I don't go near their compound. No one does."

"Do you go to Stella's house?"

She paused. I could see the wheels clicking as she pondered my words.

"You should speak to Clara."

I leaned forward, elbows on my knees in a deceptively calm pose. She leaned back. "I'm asking you."

"Uninvited Primati cannot get near her house. We can only keep watch from the road and woods," she admitted.

My eyebrows drew down. Was this a spell of Clara's?

"We think it has something to do with the eggs."

I bared my teeth in warning at her riddles. She stuttered an explanation.

"There are very old oak trees on her property. Its leaves are larger than my head. We think that's where the magick comes from. There are hollowed eggs hung in the trees. Old creation magick," she quickly finished. *Creation magick? Was it possible?*

"We noticed that only people invited by Stella or her grandfather can enter the house. Clara won't let us interact with them directly because of your rules," she continued in a thin voice.

Had I told Clara not to engage with them directly? Perhaps I had.

I was curious about the magick, whether I would also be withheld, or if I could pass through. But first I needed to speak with my brother.

If Clara's witches were disappearing, it could mean enemies were near and much sooner than expected. We would have to implement the plan agreed upon years ago. When my brother had discovered she lived.

If she were at risk of discovery, in order to protect her, Stella would be claimed by my brother as a bride on her eighteenth birthday. No one would threaten the future queen. If any tried, my armies and I would cut them down, returning to the days of heads on pikes if necessary.

Now we just had to convince Stella.

I stood and approached Bromely. She scrambled to her feet, fingers clawing at the wainscoting behind her. I reached out a hand and gently cupped the side of her neck.

She stilled, staring into my eyes while her chest rose and fell with rapid little pants.

The witch's skin was ice cold. I pressed a thumb against the thick flutter that was her heartbeat. I leaned in, holding my breath. Her eyelids went half mast, confused. My fingers probed tenderly against the fragile bones and tendons at her nape.

With a twist of one hand I snapped Bromely's neck, and watched as she slipped to the floor with vacant eyes.

Chapter 7
The Chariot

Stella

The older model Lexus rested at the side of the long drive to my house. My neighbor's curious goat was keeping a watchful eye on the silver bumper that nearly touched its fence. I recognized the car as Aunt Lena's, although the driver was too short to be my aunt.

I slowed but passed the car. The driver gave an irritated honk, scaring the goat into a leaping dance. *What now?* I pulled my VW to a stop and watched the rearview mirror. None of my Romani relations had ever come to my house with the rare exception of Mahari, who'd stopped by occasionally to speak in private with Sam. To say I was suspicious was an understatement.

Seconds ticked until the driver's door opened and then my cousin Mira stood in the road. She approached my side window and I reluctantly cracked it a couple of inches. If she were here to kidnap or kill me, I wasn't going to make it easy for her.

"Hi, cuz," she said, leaning at my window and talking through the small crack I'd allowed.

"What do you want?" I asked warily. She didn't even pretend to be wounded.

"Like my ride? Mom gave it to me."

She grimaced when I remained silent. "I just want to talk to you. Promise, nothing bad." She held up two fingers in a peace sign. I blinked. Mira was twenty-one, the youngest of the twisted sisters. She'd never visited me before. None of them had. On the other hand, although terrible together, my cousins were marginally less awful one-on-one.

"I have a present for Sam in the car from Baba," she explained. Her heavily mascaraed eyes were wide and innocent. I snorted and rolled up the window an inch.

"Listen! She said she'll send someone else over if I come back without giving it to him with my own hands. She's not feeling great today." Her cheeks and forehead were unnaturally shiny. As if she'd been exercising—or wore too much highlighter.

In her seventies, Mahari insisted on driving herself everywhere and she'd visited Sam alone before. Despite being a heavy smoker, she was never sick. Being mean gave people superpowers. But Mira was right. If I refused, Mahari would just send someone else.

"Follow me," I said shortly.

"Right behind you, cousin," she snickered, a flash of gold peeking from between her lips. It was either a gold eye tooth or a temporary something. You never knew with Mira. She trotted back to her car.

I gripped the cracked leather of my steering and rolled forward. The last twenty-four hours had been a lot, and I'd wanted time alone to study Amanda's cryptic message. Hopefully, she'd buzz out as soon as she dropped off Mahari's gift.

She parked behind my VW and joined me on the porch. "What's

with the Easter eggs?" she asked, eyeing the trees with their ribbon streams and treasures.

I shrugged. "It's just an art thing. A tradition with Sam. Come on." Revealing something, anything, personal with Mira made my skin itch. My Rom family were quick to twist information into anything that could sting later. I'm sure the vast majority of Romany were honest, kind people—but I was not related to a single one of them. Mahari's family were loyal only to one another. Anyone outside the circle, and I sat just on the line, was fair game. As usual, I took the steps two at a time, Mira breathing down my neck.

The house was quiet. I kicked off my sandals and made Mira do the same with her boots. She wore no socks and her toenails were painted a garish purple that matched her fingernails. I caught her looking at my bare toenails with a disapproving smirk. Feeling like a hobbit, I defiantly spread my toes to give her a better view.

I glanced surreptitiously around the foyer, imagining it through her eyes. It was neater than her house, for sure. Aunt Lena's house was always cluttered with random stuff and tchotchkes. I followed her gaze up the dark wooden stairs protected by a faded, wine-red carpet runner.

"Hmm. Where do you sleep?" she asked.

"My bedroom's in the attic. Sam sleeps on the ground floor now."

"You're the only one upstairs?" She looked a little impressed.

"Yup." Was she planning a break in?

"Aren't you scared to be alone up there?" she asked, ogling the ceiling.

"Never. I like it."

She fell silent, a small package wrapped in plain paper under her arm. With a start, I realized that, barefoot, we were nearly the same height. Around her sisters and usually wearing heels, Mira always seemed much taller.

"Stella?" Sam's voice floated from his study. Mira gazed down the hall, biting her lip. My head tilted, curious as to why she might be nervous. Then I remembered I didn't care. *Let's get this over with.* Visitors made Sam anxious.

We found him sitting in his favorite club chair, a fire crackling in the small fireplace. His hospital bed was pushed against one wall, and the windows offered a nice view of the backyard bathed in twilight. The small cottage on the edge of the backyard where Roger lived emitted a glow as lights were switched on. Sam's study turned bedroom was a masculine room, decorated in rich burgundy and hunter green. I pretended not to notice it also held the scent of pipe smoke.

"Hi, Sam. Where's Nancy?" Sam and I were not the most affectionate family, yet we always said hello like we meant it. I pressed my lips against the giving warmth of his cheek as he patted my back.

"Who's Nancy?" Mira asked.

"Sam's new night nurse." Although I was prone to being nocturnal, Carol had arranged a professional to stay over in case he needed medical care during the night.

"She's in the kitchen reading. You didn't see her?" he asked, eyes glued to Mira. His fingers, twisted with arthritis, smoothed at the buttons of his red plaid pajama top and I knew he was likely embarrassed to be wearing bed clothes in front of company. Sam was funny about manners and propriety.

Mira stopped her inspection of the room to step closer. Bending, she cupped her hands around her lip-glossed mouth.

"Hi, Mr. Avery. Do you remember me?" she yelled.

We both winced.

"He's not deaf, Mira," I said at normal volume.

"Oh." She pulled back in surprise.

Sam's grey mustache twitched. "I can't say that I do remember you," Sam answered. "But you do look a lot like Mrs. Mahari's people. Are you one of hers?"

Mira nodded. "She's my grandmother."

Sam looked at me with pursed lips, the wild hair of his eyebrows drawing down.

"Mira stopped by to give you a present from Mahari," I explained.

Mira plopped down in a nearby chair without invitation, curling her bare feet beneath her. "Do you have anything to eat?"

I stared at her, incredulous, before I forced a calming breath for Sam's sake. *The nerve.* I turned to speak to Sam.

"Are you hungry, Sam?"

"No. Carol fed me supper at four like a proper senior citizen. Your meatloaf was extra good, but I couldn't take that salad with those fake tomatoes." Unless it came off the vine in his own garden, Sam called all tomatoes fake.

"So, where's this present?" Sam asked, sitting up straighter.

Mira plucked it from her lap and leaned forward without standing to hand it to him.

He couldn't quite grasp it, his dexterity not being what it was. I took it from Mira and placed it in his lap.

His fingers trembled as he pulled the paper apart. Mira stared at the fire, giving him privacy. Her thoughtfulness was surprising. Sam made a choked noise and I turned to see him hold a crude cross made of dried, twisted sticks and vines.

"What is it?" I asked.

"It's a cross. Made from a Rowan tree," he gasped, turning it over in his hands, stroking the shape as he examined it with disbelieving eyes. Curious, I glanced at Mira, who regarded Sam with a sympathetic frown. Sam was somewhat religious. He'd grown up in a Quaker household but had stopped going to services years before I came along.

"Did Mahari make it for you? That was...nice," I commented, peering over his shoulder at the handmade object.

"No," he whispered. "Your mamma did."

The world bottomed out. My skin went from heated to iced in seconds as blood roared and my head swam. Outside of the decorated eggs in our tree, I'd grown up without anything belonging to my mother. Sam had told me my mom had taken all of her personal belongings with her when she ran away with my dad.

"My mom?" He nodded, eyes fixed upon the cross. Dumbly, I noticed he was crying. Sam was stoic and sturdy. Feelings embarrassed him and I wasn't sure how to react or comfort him.

"Mahari must have taken it from their apartment in San Francisco. Cleaned it out. I didn't go there myself," he mumbled. Mahari had gone to my parent's home after they died?

Mahari refused to talk about my father. Had removed every sign of him—but then held on to something that belonged to my mother? She had no right.

A worse thought came to mind. If Mahari had gone to their home after they died, wouldn't she have seen preparations for my arrival? Perhaps seen a crib or baby clothes? Yet I'd gone to foster care for months before Sam found me. Things clicked. Mahari had deliberately abandoned me. Wow. What a crap thing to do.

Sam peered at Mira through watery eyes. He was shrinking before me.

"I suppose you're here to watch over her?" His voice held a tremor as he glanced between Mira and me. I'd misheard him. It sounded like he asked Mira if she was watching over me.

She nodded solemnly, respectfully. "For tonight. Someone else will take over tomorrow."

"What are you talking about?" I asked, genuinely confused.

Sam stared into the fire. "Mira, will you give me time alone with my granddaughter?"

"The kitchen is back towards the foyer. You can ask Nancy if there are leftovers," I suggested in a dry croak. She left the room and I took her seat.

"What's going on, Sam?'

Sam lifted the cross to his nose, his nostrils flaring as he breathed in its scent. His reaction embarrassed me, as if a secret door had opened, exposing something private. Even though he didn't speak about her, I realized how deep his grief must have been to lose a daughter. He placed the cross in his lap before he raised his face, his green eyes hooded and damp within their soft folds.

"I'm going to tell you something rather fantastical. Something you will have a hard time understanding right now," he began. "I've had a long-standing arrangement with Mahari. If there is danger to you, she was to send me a sign. We agreed upon a cross as a symbol. I just didn't expect her to send an actual one. Especially this one. Vivi made this when she was young. She'd saved a bird and made this from the tree she found it beneath..." Lost to memory, he stopped speaking. Impatience strummed my nerves. "What danger?" My tone was sharper than I intended and laced with hurt, but I couldn't help it.

"The same danger that killed your mother." His voice hitched over the word *killed*.

"My mom died in a car accident," I stated, quiet on the outside.

"Your mother died of that bloody curse," he barked.

Sam was at an age when dementia or worse could set in. My belly ached with dread.

"Too many losses. Such a waste. You can't be alone now. You *will* stay inside this house." His words made no sense but his tone was commanding. It had been a long time since Sam tried to tell me what to do.

"Sam. There is no such thing as curses. This is just Mahari's gypsy nonsense. They're probably trying to shake you down for money again."

Somewhere in my subconscious was a niggling observation. Sam *was* superstitious. I'd noticed it through the years. Was it possible she'd been able to convince him that curses were real? It was their scam, after all. Convincing people to fork over cash to ward away evil or dissolve curses made against them.

"Stella Avery. You know not to use that word—it's offensive and I raised you better than that. Refer to them as Romani or Roma if you must give a label," he admonished before continuing. "I made mistakes before, thinking I alone could keep you safe. I'm too old now. I've lived far longer than I've a right to. Mahari agreed to take over when I... Mahari's people will be with you at all times. That was our arrangement. Why they gave you space all these years."

"Mahari hates me," I spluttered in outrage. And it *was* fortune-telling gypsy nonsense, complete with headscarves and fake crystal balls for cripes sakes. No way was I going to live with Mahari. No one, not even Sam, could make me.

"You don't know what she feels. But we are family and she will protect you," he said with finality. "To the Roma, family is everything." *Not this family.* Sam had always defended them, never acknowledging what I endured. He continued, ignoring my baleful expression.

"If something happens to me, Roger will know what to do. I know he's young enough for it to be unseemly, and people may talk at his being our handyman, but he should move into the house to make sure you are not alone until arrangements can be made."

Only Sam would think a thirty-three-year-old man was young. I didn't object to Roger living in the house, but the conversation was making my heart pound. In a couple of months I would be eighteen and no one would be making arrangements for me. Any talk of Sam dying spun me into anxiety and I hated it.

"Sam..."

"Enough! We can talk about this tomorrow. Right now, I just want a little peace." He raised his voice, and I flushed. Upsetting Sam was the last thing I wanted.

"I need to sleep." He placed the cross on the arm of his chair. I itched to touch it but didn't. If he'd offered it to me, I would have accepted it, touched what she had touched. But he didn't. As much as we loved one another, there was a gulf between us with my mother's name on it. I nodded, swallowing a harsh mixture of anger, fear, and sadness.

I escorted him to the adjoining powder room and waited outside as he prepared for bed. When he opened the door, I helped him sort out his evening pills and gave him water. I checked off the chart next to his bed so Nancy would know what he had taken and when. Once he was in bed, I raised the side bar and bent to turn off the nearby lamp. Sam lifted a hand from beneath the covers. His lips opened and closed. Opened again.

"Stella."

I leaned down and kissed his cheek. He captured the end of my braid and tugged. "Thick as a horse's mane," he whispered. It was something he always said about my hair, and I swallowed against the lump in my throat.

"You look like her, you know. The only one. I don't know why."

I was tired of trying to tease out facts from his strange stories tonight.

"Stella. If you get the chance...tell her that I forgive her. That I forgave her a long time ago."

"Who, Sam?" He couldn't be talking about my mother. She was

dead. Mahari?

He smiled sadly, his silver mustache gleaming in the darkness. "I told them I would never say her name again. Words have power. Everything listens."

Carol would want to take Sam to the doctor for tests. Perhaps an MRI.

"I've lived so long, Stella. I'm tired. I don't know whether I can see your story end. I don't want to," he whispered.

Tears burned, but I refused to allow them to leak out. The medication did its job, and his breathing slowed. Saying goodnight, I made sure the voice monitor next to his bed was working. I closed his door and wandered down to the kitchen, my stomach in knots.

The new nurse, Nancy, sat with a book and the other voice monitor. Mira wasn't in the kitchen. My cheeks burned, and anger coursed through me until I realized the monitor was turned off. Had it *just* been turned off?

Nancy looked up at me with a smile that failed to reach her eyes. She was a fat woman with short legs and thinning, curly hair. She'd taken an instant dislike to me, and I was thinking the feeling was mutual.

"Hi. I'm Stella. You must be Nancy. Sam's in bed. I gave him his medicines and logged them."

Her lips pursed in disapproval. She may have been pretty once upon a time, but I didn't see it.

"You should not be giving him medication. That's my job," she pointed out coldly.

She may be right, but Sam and I had looked out for each other for a long time now, and it was silly to presume I couldn't dispense a prescription without a nursing degree.

"Thanks for the reminder," I responded flatly.

Her eyes narrowed and she dog-eared her book, thumping it down on the table. Yep. I definitely did not like her. Anyone who dog-ears an Elizabeth Peters is straight up shady. "Did you see my cousin?"

She shook her head, her thin lips pressed so hard they disappeared.

Wandering the first floor, there was no sign of Mira, and I had a bad feeling about where she might be. I skipped up the long stairs to my bedroom.

Mira stood in my room, bent over my art table. She'd turned on the fairy lights covering my ceiling and her fingers were outstretched, nearly touching the completed Tarot cards.

"Hands off."

She flinched, shoving her hands behind her back. I folded my arms and she paced around my bedroom, taking in the art posters and easels of partially completed work.

She finally flopped down upon my unmade bed, sitting cross-legged amidst my blankets. *I'll have to change my sheets now.*

"They're pretty. Do you even know how to read the cards?" she asked. Still upset from my conversations with Sam and then Nancy, I didn't answer.

"I could teach you if you want," she offered.

I shook my head. "Can you please stay where you are and not touch any of my things for at least two minutes?" I needed to use the bathroom.

She held up her palms. "Consider me Elsa." I frowned and she rolled her eyes. "Frozen? The movie?" It was hard to believe she was older than me.

I cleaned up and met my own reflection in the mirror. She was a wild mess. I dragged off my hair tie and unwound my hair until it fell in waves that reached the small of my back. I tried to finger-comb it into looking neater, but then gave up, using the hair tie to create my usual messy bun. Remembering Amanda's note, I took the magazine page from my bra and unfolded it.

Stonehenge. My conversation with Carol earlier…her son Thomas worked at a replica of Stonehenge. Could she be leaving a clue to go see Thomas? We'd been in the same home school group so they knew one another. Taking the page, I returned to my room. Mira, still seated on my bed, flipped through the journal that normally rested on my nightstand.

She flung it down with a mock guilty expression when she spotted me. Fortunately, I only used the journal to doodle drawings. Nothing salacious for her to carry tales about.

I glared while shoving it into my bedside drawer but she just shrugged. "You have a very boring life."

"That's the way I like it," I said. At least that was truth for now.

I walked over to the rack of clothes that made up my closet. Mira was by my side in an instant. "Ooh. Are you changing? Can I help you find something?"

I slapped her hands away, but they returned, her nimble fingers passing over the plastic hangers. It was weird to have someone from my Rom family in my bedroom, touching my things.

'Where are we going?" She plucked out a short blue dress and held it against her frame.

"What do you mean?" I asked warily. Some "guard" she was.

She pulled out a pair of striped overalls, raising eyebrows at my taste. I shrugged. Those were super retro and I'd hemmed them myself. She put them back and kept looking.

"Well. I was listening to the baby monitor with Nurse Ratched when Sam told you to stay inside. Which means you will be leaving as soon as possible," she explained.

I grunted, outraged they had shamelessly listened to a private conversation. I was also impressed with her perceptive deduction. A half-baked plan had formulated. I was going to check out Amanda's house. See if they'd returned, and if they hadn't, to look for clues on where they might be.

Intention set, I grabbed a pair of folded dark jeans from a shelf and a holey black cashmere sweater from the rack. She looked disapproving at my selection but said nothing. Ignoring her, I slipped off my dress and began to get dressed.

"Oh. My. Sweet. Baby. Jesus. Are you wearing granny panties?"

Self-conscious, I tugged the jeans on faster.

"What's this?" She plucked the magazine page from the floor.

"None of your business," I snapped, scrambling to grab the page from her while pulling the sweater over my head with one hand.

She released it with a pout.

"Stonehenge?" She raised a single eyebrow.

"None of your business," I repeated, still embarrassed about my underwear.

They were all so *intrusive*. Pushy, overbearing, stomping on boundaries...

"At least you have good knockers. The size of apples is about right. Mom says that if you can hold a pencil under your melons then they're too saggy, and I can fit, like, a box of #2s under mine."

I gaped as she returned to the clothing rack, selecting the striped overalls and a long sleeved t-shirt. She pulled off her maxi dress and I looked away too late. She wore nothing but a pair of racy thong panties, which seemed unhygienic but to each their own.

I straightened my sweater, half listening as she chattered.

"Did you know that our family traveled all over Europe before coming to America? Mahari's grandmother grew up in Siberia." When her voice was no longer muffled, I hazarded a glance.

The shirt and overalls that were baggy on me fit her like a glove.

She struggled to fasten the bib clasps over her larger chest. I didn't know that, actually. I just assumed they'd lived here in Portland for generations.

"Mahari came to America with her first husband. He died, and she remarried Grandfather in San Francisco. We only moved to Oregon when..."

She stopped speaking and I looked at her questioningly. This was all new information. I tried to imagine Mahari as a young woman, a bride arriving in distant lands.

"You should go. To England, I mean. If you want."

I moved to the dresser and grabbed a pair of socks.

"Life is short," she pointed out.

I grunted. This was something I already knew.

Chapter 8
The World Reversed

Stella

"How long are we going to sit here?" Mira grumbled.

For the hundredth time, I resisted the urge to hit her.

If I did, I knew it would turn into a cat fight, and her borrowed car was so crowded who knows what we might roll around in. From the smell, it might be a missing pet. Fancy on the outside, the car was a mess on the inside. Which pretty much summed up everything about Mira and her sisters.

"At least you're in the front. I think I'll need a tetanus shot later." Silvan grumbled.

The car was the only reason I'd allowed Mira to come along, reasoning that no one in Amanda's neighborhood would recognize it, whereas mine was well-known to the residents here. We'd picked up Silvan for a lookout.

Amanda's house lay pitch dark, her neighborhood still. Only the front porch light of her house shone, and I knew it was set on a timer. Next door, Scott's jeep was parked beside his Dad's in his driveway, his house completely dark.

They kept a spare key hidden in one of those fake stones her mom had purchased online. It was located near the back door, and I pinched my lips, thinking about it. Her backyard was surrounded by a wood fence, so I would have to go up the drive along the side of her house to access it.

Repeating my actions from two minutes prior, I called Amanda's cell and then her home number, half expecting the sleepy voice of her father, George, to answer. It went to voicemail after several rings. No lights switched on. I trained my eyes on the side gate and spoke to Mira. "Okay. You both stay here. I'm going to check her backyard."

"No way. I'm coming, too. Mahari said I was to be on you like glue," Mira whined.

"No."

"If you make her stay in the car, can I come instead? I think I'm sitting on something damp…" Silven asked. I sighed and pinched my nose, praying for patience.

"If you don't let me come, I'll call my sisters." She raised her cell phone, hovering a finger over the screen. Shit. She would, too.

I threw my hands in the air. "Fine. Silvan, you keep low in the car and text us if you see anyone. Mira—don't speak." Silvan let loose a whispered string of unusual curse words.

Mira pouted. "I'm not an idiot, Stella."

That was debatable. I switched off her car's automatic overhead lights, so we wouldn't be revealed when the doors opened. The door handle found its way into my slippery grip and I carefully opened it, Mira following my example. Hunched over, I hurried across the street, crossed Amanda's lawn, and hustled down her driveway to the gate separating her backyard. Turning, I jumped to see Mira inches from my face. She grinned like the Cheshire cat. *Okay then.*

Unnerved by her stealth, I unlatched the gate and led the way into Amanda's backyard. Once my cousin slipped by, I latched it closed, suddenly grateful Amanda only had a cat. A barking dog would shatter my nerves at this point. I shoved hair behind my ears and searched the darkened yard.

The backyard was enveloped in darkness. Behind the back fence was an alley illuminated by a lone streetlamp, but the dim yellow light was no match for the deep shadows. I glanced over at Scott's yard and caught sight of the top of his mother's clothesline.

Cupping my hand against Mira's ear, I whispered, "There's a spare key. Just wait by the backdoor while I get it." She nodded and moved to the back steps, silent as a ghost.

I crouched next to the stones that bordered the herb garden Marion kept in meticulous order. Counting the stones, I picked up what should have been the fake plastic rock that held their spare house key. But it was heavy. A real stone. Counting again, I picked four different rocks—all real. Frustrated, I raked over the stones, trying to locate the false one.

"Do you want me to break in?" came Mira's voice next to my head.

I fell over, hand to my chest. "Shhh!"

She grinned, her gold tooth flashing in the low light. "I can break the back window. I know how to do it quietly." Of course, she did.

"Pssst," came a voice. Mira and I froze.

"Pssst." The sound was coming from Scott's side of the fence.

I turned my head, and sure enough, his face hovered over the top of the wooden fence.

Oh, boy. I swiveled to glare at Mira but she was already heading towards him. I followed, brushing dirt from my jeans.

Scott's hands appeared on the top of the fence, and he vaulted over, landing in Amanda's yard. I waited for him to straighten, a weird nudge in my chest at seeing him. He was barefoot and wore jeans and a ripped

Led Zeppelin t-shirt. I inwardly rolled my eyes at his fixation with the 70s.

"Hey," he said, hands in his back pockets.

"Hey," I returned.

He cocked his head at Mira, and she slinked into a pose that jutted one hip to the side and pushed her chest forward. His eyes predictably landed exactly where she intended.

"Hi," she cooed. Did she flirt with everyone?

Scott nodded at her before he returned to contemplate me. The dim light cast his eyes into shadows, the planes of his face in sharp relief. His tousled hair indicated he'd been pulling at it or had just woken up.

"I saw you guys from my bedroom when you got out of the car. What are you doing here? Amanda's not home," he murmured. So, my career as a spy was short lived. I gnawed the inside of my cheek. Who else had seen us? Were they calling the police as we stood here? Scott seemed to read my mind.

"Hey, don't worry. I just happened to be up, but most people on the street are asleep by ten," he said in the familiar husky voice that used to send shivers along my skin.

"Amanda and her parents are missing. I'm worried," I explained, trying to keep our conversation brief.

He surveyed her house and yard. "Hang on. I think we still have her house key in our kitchen. Mrs. Nightingale gave it to my mom, so she could water the plants the last time they went to Vancouver."

I started to protest, losing my nerve, but he was already across the fence.

I tried to ignore Mira, but there was nothing else to look at while we waited.

When I finally glanced at her, I was rewarded with a smirking grin. "Stella and Hot Guy, kissing in a tree. K-I-S-S-I-N-G," she began in a low sing-song voice. Was she drunk?

I punched her in the shoulder, missed and hit her boob.

"Ow!" She punched me harder in the arm.

"Quiet!" I hissed as she grabbed a handful of my hair and yanked.

Scott returned to the fence, making short work of climbing over.

Mira stepped away as his gaze flickered between us.

"This is my cousin," I whispered. "Her name is Mira. M.I.R.A." If questioned later by the police, I wanted to make sure he spelled her name right.

Shrugging, he paced up to Amanda's back door. We followed, waiting as he fit a key in the lock and opened the door. Standing aside, he allowed us to go in first.

I turned to thank him, thinking he would wait outside, but found his face inches from mine. I gasped, unable to help myself. I stepped backwards.

"You don't have to come in." If we were getting into trouble, he shouldn't be part of it. His mother would kill him.

"I'm already inside. What are we looking for?" His voice was the same rich bass I remembered. Sudden memories of his hands beneath my shirt and long, languid kisses flooded my brain. And in a split second those memories were replaced with an image of Alaric. He was taller than Scott. I wondered whether he was a better kisser.

"Uh. Just whether they are here, and if not, clues where they could have gone."

"Got it." He whispered with a thumbs up. I turned and led the way through Amanda's mudroom and into her kitchen.

Mira was ass-up into the refrigerator.

The fridge light illuminated the kitchen and I gasped. "Close that!" I hissed.

Her head popped up. "Relax. I was just checking. It's been emptied.

Nothing in here but a box of baking soda." That couldn't be right. Marion always kept it well-stocked with fresh produce.

I peered inside, just to be sure. She was right. Stepping to the trash can, I lifted the lid and found it empty. This morning the garbage had been half full. This morning, sitting at the table with a green juice, seemed a million years ago.

Curious, I edged my way to the bottom of her stairs. The upstairs was dark. No sound drifting down to us. I took the first step, wincing as the board creaked.

Mira flew past me, glancing back at me in challenge as she chuckled.

I glared at her daring and began to pursue. Scott tugged at my hand. I turned, unwanted heat pooling in my gut as memories surfaced. "Stella. I wanted to tell you...I really liked you. Like you."

I swallowed hard. This was the moment I'd been waiting for. Why did it feel so awkward?

"Uh-huh. That's why you stuck your tongue down that girl's throat right in front of me." The memory still wounded, whack-a-moling the butterflies in my stomach.

I couldn't see his face, but he bent his head, thick sandy hair flopping over his eyes.

"Stella...my mom didn't want me to see you."

I was shocked. His mother was always a little cool towards me, yet I hadn't known she actively disliked me. We had barely spoken more than a few words to one another.

"You broke my heart because your mom didn't like me?"

"No! I mean, I didn't know how to talk to you about it."

I tried to digest this news, half listening for Mira's footsteps.

His thumb moved across my wrist. Last year, his touch would have made my arm weak. Now it just felt annoying and I tugged my hand free. I didn't know what to think about this. Even if Sam hated Scott, I would not have broken up or hurt him so deliberately.

"I just wanted you to know. I'm sorry I hurt you," he whispered.

Mira appeared in front of us. Scott stepped back, or I pulled away, I wasn't sure which.

"The bedrooms are empty and the closets are half full. It looks like they did a runner. I didn't see a cellphone in the girlie room."

A faint voice drifted outside, from the front lawn. "Scooott?"

Oh shit. Scott's mother. I glanced at my phone to find a missed text from Silvan. *Crazy lady in pajamas on the move!*

Scott gave a frustrated grunt and hurried to the backdoor with Mira and me right behind him.

"She's been checking in on me at night. She must've seen I wasn't in bed," he explained. I bit my tongue on a dozen snarky responses.

"Dude. Aren't you a little old for your mom to be calling you home? You might want to move out already," Mira advised. I smirked, happy for once at her lack of filter. We stopped at the backdoor.

Scott faced me, his features tense.

"I'll take the key back and lock up in the morning." Not waiting for my response, he jogged back to the fence and vaulted over. I glanced at Mira and noted her grin and wide eyes. At least one of us was enjoying all this excitement. We shut the door and tiptoed through the house to the living room window where we could view the street. Mrs. Caywood was standing in her front yard in a housecoat. The woman would definitely call the police if she suspected we were here. She continued to call for Scott until I heard his baritone answer from their front porch. I scanned the street and noticed the top of Silvan's head sink lower in the backseat of Mira's car.

"Mom! I'm right here."

Mrs. Caywood turned and marched back to her own house.

Their voices mingled, rose sharply, and faded.

What time *is* it? I crept to the front entry and inched close to the grandfather clock that ticked steadily in a corner. Almost 12:30 in the morning. Sudden insight flashed as I stared at the clock hands. What if the 0200 on Amanda's note was military time for two o'clock?

"Did you see her cat?" I whispered to Mira.

She shook her head.

Racing to the laundry room off the kitchen, I noted that the cat's litter box was missing. Wherever they'd gone, they'd taken Amanda's tabby with them. I bent over my knees in relief—Dr. Pepper was a mean-ass cat that only liked Amanda. Kidnappers wouldn't have bothered to take a pet, especially one that would scratch your face off. Unless they wanted to stage a different scenario.

I bit my lip, worried Mrs. Caywood was still awake. What if she was watching the street? I had to hope that knowing Scott was under lock and key would send her back to bed. We crept back through the house, returning to the mudroom. The yard remained dark and empty. Peering around the doorjamb, I noted the absence of lights at Scott's house.

Mira shoved me onto the porch and shut the door behind her. By the time I straightened she was already hotfooting it back to the gate. I nearly caught it in the face as her giggling figure flung it wide. I kicked her, but she was so fast that my sneaker barely clipped her ankle. "Shhhh!" I warned.

She gave me the stink eye over her shoulder but never slowed. We reached her car in record time and locked the doors once safely inside. We slumped down in the seats and looked at each other, adrenaline pumping wildly.

"This is so messed up. I nearly peed my pants when she came out of the house." Silvan whispered from the backseat floorboards. We snorted, the sound melding into laughter. Big, rib shaking, can't breathe laughter.

"What's next?" gasped Mira when she could speak again. She fumbled for her car keys and I checked the time.

"Can I trust you to keep a secret?" I meant Mira. Silvan, I trusted with my life. I had no idea where the impulse came from. Asking one of the twisted sisters to keep a secret should have been like asking a snowman to visit hell and return without breaking a sweat.

Mira went still as a statue. With a solemn face, she crossed her heart with her fingers three times and then across her throat. I figured this meant *yes.*

"I think the picture of Stonehenge may refer to the fake one in Maryhill. It's about an hour and a half away." If she balked, I would go back for my car.

"I know where that is." She picked up her phone and entered an address into the GPS.

"There are a few numbers handwritten on the page. 0200. I think that means 2:00. I just don't know whether that's morning or afternoon."

"We won't know until we try, will we?"

"Silvan?" I locked eyes with his in the rearview mirror. He shrugged.

"Do you even need to ask?" His voice was resigned.

* * *

The drive was long and Mira insisted on playing too much Patsy Cline. At one point she lowered the volume. Silvan's light snore didn't falter.

"I overheard what that guy said to you. About his mom not liking you."

I squirmed in my seat, beyond mortified. I'd stopped cataloguing all the ways Mira could make my life hell, but this was probably the worst revelation.

"I just want you to know that it happens. Most people hate the Rom because of all the stories and don't want their kids mixing with us. That's why we stick together, you know? So don't worry. There are lots of guys out there."

I didn't know what to say so I turned up the volume. She took the hint, which was a miracle with Mira. It never occurred to me that Mrs. Caywood wouldn't like me because of my heritage. I wasn't even sure how she knew of it, as I didn't look like my cousins. It was terrible that that kind of discrimination was something Mira felt you should get used to.

The car lot next to Maryhill Memorial Park loomed empty but for a yellow Gremlin in the corner that appeared abandoned. Disappointment settled like sawdust in my throat.

No sign of Amanda's Jetta.

Mira was already climbing out of the car, so Silvan and I followed, stretching our legs. A breeze kicked up, ruffling the leaves overhead. The unexpected chill had me hugging myself. The cement monument that was fake Stonehenge rose high on the hill, and I was surprised to find it seemed designed to scale. Built as a memorial to soldiers who'd died in the First World War, it rested high above the Columbia River.

As we trudged up the trail a bird chirped, followed by a high trill. The call was unfamiliar and the bird making it circled overhead. Its brilliant white feathers and black face with red beak were distinctive. I stopped in my tracks to point upwards, mouth agape.

"What is it?" whispered Mira. Silvan looked up and stopped as well.

"Hold on. It looks...that looks like an arctic tern." Silvan breathed. That was pretty much impossible. Arctic terns migrated hundreds of miles west in a loop that spanned the poles. They would never be so far inland. Terns preferred colder climates, making their nests on quiet rocky beaches. The bird made lazy loops, its dark head bent as if watching us.

"I think you're right, Silvan." Its deeply forked tail was too distinctive to be anything else.

"Come on! It's almost two o'clock!" Mira tugged my arm and we followed her up the hill to the massive monument.

We bypassed the closed visitor center and its signs that warned visitors away from the park after hours. The silence was unbroken as we rounded the dark hulking shape of the memorial. The Columbia River shone down in the valley, and I breathed the fresh air in deep gulps. There was something magical about deep night, something that sparked to life.

"Stella?" I turned to search for the familiar voice.

Chapter 9
The Hierophant

Stella

⸻ ••◦✳◦•• ⸻

Moonlight cast shadows from the archways of Maryhill Stonehenge and Silvan switched on his keychain flashlight. He aimed at the entrance just as a figure dressed in tan cargo shorts and a green rumpled t-shirt stepped towards us.

"Thomas?"

"Hi, Stella. Amanda said you would figure it out."

His steps slowed as he took in the sight of Mira and Silvan behind me. Curly brown hair framed a narrow face with pointed chin. His eyeglasses gave him an owlish appearance and I relaxed a bit. It really was Thomas; the same boy Amanda and I'd shared chemistry and astrology home school classes with.

"Your mom told me you'd started working here. Amanda thinks too highly of my detective skills." I admitted. I *was* rather good at guessing the ending of most books.

"She didn't mention skills—but she did say you were exceedingly stubborn." Disgruntled, I remembered now how exact and literal

Thomas could be. He gave a short nod to Silvan but pointed his chin at Mira. "Silvan's cool but who is *she?* You were meant to come alone."

Mira scooted close and then flashed her phone's mag light in Thomas' face. The blinding illumination caused Thomas to throw up his hands while I shook my head, disbelieving.

"Who are *you?*" Mira demanded. I pushed her arm down.

"Thomas, this is my cousin, Mira. Mira—this is Thomas, a friend from school."

"I thought you were home schooled?"

"He was in my home school classes."

We were exposed here in the open. Adding to my discomfort was the fact that Mira was now pressed into my shoulder, unbalancing me while Thomas glared holes into her.

"You were supposed to come alone. I was only okay speaking to you, Stella." He wrung his hands, his sneakers scraping gravel as he shuffled backwards.

"What? Wait! Where is Amanda?" I demanded, sweeping the area for signs of my friend.

"I've failed. It'll be too late, now."

"Hold *up*," I insisted, alarmed at his reaction. Turning abruptly, Thomas dashed between the hulking pillars and ran inside Stonehenge. *Seriously?* I followed, giving chase as he ducked between and around a shorter series of stones that stood within the outer circle.

Behind me came an exhilarated war cry as Mira joined the pursuit. We reached the center of the memorial and Thomas skidded to a stop before a long stone slab that resembled an altar.

"Stop, Thomas! Why are you running away?"

He didn't answer but instead stared at the altar. Following his line of sight, I noticed a bird, with feathers so white they appeared to glow in the moonlight, perched on top of the stone slab. An arctic tern, larger than most. This close I could detect the orange-red beak among its black helmet and snowy white plumage. It had to be the bird we'd seen circling the parking lot earlier. There couldn't be two this far from their normal flight patterns, right?

Thomas fell to his knees, arms stretched over his head to touch the ground.

Silvan jogged up to us. "What's wrong with him?" he panted. I shook my head and shrugged, still scanning the dark for some sign of Amanda. Where was she?

The bird studied Thomas' prostrate form until Thomas rose to return the creature's regard, his hands on his thighs.

The tern gave another trill and took flight, orbiting once before gliding into the distance, outlined against the moon-bright sky. Mira, Silvan and I shared a look. She cocked her head in Thomas' direction and raised a finger to her temple, rolling it like a propeller, the international gesture for bat-shit crazy. Silvan emphatically nodded. I couldn't disagree.

Thomas was up in a flash; suddenly so close I recognized his soap brand.

"Come. We don't have much time. *He* thinks Mira and Silvan are okay and it's not like I have a choice now." I'd always thought there was something a little *off* about Thomas. I'd put it down to his being a little eccentric. Right now, I was worried something was clinically wrong with him.

"Hurry," he yelled and ran back the way we'd come. Mira grinned so wide the moonlight glinted from her gold tooth. Silvan pulled his small pocket knife out and waved it at me. Right. We could probably take him if he tried to murder us.

Thomas breached the outer circle of stones and took off towards the cliff, the three of us following at a slower pace. He waited with his hand upon the bark of a large hemlock tree.

"This is going to sound crazy...," he began. Mira gave a snort.

His body stiffened. "This would have been easier if you'd come alone," he accused. I shrugged and glanced at Mira meaningfully. *Behave.*

"I need you to place your hands on this mountain hemlock. You guys, too." He nodded towards my cousins. I blinked when Mira complied without an argument. She was surprisingly turning into my ride-or-die chick, tonight. Silvan stood with hands in his pockets until he saw me also lean into the tree. His sigh carried, though.

"I can get us through, but it will make things go faster if you could visualize the experience. I've been told you have some power," he said with a grin as he took a position next to me.

Power...Me? I scanned the area, half expecting a prank camera crew to jump out. If he totally cracked and asked us to sing Kumbaya they would never let me hear the end of this.

"Keep both hands on the tree. No matter what, don't remove them. It would help if you could hug the trunk a bit. No? Okay." That last was directed to Mira, who I couldn't see.

The rough bark actually felt good, and I rested my cheek against it, suddenly tired. I was both a dendrophile and a pluviophile—someone who loved rain and trees. They brought me peace in ways I never found in the company of people.

"Imagine you are melting into the tree. That you are following me, and we are becoming one with the tree..." Mira laughed, forcing my own smile. The night was beyond surreal.

"... Imagine its resin and bark, the pulse of life within its roots. Imagine our veins as just another root system. Smell the bark, feel its surface as it holds us..."

Relaxed, I allowed myself to be lulled by the imagery Thomas evoked.

I focused on the tree and a floating sensation took over, similar to deep meditation. My skin felt stretched and soft, expansive as a marshmallow over flame. The scent of hemlock resin filled my senses.

A new presence seemed to fill the void, an awareness that was different. Something much bigger than myself. So many sensations it was hard to pinpoint just one. The ruffle of wind, the rich loam of earth, the high bird trill that accompanied my journey.

"Do you feel that, Sil—" I opened my eyes, but Thomas was gone and Mira's laughter came from behind me.

"No freakin' way," Mira's voice called out.

Of course, she would refuse to play along. Thomas could probably teach meditation classes—he had mad skills, but it was very late, and this was going nowhere.

My hands stuck to the tree until, with an odd leaching sensation, I pulled free.

Turning, my knees weakened and I fell back against the tree. The Neolithic copy of Stonehenge had disappeared. The entire area had disappeared. No more Columbia River.

We stood in a small grassy field, surrounded by thick forest. The sky had morphed into a canopy of leaves and twisted tree roots that formed a dense canopy overhead. Tiny white lights fluttered like moving stars beneath the dome. They cast a gentle glow onto the clearing where we stood beneath the hemlock's branches. I turned round and round in amazement, taking in the shades of springtime green. Silvan sat upon tender grass that blanketed the ground in an emerald carpet.

Mira danced in a circle, her head thrown back and arms outstretched like a child as she ogled the lights and leafy roof above. Thomas watched her with a bemused look on his face. "Huh. That worked," he muttered.

Thomas smiled at me. A huge grin that recalled the awkward,

friendly Thomas who made study flash cards for us and told the same stupid joke about chickens in four languages.

"Welcome to my grove. Time moves much slower here. I think we might have an hour before we need to go back." He said this matter-of-factly. Because didn't we all have our own magical grove accessible by hugging enormous trees?

"Right." I pinched the tender skin of my forearm. *Ouch.*

Thomas held up a hand, a cautious worry in his eyes.

"Before you ask, Amanda is not here. She and her family are in hiding."

I stopped in my tracks. "Hiding? But she left me the note about fake Stonehenge. You were waiting." One step forward and three back. I stomped my foot, infuriated.

"Amanda asked me to tell you what I could. I'm breaking, like, a million rules right now," he explained defensively. I gritted my teeth. Oh, I was about to break something, all right.

Silvan approached us and pointed at our twirling cousin.

"What's *wrong* with her?" he asked Thomas.

Thomas dusted off his hands. "She's just a little punch-drunk from the transfer. It happens to some people the first few times. It'll wear off." Silvan scowled but I got out my phone and took some video footage of her. You never knew when stuff like that came in handy.

"So, is Amanda in danger?" Silvan asked.

"Yes—and no." He pushed his hair from his forehead and adjusted his eyeglasses.

"Stella—trust me—Amanda is more worried about *you* being in danger. Can you please let me get to what she wants me to tell you?" Annoyed by his tone, I motioned for him to begin spilling his guts.

"Not here. Follow me." Thomas walked in the opposite direction, and for the first time I noticed a canvas shelter about a hundred yards away. It resembled an African dome tent, its walls illuminated with lamplight from within.

Mira skipped after him. "This is the shit, Thomas. Do you have a girlfriend?"

Thomas ignored her even when she continued to pepper him with questions.

I followed more slowly, inhaling the oxygen-rich air. As they bounded ahead of me, a high-pitched keening sound came from above. The artic tern landed at my feet, cocking his head this way and that as he inspected me. I crouched down and held my palm up at ground level. The bird chirped sharply in admonishment before flying away. As he launched skyward, something fell into my hand. Surprised, I examined a small glass pebble. I turned it over and over before tucking it into my pocket and hurrying to where Thomas held the tent flap. I crossed the threshold and staggered. What had appeared as a simple tent from the outside had transformed into an enormous tower on the inside.

Wood gleamed from the floors and walls. My feet shuffled in a circle while I gazed upwards in awe. There were too many floors to count, each with an elaborate railing separating the circular floors from the tower's open center. The ground floor held thick wooden tables and chairs reminiscent of a university library.

Thomas gestured to some chairs. "Please sit. We don't have time to waste." We sank into armchairs as Thomas reached over his head and snapped his fingers. Vines dropped out of thin air, lowering a large whiteboard. Mira shouted an expletive, and I agreed with her. This was beyond odd. I pinched my lips between my fingertips and felt a tacky substance. A terrible thought arose. Sam and I had watched a detective show once where the villain coated drinking glasses with hallucinogenic drugs.

"Thomas, my hands are still sticky from touching the tree. It could be resin but are you sure we're not drugged right now? I mean, this is pretty strange. If you intend any harm whatsoever, please know that I *will* kill you—and then Mira's family will line up to skin you. Understand?"

Thomas crossed his arms. He glanced at Mira who nodded her head vigorously in agreement before she mimicked a gun exploding into her temple. He frowned.

"Stella, I promise—you are *not* drugged. The transfer can make some people nutty for a few minutes, but it does not cause you to see things. This place is real. It is mine alone and I promise you will come to no harm here.

"I want you to know that what I am revealing is bound by the highest secrecy. Never tell a single soul about this. If you do, *death* will follow." That last was directed towards Mira with an emphasis on "death" that reminded me of the hunchback in the *Princess Bride. "Never go in against a Sicilian when* death *is on the line."*

Mira smirked as she sat with folded arms, meeting his hard gaze.

"This is a little too D&D for me—but I won't tell," she affirmed.

Thomas cleared his voice and stood up straight. His eyeglasses were clean for once, revealing green eyes and dark eyebrows.

"Stella, you're cursed."

"Start with a softball, why don't cha." muttered Mira.

My conversation earlier with Sam still fresh, I froze in my seat. He had mentioned curses, too. What had he said? My parent's accident had been caused by a curse.

"In fact, the women in your family have been cursed for fifteen generations, originating with Lila, may she rest in splendor."

Behind him, the whiteboard's surface slowly filled with curling lines and writing. A family tree began to appear, names appearing in flourishes. At the bottom, I watched as the calligraphic handwriting completed a name I recognized as my own.

I rose and moved closer, unable to help myself. I checked behind the screen yet saw no wires or mechanical devices. Silvan appeared next to me, pointing at the names above my own. Vivian and Lasho. I didn't recognize the others.

The family tree began with a single name, lovingly rendered in scrolling font. Lila.

I tried to laugh, but what I was seeing was too bizarre. Can you pinch yourself and feel it in a dream? Maybe I was asleep in the car right this very moment. The family tree disappeared with a wave of Thomas's hand.

An outline of a palace with spires began to form, its sprawling shape surrounding three tall trees within a walled garden. Their branches rose high, leaves curling. Thomas began to speak, reciting words as if from an invisible teleprompter.

"Once upon a time the archangel Michael fell in love with a human so kind that he could not resist her grace and loving heart. A daughter, Isabeau, was born of their bond. This was just before the Creator banned such unions.

"This daughter was beautiful and gentle of spirit...also poor and taken into slavery. The Ottoman empire at that time was geographically vast, with women from Egypt, Greece, Romania and as far as Italy taken as wives and concubines against their will. Michael could do nothing. The Creator made it clear that the heavenly host were forbidden to interfere with the women and men of God. Isabeau grew up unaware of her parentage, vulnerable to the sufferings of all humankind but without the power to help even herself.

"The daughter's loveliness and exquisite voice brought her much attention, and she was taken as a slave to the Ottoman palace of Sultan Mehmet, intended as a gift. With her gift of song, kind nature and knowledge of languages, Isabeau soon captured the interest of the jaded Sultan, becoming his fifth wife.

"In those days, the highest position for a woman was to be the mother of the Sultan. She was allowed to manage everyone in the Sultan's harem. For this reason, the harem, home to wives and concubines, was a place of dark intrigue as the women plotted to have their own son become the eldest and next Sultan.

"The only males allowed in the harem were the Sultan's children, eunuchs, and the Sultan himself. With hundreds of wives and concubines, many boys were poisoned by jealous women who wanted their own son to become favored. Can you imagine how these sons must have been driven mad with isolation and paranoia? Their mothers tried to protect them from rivals by locking them in opulent rooms with only teachers and a royal taster for company."

"Throw in a bunch of paints and chocolate and that sounds like Stella's idea of a good time," Mira snickered.

"It was no laughing matter." Thomas scowled.

"Sultan Mehmet came to love Isabeau deeply. Although she was not a first or second wife, nor a Muslim, he allowed her great privileges. He granted her the right to study and learn from foreign teachers alongside his sons. Later, she attended palace meetings by his side, an indulgence his viziers hated, but could not protest without offending the Sultan.

"Isabeau bore the sultan one son and they named him Abbas, Arabic for the fiercest lion in a pride. A child so precocious he quickly became the light of his father's life and he grew up adored within the harem. He worshiped his older brothers, especially the second oldest son, Murad. Everywhere Murad went, Abbas tried to follow. The Sultan's love for his wife and son caused great worry for his mother. She felt her influence slipping as he refused to see other wives and turned to

Isabeau for counsel.

"To eliminate the threat to her power, the Sultan's mother decided to poison Abbas with sugared almonds laced with arsenic. You see, the Sultan's mother, titled the Valide Sultan, intended to hold her position for a very long time. Mehmet was frequently on the battlefield and likely to die an early death. She wanted her favorite grandson, the Sultan's eldest son, a spoiled and pampered man easily manipulated, to become the next Sultan. The eldest son had a weak-minded mother, and the Valide Sultan knew she could easily wrest control of the harem from her when the time came. The Valide Sultan chose to act when Mehmet was away, Isabeau was alone and Abbas vulnerable."

"She's got nothing on our Grandmother. Mahari would gut any one of us for a cigarette," I grumbled. Mira turned and flipped me the bird and I returned the gesture with two hands.

"Oh, my God." Thomas flicked his gaze from me to his watch pointedly.

"Can you children behave, please?" Silvan asked dryly.

"We don't have much time. Stop interrupting," Thomas chided before continuing.

"It was true that since Isabeau joined their household, Sultan Mehmet was not listening to his mother's advice. The Valide Sultan feared that Mehmet would change the law and make Abbas, his favorite son, his heir. She refused to allow Isabeau to take that power.

"Isabeau discovered Abbas with the poisoned dates. The Sultan's physicians were called, yet helpless to save him from the potent poison. Isabeau's tears fell as diamonds, such was her grief. She carried her son's body outside, next to the harem's tiled pool and beneath the stars. She called out in her beautiful voice, begging the heavens to take her life and spare her child. As she was Archangel Michael's daughter, this sacrifice was no small offering. The exchange of her life for his was accepted and the Creator breathed life into the boy."

"This is some sad shit," Mira said crudely, arms and ankles crossed. "Please tell me there is a happier ending?" Thomas pretended not to hear. His lips moved as if reciting lines from a script and then he began again.

"As Isabeau, the only child of Archangel Michael, fell in death, her love and sacrifice affected the heavens. Isabeau's soul would become an immortal star until she chose to cross over. The thirteen stars of Orion came to collect Isabeau's earthly body. Twelve daughters and one son made up their constellation. By the grace of their mother, the Goddess Danu, they entered the harem garden in human form through the great Oriental Plane trees. This was a sacred ceremony. As they wrapped Isabeau's body in gossamer sheets and carried her away, Abbas awoke to find his favorite brother Murad home from war and his mother gone. The archangel Michael appeared in human form and spoke words to the brothers before he departed as well.

"And this is where your story begins, Stella."

"Begins?" Mira gave an incredulous hoot. I nodded at Thomas to keep going.

Chapter 10
Fire

Alaric

"How dare you," Clara hissed. It wasn't her appearance that worried me. With her ponytail, purple t-shirt with—was that a Frankenstein emoji?—and fluffy pants, she looked more like a petulant teenager than the deadly Primati she actually was. I eyed her wrists, rotating at her sides. Sparks flung pink energy daggers from her aura and dripped from her clenched hands. I sighed. This was not going to be a quick conversation.

"Didn't you get my apology?" I asked, annoyed at the disruption. My hotel suite had the best view, but the sitting area was too small for an angry Clara. If I had to move to another room while repairs were made to this one, it would really put me out.

She stopped the dangerous motions of her hands and crossed her arms.

"Do you mean the delivery from Lorraine Schwartz? Do I seem a cliché to you? Rubies and diamonds are so eighties." She tugged on a sparkling earlobe and I noticed her rings. I sighed inwardly. The agent was supposed to have delivered a choice of the rare diamonds *or* rubies to Clara. She'd apparently decided to keep both.

"Did you have to break Bromely's neck? It took the last of my dragon yew to mend her vertebrae, and she's still walking around with a cervical collar."

I imagined Bromely in a medical collar. "Don't you dare smirk about it." Her voice shook with fury. Clara in a rage was both entertaining and lethal. On the other hand, dragon yew was extraordinarily difficult to obtain. The tree only grew in a remote area of the demon plane and was protected by hellcats.

"Clara, you know I wouldn't *seriously* injure one of yours. I knew by her aura that she was strong enough to survive, and I made sure it was quick and painless. She required a lesson."

Clara growled, and I frowned at her overreaction.

"If I wanted the nosy little witch *dead* dead, she would not be walking around with a stiff neck," I warned lightly.

I hated stalkers—witchy stalkers in particular, and Bromely had rubbed me the wrong way since the traffic light. Disguising her presence from me in the map store was insulting, and the scrawny witch needed to know not to pull those tricks with someone who would kill her for such an offence. I'd done her a favor, really.

"Granted she broke protocol—but she was just doing her job. Several of my Seattle and Portland coven members have disappeared in the last few days. Bromely was checking on one of my members," Clara explained. I noted the shadows beneath her eyes and felt a smidgeon of remorse. I'd taken it for granted that Clara would be able to easily heal her sidekick, not realizing she could be low on necessary supplies or that she would be juggling other urgent matters.

"What do you suspect?" I murmured silkily.

Clara shook her head, her anger drained away and replaced with worry.

"Something or someone new. I personally visited the homes of those missing, and two held the tang of earth magic—but it's buried beneath something else we've never encountered. As there are no bodies to study or ransom demands, I'm at a loss. These women would not just up and leave their family or the coven without explanations."

"Locations?"

"All outside Portland proper—and no need to use that harsh tone. For all I know, they are steering clear of *you*."

"No one but you and my guards know I'm even here," I muttered, rubbing my chin.

"I have a suspicion..." she began before cutting herself off. She knew I preferred facts over intuition.

"What are you thinking?" I allowed.

"That group you met in the woods—the one led by the sorcerer Marcus? He met you before your aura was concealed, and it was strange that he would be in my territory in such a predatory fashion." She paused, and I understood why. An outright accusation could lead to a political or actual war with the earth witches.

"I didn't sense anything powerful about him." I paced the length of the room, trying to recall anything unusual about the sorcerer. Clara folded herself onto a plush sofa, her eyes fixed on my movements. I slipped out my phone and sent a quick text to Jing San.

History was filled with deadly beta-followers who morphed into traitors. The sorcerer could be working for someone far more powerful.

Clara's voice was low as she peered up at me. "We are still looking into the background of his clan. It's an unusual one. I worry, Alaric. It seems too much of a coincidence that this is happening *after* Marcus came across Stella. What if the two are connected? What if the rumor of an Everwish is revisited? Her life would be forfeit with or without our protection." I nodded, having considered the same possibility.

I parted the curtains and looked at the wet streets below.

"Did I tell you about the first time I spoke with Stella? Murad had asked me to investigate when he first learned about her."

"You mean he sent you to kill her," Clara broke in.

I stiffened, unaware Clara had known about that. He'd changed his mind.

"She was perhaps five at the time and Sam was asleep. It was a different house then. There I was, standing in her backyard, considering what to do. In the middle of the night, Stella opened the deck door on the second floor. I watched her climb onto a chair and gaze through a telescope." A rueful smile played on my lips. I glanced at Clara in time to see her eyes roll.

"Forgive me if I'm not surprised. I can't imagine Stella ever following rules," she commented.

"Long story short, she fell from the deck and I caught her. Put her back where she belonged and made sure that the careless babysitter would never fall asleep at her post again."

"I'm guessing you made them both forget the incident?"

"Of course. But when I saw Stella standing in that river, I would swear she remembered me. Perhaps triggered as we were meeting under similar circumstances of danger. My point is that I should have known how willful she would turn out to be. It will make keeping our secrets that much more difficult." I could not magick Stella's memory from her now. She would never forgive the trespass—which meant I would only do so if her life was in grave danger.

"Alaric—"

I held up my palm. "I'll replenish your stock of dragon yew."

A knock sounded at the door. Recognizing the visitor's aura, I crossed the room and opened it. Jing San entered and offered Clara a respectful bow. Clara rose and inclined her head in return. The two had worked well together in watching over Stella these last few years. Jing San quirked a brow at me. I nodded.

"Speak freely."

"With great respect, Alaric, you asked me to remain in this disgustingly wet, strange place *for years* in order to keep Stella in the dark, only to reveal yourself. She's not one of your women. She doesn't understand…as tough as she seems, she's an innocent. She's looking at you with googly girl eyes…" Jing broke off whatever she'd been about to say.

My voice deepened to the beast's low growl as the room shrunk. "No."

Jing San lowered her eyes to the floor and hunched her shoulders. Googly girl eyes? I'd sensed a nervousness about her but not…but I did know. If signs of a girlish crush got back to Murad, he might not follow through with his plan, which placed Stella in danger.

"Never speak of this again. Either of you," I ordered. My head touched the ceiling and I snapped my jaws. Stella was as good as engaged to Murad. She just didn't know it yet. Blowing air from my nose, I forced the change to reverse until I was once more a man. She deserved to be a queen. Revered and safe among the Primati and humans.

With effort, I softened my tone. "Jing, I need you and the second guard to assist Clara. She's tracking a sorcerer, and there may be a connection to Stella." I refused to say aloud the suspicion unwisely voiced aloud by Clara. Jing looked at a spot over my shoulder and nodded. I wanted Stella to remain in the dark about the Primati community as long as possible.

Chapter 11
Death

Stella

My bottom was literally on the edge of the seat as Thomas continued his story. I struggled to recall what I knew about the Ottoman Empire when we'd covered European history. The Turks would conquer lands until the Battle of Vienna in 1683. I said as much out loud.

"Isn't that how we got the bagel?" Silvan asked, rubbing his flat belly. He was so food motivated. Mira handed him a jolly rancher from her pocket.

"I think it was the croissant." I countered. "Vienna celebrated the defeat of the Ottoman Turks with a pasty shaped like the crescent in their flag." If Thomas's story was even remotely true, then it aligned with the history I recalled reading about.

"So, what happened to the little boy? Did he just wake up and find his mother dead?' Silvan asked with a frown, his cheek full of hard candy. Mira rubbed his back and the big baby of the family let her.

"Abbas woke," Thomas continued. "His elder brother Murad kept him shielded. When the stars arrived in their human form to carry Isabeau away, it was apparent they were…different. The eldest daughter of Orion was a star named Lila. Flaxen haired in her human form, Murad fell deeply in love with her that night."

"Of course, he did. Always the blonde. Like there were no brown girls around to kick some ass and fall in love with?" Mira countered. Thomas's lips parted and then closed with a snap of teeth.

"He was captivated by her *benevolence and humility*. I'm sure he had plenty of other beautiful women…I can't do this. No one is listening and this is super-secret stuff I'm sharing."

"Ignore her, Thomas. She has the attention span of a goldfish. I'm guessing Lila insta-loved him back?" I asked.

"No way. He asked her to stay with him and she refused."

"Okay. More interesting," Mira offered, sitting back in her chair.

"Glad it meets your approval, Karen." Thomas smirked and Silvan's hand shot out to grab Mira's shoulder. I grinned. Thomas had spine. He paced as he continued his story.

"I mean, eventually she *did* fall for the guy. Lila returned a few years later to check in on Abbas and found him with Murad. She grew more intrigued. With the help of her siblings, she snuck into the palace gardens, using the magick of the great oriental plane trees that grew there. Murad taught her his mother's Circassian language. They fell in love. It changed them both in ways only holy fire and true love can beget."

"Beget? Are we still talking pastries?" Mira asked. I sat next to her. "You're thinking of a baguette. Beget means to bring something about. What did they teach you in public school?" I whispered. She twisted with a grimace.

"Excuse me. Maybe I'm just hungry and this is the longest story hour ever."

To his credit, Thomas kept talking as if she didn't exist. He was persistent.

"Time passed, and Prince Murad grew into a mature man. He took no human wife, wanting only Lila. Their entire friendship was carried out within the clandestine gardens and rooms of Topkapi Palace. When it was time for her to return home after each visit, Murad would send the eunuchs and soldiers away and stood guard to protect her privacy.

"During this time, the Sultan abandoned his harem, altogether. His grief for Isabeau had turned to rage and he embraced madness. He fought his neighbors, pushing his borders into distant lands. He gave up decision making and the Empire was overcome with corruption and war. Murad, frustrated by the way his older brothers failed to care and take action against their father, grew outraged when the Sultan began to send Abbas into battles. In time, however, Abbas become a fierce warrior with skills to match his brilliant strategic mind."

Silvan spoke up. "Of course, he did. Wasn't his grandfather, Isabeau's father, an Archangel? I mean, come on. He defeated Lucifer himself. It makes sense that Abbas would be a good fighter."

I shifted in my seat. I believed in something greater than ourselves, but hadn't given much thought to heaven and hell. Thomas spoke of angels and stars who could turn into humans as if they were real.

Thomas nodded.

"The two brothers fought side by side until Abbas surpassed his brother in strength and skill. He showed no mercy to their enemies, shocking even Murad. A rebellion sent them to a Romanian battlefield. It was there they heard rumors of a vampire demon who led the opposing army. This creature was the first of his kind and an abomination. He tricked Abbas into a trap in order to distract Murad. Murad tried to save his brother and the demon attacked. He tore Murad's throat so that he could not live and then drank his blood.

Mira and Silvan's expressions mirrored my own dropped jaw. I did not see that one coming. I mean, I knew about the legend of the Wallachian prince but it was all a myth, right?

"Are you saying that Murad fought Dracula?" Silvan asked.

"No. Not Vlad. *He* wasn't the first vampire. This creature was a general. The first of his kind and the Ottoman wars were disturbing his hunting grounds. He targeted Murad immediately. While he drained Murad of his blood, Lila felt Murad dying. Within seconds, she broke sacred laws, abandoning her place in the heavens for her human form. Her siblings were not given time to cover for her absence and her piece of sky grew dark. She transferred her energy to the forest surrounding the battle and arrived in time to see Abbas escape his trap and fight the vampire away from Murad's body. As a being removed from human emotion for much of her existence, Lila was unable to comprehend the violence of war. Having only known the peace of the palace gardens on earth, the raw barbarism of man willfully murdering other men on those blood-drenched fields horrified her.

"Lila called to her mother, the Goddess Danu, and begged her to interfere, to stop what was happening. Danu ignored her daughter's plea.

"In desperation, Lila bathed Murad in her own light, offering him her own strength. Imbued with her celestial light, he recovered and overtook the demon, draining him dry before tearing him to pieces. He then turned on Abbas."

"What the hell? He *ate* his little brother?" Mira sounded horrified. I felt queasy myself. Such a betrayal. Poisoned by your own grandmother and then attacked by someone you loved and looked up to?

"No. He did not *eat* him," Thomas clarified. "Not exactly. Murad hung onto his humanity for just an instant. He stopped feeding on Abbas and instead tried to give his blood back to him. Lila, in shock nearby, begged him to stop but he ignored her. Unable to control himself any longer, he threw Abbas to the ground and left them. He began a bloody campaign of death that ravaged the central plains where they fought for miles around. Murad, who always did the right thing. Murad who was beloved for his kindness as much as his intelligence, turned into a monster. Lila's choice to save him led to the murder of countless people. Her grief and shame overwhelmed her.

"The goddess Danu did the most merciful thing she could for Lila; allowing her to slip into a deep slumber that offered relief from her suffering. As an immortal star, without a human soul, she was unable to die as a human might. But she could sleep.

"In anger, Goddess Danu burned the cores of the Great Plane trees, preventing more of her sky children from walking the earth. She punished the three siblings who had conspired to help Lila meet with Murad by forcing them to become humans. Other stars were born to take their place. To this day, those trees stand in the palace garden as petrified shells—a reminder."

I was shaken. How easily love and happiness can turn into hell. One day Murad was doing his thing, fighting wars and loving his girl, and the next he was a monster and she'd bailed on him.

"What happened to Murad? I mean, I've never heard of a vampire called Murad. Did he die?" Silvan demanded. Thomas shook his head.

"Nearly a year passed but eventually he was able to restrain the demon inside his blood. He succeeded at controlling his hunger and became obsessed with making amends. Previously unaware of the supernatural beings on earth, he organized and led them. He instituted laws that protected humans. They say Murad believed that if he became a better monster, Lila would wake up from her slumber and forgive him. He hunted foul creatures and his army forced demons back into their own plane.

"But nothing made a difference. Lila remained a living statue in repose. Knowing she would want to be under sky, Murad ordered the construction of a tower built on a small island near Istanbul. Within this tower, Murad commissioned a glass coffin so that she was as close to the heavens as possible yet near enough for him to see her."

"That sounds like Sleeping B—" I clapped a hand over Mira's mouth but released her when her teeth sank into my flesh. Silvan raised a hand as if we were in a classroom. Thomas nodded resignedly.

"It doesn't seem like all that was his fault. I mean, it was the vampire blood that made him do it. She should have given him a chance. It was bad he killed his own little brother, though." Silvan looked gutted.

"Who said Abbas died that day? The blood Murad gave him had a different effect on Abbas. Don't forget he wasn't entirely human, but came from angelic lineage. Before the demon blood could fully change him, a blue sword, flaming with the holy fire of righteousness, drove into Abbas' heart at the exact moment the demon's blood would have consumed it. The fire cauterized the wound, sealing his heart from the demon infection. No one held that sword. It appeared in thin air and no one there that day recalled seeing anyone wield it. The rumor is that the sword was thrown by Archangel Michael himself to prevent Abbas from turning completely.

"When Abbas awoke, it was to find himself pierced to the ground with the sword. After a day of agony, he removed the sword himself. It's said that he carries scars on his palms to this day from pulling that blade. The sword succeeded in stopping the demon blood from turning Abbas into a vampire—yet he was still changed. He lost his humanity to became half angel and half demon. A dark beast with blackened wings who helped Murad take control of the Primati throughout the entire world. In truth, he was much stronger than Murad, even more vicious and bloodthirsty. As Murad was eventually crowned Noble King of all

Primatis, or supernaturals on earth, Abbas became known as The Lion, a terrifying beast in any dimension, even Hell. He became Murad's Enforcer."

Mira raised her arm.

Thomas sighed. "Yes, Mira."

"So, can you get to the point of what all of this means for Stella. I mean—yada, yada, yada—how is she cursed?" I wanted to know the same thing.

His tongue ran along his lower lip as he puffed his chest up. "Do you mind? This is my main job here," he shared in strained, dignified voice.

"Well, can't she just take some books home and study about all this in her spare time?" Mira asked, pointing upward to all the shelves.

"No. The history is oral. It's passed from generation to generation," he practically shouted.

"Ha, ha! Oral." Mira hooted.

"*Verbal* history," Thomas clarified through tight lips.

He checked the time and groaned. "We only have minutes."

If Lila slept then how did she conceive a child to begin that family tree? My family tree. This was all nuts. "Why don't you hit the highlights, Thomas?"

He puffed out his cheeks and blew air. With a wave of his hand, the palace disappeared, and the family tree appeared once more.

"Lila's glass coffin was stolen from the tower. No one knows by whom. It happened during an earthquake when Murad and Abbas were elsewhere. They found the tower empty, its walls partially eaten away as if by salt water and with no scent to track.

"We know that Lila was hidden once in Fontainebleau forest outside Paris and then moved to America when it was just being settled. It was suggested that the physical distance between her and Murad may have been the catalyst that finally woke Lila. She opened her eyes to find herself entombed within a glass coffin, inside a cave on the outskirts of Jamestown in America. She broke through the glass and explored the strange, vast woods around her. She wandered for weeks alone before falling terribly ill."

Now I was the one to raise my hand. "How do you know all of this?"

"Because my forefathers carried the story down to me. Please hold any further questions." I wrinkled my brow and he motioned to his watch again.

"Ashamed, Lila refused to return to her true celestial form or ask for help. A tribe of Native Americans found her, feverish and starving, and nursed her back to semi-health. When she remained unresponsive, they placed her in the care of a white medical man who had helped their children recover from illness and who might take her to a larger settlement. She ended up staying with him on his farm, uncomfortable with the more populated settlement.

"After several years of working side by side with this kind, simple man, Lila found a gentle love and married him. They worked the land together. Lila never used her power, afraid it would draw attention. If their crops flourished more vigorously than other farms no one thought anything of it. They were blessed with a daughter. Then another daughter. Lila and her husband were happy in a tender, borrowed fashion. It was a life she felt she didn't deserve.

"In the meantime, Murad had gone wild at the theft of Lila's coffin. He left most of his responsibilities as ruler to Abbas and searched the world for her for many years before tracking her to America. He found her in the woods, gathering kindling for a fire.

"Their reunion occurred at sunset, a bewitched time when people might be forgiven for forgetting themselves. When Lila saw Murad standing in the forest, she was overcome and ran to him. Unwilling to hurt her husband, however, she rejected Murad. She told him to return to Europe and leave her to her family."

Thomas paused, his mouth downturned and his eyes suspiciously moist.

"When she returned back to their homestead, it was to find her home on fire, one of her little daughters murdered on the porch, the scent of magick everywhere. She couldn't enter the collapsing house to save her husband and other daughter.

"She was convinced that Murad had done this deed in jealousy. She would have tried to kill Murad if she'd been able to find him then. To say she went mad is an understatement. Her misery affected everything around her as her own special magick rose from where it had been caged. It stormed for four months. The rivers swelled and flooded settlements. Chasms grew and wildfire spread where lightening split the earth. Her gentle husband's only mistake lay in saving her life, her children innocent.

"Lila renounced her immortality and begged for death but it did no good. Her choices had violated the Creator's law, and there was no response to her pleas. Her human husband had loved her. They'd brought children into the world—when her celestial directive had been not to interfere with humans. She tried again and again to die but would always recover. She became a mad, feral thing, covered in mud and wandering aimlessly from tree to tree, talking to herself. The Native Americans still speak legends of her during that time.

"No one knows exactly how or why—yet beneath a solar eclipse, Lila screamed her damnation into the four winds and the curse was struck.

"What Lila did not know was that her elder daughter had survived. She and her father had been spirited away before the fire burned their home. Her daughter inherited the curse, which took the following shape: she would grow to womanhood and attract a mate who loved her. They would procreate a daughter. She would die before the age of twenty-one, never to see her child grow up and never grow old with her lover. Undeserving of a long life by her lover's side or to watch as beloved children grew to adulthood."

I hugged myself at the reference to a curse. Could this be *the* curse Sam mentioned?

"For fifteen generations, these daughters have lived. They met their lovers at different ages. Died at different ages. But none lived past the age of twenty-one. The men always died with them. Whether by illness or by accident, always within a day. Stella, you are the last of Lila's lineage."

I couldn't stop myself. The solution for this so-called curse was so simple.

"Thomas, why didn't they just *not* fall in love, *not* have children? Wouldn't that break the curse?"

Mira nodded, snapping her fingers in agreement.

"First off, none of them *knew* of the curse. My people were forbidden to interfere. We only witness. I'm violating a lot of rules by telling you all this. Amanda found out when I…it's not important. Lila's progeny died without knowing and unable to warn their own infant daughters. Secondly, the curse is a powerful enchantment. It makes the woman irresistible to her true love, and men in general have seemed drawn to her. I suspect it also influences the woman to fall in love with an acceptable suitor. No one has survived the curse to tell of their experience. What we know is through observation."

I recalled the attraction I felt towards Alaric. The way Scott had behaved with me earlier. Could that be the curse at work? I hated the idea of anything taking my free will. Could the butterflies I felt with

Alaric be the curse? No. Alaric would make any woman weak at the knees.

"The message Amanda wanted me to convey is that Murad announced at the Primati court that he will finally take a wife. Rumor is that you will be that wife. He's convinced that he can break the curse as he's an immortal. His brother, the Lion, has been tasked to find you and take you to him. If you refuse, I think Murad's Enforcer would kill you. She thinks you should go along with it."

I stood abruptly, feeling sick to my stomach. "This is all very entertaining, Thomas. I'm not marrying anyone and certainly not an old vampire lover of my great-grandmother many times removed." The very thought was gross and creepy. My cousins led the way back to the tree we'd traveled from. I glanced back to find the tower had become a tent once more.

"Think, Stella. In two months', you'll be eighteen. No one in your line has survived past the age of twenty-one." I thought of my mom, who'd died in a car accident at twenty. I'd never believed in curses and magick. Her young death was a tragedy, a weird coincidence.

I turned to Thomas. "What's your role in all this? How do you know all this stuff?"

"My people are servants of the Goddess Danu. We've witnessed Lila's daughters all these years."

"Witnessed...you mean failed to help?"

Thomas sighed, pushing his eyeglasses up his nose. "Yes. Until I just broke that vow of non-interference. Something has to change."

"Pretending all this is real, what do you suggest she does?" Silvan asked.

"Armed with this knowledge, figure out a way to resist the enchantment. We don't know why, but Stella and her mother are the only daughters who've demonstrated any kind of special power. There must be a reason. I know what Amanda thinks but I disagree. Find a way to escape the Lion and Primati King. I'm afraid Murad's obsession with Lila will lead him to chain you to him.

"I can help you if you come with me and my family. But it means leaving Sam and your home forever. The tree that carried you here will not work again after I return you tonight. If you decide on sanctuary, just visualize me. Meditate and focus on my ability to hear you. You can also just call my cell," he added sheepishly.

I would never leave Sam. Certainly not with a pack of crazy people who believed in curses and had secret groves. I lingered over what he'd said about power. What did he mean and what had been her special power?

"Who are your people, Thomas? How can you travel by tree and create all of this?"

"I'm a druid."

Chapter 12
The Hermit

Stella

We decided to stop on the way home to eat. Actually, Mira and Silvan insisted on it and so it was that or sleep in the car while they ate. My brain buzzed too much with Thomas's words to sit alone with my thoughts in a dark parking lot. The diner she chose was one of those kitschy, twenty-four-hour places with 1950s décor complete with mint green upholstered leather booths, and revolving pies behind the broad Formica counter. The waitress arrived with our orders and we admired her fuchsia colored hair and the silver ball that glinted from one arched eyebrow.

Mira hummed as she accepted her cheeseburger with steak fries. Silvan groaned when a plate of chicken and waffles appeared before him. Pancakes slid in front of me, the whipped cream glossy and dotted with blueberries. The waitress walked to the only other occupied booth in the room where a group of men in truck driver hats dug into their meals.

I picked up my cup as Mira thrust a spoon into her strawberry malt.

It wasn't the freshest cup of java but better than none at all. I took a careful sip, waiting for the caffeine to hit.

"Thanks for being okay with stopping," she said. She tapped the bottom of an Elvis figurine that served as a salt shaker. "I'm craving greasy diner food. It feels like I've been at a rave all night." I seriously doubted she'd ever been to a real rave but left it alone.

"S'kay. You guys have gone along with me plenty tonight."

I glanced at my phone. It was four in the morning. Thomas had returned us to Stonehenge using the same hemlock tree. He'd refused to answer any more questions, just made us promise once more not to tell anyone about the night and climbed into his Gremlin. There'd been something forlorn about Thomas outside the grove now that I'd seen him there.

"So, Thomas is quite a snack," Mira said casually. Silvan choked on his food. I speared a trio of blueberries on the tines of my fork and tried not to appear surprised.

"We shared class instructions for a couple of years—that's how Silvan met him—but I really don't know him. He isn't usually so... chatty."

"Whatever you say. If he ever asks you for my phone number, though, you can give it to him." I blanked, unable to imagine two more different people than Thomas and Mira.

"Thomas? You seemed to think he was pretty lame tonight. And we're not living in the Victorian age. If you like him you could just ask for his cell number."

"Never! I would never call a guy." She looked deeply offended, her mouth rounding with shock. I raised my eyebrows over another dose of coffee. As flirty as my cousins acted, they were actually quite rigid about it being the men who chased the women. Midora's husband had asked her to marry him three times before she consented, and I knew she was crazy about him.

Mira changed the subject. "Do you believe all that stuff he said? About the curse and how the Lion is coming for you?"

I flinched. "Undecided. Are you going to tell Midora and Medea everything that's happened tonight the second you get home?" I asked.

Silvan laughed and wiped grease off his chin before offering me a fist bump.

She swatted his shoulder. "I *can* keep a secret. I don't think anyone would believe it anyway, do you?"

No. They probably wouldn't. But she'd avoided my question. I dipped a piece of pancake into maple syrup and deliberately locked gazes with her. "Maybe not. But if you do tell, I'll make you regret it. For a very long time." Facts were facts.

Mira narrowed her eyes at me. Silvan grabbed the back of her neck and shook her gently. "She won't say anything, will you, cousin? If she does, she'll have me to contend with." Mira shoved him away. "Get off." I waited with my fork still raised.

"So paranoid, Stella. I won't tell anyone," she confirmed, rolling her eyes. I relaxed and took a bite. Mira glared at Silvan but he smiled at her like a proud parent.

"So, what are you going to do?" Silvan asked me.

"I'm going to stop looking for Amanda for the time being." If she wanted to stay hidden, I had to accept it. Besides, I had new problems of my own to deal with.

"No, I mean—what are you going to do about the curse?"

There it was again. Only now, under the florescent lights of the diner, it seemed pretty silly to think my own distant relation might be the story behind a fairytale. But what if it *was* real? I mean, they must have tracked all those generations to confirm no one survived. For fifteen generations, a number I could barely wrap my head around.

I put down my fork and tore my paper napkin into strips. "My plan is simple. Not that I was likely to fall in love, anyway, but I just won't date until I'm twenty-two. Maybe even twenty-three to be extra careful. And I'll try not to be kidnapped by vampires or lions." I added what I thought was a convincingly confidant smile.

"I'm immune to those dimples. It sounds like the curse will *make* you fall in love."

"No one is immune to my dimples, and no one can make me do what I don't want to."

Mira narrowed her eyes, her jaw working until the French fry she was munching disappeared. "There is that. If anyone was stubborn enough to beat a curse, it's you, Stella." I wasn't sure if Silvan agreed with her as he muttered something I couldn't hear.

I was touched. Really, truly touched. "Thanks, Mira." She grinned.

"You know, that obsession you have with the truth isn't healthy, right? Knowing *everything* doesn't bring happiness. Sometimes people withhold truth for another person's own good." *Nope—truth is everything.*

"Did Mahari really tell you to stay with me tonight because of a curse?"

She sighed and stirred her malt while Silvan inhaled his food.

"Yes. Baba pulled the family together and told us that we were going to start taking shifts watching over you for the next few weeks. She even made up a signup sheet and everything. I volunteered for the first shift."

"Why?"

"Because I'd never seen your house. I mean, none of us have, but I've always been curious. Plus, I wanted to ask you about that guy you were with at the market. He was delicious."

"Alaric," I said, stealing one of her fries. "I don't really know him."

"Stay away from boys, Stella. I didn't like how he acted with you.

Like you're something he wants. A lot," Silvan warned. I shot him a "duh" look but his words circled again and again in my mind. Perhaps I'd had more of an effect than I imagined. Mira cocked her head but I managed a poker face until she refocused on her meal with a final comment.

"Well, with the curse, that's probably a good idea."

* * *

It was early morning when we pulled into my driveway. Emerging sunlight streamed through patches of low fog, causing the trees and grass to sparkle with dew.

"Well, my shift is over. Uncle Remi is next. He sleeps late though so you probably won't see him at the end of your driveway until ten or so." Mira said. Silvan snored softly from the backseat. I climbed out of her car and watched as she drove back down the drive. *Huh. I thought Uncle Remi was still in prison.*

When I opened the front door, it was to find the new night nurse eating a bowl of cereal. She rose from the stairs without saying anything and shuffled towards Sam's room. *Weirdo.* I didn't trust her. I followed her down the hall to check on my sleeping grandfather.

I froze in the doorway, stunned. Sam was awake and dressed in regular clothes. Nancy smirked and plopped down in his favorite club chair.

"Hey, Stella. Good morning," Sam called cheerfully.

"Good morning, yourself. You're up early."

Sam fastened a pair of red suspenders over a button-down shirt. He moved easily, the creases of pain in his face relaxed for the first time in months.

His frown was good-natured. "What do you mean? I always wake up early."

I glanced at Nancy and bit my lip.

"How are you feeling, Sam?"

"Fit as a fiddle! Haven't slept so well in years."

I itched to talk to Sam, but not with his creepy new nurse as an audience. When Carol came for her morning shift, I'd ask her about Nancy's background. We played half a game of chess and I went up to my room.

Mira's discarded clothes were still in a heap on my floor. I shoved them into a canvas tote and changed my bed linens. I then took a long, blistering shower, lingering until our ancient hot water heater surrendered and the pipes ran cold. Wrapped in a robe and towel turban, I stood in my room, undecided on next steps now that Amanda was declared safe. My bed looked so comfortable. I gave in and stretched across my duvet to stare at the ceiling. I thought of Lila in her glass coffin within an Ottoman tower. Had she dreamed? I crossed my arms at the waist and imagined being entombed on a satin bed, nothing between me and the world but a thick layer of glass. I think it would feel like a living death. It was the last thought I had for several hours.

Chapter 13
Hermit Reversed

Stella

L ater that afternoon, I stood on a street corner of downtown Portland with a to-go cup of Stumptown coffee in each hand. Tilting my face to the sky, I closed my eyelids to better feel the wetness coating my lashes and skin. It was drizzling, the kind of thick mist that Portlandia was famous for. I opened my eyes and studied the hotel.

The Regis Arms was elegant and modern, complete with a red suited doorman who'd already asked twice if I needed assistance. He was now occupied helping a couple with their luggage, and I was glad for the break in his attention while I stood on the sidewalk and mined for courage. *You can do this.*

I'd woken from my much-needed nap with an idea that would not go away. I didn't have a lot of connections in life that could help me and didn't want to involve Sam. I needed someone on my side. Someone without any self-interest who could act as a buffer in case the stories about the Noble King and Lion were real. I needed someone who could observe and see things I couldn't and who could intervene if I were kidnapped. Or, at least reliably report my abduction to law enforcement.

Unbidden, Alaric had come to mind. Hadn't he said he worked in security? That could mean anything from cyber spy to mall cop. The odds of his being in personal security were slim, but I didn't know anyone else to ask. If anything, he might have connections.

Stop being a coward, Stella. March in there and just ask him.

There was a chance he wasn't here, but he'd said he was in the city for another week. I knew a few of the hotel desk people as I'd gotten a gig here last summer, helping a contractor paint the walls across from the lobby elevators with historic city portraits. If one of them were working this morning it might make this a little less embarrassing.

I made eye contact with the doorman. He studied my holey jeans, Adidas sneakers, and grey t-shirt, his polite visage giving nothing away. I took a tiny step towards the hotel entrance, and he reluctantly swept the door open.

I swallowed against the lump in my throat and entered the lobby. It was carpeted in reds and blues with pet friendly welcome signs and a decidedly retro feel. I approached the front desk on leaden feet and carefully placed the cups on the counter next to a bowl of complementary dog biscuits. I drummed my short nails on the counter and waited for the desk clerk to finish checking in a couple. I didn't recognize anyone working. *Can you tell me if a guy named Alaric is staying here? His last name? I have no idea.*

"Are one of those for me?"

I froze, my neck prickling at the exquisitely timbered voice. I turned and looked up at Alaric. His dark hair was damp, and he wore jeans and Nikes. The rolled-up sleeves of his plaid shirt revealed muscular forearms. The fabric molded across his wide shoulders, narrow waist and chest as if custom made just for him. Maybe it was. He cleared his throat and tapped a rolled-up newspaper against his thigh. I realized with a start that I was standing in silence, staring at him.

"You really are stalking me aren't you, Stella?"

I gaped at him, flushing. If the floor swallowed me, I would gladly sink.

His lips twitched. "I'm just kidding."

His smile widened, and his curving lips were all I could focus on. That and his eyes, which were searching mine with an intensity that made my stomach flutter. He didn't appear unhappy about the idea of being stalked. He actually seemed pleased to see me. I blinked, trying to gather my wits.

"Uh. Yes. I mean, no! I brought you coffee." I handed him one of the cups and grabbed the other, holding it with both hands close to my chest. A paper shield.

"Hi. Uh. D-do you have a m-minute?"

"Yes, I have time." He gestured towards the nearby guest lounge area. As I walked towards the room, he placed a hand on my lower back for a moment, as if to guide me. The brief touch burned through my t-shirt. I wasn't use to anyone touching me so casually.

We navigated around a grand piano in the opulent sitting room to find a velvet settee in a quiet corner. I sank down on its edge; my limbs close to my body.

Two academic looking women talked across a pile of papers on the other side of the room and I felt distinctly underdressed. With a start, I realized they were both staring at Alaric in appreciation as they whispered to one another. I scowled but they didn't seem to care.

Alaric sat next to me, thighs outstretched. He tossed the newspaper next to him and leaned forward with his fingers loosely locked together, paper coffee cup between them. One of his knees brushed mine, and I pretended not to notice. Oh, but I did. I stared at the lid of my cup, thinking of how to begin.

"I'm glad to see you," he murmured.

"Are you?" I searched his eyes, but his solemn expression seemed genuine.

"Yes. Definitely."

I played with my bottom lip and his eyes darkened.

"Have you always had that habit?"

"What habit?"

"You pinch your lips when you're thinking about something. It wouldn't help you in a poker game."

I dropped my hand and sat up straight as my cheeks warmed.

"I'm sorry to just show up. I don't have your phone number."

He was suddenly holding a cell phone, thumb poised. "What's your number?"

I told him and he quickly typed it into his contacts. My back pocket vibrated.

"There. Now you can reach me."

"Thanks," I mumbled. The quickness of his request helped to quell my nerves. Perhaps my surprise visit wasn't a complete nuisance. I dove right in.

"I have a proposal for you," I said, quickly, before I could chicken out. My outburst was met with silence.

He waited; his gaze watchful. The man really had the most beautiful face. The barest shadow sculpted his jawline and mouth. I pressed a thumbnail into the soft tissue that webbed my thumb and forefinger, hoping the tiny flare of pain might distract me from ogling him like the women across the room.

"I remembered you said you were in security. What kind of security are you in exactly?" I took a sip of my Americano and pulled at the strands of fabric surrounding the hole at my knee.

"What kind of security do you require?" His voice was soft.

This was the hard part. The one I'd dreaded since forcing myself to come here.

"Before I begin, let me just say that I have some money saved up. I'm not sure what a bodyguard makes hourly, but I'm guessing it's a lot more than minimum wage."

He rubbed his face and sat back, throwing an arm across the back of the settee. I rushed on before I lost track of my purpose.

"I have reason to believe that I may be in danger." My words were rushed, and I groaned inwardly.

He stiffened and sat upright. His eyes scanned the room before they returned to me. The relaxed, friendly Alaric had disappeared, replaced with a severe, unyielding version. The hair on my arms rose with an electric charge in the air. I absently rubbed my skin.

His eyes narrowed. "What danger?"

"It's hard to explain," I began. "There's this guy that goes by the moniker 'The Lion'. I'm not sure what he looks like, but I've been told he intends to kidnap me."

He blinked. I fidgeted with my cup.

"Really? And who told you this?" His low voice hummed with intensity.

"I promised not to tell anyone about my source. Look. I know this sounds crazy. Believe me, it sounds crazy to me. I don't even *know* this person. I mean he sounds a bit arrogant walking around calling himself 'The Lion' but my friend seems pretty convinced that this 'Lion' person—" I made air quotes, "—is going to try to nab me sometime in the next week. I figure it's better to take precautions." My fingers expanded the hole in my jeans.

"Hmm," was his only reply. I cringed but plowed on.

"Also...there's a lot of weird stuff happening around me. I need someone neutral who can help me figure it out."

"And you thought of me?"

I could deny it but what would be the point. My presence here said it all.

"Yes."

His eyes gleamed with satisfaction, and his lips curved in a masculine smile.

"You're in luck. It just so happens that I know quite a lot about personal protection. I can help you, Stella."

Relief exploded, sweet and pure. My bones felt lighter with the glimmer of hope. I inhaled a deep breath—the first comfortable one in twenty-four hours.

Now I just had to make sure I could afford him.

"We should talk about your terms. How much do you charge?"

He tilted his head. "Why don't we discuss what you might require and figure it out later?"

That didn't sit well. If he ran up a huge bill that I couldn't pay it would be a disaster.

"Why don't we agree on a day rate?" I suggested.

"Let's get through today and then figure it out," he countered. I bit my lip, afraid to push him but nervous about my budget.

"Are you free today?" His tone was casual and his question unexpected.

"Yes." *Did that come out too eagerly?*

"Wait—like on the clock paid time?" I checked the time on my phone.

He grinned. "No. Free, personal time that we can also use to discuss your problem as friends." I replayed his statement several times, thinking.

"Okay. I had to drop my car off at the mechanics on Burnside just now to check on a couple of things but we can walk."

"A walk. Okay. I guess that would be acceptable. I'll drive you home afterwards." He stood. "Stay here. I need to make a quick call." Under normal circumstances, anyone telling me to stay anywhere would grate on my nerves. Surprisingly, his commanding tone didn't irritate.

He stood and wound his way through the room towards an alcove near the concierge desk. My God. The view from behind was stunning. As he passed the businesswomen, one of them called out to him, giggling. He glanced in their direction but didn't slow down. As they gawked, one even fanned herself with a notepad. I empathized.

Alaric approached the bank of elevators, pausing just past the concierge desk. Keeping his back turned, he spoke on his phone. He was alone, the concierge busy on the other side of the lobby helping a man with a bicycle.

Just behind Alaric, large glass dispensers of chilled water with floating slices of lemon and mint sat on a table. A shadow seemed to build along the wall, leaching from behind the dispensers. I narrowed my eyes. It thickened, gathering into itself. My imagination was in hyper drive.

I blinked and rubbed my tired eyelids. Looking up once more I observed a man talking with Alaric that hadn't been there a second ago. Alaric's head was bent and the man seemed to be mostly listening. He wore a suit and, as I stared, he glanced in my direction. I immediately pointed my gaze upwards, as if admiring the chandelier overhead. Nancy Drew I was not.

Trying to look a bit cooler, I pulled out my cell phone and confirmed I had one message from Silvan. He would be returning my sketchpad later.

"Shall we?" Alaric waited before me, his hands in his back pockets.

I nodded and stood. We walked through the living room and back towards the lobby. I paused, scanning for a trash receptacle to throw my cold coffee in. The cup was plucked from my fingers. Without a word, Alaric handed it to a young man at the front desk, and the man offered a deferential nod.

Alaric placed a hand on the small of my back and herded me towards the entrance, and I was too affected by his touch to remark on how I could walk fine all by myself. Standing on the sidewalk I felt a little at loose ends. The result of my quest had turned out better than expected. Alaric glanced back and caught my smile, matching it with one of his own.

"Where would you like to go?"

It was one of those bi-polar summer days. Raining one second and sunny the next. I raised my face to the sunshine, thinking. I really did have an errand I wouldn't mind running. Turning to look at Alaric, my breath caught at the expression on his face. He stared at me as if he liked what he saw. Maybe Silvan had been right. My chest pounded.

"Have you been to Powell's Bookstore? I'd like to find a book on curses."

He nodded, his smile fading. My breath caught, suddenly bereft at its loss. What had I said? *Curses?* Some people were touchy about the occult.

"I know the place. There's a café inside where we can talk." He gestured for me to go before him and we began to walk. I noticed he made sure to position himself on the street side. A few steps later and he offered me his elbow. I paused and coiled my hand around his bicep, the gesture strangely natural. His arm gently captured my hand and wrist. It was such a gentlemanly thing to do. As we walked, I peered into shop windows and looked anywhere but at the gorgeous man at my side. My fingers felt as if I were holding stone, and I tried not to surreptitiously stroke his arm like a creeper, but it was a difficult battle.

After another block I noticed a curious phenomenon. Anyone walking towards us seemed riveted on Alaric. Women and men just seemed drawn to him as we passed. Even the homeless people lying in doorways eyed his movements. This confirmed it. I was an invisible slug. No one ever watched me coming, and if someone did chance to make eye contact it was usually brief. As in, *Excuse me, Miss, you have toilet paper stuck on your shoe.*

Our silence was comfortable, and I was suddenly happier than I'd been in a very long time. We walked eight more blocks and stopped only once to retie my sneakers. It was early afternoon and people were enjoying the last weekend of summer. I felt part of the human race today. Not just an outside observer. Alaric paused in front of a window, a confused expression lowering his brow.

"I don't understand what this place is."

I read the sign and chuckled. "You've never seen a barbershop-bar-movie theatre combination before?"

Through the glass we could see barber chairs. Beer bottles lined the external windows, showcasing the available selection. A sign that read *Movie Theater* pointed towards a hallway. This was Portland at its finest. I just hoped the men cutting hair weren't intoxicated.

"This place is actually kind of famous. It has one of the oldest movie theatres in the city. You know, all red drapes and seats without cup holders?"

"I like movies," he responded simply. I impulsively tugged him towards the door.

"Let's check it out."

He followed reluctantly, eyeing the men in barber chairs. They nodded but kept up their lively conversations. I released his wrist and hustled down the narrow hallway to the theatre. A sign indicated that the first show didn't begin until four, which explained why the dark hallway and theatre ticket entrance were empty. I tugged on the theatre doors, and Alaric was suddenly there, opening them for me.

The air filled with the scent of stale popcorn and musty fabric. Low lights barely illuminated the interior space and blank screen. The screen was smaller than the chain theatres, the red velvet drapes that framed it tied back with gold satin ropes. The threadbare, red velvet seats sloped towards the screen in matching rows.

Alaric stood with hands on his hips as he surveyed the dimly lit space. I passed him and skipped down the carpeted ramp to the front of the theatre.

"Is anyone here?" I called out, thrilled when my voice echoed against the fabric draped walls. I turned to Alaric, and my heart clenched to see him smiling again. He looked so different when he smiled, more boyish. He followed me down into the theatre, watching my silly antics. I reached the front of the stage and, after making sure we really were alone, performed a little hula dance.

His laughter boomed. "You would have made a good dancer in South Pacific," he called.

"South Pacific?" I asked, swishing my make-believe grass skirt.

He shook his head, coming nearer. "It was a movie with a location set in Bali. Also, a Broadway play."

"Oh."

He stood next to me now, eyes gleaming in the low light. Shiny locks tumbled over his forehead and I suddenly wanted to know whether his hair felt as soft as it looked. We were inches apart now. His gaze drank up my face, sparking a sensation deep in the pit of my belly. "How old are you, Alaric?"

"How old do you think I am?"

I cocked my head in annoyance and he chuckled softly. "I'm twenty-two."

Some people were just old souls. Some people were just born with a charisma that seemed beyond those of us lower species. Alaric was both. I stared at his lips and wondered once more what they felt like. If the curse were true, these feelings might be a trap, and yet there was simply no way someone like Alaric would ever end up with a regular girl like me. He was out of my stratosphere. I was a simple girl, without anything special about me to hold his interest longer than a nanosecond. Right now, I was just a curiosity to him, a diversion on a pit stop.

Alaric felt safe. He would leave soon for New York, and I would never see him again. If the curse came true, which was a huge stretch to believe, then I had no more than three years to live. I'd only kissed one boy. Would it hurt so much to take advantage of a golden opportunity?

I floated forward, nervous, until our fronts brushed. He stiffened but didn't move away. So far so good. Looking into his eyes, I slowly raised my hands until they hovered near his beautiful face. Did he notice they were trembling? He seemed to understand my intentions because he bent down, allowing me to sift fingers into his silken hair, holding my breath with the sensation. I ignored the nervous butterflies and doubt, slowly pulling his face down to mine. His eyes grew darker still, his expression cold. His neck resisted for a single heartbeat, causing me to release him—and then his face lowered, and my eyes closed.

His breath warmed my lips. Then a gossamer touch. "Breathe," he whispered against my mouth. I drew in a ragged inhalation. His unique scent drugged me as surely as his presence. Something broke deep inside me, and I pressed my lips to his. They were unyielding, but madness was firing in my veins at his proximity and I couldn't stop myself. I felt everything at once. The hardness of his chest and thighs as I molded my body against his. The sensation of his hands as they rose to span my waist. The feel of his warm fingers as they caressed the bare inch of skin revealed by my raised arms. His lips were velvety, his lower lip full, tempting me to bite into it.

Before I knew it, my arms were around his neck and shoulders as I lifted on tiptoes to deepen the contact of our lips. I couldn't help an embarrassing groan escape, and it seemed to trigger something within him. He answered my sound with a growl of his own.

My feet left the floor as he held me. His lips softened, sliding beneath mine. I tilted my head, gliding my tongue lightly against the seam of his lips, testing. He pulled me closer with a low moan that made my head spin. Our roles reversed and he was now the aggressor, leading us deeper into this new universe that was ours alone. My lips were taken in the most spectacular way and heat coiled and expanded everywhere.

I felt his hand cup the side of my face and then my throat. His lips scalded my skin as he kissed the side of my mouth, my jaw, and the sensitive flesh at my throat. I threw my head back to give him better access. He groaned and nibbled my skin in fiery sweeps. I never wanted this moment to end. My hands flexed against his shoulders, keeping him close.

I searched out his lips again and he gave them to me. I was a furnace, trembling with new sensations. Kissing Scott had felt nice. This was so damn different. Alaric's kiss had become the entire world. I felt one strong arm lower to hold my hips, supporting me. His other hand tangled in my hair to tilt my head to his advantage and I hung there in his arms, delirious with this new wanting.

Alaric's lips went from feasting on mine to abruptly stilled. I whimpered, needing him to reciprocate, but he remained unmoving. I kissed his cheek, my mouth trailing in tempting sweeps along his jaw like he'd done to mine—yet he inexorably lowered his chin until his face was buried in my neck. I felt his warm breath in my hair and knew he could feel the rapid race of my heartbeat. Confusion replaced desire. Had I done something wrong?

After a few quiet moments, my heart rate decreased. The reality of what I'd just done sank in. I wiggled my ankles and he lowered me gently until my feet touched the floor. I couldn't look at him. I leaned forward, hiding my face against his chest.

Chapter 14
The Devil

Alaric

While Stella shivered in my arms, I fought the raging desire to continue our play. The beast had begun to rise, claws curling against her lovely hips. Lost in her own innocent yearning she hadn't seemed to notice, yet fear of hurting her, of my aura being revealed to all, had been the bucket of proverbial cold water I needed to rise from the fog of need she created. Her hands dropped and the loss of contact disturbed me—made me want to coax her into replacing them. I tried to recall all the reasons why this was a bad idea.

She was an innocent. My brother would soon claim her for a wife. She thought I was protecting her from The Lion. She will very well hate me when she finds out that I *am* The Lion. The big bad wolf sent to steal Red Riding Hood away. She thought she held Alaric. What will she think when she sees the beast?

Her scent was making her impossible to resist. Lavender, lemon, and a hint of freesia. Mouthwatering. I didn't crave blood as my brother and the vampires did. And yet I was very conscious of the flow of blood in her veins, the pulse unbearably tempting near the sides of her throat. My hands stroked her back, the claws gone as my control returned. I couldn't see her face, tucked as it was against my chest.

I pulled away but she stepped forward, closing the distance. Her forehead pressed into my shirt, denying me a view of her expression. I smoothed the waves of her hair, reveling in the rich softness. It was taking all my strength not to resume our kiss. I cupped the back of her head with one hand while my fingers found her chin. She resisted but could not match my persistence as I lifted her face to meet mine. I groaned inwardly when she kept her eyes closed. My sweet Stella was embarrassed. That would not do.

My fingers traced up her jaw and along her cheek bone. My black heart clenched involuntarily when she sighed. I was used to my effect on women. But Stella's sweet yearning drove dark thoughts into my head. I needed to reassure her.

"You are very beautiful." The words left without thought. I could do better.

"Thank you for the kiss. If we were in another time and place I assure you—I would want more." Was that too direct? She was so very young.

Her lashes fluttered and she finally revealed her eyes, searching.

"I am *not* beautiful. But do you mean it…that you felt it, too?" she whispered. The light was too dim to see the depth of her eyes or for her to see the truth in mine.

I held her face, my thumb lightly tracing her swollen lips. "If we continued another moment I would have you on that stage, doing inappropriate things to someone I just met."

Her eyes widened and her hands rose to cup mine.

"I would have lifted your shirt over your head and..."

"Stop!" she panted, but I noticed a smile hovering in the corners of her delectable lips. I grinned inwardly and leaned forward to kiss her hair.

"I just mean that I want you. You are very difficult to resist, and I would appreciate it if you could just help me right now in my efforts to be a gentleman."

She softened, her body curving towards mine.

"I understand." Regret swirled in her tone, and I hoped it wasn't for what had just transpired. I straightened and waited until she gave a small nod.

I clasped her hand and led her back out of the theatre. I had no idea how I was going to explain myself once she learned the truth of who I was. Was there a way to prevent it? Before we reached the end of the hall and became visible to the inhabitants of the barber shop, I tugged her to a stop. She searched my face, curious, and I pressed her against the wall. Our fingers laced and I held them over her head so she couldn't tempt me with her hands. I kissed her softly, smiling as she returned my attention. Meeting her lips with mine one last time, I drew back.

She seemed lost, her eyes the deepest shade of the Marmara Sea, stormy and wild. Tiny threads of silver wove through their depths, and I wondered just how volatile they might become if circumstances were different. Satisfaction flowed thick and heavy through my veins. The soft look in her eyes was better than any victory I could recall earning on a battlefield.

"I wanted to do that in the light so that I can remember your expression in both darkness and light." A glimmer of amusement sparked within her deep blue eyes and the silver receded. "Okay."

I released her and she tugged me closer, taking me off guard.

"I wonder where you were raised. Your accent is thicker than usual," she noted.

"I speak many languages," I said, sidestepping her question. *And your eyes shine silver, sweetheart.* Information about me was a thread. The more she pulled, the less I could stay as Alaric. She swallowed, one hand rising to touch my chest before falling away.

"There are things I want to tell you that I've recently learned about myself. About the world around us. This is so hard..." She stared at the base of my throat and began again.

"Can we just pretend today? Pretend like we might be normal people who...like each other?" Her vulnerable request robbed me of thought or speech.

"Tomorrow we can be strictly professional. After I tell you everything you may just run far away from me. I can guarantee that I won't be jumping you again if you're worried about that..." She trailed off.

Her cheeks were a fascinating shade of pink, and I knew this was taking a great deal for her to request. The idea was both horrifying and tempting. Tempting to imagine she was mine even for a single day.

Horrifying to know that such an event would make the future that more bleak. I would lose her soon. Even if Murad hadn't claimed her as his, the enchantment would likely cause her to fall in love with someone mortal—someone worthier. Today might be the only time with her I will ever have—before she finds out how I've deceived her. Then she will hate me for the rest of her possibly very short life. The thought left me chilled.

"You are asking if we could pretend to be a couple...for just today?" She nodded.

"And tomorrow we wake up as if today never happened?"

She began to nod—but then lowered her gaze. She lifted a hand and played with the buttons of my shirt. I leaned a forearm against the wall, shielding her from anyone who might walk past the windows. I stilled her hand beneath mine, mulling over her words. I had little experience with the tender sensibilities of a young girl. For centuries I'd kept my dalliances to only those women sophisticated enough to understand my interest was fleeting—and who appreciated my darker needs. I was no gentle schoolboy. Her words sparked an ache that was wholly unfamiliar to me.

As she remained silent, I realized that her energy had shifted, reflecting sadness. Her aura was a fascinating pale gold, its edges fluttering into grey-blue.

"Alaric—I'm just teasing. Of course, we can't pretend. I know that."

My gut clenched in disappointment, yet there was also relief in her taking the fantasy from me. Clara's minions would be reporting our sightings back to her. Our kiss was a one-time only mistake that could not be repeated. This knowledge did not negate the regret I felt as her hand dropped away, and she finally gathered the courage to meet my eyes.

"Thank you for...you know. I think it's best if we keep some physical distance from now on."

I nodded and resisted the urge to brush her cheekbone once more, unable to get enough of her softness. Only the image of my brother and the possibilities of spies watching us through the windows kept me in check.

"We will keep this to ourselves." I suggested, the words bitter. Once she knew the truth of who I am, and her place in my world, discretion would keep the peace with Murad. There was another reason as well. These precious moments belonged only to us. This was ours, no matter what transpires tomorrow. Her face flashed with hurt before she nodded once and locked her expression in that cool, implacable gaze I now recognized as armor.

There was nothing I could say to comfort her that would not undo the last several minutes of our conversation. I deliberately stepped away from her, and she sauntered past me, leading us out to the street.

As we walked, I kept my hands in my pockets while she remained quiet at my side. Several blocks later she seemed to rally to a more upbeat mood.

"So, you said you like movies. Which is your favorite?" she asked.

"I have many. What's *your* favorite film?" She pondered her answer as we waited for the light to turn.

"You'll laugh. Laugh at me or think I'm unsophisticated."

"Try me."

"*Shaun of the Dead*."

"What are the odds? That's *my* favorite movie as well."

"It is not," she cried, giving me a shove. I allowed her to move me several inches, glad to see the self-consciousness drop from her lovely shoulders.

"It is. I swear it." I placed a hand solemnly over my heart, pleased to see this playful side of Stella emerge.

She jutted her chin. "Prove it, then."

I fought a smile at her taunting tone. "You mean like a quote?"

"Anything."

I thought for a moment. "How about we grab Liz, go to the Winchester, have a nice cold pint, and wait for this to blow over?"

She performed a little jumping dance, delight shining in her eyes. I tried to recall other quotes from the zombie film, anything to keep that sparkle. Now it was I who felt embarrassed. She'd turned me into a foolish kid who wanted nothing more than to impress a girl. She started walking again.

"My cousin, Silvan, and I are zombie freaks. We even ran a zombie 3K last year. He loves nothing more than trying to scare me, but he never succeeds. Amanda thinks we're ridiculous," she explained. I had no idea what a zombie 3K was but if it made her this happy then I was a fan.

We crossed the street and turned, walking past a park with tents of vagrants. I kept an eye on the ones that seemed high or aggressive. The pungent odor of sulfur mixed with decay reached me, and I knew that some of these poor souls had been spelled to their addictions. I frowned, surprised Clara would allow such things in her territory.

"May I ask *you* a question?" I requested. She nodded.

"You mentioned wanting to travel. If you could go anywhere, where would you like to visit?"

"Where wouldn't I like to go? St. Petersburg, London, Paris...the list is endless."

We were nearly to the bookstore, its distinctive marque and size hard to miss.

"What do you see yourself doing in these places?"

She was silent. I glanced down, catching the blush that stained her cheeks.

It was the same look on her face from the hallway. The breath left my lungs, imagining what she might be thinking. My hand tightened on hers.

"I would...like to study art. The feedback I've gotten on my work is good, but I wonder how much better I can be if I had more advanced instruction."

"What else did you think of just now?" I was fascinated by the cause of her blush.

"Er...I may have imagined painting you, *while* in all those places."

"Stella..." I began. I could hear it. My voice consecrated the air with her name. This will end badly, I know. My punishment is one thing, but I don't want her to suffer.

There were monsters out there. Creatures willing to tear her to pieces if they got wind of old Everwish rumors. I couldn't put her at risk for my own weakness. Thankfully, she hadn't noticed my hesitation. She simply walked and I followed her off the curb and into the street.

"One more question," she began. I nodded, helpless to deny her anything.

She watched her feet as she walked. "So, do you have a girlfriend? Is that why you stopped kissing me before?" She rushed through her next words. "Because it was just an impulsive moment for me. No big deal." Her tone was casual, yet I'd noticed that she seemed unable to look at me when things mattered.

I paused in the middle of the street, heedless of waiting cars until her startled eyes met mine. "There is no girlfriend. My job is not...easy on relationships."

I didn't want her to think this doomed romance was related to a preference for another female. Hated the very suggestion she might doubt her own appeal. My work and tendency to outlive humans was partial truth. Even if she wasn't who she was, nor promised to my brother, the truth was that, when your ex-girlfriend kills every woman you spend more than a single night with, you begin to lose interest in long-term anything.

I couldn't hand a death sentence down to an innocent. Witches had exceedingly long memories, and Daria was older than most, even if she didn't appear so outwardly.

Stella nodded as she glanced nervously at the cars waiting for the lights to turn. A truck with mud splattered wheels invited injury by emitted a honk. I cast a glare at the offender, my power blanketing out in silent menace that even humans could sense. The man stayed his hand on the wheel and looked away. I followed Stella like a pup to the street corner when she tugged at my hand. We entered Powell's bookstore and it was the hell of nightmares.

I hadn't thought this through when Stella suggested it. It was Sunday and many humans had the day off to shop. I was already restraining the beast, who'd been restless since we tasted Stella earlier. Feeling trapped and in close quarters with humans was very dangerous.

A man bumped into me; nose stuck in a horror book. He apologized and I resisted the urge to throttle him. It wasn't his fault I'd been surprised. With effort, I fought back all the scents and energy swirling about us, narrowing my focus to our immediate area.

Stella beamed at me, oblivious to my discomfort. "Isn't this great?"

I grunted. She selected a canvas book tote and wandered through the crowd, into a different room. I followed, hoping it might be less populated. It was worse. It didn't help that the scent of sulfur and other magick lingered in the air. The magick was layered, some old and some as fresh as mere seconds ago.

As Stella floated happily down a flight of stairs, I stiffened in recognition of a lumberjack-of-a-man with his nose buried in a publication. He was a dark sorcerer I'd dealt with in South America years ago when he'd been suspected of helping a drug lord gain a foothold over the local government. I noted the magazine he read was called *Fashion Doll Quarterly* and my brows rose. Undetected, I shrugged. To each their own.

I tracked back to Stella but she'd disappeared. Rattled at how quickly she'd vanished, I scanned the area, trying to spot her golden hair. I was tempted to open my powers, to locate her by scent instantly. The presence of other Primati prevented me from choosing this path. I did not want to be recognized unless ready to end this persona altogether. I stalked along the landing, relieved when I recognized her fair hair and humming voice between stacks.

I touched my chest, the tightness unfamiliar. What if she'd been grabbed or worse? Stella was a firefly, a bright light meandering where she wished on a whim. Her willful disregard for her own safety caused the beast within to pace and roar as I made my way to her side.

Crouched in front of a shelf, Stella smiled into a book, and the tightness eased somewhat with her proximity. I was finding it hard to remember why I didn't just place her in the holding tank I kept in the basement of my New York apartment building. But that would realize her fears. The Lion kidnapping her. Who'd told her about the Lion and how much did she know?

The curve of her spine was mesmerizing. My fingers itched to explore it, and I inhaled deeply, thinking of anything to distract myself.

"Do *you* have a boyfriend?" I wished the words back. I knew from Clara's reports that she didn't have a boyfriend. Even if she did, he wouldn't matter now that Murad had laid claim. I had no business asking her in the first place. We'd just decided not to engage in any further flirtation, hadn't we? I should keep up my side of the agreement.

Her shoulders froze as she looked up.

"Not even close. I mean there was someone a year ago but not any longer." She trailed off, not meeting my eyes.

Well, Fuckall.

This was news to me. According to any account I'd read, Stella had shown no indication of a boyfriend. I felt my body begin to expand, the change happening. I fought back the beast, tried to think of ice cream, daisies, whatever shit I could come up with.

"Are you okay? You look a little warm." Stella stood, concern in her face.

I was afraid to nod, move, or do anything at this point. I needed every bit of focus to reel back the burning desire to change shape. This lack of control hadn't happened in hundreds of years. I scanned the room, desperate for a way to distract her. Gritting my teeth, I leaned towards a shelf and plucked out a book.

"Here," I said, thrusting it beneath her nose. She took it, inspecting the cover.

"*The Little Prince* by Antoine de Saint-Exupery," she read aloud. "I love this book!"

She did? It happened to be one of my favorites as well. Grasping for control, I took the book and turned it to my favorite section. Jabbing the page with a finger, I gave it back to her. She read it aloud.

"*You—you alone will have stars as no one else has them...In one of the stars I shall be living. In one of them I shall be laughing. And so it will be as if all the stars were laughing, when you look at the night sky...you—only you—will have stars that can laugh.*"

She looked up, her eyes shining. "How did you know this was my favorite passage?"

Did I know? I thought back to the reports I'd scanned. I didn't recall anything about Antoine de Saint-Exupery. I'd known the pilot-writer personally.

At this moment, I didn't trust my self-restraint while the lingering ghost of another male in her life stirred the beast. The enclosed space with so many humans and Primatis in the area put me on edge, while I remained in human form and Stella's scent was compounding the strain. How was I going to manage eventually seeing Stella on my brother's arm? The very thought splintered my control.

"Stay here." I gritted my teeth in a grimace that puckered her forehead in confusion. "I have to find something." I hated to leave her, but this was as safe a place as any. I had to make sure I could keep myself in check near her. I stalked away, ignoring the hurt on her pretty face.

Minutes later I was on the street, striding in barely human steps. My expression must have held a warning as mortals leaped from my path. Having a temper that was rare but legendary was the result of the demon I kept at bay within my blood. My dual bloodline was a blessing and a scourge. The vampire-demon dampened much of the empathy that had caused me so much suffering and conflict as a human. In turn, he needed an outlet for his rage and blood thirst. I'd spent an entire week as a good boy, if I didn't count the witch in the map shop. The beast in me wanted to rise.

I found a quiet alley and called to Grayson. He materialized within seconds, a glass beer bottle in hand. I looked pointedly at the bottle.

"Forgive me, Sir. You have unexpected guests and they wanted to try the local IPA."

"I don't have guests, Grayson."

Grayson remained silent, already sensing my mood and knowing it best not to challenge me. I sighed. "Who?"

"Noble King Murad and a few others."

I punched the brick wall, dust and mortar flying. It felt good so I did it a few more times. A nearby metal door creaked open, and a man with an apron gave us a startled inspection before closing the door with a hasty thud. The scrape of a latch followed. My chin sank to my chest as my palms met bent knees. Could I not catch a fucking break?

I straightened. "What does my brother want?"

Grayson cleared his throat and avoided eye contact.

"He says that you're not answering your phone and he was concerned."

This was accurate. I'd been avoiding giving my brother an update, hoping to buy time.

"He cannot use your bond to communicate when your aura is locked," Grayson pointed out unnecessarily. This was true. It had been nice being the only one in my head for a few days.

"Sir—he let Demir out."

I stopped breathing. "What did you say?"

Grayson stared at me. "He said he let her go because he needs the Covens to convene a full Council, and they cannot meet as a Council with the Earth Queen buried in bedrock."

"It's only been five years." Daria Demir had been sentenced to fifty years for ordering the murder of a young child in retaliation for a debt the child's father owed.

"Yes. But you were not available to counsel him on his decision. He also thinks with Samhain coming up in two months that Stella will need help preparing for the ball and the wedding. He heard Stella may have power and wants her to have guidance."

How had he heard she had power? I shook my head. With Daria loose, it was wise that I would be distancing myself from Stella immediately. Her jealousy was lethal.

"Who else is with the King?"

"Only Queen Theresa and the guards attending them, Sir. I located a suite with atrium view at the Nines hotel for his Noble Highness. Queen Theresa will be taking an empty house during her stay. I thought you might prefer the privacy."

A loyal friend, Tess was never far from my brother.

"Thank you, Grayson."

"Anytime, Sir."

I checked the time, frowning when I saw I'd been gone for nearly thirty minutes. Stella will think I abandoned her again. She was relatively safe in the bookstore in daytime. Safer than by my side when I was not in full control. I shook my head and retrieved my cell, pressing Murad's name in my missed calls queue.

While I waited for my brother to pick up, Grayson held out a pair of Wayfarer sunglasses. I glanced at the gray sky and frowned.

"Your eyes, Sir. The bond on your aura is fracturing."

Chapter 15
Temperance

Stella

Alaric had walked away from me. Again. He'd practically shoved *The Little Prince* in my face before he'd ditched me. A woman in a sundress I'd seen make eyes at him earlier stepped in front of him, a question on her lips. He maneuvered around her so fast her audible gasp carried back to me. I wished I could read his mind. Sighing, I put the book back and continued my mission. A store employee pointed me towards the magic, witchcraft, and paganism section. I wandered through aisles, keeping a look out for the vanishing Alaric. Giving him the benefit of the doubt, I pulled my phone out and sent him a text, letting him know which section I would be in.

Our kiss in the theatre replayed in a loop in my mind, and the memory had me flushing. The feel of his hands on me were a revelation. I'd always judged girls who fell fast, yet here I was—on fire for a man I'd barely known for forty-eight hours. I'd thought I was in love with Scott, yet I'd easily kept him at arm's length. With Alaric, it was as if he were a magnet for every cell in my body. Perhaps impending death was changing me. There were enough closed doors in my present and possibly my future. Even if the enchantment Thomas referred to could be broken, today with Alaric will be one of my best memories. I couldn't imagine anything better.

Stop! I had to force back these feelings because they had nowhere to grow. Obsessing over a beautiful stranger was a distraction I couldn't afford with this curse to figure out. I finally found the right shelves and stared in awe at the assortment of occult books. Who on earth read, let alone wrote all of these books? I scanned the stacks, looking for anything helpful on how curses worked.

After several minutes spent trying to identify topics, I shook my head, overwhelmed by the selection. There was even a *Wiccapedia for Dummies*. I found a shelf of herbal cookbooks and alchemy notebooks, even recognizing some I'd seen in Marion's store. A few gave off a creepy vibe and I deliberately kept my distance from those. On the last shelf I discovered a thin book on druids and placed it in my tote, along with a copy of *Practical Elemental Magick*.

Rounding a corner, I ran into a bookcase with locked glass doors. Its wood shelves held crowded displays of tarot card decks of different styles and sizes. Some were used and claimed to be collectors' items. With a start, I noticed a Polaroid picture of a Tarot deck that resembled one of mine. My breath fogged the glass as I squinted to read the handwritten scrawl on its accompanying index card.

The deck was called the Scion Deck and interested customers were instructed to speak with the helpdesk for more information. I stared at the image. It looked very much like an Empress card from a Major Arcana deck I'd painted two years ago. I recalled using a great deal of green in that set.

"They can take them out for you if you want to look at them," said a girl my age. She had ebony hair, skin so pale it was translucent and wore a long dress with fingerless gloves.

"Thanks. I think I'll ask about this one," I said, tapping the glass in front of the Polaroid. The girl peered over my shoulder.

"Oh. You must be rich. The Scion decks are the most expensive in the world. I doubt they really have a set here. They're too rare. I hear it's because any reading given with that deck will actually come true."

"Really?" I murmured. I squinted but the photo still resembled my work.

"Umm hmm. There are about six sets worldwide, and all of them hand-painted by this mysterious master they call the Scion."

"The Scion?"

The girl shrugged, her eyes bright as they held mine. "Some guy. He only signs with a star symbol but they call him the Scion." My skin flashed cold.

What were the odds of another person using a star as signature?

"The artist is a man?"

She shrugged again. "That's what I heard."

"You seem very knowledgeable."

She offered a shy smile. "I pay attention. Plus, I do tarot readings so I know about different decks." I took out my phone and snapped a quick picture of the Polaroid to share with Marion later. Maybe the girl could help me. "I'm looking for a book on curses. Maybe you could recommend one?"

The girl beamed and immediately meandered towards a section in the middle of the aisle. A man hunkered upon a stepping stool nearby, a pile of books at his side and a large volume in his lap. She sidestepped around him when he didn't budge or look up. Losing oneself in a great book is the sweetest experience and one I couldn't begrudge anyone.

"The thing is, most books on magic will have some information on curses. Light Wiccans won't go there because whatever you put out in the universe returns thrice fold. There may be books on how to break curses..." She flipped through titles as I surveyed the books nearby.

The man at our feet stood. He was of medium build but seemed more muscular once upright. He offered a slight smile. "Sorry. I couldn't help overhear your conversation. Might I recommend something?"

He was good looking, with dark eyes, tanned skin and thick brown hair. He reminded me of a model in the back of one of Amanda's fashion magazines. Attractive if you liked pretty men. I preferred Alaric's rougher exterior. The girl eyed me questioningly.

I shrugged, nudging the spine of a book until it aligned with its sisters on the shelf.

"Sure."

He smiled with warmth and I couldn't help but return it. It was a nice smile.

The girl stepped between us, placing a hand on his shoulder as if to maneuver around him. Before I could move back, she placed a hand on my forearm. The man touched my other arm.

I pulled away, but the girl whispered something, and the bookstore vanished.

When I opened my eyes, it was to see an elaborate four-poster bed with mustard-colored bed hangings. Panicked, I sat up and immediately the room spun. I rubbed my temples, trying to shake off the unpleasant sensation.

"Gently," a soft voice murmured. "Give yourself time to acclimate. Air transferring at this distance might make you feel a little woozy."

I followed the voice to where two figures sat in matching chairs before floor to ceiling windows. Heavy silk drapes were pulled back to reveal darkness and I saw the room's reflection cast there—how long had I been out?

"She's strong. As a human her recovery should take longer, don't you think?" asked the man from the bookstore. His voice was smooth and pleasant. A voice made for stories around campfires. The girl with ebony hair responded, her eyes watchful.

"That is because our Stella is not entirely human. Haven't you felt that yet?"

He cocked his head, studying me. "I think Stella is curious as to why we are talking about her while she sits here wondering what is going on. Apologies, Stella."

They know my name. I tried to stand but only got as far as sitting on the side of the bed, legs dangling. I was glad to see they hadn't moved any closer. In fact, they sat still as statues, watching me with similar expressions of concern.

I tried to think. The girl said "transfer," which was how Thomas had explained moving from one place to another through trees. Were they also druids? This transferring business had been different than with Thomas. I couldn't remember the experience for one thing. I shook my head, angry and disoriented.

"Who are you? Where am I, and what just happened?" I flexed my fingers atop the silk coverlet and tried to look tough versus like Little Miss Muffet. It was hard. Although I was sitting on the side of the bed, my toes were nowhere near the floor. I gauged the distance I'd have to run from the floor to the open door I'd spotted over my right shoulder.

The man leaned forward, placing his elbows on top of his knees. He wore a navy shirt and dark pants and seemed at a loss for words. He glanced at the girl. She nodded and untucked her legs, swinging them forward to face me.

"Stella, my name is Tess. We're at my home in Scotland. This man—" She motioned to the man, "—is a good friend of mine. His name is...Murry and we brought you here to explain some things. After we talk, we'll take you back exactly where we found you and almost no time will have passed." Murry gave Tess an odd look.

I waited, expressionless. Thomas had made me promise not to reveal our discussions and Scotland sounded super farfetched.

"In the interest of earning your trust, I want to reveal my true self to you. Don't worry, I won't turn into a lizard." She half laughed and I realized she was uneasy. It went a long way towards humanizing her, and I had a weird feeling we could be friends under different circumstances.

"If your *true self*," I said, using air quotes, "involves mind control, snakes or mice, I am hella outta here," I warned, my hands closing into fists.

"What a strange imagination you have. I promise, no one will influence your mind with magick." She smiled and raised her hands in front of her face. This day could not get stranger.

She remained silent and I stared, uncertain of what was supposed to happen. Her hands changed. Not a lot but then the veins became more prominent and a few freckles appeared. She slowly opened her hands to reveal her face. She'd aged perhaps fifteen years and was stunning. Thick black hair fell straight behind her thin shoulders. She was a little taller, her skin so pale she could have been an albino were it not for her sooty lashes and large eyes. They were the blue of a hot summer day and an endless expanse of pure, cloudless sky.

"I know this is difficult to understand. I hope by demonstrating real magick, it might be easier for you to accept as truth."

"T-t-truth?" My nerves betrayed me. If this was a trick, it was a really good one.

"Truth that magick exists. Murry thought you might have an easier time of it if you saw it for yourself. Also, that you might be more comfortable meeting him with another female present," she said, gesturing to him. I shook my head, but the room remained exactly the same.

I have very thoughtful, sexist but honest kidnappers. I should buy a lottery ticket later, I was so, *so* lucky.

"More comfortable for what exactly?" I asked, narrowing my eyes.

Murry raised his palms and spoke gently. "I mean you no harm. Have no fear of that." He rose, watching me warily as he did so—as if I might freak out. I was tempted to act a little crazy just to mess with him, but it was too much work with my head starting to hurt.

There was something very appealing about both of them, and I realized with a start it was because the man seemed familiar somehow. Trustworthy in a he-won't-chop-me-into-pieces-with-an-ax kind of way. My curiosity warred with anger at being taken without my permission and a desire to return to the bookstore.

He walked to the foot of the bed and paced the area with hands in pockets.

"Stella, we found you today because...uh...because there is a world beyond the human world that you don't know about yet. That's right. And unfortunately, you cannot remain in the dark any longer."

I glanced at Tess and found she'd swung her legs over one arm of her chair, settling in as she watched Murry. A huge bowl of popcorn had appeared on her lap, and she placed a kernel daintily into her mouth. With a start, I found a similar bowl on the bed next to me. Wicked trick.

"You are related to someone very dear to me. Beginning with this person, every female direct descendent in her line has been the victim of an enchantment. We happened to be visiting...and when you asked that book shop woman for information on magick and curses I thought you might already be aware of something." He stopped abruptly, resting a hand on a bed post to examine me with hopeful eyes. "Are you? Already aware of something?"

I shrugged and raised the bowl of popcorn, giving it a sniff. My stomach growled with the warm scent of freshly popped popcorn with butter. I glanced at Tess and she winked. I scowled and placed the bowl on the bed. For all I knew it could be poisoned.

"Oh. Alright then. Where was I? The enchantment. I only discovered it existed—and you—about eleven years ago." *Six*. I would have been six.

"I've had your family tree researched, and it's quite remarkable. The one thing your ancestors have in common is marrying, carrying a child— always a girl—and then dying before the age of twenty-one. Their husbands always died with them or within the same hour. Twenty years, eight months was the oldest survival age we found. Many actually died around eighteen years..."

Tess loudly cleared her throat, and Murry frowned. "Oh. Forgive my insensitivity, Stella."

"It was also a different time for most of those years. People married very young," Tess added.

The idea of a family tree intrigued me. How could I get my hands on that? I wanted to ask questions, but Murry seemed on a roll, and I was curious how his version might differ from the one Thomas shared.

"Your ancestor, Lila, was enchanted after her family was murdered." He said her name as if naming a rare flower or a wondrous new species of butterflies. "I was nearby and heard the screams as she ran to them. We believe that the druids murdered her family and that the enchantment was woven by someone working with them. The druids are a secret sect of mystics, men and women, who believe themselves protectors of magickal knowledge. Creation magick. The problem is that magick users sometimes disappear with the scent of druids lingering where they were last seen.

"My soldiers and I hunted and captured three of those druids in the woods that night, human blood on their clothing. Before they could be questioned about the murder of Lila's family, they committed suicide with poison. I think someone very powerful rewarded the druids for the murders. I've been rooting them out ever since."

If I believed this man, Thomas should have been just another human. No hidden grove and without the power to transfer himself and two girls through a tree. Could Thomas be setting me up with lies? Had his family been behind the murder of Lila's family—and ultimately the curse itself? The theory would go a long way in explaining how his group had kept tabs on my family all these years. There was just one problem. I didn't believe Thomas or his mom were capable of murder.

"Have you spoken with other, er…druids? Asked them?" I questioned.

"They are not so easily found. I've discovered only four of their hidden groves, yet the towers they hide are always empty."

"No records at all?" I asked.

Murry's brows drew down. "That would be good of them, wouldn't it? Unfortunately, the druids never leave records behind. They share information through the telling of tales between generations. I know they're behind this. The druids worshiped your ancestor—my friend. They were not very happy when she became my friend and lived as a mortal. I've searched for years, looking for a solution to the enchantment. Some call it an Everwish. A desire so intense it is brought to life and endless. In my lifetime, I've only known it used once. There is a theory that only someone with my friend's blood can make an Everwish."

He paused, his shoulders curling inward. "She wasn't always mortal. She was once—a goddess. I can share more later. There is something more important I need to discuss with you."

I waited, my brain thrumming with the word "goddess".

"Um. You see, we think that if we can break parts of the spell, we might be able to circumvent it entirely."

I sat straighter. Not dying was always good.

"I may appear human, but I'm immortal, Stella. I was thinking that if *I* married you, platonically of course, and you remained chaste—" he flicked eyes to the bed, flushing "—that together we can...well, I'm hoping that your passing the age of twenty-one *alive* might break the enchantment for good. Your ancestors all had husbands who died. Death does not seek me. As your official lover in name, if not in fact, my inability to die, coupled with no child of our union, *should* keep you from dying as well. Anchor you, so to speak."

I was stunned. Could it be that easy to outwit a curse?

"Why would you want to do such a thing? What's in it for you?"

He met my eyes with great sadness. "Isn't saving the life of my friend's daughter not enough? I would give my life a thousand-fold to have her whole again. This is the least I can do." Tess sniffed, drawing my attention. She'd turned to stare out the window, her shoulders rounded.

"I appreciate your kind offer. I do. It's not every day a girl gets a marriage proposal. I just don't understand how that would keep me safe from the druids."

Murry smiled and there was a glimpse of a deadly predator in his eyes and white teeth. I swallowed. "That's not something you need worry about. I almost always get what I want," he assured me coolly.

Tess joined Murry at the foot of the bed with graceful steps. Her eyes were shining as she motioned towards him with a wave of her wrist.

"Stella, may I introduce you to the Noble King, Murad? Murry is what I call him when it's just us."

The room shimmered as my heart began to race and my jaw unhinged. Murry was the scary Noble King? This kind man with the vague air of a handsome teacher was the demonic vampire Prince that murdered innocent women and children?

"Murad the Noble King, brother of The Lion?" I gasped, forgetting I wasn't supposed to know that much. But if Thomas and his group were the bad guys, did I owe him my silence?

They both stared at me. "How do you know about my brother, Stella?"

"I gave my word not to say anything." I spluttered.

Tess began to speak but Murad held up a hand and she froze.

"A promise is a weighty thing. I suspect this source is also why we found you looking for books on curses?" His warm brown eyes were sympathetic and somber.

I nodded.

"I won't require you to break that promise, Stella. But please know that if you ever wish to share or otherwise have questions, you can come to me. If you know anything about me or my brother then you know that we are very powerful. We keep peace between the supernatural factions and protect humans. My brother is known as The Lion with good reason. He is the Enforcer of our laws and can be very frightening—he keeps to himself mostly as those who weigh and mete justice often do. I'd hoped to introduce you, but he had other business. Once you hold the position of my wife, no one will dare try to touch you."

The idea of being a queen, to anyone, anywhere, was pure fantasy. Something I had never, ever imagined possible or even wanted. Unless it was Queen of ass-kicking and taking names. Maybe Queen for a day...maybe I really did want to be a queen.

"Not only the Lion, Murad," Tess murmured. She held my eyes. "The Noble King's subjects— most of them—will also protect you with *our* lives. There is much for you to learn, Stella. There is great magick in this world and within other planes.

"I am the Sky Queen. One of five Elemental Clans of Witches, and we have a Grand Council in a few weeks. You will be presented to the Witch rulers, and at Samhain we will present you to the leaders representing the rest of the Primati world. Primati is what we call beings who were created before man took dominion by the Creator's decree. It means those beings who came from above, first."

Murad continued when Tess paused, his fingers loosening the fabric at his neck.

"You should know that there are those who believe being first means best. Humans came second in creation and are sometimes referred to as Ancilla. I don't believe this. The strong should protect the weak, not prey upon them.

"If you agree, we will be married at the Samhain ball for all to witness. No one will dare harm you under my protection as wife. No one but Tess, my brother and the two of us will know that this is a marriage in name only."

Taking a chapter from Silvan's book, I raised my hand. Frowning, Murad nodded stiffly. I noted his reaction. Murad the King wasn't used to being interrupted.

"So—what is your relationship?" My pointer finger wagged between them.

They both smiled; Murry actually chuckled.

"Us? We're just friends." Tess's tinkling laughter fluttered in the air like gossamer winged hummingbirds. "Platonic friends. You see—your ancestor was my sister."

"Wait. But if she was a goddess, wouldn't that make you one, too?" Thomas had said star, not goddess but I kept that to myself.

Tess looked sad as she folded her hands at her waist.

"We were stars, child. Not goddesses, although our mother was one. My two siblings and I were changed to earthbound creatures with certain gifts and tasked with witnessing our sister's pain after she'd made certain decisions..." She flicked her gaze to Murad, and every aspect of him faded into a facsimile at her words.

He looked terrible, gutted even. I had a hard time reconciling this Murad with the Lothario who romanced a star into falling from the heavens.

"But that was long ago. With our gifts my sister and I chose to lead different witch covens. Our brother is rarely seen."

I realized suddenly that I had maternal family. At least two new aunts and an uncle, although very far removed. "Does this make us related? Like—can I call you Auntie Tess?"

I grinned and she grinned back.

"In private. It might be better to avoid the familial title when at court or in front of others. Until you pass safely into the age of twenty-two, I'd rather not remind anyone of your ancestry. There is a great deal of jealousy within the Primati. There are some who will not like you just because you are human."

"At first," Murad growled.

"That makes sense." I nodded; my world blown wide open with discovering that a piece of my mother's genetic code somehow lingered in other living souls.

"Can I tell my grandfather or friends about this?" My thoughts were of Alaric. How could I explain to him that I was suddenly engaged and no longer required his services? He would think I was a liar—not that it mattered. He would soon return to his life in New York and forget all about me.

Tess folded her hands in front of her. "It's best if you keep this to yourself until after the Coven Council. You will not be able to return to your home after that meeting and reveal."

"No. I cannot abandon my grandfather." This was a deal breaker.

"Oh, you misunderstand. Sam can join you in your new home, after the Samhain wedding." Tess clarified. Murad approached and took my hands.

"Stella, I promise you that Sam will be kept safe. I owe him more than you know."

I tugged my hands from his cool fingers, uncomfortable with being touched so casually, potential fiancé or not. Sam would not leave our house, no matter what.

"Where is your home, exactly?" I asked, buying time.

"Paris. The outskirts, actually. I had a home built there many years ago, and I hope very much that you and Sam will be happy there. You'll never want to leave the grounds."

Perhaps he didn't mean that last statement to sound like a prison, but would that be the case for three years of my life? Paris sounded beyond my wildest dreams, but not from the vantage point of a cage.

"Of course, whatever you wish will be reality. I heard you enjoy art and Paris is home to many opportunities. I enjoy painting as well," he offered shyly.

Tess gasped. "Don't let him fool you, Stella. Murad is one of the finest oil painters ever known. Many of his pieces hang in museums around the world under other names."

I regarded him with new eyes. Oil paint was a medium I'd experimented with for several years and I had a lot to learn about.

"Tess is being kind, but if you are serious there *are* opportunities for you. There's the Paris College of Art, the University Paris Pantheon-Sorbonne, or we can even arrange private instruction if you prefer. I want you to be happy, Stella. Once you pass the age of twenty-two you can be free. Until then your safety and happiness will be my privilege to safeguard," Murad said earnestly, pressing a palm to his chest.

"I would need to explain everything to Sam so that he understands. He's not young anymore."

Murad nodded. "If Sam goes, I promise he'll receive the best care money can buy. I'm a man of unlimited resources." Unlimited resources? I didn't want to owe anyone anything. But this offer was a solution better than any I could hope for.

"And I don't need to leave right away?"

"No. You'll have a week or so to tie up ends in Portland."

One week to figure out an alternative. Ignoring the hollow pit in my stomach, I stuck out my arm, hand extended. He looked at it for a moment before wrapping my hand carefully with his own. I shivered at the chill of his grip.

"It's a deal," I said simply. He smiled and his cool grip firmed around mine.

Chapter 16
The Star

Stella

Tess magicked herself to once again resemble a teenager and brought me back to the bookstore as promised. We sat at a table within the crowded in-store coffee shop and she pulled out a flask. I gritted my teeth against the vertigo that caused my brain to swim and pressed my forehead against my folded arms, the table's surface cool against my skin.

"Try this. It's a combination of dark chocolate, orange peel, and hot milk. I find it a very helpful remedy from air transfer when people are still new to it," she offered. I took the elegant silver bottle and sniffed the contents. "You mean it's hot chocolate?"

She smiled ruefully. "Yes—a variety anyway. It's thicker than your American version." I took a tiny sip. It was bitter yet so delicious I took another pull. The dizzy sensation faded fast.

"Chocolate makes everything better," I said. This was a universal truth in my book. Right up there with real girls can drive stick and people should mind their own business.

"Yes, it does. I think I embroidered that once on a pillow." Tess grinned and I couldn't help but smile back.

"Did my grandmother, removed a million times, look like you?" Her smile faded.

"Stella—there is no easy way to say this, so I'm going to be blunt. I think you prefer that style of communication anyway. My sister Clara has been responsible for looking after you for quite some time. I just learned that you've been given a unique potion to maintain an enchantment on your looks for the last five years."

My jaw dropped as she continued, biting her lip as she continued.

"These are commonly distributed in heavy liquids or thick yogurts and puddings. In your case, they were given with the very best of intentions. You were showing signs of being a terrific beauty. The concern was that you would attract a love interest too soon, sparking one of the parameters of the curse, and so the objective was to mask that a bit."

"Someone made me ugly?" How does that even work? How would anyone have access to tamper with what I ate or drank for such a long period of time? Thomas's mother Carol came to mind, but she had only been with us for the last two weeks.

"Nonsense—do *you* think you are ugly? But in the coming weeks, with the drinks no longer ingested, you'll find yourself changing to what you would be naturally—if unsuppressed. Just be careful of unwanted attention. I hope by expecting it you might better handle it. We can't have you succumbing to the charms of an insistent suitor after all this."

I literally had no words. The list of indignities kept growing. I liked what I looked like. I was *me*.

"Tess, leaving out the notion that my looks might be better or worse, the idea of being manipulated in any way without my permission is just…infuriating. I don't like secrets."

She nodded sagely. "I agree. Which is why I'm telling you about it. It's been agreed to discontinue the practice, yet I would not accept food or drink from anyone you do not trust."

I screwed the cap back on the silver flask and handed it back to her.

"So, what's next?" I asked, checking my phone. No messages and only twenty minutes had passed since I'd last texted Alaric. I was sure we'd been gone much longer.

"Keep to your normal routine for the next few days. When it's time, Clara or I will escort you to the Council meeting. We wish to leave early in order to do some shopping. I think a week will give us the barest minimum amount of time as we have seamstresses on retainer. We know all the best designers still maintain showrooms for such purposes in Paris and Manhattan. Why, I recall the days when Coco Chanel herself would pour the champa—"

"No, I mean next for Sam?" I tapped my foot. Tess looked taken aback but recovered smoothly.

"On it. Assuming he agrees to the move, Murad is likely already making physical arrangements."

"I get to tell Sam," I insisted.

"Of course. I doubt he would listen to anyone else. This is a big change," she agreed.

"Now, tell me your shoe size and measurements and I'll—"

"I hate shopping. It's tedious and boring. Let's skip that part," I cut in flatly.

She paused; her bright smile uncertain. She seemed confused so I spelled it out for her. "That's a hard *no* on shopping. I already have clothes and I know what I like. I don't need a bunch of people telling me what to wear."

Her doe eyes widened, her lips rounding in horror before they parted and closed several times, soundless. I fidgeted in my seat when she continued to stare without speaking. Perhaps I was disappointing as a newfound, far-removed niece.

"So anyhoo—I better get going. Thanks, Tess."

I stood and paused, but she remained frozen, staring at my empty seat. I said an awkward goodbye. Leaving her at the table, I made my way back to the occult section. Alaric hadn't responded to my prior text and I pinched my lips, considering the odds that he might have truly ditched me. I could always call Silvan for a ride home--my original plan.

This would be the last time I saw Alaric. I no longer needed a bodyguard now, did I? Perhaps I could still hire him for the next day or so? The idea of people spying on me and trying to feed me potions was insane. But then what if my being near Alaric put *him* in danger? No. I couldn't let that happen. Whatever happened, I had to protect him from these crazy events.

When I found the occult section again, a girl dressed in steampunk Goth was putting books back on the shelf. She wore heavy makeup and pigtails. A black scarf covered a cervical collar, matching her clothes and metal accented boots. I patted the tote bag looped over one shoulder, ensuring the books I collected earlier had made the transfer with me.

"Isn't it rude when people don't put books back properly?" the girl asked. I pretended not to hear her. Being sociable had only led to surprises for me this week. I was at my limit.

I felt him before I saw him. Then his scent was everywhere.

Grinning in relief, I twisted to spy Alaric standing at the end of the aisle. His gaze was warm before he glanced past me. A sharp whimpering sound rose and I turned back around.

The girl appeared absolutely terrified. Her arms outstretched, she backed away when I took a step towards her. She tripped over a low bench that sent her sprawling. I tried to help, but Alaric grabbed me by the shoulders and pulled until I was behind him. He paced towards her and the frightened girl ran like an electrified squirrel.

We were alone once more and I frowned at the back of his head.

He turned and noticed. "What? That was weird, right?" he asked, innocence personified.

"What did you *do* to that poor girl?" She was clearly unbalanced, but had he made a rude face at her or something?

He appeared wounded, touching his hand to his heart. "Me? You saw her. I was nowhere near her." He shook his head. "Portland is so weird."

"Umm hmm. It's so weird," I agreed, eyeing him pointedly.

He was suddenly in front of my face, sniffing my hair. "Where have you been?" he asked roughly.

Did I smell differently? I tried to surreptitiously sniff my shoulder. I didn't recall any odd smells with Tess and Murad. Did transferring leave a scent?

Alaric looked into my eyes, searching. I kept a blank expression on my face and shrugged. I might not lie as well as my Rom cousins, but I'd picked up a thing or two on how to evade the truth. He stepped back into the main aisle of the store, scanning the area. "I think we should go. Did you find what you needed?"

I nodded and he escorted me to the checkout desk, where I placed my new tote and books. I pulled out cash, but Alaric was already there, insisting on paying for my purchases.

"What are you doing?" I whispered as the clerk accepted his payment.

"While you're with me, I pay," he replied tersely.

"I appreciate the gesture, but I can pay for my own books."

He accepted the tote from the bored clerk and indicated I should walk in front of him.

I stood rooted in place, waiting for him to acknowledge my

statement. He smiled lazily and leaned forward until his mouth was near my ear. Tingles ran along the sensitive skin of my neck as his breath fanned over the shell of my ear.

"No," he said in that bourbon-tinged tone that made my stomach do Olympic-worthy summersaults.

He walked away with the bag, and I followed, the world tilting as I struggled to put one foot in front of the other. It was hard to refuse him anything when he used that voice, and I was afraid of encouraging any further conversation that might cause him to repeat it. I might do something crazy like attack him again. It had taken him a single word to erode my willpower.

We exited into sunshine. As we turned to head back to the hotel, a thin man with shaggy hair touched my elbow. He stepped too close, his long arms swinging restlessly into my personal space as I tried not to react to the overpowering stench of his unwashed body.

"Do you have a light?" he asked, his tone aggressive. I glanced at the open sores and telltale track marks on his arms.

"No," I responded, maneuvering around him. "I don't smoke."

Alaric turned at the sound of my voice just as the man spoke.

"Bitch." The man spit at the ground.

Between blinks, the man was dangling against the building by his throat, Alaric holding him with one hand.

"What did you say to her?" Alaric muttered. The action was shocking enough. The quiet rage in his voice sent icy fingers down my spine. Passing skateboarders whipped out their cell phones and I quickly grabbed at Alaric's arm. The man's face was wild and getting redder by the second. It was clear he couldn't breathe let alone answer the question.

"Stop! Alaric, stop! Please!" I squeezed his wrist, digging my nails into his flesh when he paid no attention. He exhaled slowly through his nose, his face a cold impassive mask while the man's eyes began to protrude from their sockets.

"Alaric! Stop this now! You're killing him." My voice was low but panicked. The sudden violence of Alaric's actions was upsetting. This was overkill and he was so immovable. Something in my tone got through to him because he turned and locked eyes with mine. He released the man in one motion, allowing him to fall to the sidewalk in a limp heap. I bent down but refrained from touching him.

"Are you okay?"

The man squinted up at Alaric as he rubbed his neck. He gave a jerky nod. A green bill landed on the man's chest.

"Buy your own damn matches. Don't accost any more women on the street," Alaric warned tightly.

He lifted me unceremoniously by the elbow. I resisted, furious, yet found myself quickly on my feet. When he allowed me to wrench away, his glare was unapologetic, a muscle jerking in his cheek. After assuring myself that the man was comfortably breathing, I stalked down the street. Several blocks later I cooled down enough to care whether or not Alaric followed. I glanced over my shoulder and spotted him several steps back.

The pedestrian light flashed a warning to stop, and I turned to face him when he reached my side. His eyes were steady, and I dropped mine to stare at the sidewalk. When I put my hands in my pockets, he mirrored my gesture. I may have overreacted by storming off, but his physical strength and quick moods were putting me on edge. I was struck with how little I knew him.

He was the first to speak. "I'm sorry."

"For what exactly?" I questioned. He looked at me stonily until I realized that was all the apology he planned to offer. There was no point in dragging this out. We were about to part ways forever.

"You might want to look into anger management classes," I suggested.

He smirked and averted his eyes to the sky.

"Okay, I'm not sorry. He shouldn't have called you that. If no one checks him, he might feel emboldened to get physical with the next person he perceives as weaker," he said with a cold edge to his voice and eyes. Wow. He was pretty unyielding on his opinions.

"First of all, who says 'emboldened' anymore? Secondly—I understand and appreciate your defending me if you thought I was in danger. It was just a bit much to hurt him like that."

"Hurt him? I didn't hurt him. I just made sure he thought about our conversation every time he swallowed for a day or two. That was just being a kind, considerate citizen."

The man was the very definition of stubborn. I threw up my hands and he met my hard stare with calm confidence. He wasn't sorry in the least.

We walked in silence back to the hotel. My steps felt increasingly leadened as I realized each stride brought us closer to goodbye. Instead of returning to the entrance, Alaric led me down the parking ramp into the underground garage. The attendant saw Alaric and rushed to collect his vehicle.

I told Alaric my address, offering simple directions. I expected the typical rental car. When the attendant reappeared with a rumbling motorcycle, my breath caught.

"I've never ridden on a motorcycle before." I gasped, my eyes glued to the gleaming metal rolling to a stop. The attendant parked, a huge grin on his face. Alaric touched his hand with cash, and the man accepted it with a laugh.

"Dude—it was an honor just to ride through the garage. Thanks, man!"

Alaric's lips thinned and he ignored the fist the man held out for a bump. The guy took the hint and walked away as Alaric removed a single helmet from the back of the bike.

"Don't be nervous," Alaric said. "You'll be perfectly safe. Just make sure to lean with me on turns, keep your feet where I tell you and stay still otherwise." He tucked my tote bag into a leather satchel secured to the bike and then turned me towards him, lingering fingertips on my shoulders. He placed the mat black helmet over my head with the visor up as I strained to get a better look. The bike was onyx and steel, its lines both dangerous and beautiful. Like Alaric.

"Are you okay? I can have a car brought round if you prefer," he offered. Sam would never, in a million years, be okay with me on a motorcycle. He thought they were deathtraps, especially on Portland's often rain-slicked roads.

"Are you kidding?" I grinned like a maniac and bounced on my toes. He blinked.

"This is amazing!" I squealed in wild elation as I looked up at him. *Best. Day. Ever.*

He returned my grin and reached out, brushing my cheekbone with his knuckles. I stopped breathing and he chuckled before seating himself, steadying the bike with sure hands. At his nod, I threw my leg over to straddle the bike behind him, just like I'd seen in the movies. He directed where to place my feet and offered a few more instructions.

"Don't you need a helmet, too?" I yelled over the bike's raucous growl as he revved the engine. He shot me an exasperated look and grabbed my hands, placing them around his waist.

Oh. This was better than I could have imagined. I slid as close as possible, for safety's sake, and held his waist tightly. I felt the vibrations of his quiet laughter and wished I had the nerve to lay my head against the tempting expanse between his shoulders.

Alaric steered us up the ramp and into the streets. It was a short ride onto the parkway, and I thrilled at the sensation of wind ripping at us as we sped up. Once we left the city behind, he drove even faster. I leaned back a bit, feeling the ends of my hair whip back as I marveled at the blurring landscape. We flew past cars and Alaric leaned us expertly around curves and between traffic.

At one point, a couple of heavy black SUVs with tinted windows sandwiched us. I looked from left to right, wondering at the coincidence. Alaric revved the bike and we quickly outpaced them. The Colombia River came into view, and I couldn't resist the urge any longer. I leaned my head against his back, wishing the barrier of the helmet away.

Much sooner than I wanted, we were driving up to my house. Alaric slowed the motorcycle to a purr and cut the engine. He held the bike steady as I dismounted and then stood close to me. My legs wobbled a little from the ride, and I couldn't figure out the chin strap. Alaric took over, relieving me of the helmet.

"You did great. How are you feeling?"

"Fantastic!" His eyes remained serious, and I realized his mood had changed. Stern Alaric was back. Should I tell him that I'd changed my mind about his help?

"So, this is where you live." He glanced around, his eyes lingering on the silk-tied eggs that waved in a sudden breeze.

"It is." The sense of ending was acute and all encompassing.

"Take care, Stella. I have some work waiting for me, but I'll be in touch," he said, mounting the bike. For a moment he hesitated, feet planted as he rested one hand on a handlebar, the other on his thigh. I stepped hesitantly towards him and he glanced away, starting the engine.

"Just make sure you lock your doors tonight." He looked up at the trees when he spoke, his tone commanding. I watched as he roared down my drive without a backwards glance, waiting until he disappeared from view.

Loneliness pierced as I swung my new tote bag over a shoulder. There were so many secrets and Alaric was mine. A brief touch of something delicious and special and this sudden ache for him was a small price to pay. I went into the house and called for Sam. The house was eerily silent. I checked Sam's room and then the kitchen, but the house was empty.

Tracing my steps, I found a note propped up against the salt shaker. Carol had called out and Nancy had taken Sam into town for an early supper and movie. I was torn between feeling glad for him and anxious about Nancy's ability to take care of him while out and about.

The aloneness I felt was overtaken by an overwhelming desire to feel grass between my toes. I threw my things on the stairs, kicked off my shoes, and walked barefoot outside. The yard was peaceful, the leaves still damp from earlier rain. As I moved off the porch a blue Steller's Jay landed near the glossy green hedges, startling a lean bunny. The rabbit raced across the yard, escaping into the forest. I closed my eyes, raised my face to the sun, and dug my toes into the soft ground. For as long as I could remember, being outside made me feel connected to things greater than my petty problems.

I imagined energy flowing from the earth, traveling up through me and into the sky. A growing flood of peace began to take the edge off the loneliness. I focused and heard the drone of bees and the tinkling of porch chimes coaxed by the caress of a light breeze. The rumble of a car engine intruded. The occasional backfire burst was familiar, and I lifted a hand over my brow as Silvan's rusted red Subaru Forester came into view.

As my cousin parked beneath the great oak trees, I went to greet him and stumbled when I saw the person exiting the other side. *Amanda!* I sprinted to the car and halted within an arm's length of my best friend, shocked at her disheveled state.

She wore torn grey jeans with a yellow t-shirt and sneakers. Her clothes were dirty and she held her left arm across her waist as if it hurt. The ponytail I'd seen her wear last was now in greasy wisps, and she had scratches on her cheek. She offered me a wry smile, and I didn't know whether to hug or throttle her.

Deciding to do both, I threw my arms around her before jumping back at her cry of pain. She patted my shoulder with her good hand.

"Hey, Stella. I think my ribs are cracked."

"Where have you been? What happened?"

She glanced at Silvan and then walked beneath the great oaks, peering up at the branches. Silvan came to my side, leaning back to cup his elbows behind him. His thick hair was mussed as usual and he'd changed into one of his endless supplies of black t-shirts and grey jogger pants.

"I found her hiding in my backseat."

Amanda wandered aimlessly across my yard, her head turning in different directions as if listening for something. We watched her, my heart pounding in both relief and confusion at her odd behavior.

"Did she say what happened?"

Silvan shrugged. "The only thing she told me was that she was punished."

My skin crawled. George and Marion Nightingale were kind people. I couldn't imagine them ever hurting Amanda. Silvan kept talking as we walked.

"I asked her why and she said only one word. She said your name, Stella."

Chapter 17
Strength Reversed

Alaric

———⸱⚬❦⚬⸱———

My men were waiting for me at the end of Stella's driveway. I signaled for them to follow and rode several miles before pulling over at a closed logging facility. The black Escalades parked, their engines running. The windows rolled down as I approached.

"Is there a reason you decided to become obvious?" I asked darkly. My anger was self-directed but the guard who paled in the driver's seat of the first car didn't know that. I'd been so wrapped up in Stella that I'd forgotten to notify my team to stand back. For brief moments it'd only been Stella and the Pacific Northwest landscape. Then the Escalades had levelled out with us on the highway, bringing me back to reality and my responsibilities. I only hoped Stella hadn't noticed them.

"Sir—" the man's mouth gaped, but then he said soberly, "Grayson notified us that Queen Clara found the girl's friend. He asked us to find you as you'd requested an immediate update. Apologies if we were indiscreet."

The highly skilled soldiers in the second vehicle wore identical expressions to the first. They were too well trained to reveal the heightened anxiety my displeasure was causing, yet the scent of fear, betraying tics and tell-tale gleam of perspiration on their muted faces revealed their state. I stepped away from the car, only to realize upon release that my grip had indented the door's window frame. To his credit the driver kept his gaze trained on my face.

"Where is Clara?"

"Waiting for you at a motel, Sir. I sent the location to your phone." I checked, recognizing the area. It was definitely not a place I imagined Clara would visit willingly. This team was new in rotation and I wanted their respect, not fear. Humans were not as noticeable as my Primati soldiers when dealing with mortals, but they required more patience. I peered into the distance, speaking quietly.

"Return to Grayson. I need one of you to return the bike to the garage. I'll check in later." I caught myself and made eye contact. "Good work." I said. The men nodded and a volunteer stepped out to take careful possession of the motorcycle. I watched in silence as they returned to the road.

The lumberyard was filled with hundreds of enormous, stripped logs, many already chained on trucks for transport. I moved between rows of the damp, fragrant wood, avoiding the human security cameras I'd noted when we'd entered the lot. Stella was on my mind. Her fearless enthusiasm, her quicksilver moods, and her surprising appreciation for zombie films. The way her eyes lit up with mischief, and the way she'd fiercely protected that drug user from me, even after he'd assaulted her. Her arms holding me tight while she laughed without care into the wind. The lost look on her face when I'd left her. Creator help me. I was falling for my brother's claimed queen and Murad rarely changed his course once his mind was made up. Closing my eyes, I transferred.

* * *

I held myself as shadow for a moment, observing. The sky was grey and the motel's parking lot held a smattering of cars and a cluster of smoking men. A man and woman exited a room on the ground floor, objects in their hands. They left the door ajar, a sickly yellow light illuminating the doorway. I found Clara sitting in her red Mercedes, facing the motel room. I appeared next to her, startling her in the midst of raising a cup to her lips.

"Damn you!" she hissed.

"You called." I responded dryly.

She patted her dark jeans, brown splotched white blouse, and splattered steering wheel with paper napkins, the scent of coffee redolent in the air.

"A little warning!" She glared, but there was little heat to it. She tossed the napkins in the backseat and leaned back in her seat. Her mass of hair was twisted into a tight ballerina bun, highlighting the strain in her pretty face.

"What's happened, Clara?"

"Do you see that room over there?" She nudged her chin in the direction of the action, her hands gripping the leather steering wheel. I nodded.

"That sorcerer, the one you released from the forest? He was holding Stella's friend Amanda there. *My* witch. *Mine.* My people found her two hours ago, and it looks very much as if he planned to kill her. I rendered him unconscious with a sleeping spell and wrapped him in enchanted chains, sent a message to Grayson and dropped Amanda off at her mother's store." She lowered her chin. "When I returned to question him...he'd escaped. He'd been alone in that room with three of my clan watching from outside."

I held still, considering her words. I disappeared in a flicker, finding Grayson and instructing him to triple the shadow guards surrounding Stella's property immediately. I reappeared in the passenger seat next to Clara. She was still staring hard at the activity across from us. Clara was clearly unnerved. I made an encouraging sound and she pinched the bridge of her nose.

"We'd turned off the lights and sealed the room from the outside. He should not have been able to move an inch from the seat we placed him in. No one has ever escaped my holding chains. Ever. He had help, Alaric. Someone very strong."

That help would have to be extremely powerful to get the drop on Clara. This explained her agitation. I thought back to that afternoon on the river. Had I been so bothered by seeing Stella that I had overlooked the sorcerer as a threat? If so, this was on me. Stella was a distraction I had to purge.

"Did you recognize who it might be?"

"I had a faint sense of recognition to the power used but it was concealed. Like a memory copied a thousand-fold and mixed with other signatures—it was too faint and meant to elude me. I'm worried, Alaric." She released the steering wheel and crossed her arms over her middle as if cold. "He was questioning Amanda about Stella."

Chapter 18
Strength

Stella

The moment we crossed the threshold into the house, I shut the door and secured the lock. Amanda bended with a wince while Silvan headed towards the kitchen.

"Can I have some water?" She was pale, with violet circles beneath her eyes. I noticed blue and plum bruising around her neck. The sight left me nauseous and freshly angry. Whoever made those marks would have to die. I hoped she was ready to tell me everything.

"Of course." I followed her as she made her way to the kitchen. She knew her way around, but I pulled a chair out and then poured her a glass of cold water from the fridge. She gulped it greedily.

"Here you go." Silvan extended a baggie of ice covered by a dishcloth. Amanda placed it against her neck.

"Thank you," she said softly. Silvan smiled sweetly and then began heating up large chunks of leftover meatloaf in the microwave.

"Oh, and Stella—I'm staying over tonight. Uncle Remi got caught breaking parole this morning, so I volunteered to be your bodyguard today," Silvan said over his shoulder with a wiggle of eyebrows. Amanda choked on her water. I decided to focus on one problem at a time. Mahari's ridiculous games would wait.

"Are you hungry?" I asked. She nodded around her water glass. Amanda avoided meat, so I made her thick slabs of toast with honey and then peeled two apples.

"Silvan do you want to come upstairs with us?" We watched in fascination as Silvan shoveled in bites of meatloaf larger than his mouth. Cheeks bulging, he glanced between Amanda's lowered gaze and my face and shook his head. I burned with questions but she seemed too fragile for an interrogation just yet.

Amanda rose stiffly, favoring her side. She kept the icepack while I carried her plate and a fresh glass of water to my room. As soon as we reached the top of the stairs she headed for my bathroom.

"Would you like to take a shower?" I asked her through the unpainted door.

Her voice was faint but enthusiastic. "God, yes. Can I borrow some clothes?"

I turned but then a terrible thought came to me.

"Amanda—is there any reason why you should hold off taking a shower until *after* we go to the hospital and file a police report?"

The door jerked open so fast I nearly fell. Her eyes were wild again.

"No police! No way. I haven't been assaulted that way, okay? Please, just don't call anyone. Please, Stella!" Relief hit and I nodded.

I brought her a pair of my capri leggings and an oversized Dunder Mifflin t-shirt with a new pair of underwear. She didn't speak but nodded her thanks before disappearing behind the door again.

"Just don't lock the door," I called. "If you fall, I'm not sure Silvan and I could break the door down." She sniggered. The sound was better than any assurance she could give, and I felt a fission of hope that she might really be okay.

I tidied my room while she showered, knowing if I didn't that Amanda and her OCD would do it for me. Quicker than I expected, she resurfaced with wet, dark hair combed behind her shoulders. She joined me on my bed where we sat cross legged across from one another, just like we used to. I could tell by her cautious movements that her ribs were hurting. I would have to find some way to convince her to go to the hospital.

"Thank you, Stella." she said, before taking several quick bites of toast. I'd added two pain relief tablets to her plate and was pleased when she took them. When most of her food was gone she sighed and wiped her mouth with a napkin.

"You make great bread," she complimented. Amanda pushed the plate to the side and took off her necklace. It was one she wore every day, the amethyst about half the size of my pinkie finger. She exhaled in a rush and sat up straighter.

"Stella, you are the only sister I've ever known. We became friends before I knew any of the stuff that I'm about to tell you," she began.

Uh oh. This felt like a warm up before the curveball.

"When everything happened at the river, it was the first time I saw you do anything like it. When you jumped from the cliff, Marcus was telling the truth. You didn't fall like a normal person influenced by gravity. You literally floated most of the way down. Do you remember *feeling* anything different?"

I shook my head, my eyelids prickling with heat. Hearing Amanda tell me this made everything else I'd been told in the last twenty-four hours seem possible and much more real. She sighed.

"The man we met on our hike, Marcus, is a sorcerer," Amanda rushed out. She paused with a wince, as if expecting me to interrupt. I waved impatiently for her to keep going.

"Which is a magical dude on the dark side. They usually follow the law but have big egos. If they go mercenary it's hard to catch them. Once they sign a contract with a client, the best ones never give up." She paused and I knew that look well enough. She was about to say something I wouldn't like.

"I know this because I'm a witch myself. So is Mom. There are five different clans of witches, and each have a kinship to an element.

"Mom and I are water witches. That was why I had you stand in the water. Water witches can transfer only through flowing water. Rivers, creeks, oceans. Marcus realized who I was by my clan mark." She held up her tattoo of blue waves. "If he tried to take you, I was prepared to transfer you somewhere safe. If he touched the water, I'm pretty sure I could have transferred *him* somewhere else. Transferring is when—"

"I know what transferring is."

Amanda pressed her tongue into her cheek and slapped her knees. "Right. Thomas must have explained that. Okay, then. You asked me why you couldn't move. I'm not as old or skilled as Marcus, so I couldn't prevent what happened. He used his power to convince your mind to follow his instructions. He tried to force you to come to him and to give him information. I counteracted it. I actually tried to make him leave, but he was too strong for me." A shadow crossed her face.

"I tasted it," I whispered. She nodded.

"Our magic has a flavor when used to take someone's will. Marcus is an earth sorcerer. Their magic often tastes of burnt wood. We're not supposed to use it. Taking someone's free will is a terrible breach of etiquette. It can actually be a cause for defense if one witch murders another. If their memory can be read and it's confirmed they were forced to do something harmful against their will then the influencing witch could be put to death, depending on the crime.

"It rarely goes to trial or is made public, because if you're too weak to ward off someone taking over your will then you are not likely going to survive the encounter to tell about it. Either because the perpetrator wants you dead or because your own coven puts you down for being a weak link capable of placing them all in danger."

I shuddered, remembering the taste and the awful feeling of not being able to control my own body. If what she was saying was true, being a witch carried enormous risks. A lot scarier than I'd imagined.

"If you are water and Marcus is earth, then what are the other three?"

"Next is the air clan-they live mainly in Europe and the poles. Then there are the Fire witches, who I've never met and are kind of persona non grata for the last few centuries. They can transfer through flame. A group of them tried to raise demons on this plane and the experiment did *not* go well." She shook her head and rolled her eyes. Right. Those pesky fire witches and their crazy ideas.

"The fifth clan is Spirit. These are nearly extinct and rumor has it they can transfer through living trees. American Indian shamans and a tiny group of Buddhists are the only ones I'd heard mentioned who could do this before I met Thomas. Was he able to tell you everything?"

"If by everything you mean about the curse, then yes," I said.

She breathed a sigh of relief. "Good. I thought having Thomas show you his grove might help you believe it's real. You're a show-me kind of girl."

She did know me well. I quieted, realizing just how little *I* knew about my closest friend. She knew how much I valued honesty, and yet she'd been forced to keep secrets. I loved solitude and getting wrapped up in my art. And all this time, Amanda had been adjusting to an entirely different world. I felt disconnected and sad. How could I have been such a bad friend not to notice?

"What about George? Does he know about all this?" Amanda's

Dad was the most normal guy on the planet. I couldn't imagine him being part of all this.

"Dad knows. He's not a witch but male witches or wizards in general are highly regarded, because there are fewer of them and they tend to be powerful."

"Speaking of *which*, pun intended..." Amanda removed her necklace and held it cupped in her hands. She closed her eyes and ran her fingers along the violet prism. She frowned slightly but then something happened. The crystal grew, lengthening into a glowing purple cylinder roughly the size of a conductor's baton. Tossing it, she caught it in one hand, and waved it gracefully before my incredulous eyes.

"This, Stella, is my "Pagatio," or wand. Most witches have them. They are concealed as stones or crystals and only reveal themselves to their witch soulmate."

"That is the coolest thing I've ever seen." I wanted to touch it but was afraid I might get zapped. The bar of amethyst literally shimmered with energy.

Amanda giggled. "Isn't it! When I got it at thirteen, I wanted to tell you everything, but Mom wouldn't let me. There are all kinds of ceremonies and instruction classes in order to learn how to use your element power. It's a big reason I was homeschooled."

"Where did you get it?" I wanted one. I wanted one badly.

"There are special conventions in protected warehouses where witches search for a crystal that attunes to their individual magick. Mostly novices but sometimes a witch outgrows or loses their Pagatio and seeks a new one. Collectors find them all over the world.

You can't imagine, Stella. There are enormous bowls and tables filled with diamonds, opals, quartz, citrine, jade and emeralds—so many that the air sparkles when they allow the novices to enter and their magick searches for a match." Amanda's eyes were starry, and I smiled wistfully. She leaned close and whispered, "I've buried a number of crystals around the edges of your property."

I pulled back and saw she was serious.

"Why?"

"Protections. You never know. But you have deeper magick here. It's like a low vibration I've never felt elsewhere."

"You sound really excited about crystals—about your...Pagatio?"

Amanda took my hand with earnest eyes. "Stella, do you remember how you felt when you first heard Radioheads's Kid A album?"

I nodded.

"It's like that."

"Wow."

The strains of a violin rose from the stairway, and we jumped at the initial shrieking of strings being warming up. Silvan must have collected his violin from the car. We stilled, waiting until the haunting strains of Barber's *Adagio for Strings* filled the house before sharing a smile. It was one of my favorite songs, and Silvan often played it when he knew I was upset or sad.

"So, what happened to you?" I asked quietly. She lowered her chin and picked lint from my comforter before meeting my gaze. Her hazel eyes held mine without flinching.

"I'm sorry. We left because I knew you would not let things go about what you saw at the river. We were sworn to secrecy and didn't have permission from our clan's Queen to reveal ourselves."

"What are you still hiding?" I struggled to keep my expression neutral, to not betray how much this mattered. She looked down at her wand, fidgeting with it.

"Please don't ask." She averted her eyes to the floor. I folded my hands in my lap and resisted the urge to throw the plate across the room. Didn't I have my own secrets now? As much as I craved to tell her about

Alaric, he felt too private to share. The trust between Amanda and I too tender. So, I shared another secret.

"It seems a lot happened to us both today. I think I'm engaged." I deadpanned.

Amanda's eyes widened in horror. "It's too soon for the Noble King to find you. I thought you knew of the enchantment, Stella? You can't marry or you'll fulfill the curse. I leave you alone for *one* day. Please don't tell me Scott wheedled his way back into your good graces."

"No. Not Scott." One day I would have to tell her about breaking into her house.

"Have you ever met the Noble King?" The name flowed from my lips.

She gaped before snapping her teeth together, swallowing several times. "Once. He is...very handsome. I got to meet him at my coming out. That was our trip where we said we went to Alaska, but we really went to Paris."

I frowned at her admission. "But you brought me a wool scarf and hat from Alaska.'

Amanda flashed me a sheepish grin.

"Internet shopping," she explained. *What the...*

"How did you meet the Noble King?" she asked hurriedly.

"At a bookstore. Did you *really* go to Paris?" I countered. She nodded. I shook my head. I really didn't know my dearest friends as well as I thought I did.

"I met Murad and he wants to help me. He thinks his immortality might save me from the curse."

She nodded, thoughtful. "Wow. You call him by his first name? I'd hoped you might have laid low after Thomas told you about the declaration to marry you but that would just not be you, would it? I've thought about it a lot, and it would give you a lot of protection to be

Noble Queen. If anyone tried to hurt you, all the factions would rise up to prevent it.

"Stella, I've known you a long time, and trust me when I say this. You are a passionate, impulsive person. You leap without looking and stay focused on what you want until it's yours. It's what I both love and find most frustrating about you.

"But what if you fall in love with someone else *after* the curse is broken? Will there be consequences if you leave the King—what if he won't let you go? There are rumors that he mega-stalked his last fiancé. His power is rather scary and rumor is that he doesn't forgive easily." She gingerly cradled her side and I handed her the ice pack.

"I don't know the guy, but I can guarantee he'll never fall in love with me. I'm just trying to survive to middle age here." Amanda opened her mouth to speak and then closed her lips with a grimace.

"Your turn. How did you get those injuries?" I pointed to her neck.

She cupped her throat gently before dropping her hand.

"Marcus," she whispered, shame swirling in her voice. It made me want to break him.

"The hiker-sorcerer guy?"

She nodded. "I was supposed to meet Mom and Dad at the ferry. I told them I had to return books to the library but instead I spoke with Thomas and then left you that note about Stonehenge. When I left the market, Marcus was waiting for me. He surprised me at the car and told me he had you. He threatened to kill you if I didn't come quietly and then he took me to a motel near Beaverton." Her voice had lowered to a whisper. My jaw and hands clenched.

"I'm not a very good witch it turns out. I was too petrified to work a single defensive spell, and when we got to the room and I saw you weren't there, it was too late. I tried to fight but it was pathetic. He held me down and when I came to, I was tied to a chair," she gave a rough laugh. "Better than dead I guess."

"Oh, Amanda." Fury held me rigid.

"He lied to you, of course." My voice was tight. "I was at the market and found your note just after you left it beneath the door. What—what happened when you woke up?" Amanda noticed my clenched hands and her face relaxed into a slight smile I knew was meant to reassure me.

"It was like something from a movie. Bad carpeting, old cigarette stench—a total cliché. Marcus hurt me, wanted to know how to find you. When I refused, he took my wand. That was the hardest part, actually. Once a crystal attunes to a witch it becomes part of you. Taking it from me was painful." Her hands twisted in her lap.

"How did you get free? How did you get your wand back?" I ground my molars. Marcus was going down, no question.

"Clara rescued me." Amanda said, as if she still couldn't believe it. "I got lucky that she and some of her clan leaders were in the area looking for someone else. They tracked Marcus because he held my Pagatio to keep me from screaming. Clara can feel us at the end of our magick. She knew it wasn't me. I was also bleeding and blood has power. It amplifies. I used my magick to send her an image of my location before he stopped me."

"Interesting," I commented, meaning it.

"She's the Water Witch Queen and the leader of our Clan. She lives here in Portland but leads all the witches in North America. It's a huge transgression of territory for one Queen to kidnap another Queen's coven members. His ink marked him as Earth coven," she explained. I recalled his tattoo of twining red roses.

"Where is Marcus now?"

"Likely in a magickly enforced cell awaiting trial. Clara drove me back to my car before I saw what happened to him," Amanda said.

"She just dumped you at your car with broken ribs? No hospital?"

How uncaring could this Clara be? I swung my legs over the side of the bed.

"Witches are different, Stella. Clara couldn't heal my ribs just yet. She needs supplies. So, no need for a hospital. I just have to wait for her to come round tomorrow." She looked away, using her finger to arrange the crumbs on her plate in neat lines.

Tess had said that Clara had been feeding me ugly juice for the last few years. Then realization dawned...how Clara had access to my food and drink; I think I was looking at her.

The thought formed, circled and settled into my gut like a missing puzzle piece. All the green juice she and her mom gave me. The health drinks Marion was always experimenting with and asking me to try. At least two or three times a week. I shared meals with Amanda and her parents pretty regularly. The betrayal of it washed over me like a tsunami. Needing distance, I walked over to my work table. I picked up the Empress tarot card while listening to the roar of blood in my ears. How do you accuse your best friend, the one you trust the most, with such a deep betrayal?

"Amanda—have you been giving me concoctions to make me look—different?" I slowly turned to see Amanda unfolding herself to stand. I was considerably less sympathetic to her obvious pain than I'd been a minute ago.

"You know. Stella—I know how funny you are about trusting people. I know how this may seem, but please just hear me out." She held her palms out as if I were an animal preparing to attack. I arched a brow and remained calm. When I didn't erupt in flames, she put her plate on my dresser and eyed my overflowing wastebasket.

"Mom and I were approached by Clara when you and I first started homeschool classes together. I wasn't even an official member of the coven, yet. I didn't know it then, but Mom has been tasked with keeping an eye on you for years. She reports anything unusual. It was for your own good—to help you hide." Frowning at my waste basket, Amanda worked the bag from the bin. The container fell to its side and rolled in my direction. I kicked it and Amanda sighed as she tied the bag.

"Queen Clara asked Mom to deliver an enchantment that would tone down your beauty so that you wouldn't start getting the wrong attention. It also masks your natural aura—the thing that really makes you attractive. She said that the fewer people noticed you, the better chance you would have of staying under the radar."

I leaned back against my art table, my nails curling against the wood.

"Do you realize how messed up that sounds, Amanda? Because if a girl is pretty, she will automatically be a tramp or fall for the first guy who pays her any attention? What happened to free will? Why is it the—" I jabbed my chest with my thumb "— girl's fault?" I didn't care about the pretty part but it did make be angry that I was the one who got messed with. Amanda beseeched me with earnest eyes.

"Stella. It's the *curse*, not you. The curse intends to make you fall in love and for your best match to fall in love with you. There was no guarantee a deterrent would work. Love is in the eye of the beholder, after all. They just needed to try to narrow down the odds—and number of suitors. What if a photographer took your picture?"

I wasn't willing to concede anything in my current frame of mind.

"What did you give me to drink, anyway? If you say anything about eye of newt, I'm kicking you down the stairs, injured or not." She gave a trembling, relieved laugh.

"No newts. I think the main ingredients are trace copper and a special lichen. Like most enchantments, it's more about the intentions of the witch that creates the spell. In appearance, it's a finely ground powder that smells a little like moldy pennies but is tasteless."

Beyond disgusting, but I could deal with moldy pennies much better than about a million other things I could think of. I watched as she returned my wastebasket where it belonged. I hated what Marion and Amanda had been an accomplice to. That they somehow "reported" on me to strangers. My heart hurt.

"So, our friendship was a lie? Marion being nice to me, you being my friend—you were just my jailors?" Amanda rushed to stand before me. When her palms grasped my forearms, I tugged away without thinking. The hollow sensation in my chest intensified at her hurt expression.

"No! Never! We became friends naturally. On our own. Nothing can take that away from us. If we weren't real friends, Mom would have found other ways to get you the drinks. Maybe worked as a barista, considering how much coffee you drink." Her joke fell flat and I ignored the tears in her eyes.

"She truly loves you. I do, too. And I am so, so sorry for deceiving you. I wanted to tell you so many times. Telling you before now would have just put you in danger. I know you. You would have run away or taken out ads in every major newspaper looking for Clara. What does your gut tell you is truth?"

My gut told me that the affection from them both was genuine—even if my brain screamed "traitors." Amanda's expression turned a little more desperate, her eyes pleading.

"No one even *knows* about Thomas. I found out about him on my own. *I* was the one who asked him to tell you about the curse. If Mom found out, or Clara does, Mom and I could be expelled from the coven. In case my memories are viewed, Thomas and I speak in vague terms, and no one would guess who he is without context. It's why you and I cannot speak about him in detail right now," Amanda confessed with a meaningful squeeze of my hand.

"I just can't wrap my mind around how easy it's been for you and Marion to manipulate everyone. I mean, your mom goes to a Baptist church every week. How does that support being Wiccan?" I scoffed. Trying to unravel all the lies was giving me a headache.

Amanda frowned. "We are *not* Wiccans. Wiccans are humans who, for the most part, have no real power. They call themselves witches and form a religion. Mom never lied about her beliefs. Primati witches are only one part of the Primati, Stella. You have a lot to learn. *I* have a lot to learn myself, and we're inherently secretive. Just take it slow and keep an open mind."

"I need time to think about all this," I whispered.

"We don't have time, Stella. I understand you feel betrayed. Everything I've done has been to protect you. I hope you will eventually see that. Right now, we have to figure out something much more important. Can we call a truce and tally up later?"

This was so like Amanda. Rational and busy planning everything and everyone.

"That depends. What will happen to me now that I am not gagging back your mom's ugly juice?"

"It's not ugly juice, Stella. I don't remember exactly but apparently there were signs that you would strongly resemble the first of your family line—Lila. Her beauty was otherworldly and led to obsessive love. To answer your question—I just don't know. I guess with time your looks might change. But you will always be *you*, Stella."

She was reading my mind again. Knowing what to say as she had since we were kids.

I lowered my head. "You know I'm going to have to get back at you in some horrible, terrible way—right?"

A huge smile broke across her face, and she clapped her hands in excitement like the nerd she was. "I know. I'll deserve it, whatever it is."

"So now what?"

"We have to open a three-hundred-year-old cold case, Stella. I've overheard things that make me think whoever was behind Lila's family being murdered will also try to harm you. Someone hired Marcus. Everyone seems to blame the druids, but I'm not convinced."

"You mean Thomas and his family?"

"I can't imagine Thomas hurting a fly—can you? Whoever they are, I think they will do everything possible to kidnap you before the curse does its job. Not that I will allow that to happen. That curse will have to go through me and my clan first, Stella."

Silvan's voice called up the stairs. "Ladies, I'm bored. Can we get pizza?"

He just ate! Amanda mouthed. We shared a tentative smile.

"Do you mind if I stay here tonight? I'm not ready to join my parents yet, and I'd rather be here with you." Once more she touched the amethyst resting at the end of its golden chain.

"On one condition. No more lies from here on out." I meant it. I held out a pinkie and she solemnly hooked it with her own.

"Yes," she agreed. I moved towards the door but froze, pivoting back to my friend.

"One more question." She nodded, biting her lip.

"How does one kill a sorcerer?"

Chapter 19
Judgment Reversed

Stella

Uncle Vang and his burley sons blocked the road to Mahari's house. The sun had just passed behind the horizon, and barrels of fire burned on either side of the street. As their neighborhood was just outside city limits, and exclusively comprised of family, there would be no pesky complaints to the HOA or police.

Amanda clasped and unclasped her hands while she looked down at her lap to avoid seeing the fire. I made a mental note to continue research on her phobia. Last night had gone uneventfully after the call with Marion. After a pizza run, we'd said goodnight to Sam and made Silvan a fluffy pallet on my bedroom floor with old quilts and a sleeping bag. I'd only woken once, when the low rumble of a motorcycle invaded my dreams.

We'd slept late and to my surprise, Nancy had been pleasant with Amanda and Silvan around, even taping up Amanda's ribs and placing salve on her bruises.

Tonight was the evening of the total solar eclipse and Mahari had insisted I come to spend the night. They were having a family party.

"I feel weird," Amanda informed me for the tenth time.

"You *are* weird," I retorted with a grin.

"Ha-ha. What if they kick me out?" They might actually. I hadn't waited on a response to my request to bring Amanda. Oh, well.

The side mirror reflected my smirk when I rolled down the window.

"Hey, what's up, assholes?" I called out.

Uncle Vang peered into the car. "You have such a potty mouth, girl. Someday someone's going to do something about it."

"You're right. Someone should do something about it. Shall I tell Mahari it should be you?" By rights, Uncle Vang should be the next head of the family, but Mahari didn't trust his ability to lead. I'd heard he was kicked in the head by a horse in his youth and experienced a personality change afterward. All I knew for sure was that he was a bully, and you shouldn't show weakness to bullies. His five sons, also known as the Vano boys, took after their father so it wasn't likely the kick that made him a jerk.

Amanda whimpered and I turned to see my cousin Joseph licking her car window. Really. The things they did to get a rise out of people. I shook my head. Vang waved us through and I drove past a series of yards with children running around with sparklers. Amanda shrank in her seat. "Aren't fireworks illegal this time of year?" she muttered.

At the end of the cul-de-sac, I parked in front of the pink monstrosity that was Mahari's house. A separate trailer in the back of the property was kept as a bathroom station. Mahari was old world Roma and felt bathrooms should not be anywhere near living quarters. She found it repulsive that Ganji prepared food in the same building where they used a toilet. It was one reason I usually stayed with Silvan and my aunt Lemontina in their modest ranch across the street. They used their entire house and had zero hang ups.

"Are you ready?"

She shook her head. I couldn't blame her. Over the years, Amanda's exposure to my Dad's family had been brief and unpleasant.

"Come on," I urged, getting out of the car. I wore a black halter top that covered my chest but left my back, arms, and stomach bare. It would make my grandmother crazy to see so much skin exposed in public. My black silk harem pants were another thrift store find. Black boots and a multitude of mala bracelets completed the look, as did my loose hair, kohled eyes, and tiny gold hoop earrings.

Amanda's bruises were more vivid than the night before, having deepened into a mottled purple and green, but the extra sleep had helped. She'd borrowed a summer dress she'd given me last year. It was white-eyelet cotton with capped sleeves that ended at her knees in a swish. Her shiny hair was parted in the middle into a low ponytail and she looked terrified.

"Stella!" Mira called. She wove her way down the steep incline of the front yard towards us, Medea on her heels.

Amanda patted the cross-body purse I'd loaned her. It held a can of bear spray that I'd instructed her how to use it on my family as makeshift mace, if the situated warranted it.

"You found Amanda? Wow. Where have you been?" Mira asked, breathless.

"Uh. I was with my parents," Amanda shared with a nervous eyeroll towards me.

Mira stared pointedly at me. I shrugged. "She thought she was helping by staying out of sight."

"Hey, Mandy," Medea said. Amanda winced at hearing the hated nickname but didn't correct her. Oh, boy. I knew Amanda was traumatized but hoped I wouldn't be knocking heads for both of us all night.

"Cut it out, Medea. Amanda is Stella's guest. She can have sanction for tonight," Mira told her sister. Sanction is what my cousins called a truce of any kind. They were rare but honored. Medea's overly plucked eyebrows arched at Mira but she snapped her teeth shut.

"Where's your overnight bag?" Medea asked. That's right. I'd been instructed to spend the night.

"I didn't bring one," I said bluntly. If they pushed me on this, we were so outers.

Medea and Mira glanced at each other but surprisingly dropped the topic. We trailed the M&Ms up the hill and around the house to where the party was already underway.

The cul-de-sac was surrounded by more than thirty miles of state park, and the backyard was really more of a big field. A handful of house trailers dotted the perimeter, and in the back corner was a collection of painted caravans that Mahari amassed out of nostalgia. Campfires dotted the field, surrounded by chairs filled with raucous adults drinking and laughing.

The children were allowed to stay up late during new moon celebrations. Italian wedding lights illuminated a circular area where the children took turns riding ponies bareback under the watchful eye of several older cousins.

Near the back of the house, tables were filled with breads, vegetables, meat rolls, and bowls of sour cream and pickled red cabbage. We wandered closer and Amanda's eyes widened at the huge black pots hanging over fire pits. My aunts attended them, and from the smells I recognized paprika soup and a garlicky goulash. Desserts, water, and soda cans were dedicated to one round table. My favorite cousin exited the house and walked towards us.

"Hey, ladies," greeted Silvan. He was dressed in trousers and a white button-down shirt with shiny black shoes. He already had his favorite violin in hand, its spruce and maple wood gleaming in the firelight.

"Hi, Silvan. You look very handsome tonight." Amanda complimented. Flushing, he carefully clutched his violin and horsehair bow in one hand and offered a deep bow.

"I thought I'd dress the part tonight," he said, his hair flopping in his face before he brushed it back, straightening. He looked kind of grown up to me tonight.

"Where are you playing tonight, Maestro?" I asked.

He nodded towards a flat wooden stage area where several men and women were warming up instruments.

"Can I help you set up or anything?" Amanda offered. I suspected her offer was as much to get farther away from the M&Ms as it was to hang with Silvan. He flushed, and Medea and Mira smirked at one another. He held out his instrument. "This is it, really. Not much of a setup. You can hang out with me by the stage if you want. It's about time I collected a proper groupie."

"Consider me a groupie, then! Although that term is a bit sexist. Do you ever hear of a man being called a groupie? Not usually. I mean, the term dates back before Woodstock even—all the way to the mid-nineteen-sixties when young girls offered favors to get close to a band. Maybe I could be your most supportive fan? Oh! How about a very enthusiastic admirer?" Amanda's voice trailed off as they walked across the field and out of earshot.

"Your friend is going to blow up her brain thinking and talking so much," Medea said with disapproval. I smiled, knowing Amanda's chatter was caused by nerves. The fires were not helping her chill out. I should have remembered they often started those for celebrations.

"At least she gave you an excuse to stay in. Aunt Lemontina and

Cousin Val said you didn't leave the house all night after picking up pizza." Mira smirked.

I knew it. It was too good to be true that they would only send Silvan to spy on me.

"Let everyone know that Amanda is to be left alone tonight, okay?" Medea didn't respond but as she ghosted away her head bobbed once.

"Mahari is in the blue caravan waiting for you," Mira said quietly. I jerked. This was the first time I'd heard of anyone going into the blue caravan. It was off limits.

She nodded. "I'll walk with you."

We took a few steps when Silvan's violin sang its first sweep. Mahari could wait.

I wasn't the only one drawn to the rustic stage. Adults and children alike began to gather around the musicians. Silvan was already warmed up, his shirtsleeves rolled to the elbows. He must be trying to impress Amanda as I recognized the tune selected was Havanaise Op. 83, a complicated piece that featured plenty of solo action. It was a flirty, uplifting melody, and my Aunt Cecelia accompanied him with her cello as my cousins wove in with their own violins. The guitarists sat back and watched.

Inspired by the popping of a campfire, the song began as a slinking melody that built into a Cuban rhythm. Silvan's hands and arms danced with the rapid asides and smooth progressions. The music floated like stardust and the entire field of Romani fell silent. A breeze rippled the tops of the massive evergreens encircling the yard.

The high notes were so delicately rendered that it seemed the trees themselves swayed with the scales. I rubbed my bare arms, shivering with the beauty of the moment. The song concluded with a single high note that trembled into the night.

Everyone jumped and applauded. Fingers in mouth, I offered my own ear splitting whistle. Silvan gazed at the ground with a humble bend of his head. The claps faded as he began another song, a more modern tune that the guitarists picked up easily. Mira and I resumed our walk towards the blue caravan concealed in the farthest left corner of the field.

The vardo was an old-fashioned model with a curved wooden roof and six wheels. A small chimney rose on its left side, above a painted doorway. It was lacquered in shades of blue and gold and usually kept under protective tarps. Mahari kept it padlocked at all times and we all knew to never, ever enter it upon pain of a random uncle's heavy leather belt. I was nervous that she wanted to meet with me there. It was a forbidden place that seemed the epitome of this wild, secretive family.

Torches spiked the ground around the caravan. The tarp had been removed, and the structure gleamed proudly in the firelight. I climbed the short steps and paused before the door, unable to knock.

Mira placed a hand between my shoulder blades, and I was touched to have her support. Maybe we really had achieved a breakthrough after all these years. Then she shoved me hard, knocking my head against the door. I whipped around but she was already dancing away.

"Like a Band-Aid..." she sang.

I rubbed the goose egg already rising from my forehead, ready to leap after her. Then it was too late to change my mind. The door swung open and Mahari appeared in the doorway.

She was not much taller than me. Her dyed brunette hair touched her shoulders and her lips were heavily lined from years of smoking. Her dark brown eyes raked the area behind me and then she turned her back to walk deeper into the caravan. I followed, closing the door behind me but leaving it unlatched.

My imagination had always envisioned colorful silks and cushions inside. In reality, it was small and crowded with a musty smell. A battery-operated camp lantern hung above a small table, and a few candles dotted a counter top. Mahari sank into a chair at the table and motioned for me to use the only other chair.

A bottle of *rosé* wine sat on the table next to a worn deck of cards and two small glasses etched with silver. The bottle was half full and her glass was nearly empty. She refilled her glass and poured a small quantity in the second glass without asking me. I folded my hands in my lap and waited.

She studied me, took a sip of her wine and smacked her thin lips. Reaching into a drawer at her side, she retrieved a photograph and laid it onto the table in front of me. A laughing young man leaned against a car. He was thin and tall with thick, wavy brown hair and mischievous eyes.

"That—" she tapped a thick fingernail on the table above the man's face "—is your father."

I blinked hard, trying to focus on every detail of his face. He was exactly as I imagined. I used my fingertips to draw the photo closer to me. Another picture landed on the table. The image was of the same man with his arm around a petite woman. She had straight blond hair and a happy smile. Their arms wound tightly around one another. In the background I recognized the Golden Gate Bridge. Mahari's thick Slavic accent drew out her next words.

"My son—Lasho."

I couldn't meet her eyes. She'd had these and never shared them with me. Had probably known I existed and allowed me to go into foster care. I focused my attention on the faces in the photos. My parents.

"I don't like to talk about him. When you love someone too much, holding on can create ghosts or worse. That's not good for their soul, and it's not good for you.

"But I want to tell you something about him now. He was strong.

He was good with business, but he loved to write his poems more. We lived in San Francisco then. I had a pretty good income coming in and the family was solid." I heard her glass as she lifted it to her lips for a noisy gulp and then the *thunk* as she banged it back on the wood table.

"Your mother was a runaway," Mahari continued, a note of derision in her voice, "She arrived in San Francisco and lived in a tiny room over your Aunt Lenora's tarot shop. Vivian had an adopted brother visit her at the time. I forget his name." *Brother? My mother was an only child.* Perhaps Mahari was drunk.

"One day she ran into Lasho in the shop and that was it. My boy was bewitched. She got him into all sorts of trouble. But he loved her. I'll give you that. You live awhile you start to recognize true love. They would have died for each other, your parents. Perhaps they did."

I raised my face to hers. "How would you know what love looks like?"

She stood and retrieved a yellowed package of cigarettes and a translucent purple lighter from a cabinet before sitting down heavily. She lit a cigarette and blew the smoke over my head. She wore a loose brown dress with a crocheted vest I knew she'd knitted herself.

"You're lying, anyway. My mother was an only child." Sam would have told me if he had an adopted son. She gave an infuriating shrug.

"I'm an old woman now. There is no reason to lie. You think *you* know what love is? As far as I know you love three people." She raised three fingers around her cigarette while picking a piece of tobacco from her tongue. "I know my Silvan is one of these. He is beloved by many in our family, but I know your heart is small. He holds a large part. You know there is power in the number three? I wonder what would happen if it becomes four?" Her eyes slid craftily over my face, and I clenched my jaw. Before I could respond, she spoke again, tapping ash from her cigarette once more.

"Did you know I was born in Siberia? My family was poor but we had what we wanted and were very good with the horses. The Gadjo women would come to hear about their husbands from my mother and her sisters. They would do some *dukkering* to put food on the table—lift bad things and help them bring their husbands back to them. That kind of thing. The women in my family could read fortunes in firelight. Most can use tea leaves or hands but we—we could read the flames."

"In the war our men were pressed into the army. So, we moved west. And were taken into concentration camps by the Nazis. I married an older man to save myself. We came to America and started over." She blew out a perfect smoke ring and then another that passed through the middle of the first.

She tapped the deck of cards. "Pick," she said shortly.

I cut the deck and began to flip over the first card. Her hand clapped down hard upon mine.

"No! Play with them first. Feel them. Focus and then pick."

I placed the photos carefully to the side and pulled the cards towards me. I shuffled them several times and even closed my eyes to better feel them between my fingers. One card seemed to fall out of the others. I pinched it between my fingertips to slide it back in the deck but it seemed to have a restless energy. It didn't want to be returned. Opening my eyes, I placed the card on the table.

The King of Diamonds.

Mahari grunted. "When bees drink the honeysuckle, red lips shall reveal love."

"Excuse me?"

"You pulled the King of Diamonds. That's what it means." She grunted and shuffled the cards again. I could see her doing this all night. Controlling the conversation with vague rabbit holes. What I really wanted to know was too painful to leave to her shenanigans.

"You must have known there was a baby. Why did you abandon me?" I asked, lips numb with emotion. Now that the words were out there, would any version of the truth make it better? She didn't seem to hear me. She flicked ash into her empty glass and tapped her knuckles three times on the top of the neatened deck of cards.

A scream rent the air. Then shouts.

We stared at one another, and color drained from the old woman's cheeks. We jumped up at the same time, chairs scraping the floor. She hurried from the caravan, and I vaulted the steps, landing near her.

"There's a circle. No one should be able to get through," she muttered.

I ran before her to the center of the field. It took me several seconds to comprehend what I was seeing. Figures in black clothing and hoods carried guns and large knives. A few restrained children, knives to their throats as they screamed or whimpered. The adults stayed back, terrified of making the wrong move and seeing their children hurt. One such figure held Midora down on the ground, a blade pressed vertically against her throat as if ready to saw through her flesh and into the earth.

Mahari yelled something in another language, and the barrels of fire became columns of flame that rose into the sky.

"I wouldn't do that if I were you," taunted a vaguely familiar voice. I searched for its source and found its speaker on the makeshift stage. He clasped Amanda with an arm around her throat, a gun to her temple.

"Marcus," I whispered.

It couldn't be. Amanda said he was history.

"There she is," he chortled. "Come closer, dear. I've been looking for you."

I took a step forward and met Mahari's arm.

"What do you want?" I screamed, thrusting Mahari's arm away. It returned, smacking into my belly.

"I want you to come with me. And no witnesses." He smirked and jammed the gun harder into Amanda's head. She gripped his arm, eyes wide and terrified, but did not cry out.

No witnesses? Did he mean to kill everyone here?

There were shouts and tussles as the family comprehended his words. I saw Midora's husband nearby, on his knees and helpless to interfere while the blade pressed firmly into his wife's throat. Midora herself looked pissed off and I noticed her hands curled into the dirt as if preparing to grab handfuls. Knowing Midora, she was preparing to fling them into her attacker's eyes, despite the fact that he wore a mask.

I searched the crowd and found Silvan on his knees with the rest of the musicians, his violin smashed on the ground. Air filled my lungs with a tiny measure of relief that he was okay. We could always replace a violin.

Marcus felt for Amanda's necklace and jerked its chain from her neck. Amanda gave a whimpering shriek, but he clutched her tighter, tapping the gun's muzzle against the side of her face.

"Worked like a charm. Ha! Literally. I placed a locator spell on her Pagatio and she didn't even know it. I knew she would run straight to you. Useless little witches today..." he crowed as he tossed Amanda's Pagatio to the stage floor.

"Run into the woods. To the south," whispered Mahari.

"No!" I replied fiercely. I would not abandon my friends and family. I pushed my way past her arm and approached the stage. Marcus wore no hood and his red hair shone in the light, matching the maniacal intensity of his gaze.

"That's it. Come closer." He loosened his grip on Amanda, swinging her away from him with a grip of her hair. She cried out in pain and I nearly shrieked in frustration. There had to be a way to negotiate with him to let her go. Let them all go.

"I'm here! I'll come with you if you want. Just leave everyone here alone," I said, trying hard not to sound demanding.

"You will come with me no matter what." He grinned. His confidence made me stumble.

"Why do you even want me? Did I run over your dog in a past life?"

He started to reply but I watched in horror as events played out in slow motion. Amanda's hand reached into the cross-body purse, withdrawing the bear spray I'd given her. She thumbed off the cap and sprayed it into Marcus's face. It mostly missed his eyes but surprised him. Silvan jumped up and rushed across the makeshift stage to tackle Marcus at the knees.

Marcus fell backwards and fired several shots into Silvan's chest, the sharp sounds echoing within the clearing. Silvan fell, his back striking the edge of the platform before he slid, his head landing on the ground. The spread of scarlet against his white dress shirt. His hands grasped at his chest.

Then Jing San was there. She wore black, too; her hair tied back and a wide sword in her hand. My hands trembled as Silvan's boss brought the sword across the neck of one of the figures holding a little girl. His head fell and his body seemed to fold in upon itself. One of my uncles grabbed the girl, pulling her from the dead man's grasp.

I ran to Silvan but Mahari was already there. She opened his shirt and removed her vest, pressing it against his laboring chest. Blood trickled from his lips as he glanced wildly in my direction. His eyes were bewildered and beseeching at once. My vision swam, his image distorted as I tried to help. I was muttering something. Repeating it over and over. *No. No. No. No...*

Screams filled the air. Mahari instructed me to keep pressure on his wounds and then left us. The air warmed and brightened as fire erupted across the field. There was so much blood. Far too much. The wet heat soaked my hands up to my wrists. I glanced around, frantically searching for help. Someone to call an ambulance. Everyone was running around. Marcus's followers were doing their best to cut down my family. A figure in black marched towards me but then Mira was there, taking the brute force of a punch before several male cousins jumped in to help her disarm and tackle the man to the ground.

Then I saw Alaric in the firelight. He picked up a large man as if he were a rotted branch and broke him in half across his knee, his torso to the side of his hips at an odd angle. The man screamed and kept screaming as Alaric kicked him to the side. *Impossible.* I looked across the field as Jing swung two swords as if performing a ballet. Her movements were lightening swift, her swords dripping crimson.

Silvan's gasps brought my attention back to him. He couldn't breathe! I removed my hands from his chest and dragged him backwards by his armpits until he lay even on the ground. *What should I do?* I raised his head, placing it on my lap and then reapplied the pressure. I closed my eyes, begging God to intervene. Fiercely promising anything to save him.

My breathing slowed and I focused on my hands. I imagined light moving from my body to Silvan's. Offering all my life energy to flow into his. I chanted over and over again, "Live. Just live." Silvan, with his sweet mischievous ways, his talent and unwavering loyalty, couldn't leave me alone. Liquid covered my cheeks and dripped onto his hair and face. I rocked us, begging him to stay with me. My hands, slippery with his lifeblood, kept applying pressure.

"Stell..." he whispered between awful gurgling sounds.

"I'm here, Silvan. I'm here. I'm not going anywhere. You're safe." My hands began to burn, but I refused to let up on the pressure. I kept visualizing the light, telling him again and again that I *would never leave him.* I bent and kissed his forehead.

"No, Stella!" Alaric roared. He stood over us, horror etched on his face. Mahari appeared next to him, her expression aghast. *What?*

I looked at Silvan and he was very pale, his chest unmoving. He wasn't breathing. I shook his shoulders. "Silvan? Silvan?" His eyes stared without blinking. I felt it then. The absence of him. Silvan was no longer there. He wasn't *here* anymore. I was holding something but it was no longer Silvan. I stared hard, looking and looking as ice crept into every part of me.

A high keening cry broke the night, followed by wails of agony. As Alaric pulled me away from Silvan's body, I noted that some of those awful cries timed perfectly with the ravaged sensation in my own chest and throat. The world dipped as my feet left the ground and my eyes closed tight against the terrible night. My first rule of life was true for a reason. *Don't get attached.* Not even to your own life. People who had something, or someone, to lose always lost it. I attracted death for anyone idiotic enough to care about me. My parents and now Silvan. Possibly for a future lover who I would doom to the grave.

I welcomed the muffling sensation around me and pulled it closer, vaguely recognizing Alaric's voice mixed with others. Movement. The voices grew distant as he continued to travel away from the field and its bright firelight. I was placed upright, Alaric's hands holding my face as he shouted. Like a cranky radio station, his voice rose and fell in volume.

"Can you sit on the motorcycle? Answer me, Stella!" *What?* I heard him curse as I sank back into the comforting darkness, my body falling towards the street pavement. I was caught, my form moved, positioned facing Alaric on the motorcycle. My arms were threaded through a jacket and then the roar of the motorcycle rumbled beneath us as Alaric's arms caged me close. My cheek sank against his chest.

For a long time, I was aware of nothing in particular. Time passed with only the bike's rumble and intermittent motion as we leaned this way and that. Stopped and moved again.

I gradually noticed that my legs ached and I realized they were draped over his thighs and around his waist, locked behind him. My arms were wrapped around him, and I was burrowed into his warmth. Flashes of Alaric hurting the man from Mahari's field entered and left my mind in quick sequence. His arm curled around my back, holding me closer. I shifted and soon felt the bike slow. The crunch of gravel and then the smooth hum of wheels on blacktop.

Alaric brought us to a stop and held me for a long moment. He spoke quietly into my hair in French, and I recognized only *petite etoile*— little star. I shuddered and lifted my head to squint at harsh lights. We were parked behind a truck stop.

"Stella. Do you want to clean up?" Alaric asked gently. I shook my head. He sighed and dismounted the bike with me in his arms. He waited patiently as my feet found the ground. I hissed as the blood began to pump through them again. He held me close, rubbing my arms.

"You need to walk around a little," he said in a low, soothing voice. On autopilot, I followed him as he steered us towards the ladies' room entrance at the back of a low building. He escorted me into the bathroom, then nudged me until I shuffled towards a row of rusty sinks and turned on a tap. I raised my hands but they were covered in the long black leather sleeves of Alaric's jacket. I was a wind-up toy, hitting a wall with no ability to help myself. He removed the jacket for me.

I placed my hands beneath the freezing water and looked down at myself for the first time. Screams ripped from my sore throat. My hands were covered in dried blood up to my elbows. Most of my clothing was wet with blood, parts of my silk pants stiff with it. I raised my head and viewed my reflection. Mouth gaping, eyes dead and feral at the same time.

Alaric shushed me, turning the taps until the water ran warm. He massaged soap gently into my hands and arms and rinsed them while I stared blindly at the girl with specks of blood on her face. My mind grew thick, as if cotton were stuffing itself around every nerve ending—yet I was aware when he ripped the towel dispenser off the wall with muttered frustration. I heard a feminine voice and Alaric's sharp reply.

Then he placed my arms once more into his jacket; bundling me on the bike again so that I faced him and I buried myself in him as he started up the motorcycle. As he rebalanced the bike, I raised my head with a great deal of effort.

"Did I see Jing San hack at people with big knives?" I could not tell what was real and things were hard to absorb.

"Yes. But they were wakizashi and only the bad people. Don't worry. Your friend Amanda is safe. Shhhh, now."

We rode for a long time. I nodded off and was awakened by Alaric's hands on my back, rubbing circles. I opened my eyes and lifted my head. We were stopped, in complete darkness with only the wind and gentle patter of rain on leaves for company.

"We're in the heart of the Olympic Forest. I'm taking you somewhere safe," he said. I didn't reply. The part of me that thought and felt were far away, leaving behind just this person now, who followed directions but otherwise was a shuttered, one-dimensional object.

"Can you walk?" he murmured softly. I thought and then nodded.

When he stood me on my feet it took several minutes to get feeling back in my legs, the pins and needles oddly comforting. When he was satisfied that I wouldn't collapse, he parked his motorcycle deep beyond the dirt road we'd stopped on. I whimpered at his absence, hugging my middle and he reappeared immediately. Taking my hand, he led my stumbling form over uneven ground and damp fallen logs as we made our way into the dark forest. Soon after, he cursed and swung me up into his arms. I didn't complain. We moved much faster. The cool night air smelled clean and earthy beneath the light drizzle. Tiny dancing lights seemed to guide Alaric's steps. At first, I imagined it to be glowing honey fungus on the trees but then the lights darted from tree to tree. Lightening bugs couldn't live in this climate and I'd never even seen one before. I waved at one that flickered near my face and it zipped over Alaric's head.

Time drifted until Alaric finally came to a stop, releasing me with gentle hands to stand once more. We stood in a tiny clearing brightened by moonlight. An enormous Sitka spruce tree loomed overhead, surrounded by tender saplings. It was so huge my VW could probably fit inside with plenty of room. "Thank you, TirieFliuch," I thought I heard Alaric whisper. Then he lowered his face to my neck.

"Please trust me, Stella," Alaric murmured. He turned my unresisting form and pressed me against the tree, the bark rough beneath my cheek. I leaned into the tree, hugging it. He caged me between his arms, pressing my hands with his on either side of my face. The air grew warmer and I closed my eyes, inhaling the spicy scent of tree bark, feeling Alaric's heat behind me and thinking of nothing. I was empty. The air cooled and I opened my eyes to a new reality. We were on a rooftop, the lights from nearby buildings illuminating a city landscape.

Chapter 20

The Hangman Reversed

Alaric

———·⚬❧·———

Dawn was still hours away when we stepped from the large Hemlock tree onto the roof patio of my New York City building. Transferring through a living tree with roots on another plane was something better suited to the most experienced travelers. I hoped it hadn't damaged her. I hoisted her into my arms and carried her through electronic doors set to my voice. Light as a thistle, she shivered, her lips faintly blue.

I bit my tongue until blood flooded my throat to stave off a roar of frustration. She was clearly in shock, and I'd just forced her on an hours long motorcycle ride. Even with the jacket and summer weather, it had been too cold, had taken too long.

I strode through the penthouse; Grayson appeared and then melted into shadows when he saw my expression. My path was unerring as I walked us to my bathroom. Behind a thick glass wall and door lay a blue tiled shower room large enough for the beast. The shower held four massive shower heads and, without releasing the traumatized girl in my arms, I turned them all to a hard rain effect.

A white leather chair sat before my soaking tub, and I placed her there to remove her shoes and adjust the heat flowing beneath the white ceramic floor tiles. Unwilling to sever our physical connection, I scooped Stella up. Once the shower's glass wall was fogged over, I walked us into the shower room.

She gasped when the water hit her skin but was otherwise silent. I placed her on one of the wide-tiled benches along the shower wall and eased the jacket from her. She behaved as a doll, obediently following my quiet instructions without any sign of that indomitable will I'd come to know in her. This was what alarmed me most. Tears periodically streamed from her eyes, mixing with the water sluicing down her face. Occasionally she sobbed outright and when those black moments hit, I stilled to offer my body until the storm depleted itself.

I worked blood from her hair and lathered shampoo from a black bottle into the silken strands until the air was thick with the lush scent. Adjusting a wall jet, I turned her, working the suds from her hair until the water ran clear. I then set about cleaning the blood from beneath her fingernails, striving to be gentle while my body tremored with rage. Her limp compliance and silence put me on edge. The Stella I'd come to know was a wild and vital girl. A fighter. This biddable Stella was unbearable.

I knew that her cousin had been important to her. She'd experienced so much loss in her young life. Her parents and now Silvan. More than anything I wanted Stella to survive. To grow old in peace, surrounded by loved ones. I would make this happen for her, even though it meant I couldn't be part of that future. For the first time in my long life, I wanted something more than the role I'd been thrust into. The justice bearing cold one without any desires of my own.

The memory of my mother was more distant than I could bear—

yet one memory still emerged as fresh as the day it occurred. It was summer and as a treat I was allowed tutoring on the terrace of the great palace. As I struggled over an abacus, Murad had been practicing sword fighting in the courtyard with an Italian instructor and our older brother. I could see them below and my young feet had swung restlessly, wanting to be part of the yelling, clanging action.

My mother, always knowing what I was feeling, had touched the top of my head and asked my teacher to leave us. She told me that Murad might never be Sultan, but he would be a great man. I had to study and make sure that I was able to help him one day as his nature was an impulsive one. My role would be to support my brothers, to stand for right and to be their strength. For over five hundred years I've been the noble Lion, the strong one while Murad fell into despair and madness over Lila. For the first time I felt the bitter burn of resentment for my brother's weakness for her, and how it had taken over my own life. And yet, Stella's happiness was fast becoming my only desire. One that was taking precedence over duty. Perhaps we brothers had inherited the same weakness.

I washed the bare skin of her arms and back and held her beneath the spray until the water that streamed from her clothes was devoid of blood. When she appeared to fall asleep, I turned off the water and carried her from the shower. Enveloping her within enormous white towels I towel-dried her hair as she sat, silent and wrapped within her own mind.

"Stella. I need you to get out of these wet clothes. There is a robe on the back of the door. I'm going to leave the room to give you privacy. Can you please undress and put the robe on?" Eyes drooping, she bobbed her chin once. She remained in the chair as I exited the room and shut the door behind me.

I went into my dressing room and quickly changed into dry jeans and a plain white t-shirt. I returned to the bathroom door to find it still closed. I rapped softly and her voice responded, albeit faintly. "Coming."

The door opened and a confused Stella stood in the doorway. She swam in the giant white robe, the sleeves nearly reaching her knees. She'd tied the belt around herself thrice.

"I'll have to find you clothes later."

"I want my own," she replied sleepily. Relief coursed through me at the sound of her voluntary response. Stella was still here. I'd seen this reaction before in shocked humans. She just needed to stay walled off until her mind could accept the loss.

I gathered her small hand in mine and led her to a door across from my own bedroom. I never had overnight guests but this was one of several additional bedrooms. It was decorated in neutral creams and yellows. Blue pillows and vases provided what my decorator had claimed were tasteful accents.

She stopped inside the door, staring at our hands. She turned my palm over and, reaching for my other hand, traced the long scars lining each one without saying a word. It was more intimate than I could bear. The scars were the few wounds on my body that had remained after my turning, and they brought me back to that horrific day. When I'd woken to find myself pierced through with the Sword of Righteousness. The agony as I pulled the hot blade from my own chest. The mark on my chest and the scars on my hands were a reminder that I had survived a fate worse than death—immortal damnation as a vampire demon with angelic strength. Instead I remained a portion angel and the rest demon. There lies my prison. I could not leave my brother alone in his suffering. I kept him sane, his humanity close.

"Alaric—who are you? I'm not stupid. You're one of *them*, aren't you?" she asked quietly. Saying the words or not would not help push back this moment. She needed truth. I saw it in the raw, bared soul visible within the depths of her eyes. She was afraid of the answer, yet needed it all the same. I was the most despicable of creatures, because I couldn't give her everything. Not tonight.

"If you mean a Primati, then yes. I am one. I knew you were in danger tonight and came." The admission was the most I could offer. I watched as her vulnerable stare became tinged with despair. A wave of sensation swirled beneath my breastbone.

"You must have laughed at me. Poor Stella, so naïve. You aren't the only one, you know. I didn't know about Amanda. I didn't know there was a whole freaking world of people performing magick on me for years." Her low laugh cracked, transitioned to a sob before she swallowed it back, her lips tight. I had no idea how to comfort her.

"No. Not poor Stella," I insisted, knowing I was creating a terrible mess of this. "Do you really want to know everything, Stella? Can't we just leave it alone for now? I'm your friend and I want to help."

"Help? Right. Because you're like, what? A wizard?" She was crying again and I hurried to stem the tide rising beneath her surface.

"Reality will come soon enough, Stella. I can offer you a safe place for a week or two. After that we can return to whatever awaits us." I expected a fight. It hurt when her eyes dulled once again. She said nothing, just leaned forward until the top of her head rested against my chest. The strange sensation in my chest intensified.

My hands rose tentatively behind her slim shoulders, smoothing her wet hair down her back. We stood there for several minutes, and I felt the moment sleep began to take her. I lifted her in my arms and she allowed it, her head settling upon my shoulder. When I pulled down the duvet and helped her into the king size bed she immediately turned to her side and curled into a ball, away from me.

"Stella? You have your own bathroom. The door is across from the foot of the bed," I said. She didn't utter a sound. I crossed the room and closed the cream silk curtains with their black out panels, shutting her off from the intrusion of approaching sunlight.

"If you need anything, just call and I'll hear you." I offered, uncertain if she heard me. She remained quiet and I left her to slumber's seductive embrace. For several moments I listened outside the door, relieved to hear only her deepening breaths. Her cries had eviscerated me more effectively than any enemy blade.

I prowled the halls to my study. With Stella safe, it was time to hunt. Marcus had disappeared from the field the second we'd reached it. I would find him and bring his head, along with whoever was behind the attack, to Stella as a prize.

* * *

"It's been ten days, Sir."

"Your point, Grayson?"

"It's not healthy for a human to eat just one small meal a day. She only leaves the bed or the garden hammock to use the washroom, paint, and eat one meal a day. One meal, Sir. I was thrilled when she asked if she could request food but she only asked for sunflower seeds. Raw seeds, Sir. She is wasting away."

I'd never seen him so worked up before. Grayson had taken it upon himself to personally prepare Stella's meals. He'd coaxed her to eat his soups and comfort food with intermittent success. It was true she spent most of the day in bed with the curtains drawn. Recently she'd taken to painting from the rooftop garden in the late afternoons, falling asleep for an hour or two on the hammock Grayson produced especially for her after finding her curled asleep against the magicked Hemlock. She would wake and continue painting by artificial light until early morning and then she sought me. I was never far.

When she did sleep it was always in my arms. The first night she'd awakened screaming from a nightmare, panting so hard she'd nearly lost consciousness. When I'd tried to wake her, she'd pulled at my clothes until I joined her. She'd tucked herself into my side and I guided her through the panic attack until she regained control. Within minutes, she'd fallen asleep, fingers still tight on my shirt. We didn't discuss it then or in subsequent nights—yet I always ensured she remained under the covers while I stayed on top of the duvet. I wanted no hint of impropriety that could lead to her feeling guilty later. Or my brother to question.

She'd risen from her grief only once, when Sam had insisted on a conversation to assure himself that she was alive and well. She'd tried during those brief moments to become more animated and reassure him she was fine. When she'd suggested she return home, he'd erupted, insisting that she stay where she was if it wasn't safe in Portland.

I had some of Stella's clothes and personal items flown here, hoping it might cheer her up. Her cell phone was found and delivered, but she had yet to pick it up. I'd read her messages aloud, hoping to stir her interest. Lots of entreaties from Amanda. A few versions of, 'We're all sad, get over yourself bitch and call me' from her strangely rude cousin Mira. An inquiry on her welfare from someone named Roger that I was more than a little curious about. She'd explained he worked for Sam and responded to none of the messages.

Her paintings were dark, impressionistic canvases without subject. She often left one unfinished before beginning a new one. They were disturbing. Compelling and unformed, I suspected they would have an emotional effect on someone more vulnerable to magickal properties.

"What do you recommend, Grayson?"

"Get her outside this building. A change of scenery will do her good. It's not right for someone so young to just give up on life."

"She's grieving, Grayson," I replied gruffly. He sighed.

"We know what that did to someone else," he said simply before exiting my study.

I did recall. I'd arrived in America at my brother's side just after Lila had found her family slain. She'd been as a trapped animal, entombed in a grief so profound she'd never recovered from it. Lila was a different being, however. A celestial creature given to extreme emotions as a human. Lila had also lost her own children. Although Stella's cousin was dear to her, there was no comparison to the pain of losing a child. Stella would rebound.

Grayson was right, however. I could no longer allow her to hide from the world when the Grand Council and Samhain Ball were so close. She needed to be stronger and made ready for this next stage in her life. A human lifetime in which the Alaric she thought she knew would disappear. When she would only know me as the Lion. The Enforcer. She deserved a family of her own one day. The future Lila never had. I sighed, steeling myself for what would come next. With a few whispered words, I lowered the mystical barrier around the property I'd erected when we first arrived. I picked up my cell to call Murad but he appeared in my study before I could pull up his name.

"You bloody wanker," he yelled. My eyebrows rose. He must be spending time in London. He always reverted to the bloody-somethings when in the U.K. for longer than a day.

"Where is she?" he demanded,

"Ease yourself, brother. She's safe."

"Why on earth have you shielded her from me for two bloody weeks? And not answered your bloody phone!"

My brother stalked my office, scowling fiercely. He wore a finely tailored three-piece suit, which usually meant financial meetings. London then. I leaned back in my leather chair, waiting patiently as he got it out of his system.

"I should kill you for this. Aydin Bey would have strung you up by your intestines," he lashed out, bringing our younger brother and former pirate king into the mix.

"Aydin was a legend, true," I admitted.

"I looked everywhere that night for you until Grayson informed us you were in hiding with Stella. You never hide. Your transfer left no trace, so no one knew of your whereabouts. I guessed immediately you were here, but this place has been impenetrable." Murad was vamping out as he paced, the whites of his eyes scoring with tell-tale crimson flares as his face grew more angular. He continued angrily, "I've had people stationed around the block and in flight overhead, but no one has been able to enter the building." His voice had deepened, his human façade sharpened into something absolutely lethal.

This was the reason for our motorcycle ride to the hidden, sacred grove in the Olympic Mountains. Demons were deadly hunters, their sense of smell tied to the *taste* of the scent. If I'd transferred us through the demon plane, Murad and many others would have tasted my passing. Even worse, they would acquire knowledge of Stella's taste as well. Allowing them to gain hers would have added to her vulnerability. The ancient tree had allowed us to transfer without notice.

"Where is she?" he demanded with an enraged glare.

I stood and walked over to the office's floor-to-ceiling windows. Fifth Avenue was bustling. A bus deposited a group of teenagers at the corner, their faces laughing at something one of them said. I tried and failed to imagine Stella in their midst.

"She is not recovered, brother. Her grief over the boy runs deeper than I expected."

Moments passed and Murad sank into a sofa. He was silent for a long time, his forehead pressed to steepled fingers. I watched him with sympathy. He had much experience with grieving females.

"They are steadfast little things, aren't they brother? These women of stars," he finally stated wearily.

I studied the park below. "Yes. They are."

"Did you know they refused to have a funeral for her cousin?" Murad informed me.

"Why is that?" It seemed a curious thing. My research had been thorough, and Mahari had more than enough funds for a grand funeral of considerable proportions.

"Clara said they refused to explain themselves. As far as we know they buried him in a backyard. We can't get near them without causing more trouble. I assume Jing is here with you?"

"Yes. She's been in and out as we search for Marcus and whoever led the attack. Those we managed to keep alive and capture told us nothing. Which means they knew nothing. Jing's interrogation tactics are effective. They would have broken," I said matter-of-factly. Murad nodded.

"Where are they now? Perhaps my own techniques could persuade them." My brother seemed restless, eager.

"Too late. Bodies are in the incinerator, their heads floating on pikes in the demon realm with bounty signs offering a great sum for information." I refrained from telling him of the one remaining prisoner waiting in the basement of this building. He was taking a long time to heal, but once his tongue grew back, we would play some more. He had to know something that would lead me to Marcus. No one stayed hidden from me for long.

"Clara and Tess will be here soon. They want you skinned alive for taking Stella away and shielding her for so long."

"Yes." I acknowledged, not really caring.

Without preamble, I strode from the room, knowing my brother would follow. I led him to the living room where Grayson had placed Stella's art to dry atop cloth tarps. They leaned against two walls of the enormous room. My brother was speechless as he took in the violent swirls of deepest grey, cobalt, and red. Red tears streamed from his eyes. "Where is she?"

Chapter 21
Star Reversed

Stella

Time passed without meaning. The entire world had shrunk to remembering that Silvan was gone and brief moments when I would forget. In the forgetful spaces, there was sleep, my paint brushes, Alaric…and the bird. The arctic tern had appeared in the garden about a week ago. Watching him inspect my latest canvas, I recalled the raw sunflower seeds requested from Grayson. After cleaning my brushes in the outdoor sink, I dug a hand into the loose pocket of my jeans and pulled out a handful of the seeds.

"Want some grub, Bird?" I emptied my offering onto an outdoor table. "Maybe you could tell your friend Thomas that I'd like to speak with him," I suggested, feeling more than a little foolish. Thomas had believed the bird could communicate, but so far I didn't see how.

A sparkle flashed, and I poked through the seeds to find a small glittering stone. The bird made a series of excited "Kee-ee" sounds. White feathers set off his black eye mask and orange-red beak, giving him the appearance of a scolding bandit.

Raising the stone to the light I recognized it as the same stone Bird had given me that night in Thomas' grove. It had been in my jeans pocket this entire time. I thanked Alaric silently for bringing me my own clothing.

I drifted over to the standing hammock. Lying down, I absently kicked off into a slow swing before holding the stone up to afternoon sunlight. It was small, perhaps the size of my thumbnail. Its brilliance reminded me of a diamond, yet the center was milky with a strange shimmer. It felt content in my hand and I squeezed it within my fist a few times, trying to think of what it could be. Bird flew closer—making soft "kip" noises as he watched me.

"Sorry, Bird. I won't lose it again." I stood and tucked the stone back into my pocket. He seemed appeased as he tapped his feet and nabbed a seed before taking flight towards Central Park.

I wandered to my room and changed into a soft t-shirt and a pair of Silvan's old sweatpants he'd outgrown years before. Exhausted, I crawled into the huge bed and curled beneath the covers with my crystal treasure. I knew that Sam would not always be with me. The thought of being alone in life had been an ever-present specter. But Silvan had been so young. Alive. Any future I'd imagined, Silvan was a cornerstone. How could so much potential just disappear...his life-force no longer exist?

I could still feel him sometimes—and then my mind would remind me that it was impossible. He would never be with us again. I would never hear him tell his stupid zombie jokes. He would never become an adult. He would never fall in love and realize his dreams of becoming a master violinist. So much wiped away, and yet the sun kept rising with ridiculous oblivion that he was no longer alive beneath its promise. I'd come to hate those sunrises. Sleep was a reprieve. Sometimes I would wake and be okay for several seconds until the inevitable happened. I would recall that he died. Realize something that was forever lost; his dimpled smile, the way he set himself adrift in his music, our shared love of popcorn, our mutual hatred of hot weather—and the sobs would begin unabated until fatigue took me into blessed sleep.

In the darkest moments I would recall his bravery at trying to save Amanda. The fear in his eyes when he struggled to breathe. Thank goodness for Alaric and his ability to keep the worst at bay. He would stroke my hair and guard against the awful pain until I could drift off.

Once I dreamed that I was in the body of a woman, crying in the rain with such loneliness I woke up clutching my aching chest, crushed by the sadness choking me. I dreamed of a blonde girl who could make dandelion wisps dance at will. I dreamed of Sam, a younger, stronger version with a shockingly full head of brown hair. I even dreamed of waking in a coffin. Clawing uselessly until my screams shattered the glass above.

I kissed Bird's stone gift, feeling it warm against my lips and wishing that it might help keep the nightmares away. Then I put it in a zippered pocket so it couldn't be lost in the twisted sheets. In time I heard my bedroom door open and anticipated Alaric's weight on the mattress behind me as he would sometimes lie down with me between his work. Then the room was filled with bright sunshine as the curtains were thrown back. I hissed and buried my face in the covers.

"Stella Avery. Sam will be so disappointed in you," came a hard male voice.

I went still, terror freezing my limbs. That was not Alaric's voice. Where was Alaric? I imagined Marcus at the foot of the bed, leering over me with a large knife. Before I could move, the covers were ripped from me in a forceful yank. I scrambled towards the headboard, unable to see for the tangle of hair in my face. I screamed for Alaric and he crashed into the room.

"What are you doing?" Alaric roared, standing over me.

"*Kardeşim*, stay out of it," the man said. I pushed my hair from my eyes and gaped to see Murad watching me from across the room with a stormy expression. The Noble King looked me over, his expression softening.

"Stella, dear. When did you last eat something? You're wasting away." Murad scolded gently. I hated that he used the word, "dear". It was what Marcus had said.

I glanced down at my jagged fingernails, suddenly ashamed. I longed for the sanctity of my darkened room and blankets. I squinted at Alaric, beseeching him silently, but he just looked at the wall above my head, his handsome face an impassive mask. My voice was rusty with hurt. "I eat."

"Um hmm. Well in that case—how about you come and take a walk with me?"

I stared at him in amazement. The last thing I wanted was to leave this room. I didn't want sunlight and people. I craved what every wounded animal wanted. A peaceful cave in which to lick my wounds or die.

"You are worrying Alaric, sweetheart," he said kindly. My eyes shot to Alaric, but he was glaring daggers at Murad. The last thing I wanted was to cause Alaric distress. He'd been my rock in a tsunami-whipped sea. Deep down, though, didn't I already know that I'd taken advantage of his unjudging care? Distracted him from his normal life? He must be tired of having a guest all the time.

"How about a compromise? If you come with me now for a single hour, a short walk, then I will not ask you to eat or even comb your hair," Murad coaxed with a gentle smile. Panic rose at the thought of stepping out of my haven—yet a short walk seemed a reasonable exchange if it meant putting Alaric at ease. I ran my hands through my hair, feeling the tangles. When was the last time I'd washed it? A few days…perhaps longer. Warmth crept into my cheeks.

I slid to the edge of the bed and stood slowly. Alaric kept his distance and it hurt. I'd gotten used to his solicitous presence and touch. But he wouldn't touch me in front of Murad, would he? For all intents and purposes, I was the King's betrothed. Murad might be a decent ruler to his Primati, but he was still a king. I didn't want to get Alaric in trouble.

When I returned from the bathroom, it was with clean teeth and my hair twisted in a low bun. Alaric was gone and Murad was sitting on the edge of the bed, holding a pair of my sneakers. I put them on and we walked silently to the foyer where a pair of ornate gold doors embellished with snarling lions parted to reveal an elevator.

When the doors opened to a lobby, I hesitated. Since arriving with Alaric, I hadn't left the apartment, although I knew we were in New York City from Alaric and the long hours spent staring out at the landscape. We passed through two security sections until a doorman held the door for us. His examination of us was discreet but thorough. The world shifted the moment we stepped outside into the humid air. Murad paused infinitesimally and the doorman moved inside so fast I barely saw his retreat. Weird.

For September, it was hot. Much hotter than back home. The dense flow of people was uncomfortably close, one or two giving me a dirty look as I stood like a stone in a river. Murad touched my elbow and moved us in the direction of Central Park. My shoes might as well have been lined with lead. To his credit, Murad kept to my unhurried pace, somehow discouraging others from bumping into me. In time we passed vendors selling used books. My senses were on overload. The thick odor of subway exhaust wafted in blistering waves from sidewalk grates. Sour garbage and warm pretzels added to the complex layers of scent around us.

"So you're a—you-know-what—but you can still be outside in the sun. How is that possible?" I asked, too embarrassed to say the word "vampire". Murad leaned close, as if to hear me better.

"What was that you said? A you-know-what? Do you mean a good-looking investment banker?" he teased. I rolled my eyes and he laughed softly.

"I *am* a vampire but I'm also more than the stories report about our kind. We've had plenty of time and money to invest in the entertainment industry and its false portrayals. There aren't many in the world today and each continent has a group that call themselves a family—who act as an oligarchy for that part of the world.

"Many of us can be in the sun, although those with the greatest longevity prefer to keep distance from humans during daylight hours. Less temptation that way. A particular issue for younger vampires who don't get enough sustenance." It was on the tip of my tongue to ask him what he meant exactly by "sustenance" but then he brought us to a halt in front of a massive stone building with fountains and imposing marble steps leading up to its entrance. The steps were crowded with people who were lounging, taking pictures or eating. The scent of hot dogs made my stomach take notice.

"This is it. The MET," he announced, gesturing to the building with its colorful banners. The Metropolitan Museum of Art. My heart raced. I'd studied its collections online and in books. Mark Rothko and Van Gough under the same roof. There were even Egyptian mummies, which I'd always wanted to see. I turned to him, energized. "Can we go inside?"

Murad responded with a huge grin and gestured towards the entrance. I soaked up every detail of the interior hall as Murad paid our admission fees. Once we reached the bottom of the main marble staircase, he pulled me aside, waiting until my awed gaze shifted from the spacious ceilings to his face.

"I have several paintings on exhibit here. All under aliases. The museum likes to move things around and rotate collections, yet I'm hoping the piece I want to show you is on display. I want to play a little game and see if you can find this painting without any help from me." I frowned uneasily. The museum must have thousands of paintings. No way would I be able to find Murad's without knowing his style or the name he'd assumed.

"Take your time. Meander. I have all the time in the world," he said calmly. I shrugged. If he wanted to follow me around while I soaked up the museum, he was welcome to it. There was no way I could locate a painting with so little to go on. I wandered, noticing the startled glances of a few people we crossed paths with. Murad would nod with a tight smile, and they would bow their heads deeply, hastily moving from our path. It was an unwelcome reminder that he was more than what he seemed and that the world I *thought* I'd known was really much more complex.

He followed me patiently as we explored the Egyptian wing and ancient Greek grave stelae before making my way up the wide marble staircase. According to the map I swiped from a kiosk, European paintings here were categorized by type and time period. I stood mesmerized before the brushstrokes of impressionist masters and great artists who'd captured iconic imagery with passion and sly wit. Many I'd seen in books or posters. As we walked, a mild tugging sensation took root in my chest. I noticed that Murad began watching me with a half-smile, as if anticipating something. The longing intensified as we moved room to room. I hurried across creaking parquet floors, my eyes scanning and discarding as I went. Once I even wormed my way in front of gawking tourists and was reprimanded by security guards who hushed when Murad came to my side.

When I entered the room, it was as if we'd entered the hushed sanctum of a house of worship—one in which generations of hopes and prayers had permeated the very structure. The oil painting filled almost an entire wall in the smallish room. A polished wooden bench sat before it. I approached slowly, along the edge of the opposite wall, stalking it. The frame was old and decorative, its paint flaking away in places to reveal wood. The painting itself appeared at first glance to be a jumble of dark hues with no form. It was a reconciliation that made no sense.

I drew nearer, sitting on the bench. I stared and stared, knowing I was witnessing something both mysterious and authentic in a mad world. The colors lightened and I gasped. What I had taken for a mass of brown and russet strokes became a forest at nighttime; the sun's dying light caressed bare branches and hidden places. Fallen trees lay on the forest floor, giving life to a future ecosystem. It was the grandeur of nature and its fallow season fully understood and executed. Details came to life as my eyes adjusted and contrasts appeared. I stood and stepped close to the canvas. Two tiny figures walked through the forest floor. A third figure appeared as a half face and shoulder, peering out between a tangle of branches.

The painting continued to lighten the more I studied it. Leaning over, I read the simple white placard beside its frame. *The Woods Before Dawn* by William Carter. He'd used an alias.

Murad stepped near and handed me a white handkerchief. I accepted the soft cloth, wiping my face before blowing my nose. I silently dared him to say something, but he only smiled ruefully. He really was very handsome. I wadded the fabric into a ball and sank onto the bench.

"Is this your painting?" I asked quietly.

"Yes." He sat next to me and placed his palms against spread thighs. "It is."

"How...why?"

He leaned forward, his hawkish gaze on the painting for what seemed an eternity.

"Many years ago, in my search for Lila, I followed a tip from an informant that led me to Fontainebleau Forest, outside of Paris. It was less populated then, very rural; Clara and Tess joined my search, thinking she might reveal herself to them, if not to me. No one confessed to seeing anything useful, least of all a sleeping woman in an elaborate glass box." His half-smile was sheepish as he cleared his throat.

"But I *knew* she'd been there. I felt her there in my bones. So close. The agony of hope is something I have lived with for a very long time." The tightness of his voice resonated with the uncomfortable pain in my own heart. Without thinking, I touched his hand and he was suddenly clasping mine. It felt nice.

"I understand your grief, Stella. Lila was lost in her own anguish over my savagery. I caused it. I lost the love of my life to something I had no control over. This painting was my outlet and what you feel when you see it is likely a shadow of intense longing. Alaric showed me your work and I felt grief. I think you have the ability to paint magick into your art. Certain humans over time have held this magick but not to the degree of your work. It is rare even among the Primati."

I studied the painting with fresh understanding. He'd painted Lila peering from a tangle of winter branches, elusive within the enormous landscape. Without careful study, she wasn't immediately visible, adrift as she was in the dark. I ignored the magick comment, figuring he meant it figuratively.

"As to why you were drawn to it—I've noticed over the years that humans who are sensitive in nature seem the most affected by it. I worked off and on for over twenty years on this piece. Perhaps imbued it with a piece of my soul, if I were capable of having one." *I would never want a soul so bleak, no matter how beautiful,* I thought. But wasn't all observed art like touching someone's soul?

"It certainly has a magnetic quality. I think I could sit here and look at it for days," I said truthfully.

"And that is the trap, Stella. It is not healthy to wallow in our sorrow. Grief is love in equal proportion, but whereas love is selfless, its equal measure in grief can become a madness that consumes as surely as a black hole upon the cosmos.

"No one can tell you when your grief for Silvan is ready to evolve into something you can live with. That's okay, Stella. Just know that I understand what you are going through, and you're not alone."

His words broke something fragile inside. *You're not alone.*

"It was my fault," I whispered. He stiffened beside me.

"Amanda didn't want to come but I made her anyway. If Amanda hadn't been there, then Marcus wouldn't have found me there, and Silvan would still be alive." The words left me in a rush. There was no relief with sharing their weight.

Minutes passed and then Murad spoke in a calm, measured voice.

"I will say this but once. It was *not* your fault, Stella. What happened was the result of a thousand small decisions by many people, over many years, that had to have occurred beforehand. It is the web of life itself. One day you will see this clearly, but for now you can only feel and then release this undeserved guilt." He patted my hand.

"Let it pass through you like a fog, moving through you to the other side." We sat in silence for a while longer, studying the painting. As it became harder and harder to lift my eyelashes, Murad stood with a reluctant smile.

"You're tired. We should go back."

We strolled back to the apartment building in comfortable silence. There was no identification of the penthouse on the floor selection buttons but Murad typed into a keypad. As we entered the elevator, I forced past a new shyness to make eye contact. "Thank you."

He nodded with a tilt of his chin. The elevator opened to melodic peals of laughter. Alaric stood near a grand piano in the living room, a beautiful strawberry blonde hugging his arm as she smiled up at him. My entire focus zeroed upon the exact spot where she leaned against his arm. He seemed at ease, as if they were old friends.

"Stella!" Tess leapt up from a couch and hugged me. It was a very brief embrace. "Uh, when was the last time you showered?" she whispered in my ear. I flushed, folding my arms and trying to appear smaller. When did everyone get so opinionated over hygiene? The Titian-haired beauty approached. I glanced at Alaric, who greeted Murad in muffled tones. His overt disregard stung.

"Hi, Stella! I'm Clara. I've known you since you were six years old but you wouldn't know that. I'm very glad to finally meet you in person." *Clara?* We appeared the same age. How could she be the leader of an entire continent of witches? Who would ever take her seriously?

"I know who you are. You allowed a monster to kidnap my friend and murder my cousin," I hissed. Tess gasped and Clara's smile faltered. The men's conversation fell silent, and Alaric appeared at my side. Clara studied me with narrowed eyes before flicking her gaze towards the men.

"Oh, relax. I'm not going to turn her into a toad," she said, her upper lip curling. I raised an eyebrow but refrained from making a snarky comment. Something told me she wasn't Queen of a heck load of magical beings because she was pretty.

"You're right, Stella," Clara said, crossing her arms. "I failed Amanda and you. I thought I'd contained the sorcerer but he escaped. I'm doing everything I can to rectify my underestimation of his benefactor and bring them both to justice.

"I'm also very sorry for the loss of your cousin, Stella. He seemed a sweet boy and I'm sure many people will miss him."

Her apology reeked of sincerity, damn it. Alaric avoided my eyes to stare at my throat. Throwing a fit was not going to make any difference. In fact, it might make things more uncomfortable for Alaric to have important people argue with a guest in his home. I nodded. The tension eased and Tess breathed an audible sigh of relief. Murad and Alaric drifted back to the living room.

"How's Amanda?" I asked.

"Amanda is quite sad actually, but that's to be expected with losing a close friend and then another disappearing. She hasn't touched her Pagatio since that day, despite our assurances that it's been cleansed. You'll see her soon at the Grand Council." It stung that my staying away had left Amanda to cope alone. I missed her but couldn't bear to talk about Silvan right now with anyone. Even her.

Tess tapped Clara on the arm. "Speaking of the Grand Council, before your betrothal can become official, you'll need to be a member of the Primati. Joining a witch clan will expedite your claim and give you credibility. Don't worry about the vote—it's really just ceremony." *Wait. There was a vote?*

"The dressmakers will be here in an hour, Stella," Tess said with restrained excitement.

"Dressmakers?" I asked, confused.

"She means stylists," Clara responded. "The stylists are coming by with selections from a few upcoming fashion collections."

" You said that you don't like to shop, so I thought you might prefer this instead. They'll come here so there's no need to worry about claustrophobic dressing rooms and prying eyes." It took all my will power not to mirror Clara's rolled eyes.

"Don't forget to tell her about the hairdresser and makeup artist from Henri Bendel," Clara added, eyeing my greasy, messy bun. My "look?" What was wrong with the one I had? Nothing, that's what. Trying too hard was worse than not trying at all.

I couldn't fault Clara's envious looks, but I eyed her unusual combination of white crop top, green and white striped cocktail skirt, and pink shoes. She noted my once-over with a mischievous grin and twirled.

I crossed my arms. "No."

"We've gone to considerable trouble to make these arrangements. Just pretend you're playing a part. If not for yourself than for Murad," Tess pleaded.

"Considerable trouble? You made one phone call, sister. I was there. But you are right about Stella dressing for the part. Murad can't have his future queen in rags, can he?" Clara's thoughtful gaze moved to where the men were still engaged in a deep conversation. Did she just call my clothing rags?

"Stella, maybe you want to go take a shower before they arrive?" suggested Tess.

" I *was* already planning to take a shower…anyway." Tess nodded while Clara hid a smirk. I stomped away, veering my path through Alaric's bedroom and into his bathroom. You know what? They could just wait. I'd take a bath instead. Perhaps the unwanted visitors would take a big hint and *leave*. I didn't need a stylist or anyone else to judge me right now.

A knock sometime later startled me from a drowsy soak, the bubbles long gone. Alaric? Instantly awake, I prepared to give him heck. How dare he throw me to the wolves like this? I climbed out of the tub, wrapped myself in a towel and flung open the door.

Clara and Tess stood in the doorway. Tess stared at my dry hair with a frown, covering the rounding of her mouth with a slim hand.

Clara's expression morphed from surprised to gritty determination. I took several steps back, not trusting that look. I'd seen it on Midora's face several times, just before her sisters sprung an ambush.

"Stop, Clara!" Tess cried as Clara pushed past me to enter the bathroom. "Give her a choice."

My eyebrows shot up. *A choice about what?*

"Fine. She makes us wait an hour for her, which is downright rude, but you want to give her a choice." Clara snapped. She leaned against a sink and crossed her slender arms. Tess followed her into the room with an apologetic wringing of hands.

"Stella. I know you better than you realize. I know you want to tell us to fuck off—yet trust me when I say that you will want to feel your most confident before the Grand Council," Clara said in a clipped voice.

"Especially since Daria Demir, the Earth Witch Queen will be there and she's both paranoid and ambitious," added Tess. Clara nodded tersely.

"Daria is bat-shit loco and just coming out of the ground as punishment for a serious crime. Stay out of her way. We need her there to have a formal quorum of votes so she can't challenge you in the future. In exchange for her cooperation, Murad agreed to allow her to circumvent her sentence," Clara continued, her voice thick with disapproval.

"Murad is doing this for you, but she won't be grateful. Don't engage her in any way. She has an obsession with power and you'll be seen as a threat. Just stay clear of her," Tess warned.

If they knew me at all then they would know they just placed this Daria on my top three most fascinating people list. I couldn't wait to meet her. But not under these circumstances.

"Listen—I know that Amanda mentioned something about my jumping off that cliff, but I have no power. Please don't get your hopes up. If I'm tested or whatever, I'll fail. So, you can just send my regrets to this Council or cancel it right now. If it means not marrying Murad, that's okay by me. I don't know why you think a curse can be broken after so many years, anyway." Clara shook her head as if she'd never seen a denser human being.

"The Grand Council was scheduled long before you, Stella. We call one every Autumn Equinox. We're just adding your membership into the Primati to the agenda," Tess said before picking up a small white cake of soap from the sink. She walked over to the soaking tub.

"As far as the curse is concerned—we think that it may have grown weaker with time. There's value in making an effort to break it. Watch, Stella. Do you see how calm the surface is?" Tess dropped the bar of soap into the center of the still filled tub, creating waves in the blue and green sparkling water. I may have gone overboard with the bath bombs Grayson had placed under the sink.

"Enchantments are like these ripples. It's about intention. See how the ripples are stronger from the epicenter and then get much smaller, fading as they expand? I think Lila's curse is like this. The original enchantment was devastating, but subsequent generations have served to weaken it. This is why I think your mother demonstrated some gifts. This is what led to her being discovered.

"There were rumors about a human girl with power living in San Francisco. She died before we could meet her and determine the truth of any power she held. There's no reason *not* to believe you will have even greater strength; the enchantment's original intention came into being so long ago it might not even affect you."

"As long as you take precautions. Avoiding romance until you pass twenty-one is a good start. Marrying Murad is insurance. He's immortal, and the marriage will be in name only but technically, a marriage makes him your mate," added Clara.

"What if I'd been born gay?" I asked, curious. Tess tilted her head while Clara tapped her chin in thought.

"That wouldn't really solve the problem," Clara said slowly. "You would still fall in love with a mortal, and as a woman, you're still presumably able to give birth as there are several options in the modern world. The enchantment would likely lead you to want to try to procreate," she said. I shrugged. It wasn't like I could change who I was anyway.

I sat on the edge of the tub, considering.

"What choices were you talking about when you first came in?"

Clara positioned herself in front of the door and jutted her delicate chin. "We can take you into that shower and scrub you within an inch of your life—or I can perform the same with a magick spell. What's it to be?" Clara asked.

I scowled. I didn't want anyone using magick on me ever again. But the thought of being manhandled naked seemed an even worse choice. Something about the gleam in Clara's eyes told me she'd be a fierce opponent in a tussle. I was suddenly exhausted.

"Magick," I chose. Clara rubbed her palms together.

"You're gonna love this," she promised, her smile feral.

Chapter 22
Justice

Stella

I fidgeted before Tess and Clara.

"Well. I would say your bonding spell on her looks has dissipated," Tess murmured to Clara.

"Safe to say. I just can't get over the resemblance," Clara muttered.

Whatever spell Clara had cast, my scalp and body felt squeaky clean. She'd then spoken some words and my hair had dried. If there was ever a reason to learn or be skilled at magick it was to save time getting ready in the morning.

"Can I look now?" I asked for the umpteenth time. Alarmed by their silence, I turned to face the mirror and jumped. When I raised a hand to my cheek, the girl in the mirror did the same.

"What did you do to me?" I whispered.

"I think the cleanup spell may have cleared away the last of the physical bonding enchantment. It detoxes anything that doesn't belong," Clara said as her wide eyes wandered over my reflection. Apparently, I wasn't the only one in shock. Tess appeared just as unhappy as I felt.

"If it removes things then why am I wearing makeup?" I squeaked.

"That's just an enhancement spell. It was meant to dry and trim up your hair a bit—darken your eyelashes. What you see is almost entirely you, Stella," she said.

I stared at the stranger in the mirror. I looked older somehow. My thick blonde hair now held platinum highlights. Siren waves fell across my shoulders and down my back. My eyes were a more vivid shade of blue and fringed with sooty, long lashes. I peered closer and noticed freakish silver strands of color streaking from my irises.

Even my eyebrows were perfectly groomed and symmetrical. I rubbed my lips and checked my fingers. No trace of lipstick, although my lips were fuller and a rose shade unlike their usual color. My body seemed a little fuller in places as well. A thought raced and I checked my thigh. Nope. The pale line I'd acquired from being thrown from a horse was still there. Relief filled me at that at least. I'd earned my scars.

"She looks just like a petite version of Lila. How is this possible after so many generations?" Tess gasped with a dumbfounded expression. Anger flashed, and my hands squeezed into tight fists.

"No more. No more secrets and no more deception. I mean it! I'm tired of being a plaything." I turned back to the mirror and tried not to hyperventilate. Throughout all of the recent craziness, I was still me. The same boring but "me" face. I swung around on Clara.

"Turn me back to how I normally look," I demanded.

She shook her head, stepping backward. "You just told us not to do magick on you. Not to deceive. This really is *you*, Stella. If I change you back, *that* would be the lie." Tess jumped in. "Clara is right—but witches with skill can change their appearance. This is not the end of the world if you want to one day change your appearance," she sympathized. Clara frowned at her and Tess shrugged. I floundered for a moment, working out what I wanted to say. Then a pounding at the door interrupted us.

"Stella! Are you okay? I felt...I thought I heard raised voices." It was Alaric.

I freaked out, frozen, while Tess moved to open the door. As she turned the handle, I grabbed a towel off the sink and covered my head. When the door thumped open beneath the force of Alaric's hand, I pushed past everyone and ran to my bedroom. Locking it behind me I hurried to the closet. Grabbing undergarments, I added a pink patterned peasant skirt and a navy t-shirt and quickly dressed.

A discreet knock sounded just as I pulled the shirt over my head.

"Ms. Avery? Stella—Alaric asks that you join them in the library." Grayson. From experience I knew he wouldn't leave unless I acknowledged him.

"No." Seconds ticked by.

"Stella. He's very worried about you. If you don't come out, I'm afraid he *will* make a scene coming in here after you," Grayson said calmly. Which would raise eyebrows from Murad as to why Alaric cared so much about my well-being.

I paced the room and sighed. "Give me a few minutes." Silence loomed. I hurried to my dresser and grabbed a hair tie, pulling my mane into a low messy bun. A glance at the mirror proved that it just made my face stand out even more. I had like, zero pores and the girl in the mirror started looking terrified again. I pulled off the tie and moved hair close to the sides of my face, hoping it would distract from the changes. Shoulders back, I left my room for the library.

It was crowded, Jing having returned from wherever it was she'd gotten to. I stood in the doorway; eyes downcast to hide the nerves fluttering in my stomach. I refused to seek out Alaric, still annoyed with his ignoring me and putting me in this predicament.

"My God," Murad muttered. I glanced up to find him approaching with purposeful steps. I tensed as the inhumanness of his movements, noticing that his eyes had darkened to deepest red. There was a stillness to the room that confirmed I wasn't the only one to notice Murad's lack of control.

"Lila?" he growled. The astounded hope in his claret eyes softened my anxiety. Oh, God, he thought he was seeing his lost love. I blinked rapidly to clear my vision. As he drew nearer, the hope in his expression faded, replaced with chagrin.

"No. Of course, you aren't Lila. You're Stella," he murmured apologetically. He blinked and his eyes were once more a warm brown. I was just glad he was moving normally again. That glimpse made me realize that Murad was much more than the façade he presented.

"I'm sorry, my dear. For a second, across the room...but of course you are yourself," he said. I allowed him to take my hands and stood passively as he pressed his lips to the back of each one. I squeezed his hands, feeling guilty for causing him pain.

"The resemblance is uncanny," he explained.

"She doesn't look any different to me," boomed Alaric, and I found him much closer than I'd thought. He was scowling. It was the most perfect thing he could have said. Maybe it would be okay. He looked away and my heart sank.

"Agreed. Stella is just as ugly as she ever was," Jing San added blandly. Laughter bubbled up from my throat, the sound more hysterical than amused.

Murad's shoulders rounded. I couldn't imagine what he must be going through. Impulsively, I put my arms around him. It felt good when he hugged me back. Now that I knew his story, I better understood how upsetting this must be. He pulled away, taking my hands again.

"I'm sure this is a shock to you as well. Especially coming on the heels of such a loss. What do *you* need right now, to feel alright with this?" Murad asked. His earnest interest in my well-being made it easy to respond.

"Time would be nice. If everyone can just leave us—me—alone for a while. I promise I won't fall back into sleeping all day. I just don't want to talk to strangers and try on a bunch of clothes." I didn't look at Clara and Tess but they had to understand I was referring to them. I didn't give a flip if they thought I was being uncooperative. Between the museum trip and the shock of my reflection, I'd hit my limit.

Murad nodded. "Consider it done." I blinked. That was way easier than expected.

"Murad! We need to at least take her measurements," Tess yelped, fluttering her delicate hands.

"Murad is right, Tess. This was a big shock and we need to let Stella come to terms with it," Clara said. There was a speculative gleam in her eyes and I expected retaliation. Tess flipped hair as shiny as a raven's wing behind her shoulders.

"Ugh! Of course. Our Noble King has spoken." Her lips twisted wryly as she continued, "I suppose we can handle any last-minute alterations—Murad, why don't we go have cocktails at Tavern on the Green? We haven't done that in ages." Tess looped her arm through his and gently tugged. He stood immovable and she stepped back when he bent to kiss both of my cheeks in the European fashion. As he leaned in, I saw Tess frown over his shoulder. She saw me notice and offered an encouraging smile. She was trying to distract him. Gratitude swelled to have her at my back.

"You are a survivor. Never forget that," he whispered before pulling back. He eyed Alaric. "Take care of her." Alaric nodded, as did Jing. I followed the group to the elevators. The evil wink Clara gave me, while the others were turned away, only confirmed my suspicions. When they returned for me in three weeks I expected to be presented with the ugliest dress in creation.

The elevator doors finally closed, to my immense relief.

"Well, you just earned a reprieve. Use your time wisely," Jing San said before disappearing deeper into the apartment. I hadn't yet figured out where she went to and I'd never seen her leave by the elevator. Alaric studied me impassively and I pushed a loose strand of hair behind my right ear, self-conscious. He broke the silence.

"I've arranged for your artwork to be crated tomorrow. They'll be shipped to his Majesty's home—Murad's home in Paris," he said stonily. I didn't give a fig about the canvases, and I didn't like him planning to get rid of me so quickly. Before he could step away, I latched onto his wrist. He froze, then tugged easily from my grasp.

"Wait! Can I talk with you?"

He crooked a finger over his shoulder and continued long strides to his office. I followed his broad shoulders, a lump of nerves in my throat. Alaric deliberately kept the door wide open. I waited for him to move away and then closed it firmly. When he sat behind his desk, I refused to let him hide behind it. Moving to his side, I planted myself on the corner of his desk, facing him. He pushed my skirt away from his legs and looked towards the wall of windows with a bored sigh. I drank in his gorgeous profile. His white dress shirt lay open at the neck, its sleeves rolled-up to reveal strong forearms. He didn't look over twenty-three years old but I'd recently learned that with Primati, looks can be deceiving.

"How old are you?"

"A lot older than you," he responded coldly. His aloofness seemed infinite; the tender companion I'd spent the last weeks with had disappeared with the arrival of Murad.

"I've been told witches can change their appearance—mask their age. And it made me wonder how old you are. Are you over a hundred?" I persisted.

"Stella, is this what you wanted to discuss with me?" he asked, his jaw tightening.

"Why are you acting like this?" I responded with testiness.

"Like what?"

"Like someone different from the man who's been sleeping next to me. Who seemed to care about whether I lived or died?" A muscle jumped in his jaw but then he picked up a piece of paper from his desk and read from it. I bit my tongue and prayed for strength. Confidence surged when I noticed the paper was upside down.

"It's the spell removal, isn't it? I look different. You don't like it."

"It makes no difference to me. You were fine before and equally so now. Your appearance is unrelated to the content of your character. I meant what I said before."

A non-answer. Could I get a witch to alter my appearance to someone he might find more attractive? A brunette beauty with dark eyes or to become taller? Was it possible? Was it worth gaining his admiration? My stomach roiled. As much as I hated not feeling connected to what was in the mirror, the changes weren't stupendous. I knew in my gut that I couldn't—wouldn't change my physical self for someone unless it was for *me*.

"I believe you. I know I would like you even if you looked different. Do you like *me*, Alaric?" He met my gaze then, and I drew in a breath at what I saw. Stormy eyes tinged with despair and longing. They told me his secrets.

"Do I like you? Of course, I *like* you," he said harshly, glancing away. I inched closer. "Do you *more* than like me?" This mattered so much. He had to accept this.

"What is it with these school girl questions? You're engaged to someone. Royalty no less."

"I don't see a ring on my finger," I said. He frowned.

"I'm sure it's an oversight and he will give you one soon." Desperation clawed up my spine. I was not a girl who considered things, making checklists of pros and cons. I launched forward, landing sideways on his lap. His hands were trapped by my flowing skirt, giving me time to place one arm around his neck, while the other turned his gorgeous face to mine.

"Damn it, Stella," he whispered furiously. "Stop this." He turned his head but didn't shove me off his lap, though he easily could have. Hope surged.

"I don't care. Look at me," I begged. Baleful eyes met mine and his jaw clenched. Before he could speak or shove me away, I pressed my lips to his. Once, twice, and then I lingered, investigating the shape of his mouth. His lips were hard and unyielding—at first.

Then they crashed upon mine as he straightened, meeting my reckless exploration with a hunger that matched my own. There was a hopelessness to his kiss that I tried to erase with soft reassurance. His warm hand drifted beneath my skirt, cupping the skin of my outer thigh, startling me. His hand moved no further, yet his caressing fingers electrified, causing me to tremble. I clutched him closer, wanting to dissolve into him, yet also needing to remember what I'd set out to accomplish.

I pulled away first this time. At first he refused to allow it, crushing me closer. Self-satisfaction sunk warm and deep into every cell of my body. I was making him admit with his kiss what he couldn't say out loud. He finally leaned his head back against his chair, his eyes never leaving mine. There he was. The boy from the movie theatre.

"Stella, you are, without a doubt, making this worse. We have to stop." His voice caressed my name, belying his words.

"Why did you save me—bring me here?" Boneless, I tried to focus on anything but his lips. My heart was galloping a mile a minute, my every sense prickling at his nearness.

"Duty?" he suggested darkly. I shook my head.

"I think you more than like me. I more than like you, too."

"Stella..." he groaned.

"Wait. Hear me out. To be honest, I wonder myself if it's the enchantment at work. What I feel seems *real,* though. You were there for me when I needed you, but it's more than that. I only feel complete when you're in the room. I've felt this since that day in the woods." He jerked and I touched his throat with one hand, willing him to understand.

"You're also forgetting that I *am* going to die. We *all* die. Well, maybe not you for a long time. But I would rather live a short life that *I* choose over a life that other people decide for me. Losing Silvan, knowing how fragile life is, everything seems much clearer." He leaned his head back against the chairback, eyes hooded and indiscernible.

"If there's a chance I can break the enchantment, then great. But whether I have one year or two hundred, I want to spend it with the man I feel something for. I choose you. You just need to accept it and get over all this chivalry. We can find a way." There. My cards were all on the table. Alaric tried to lift me off his lap but I clung to the tall leather seat back.

"Wait! I'm not stupid, Alaric. We don't have to do…the deed," my cheeks warmed, "until we get past this stupid timeline. Murad is just doing me a kindness—as a family friend. I know you must be impressed with him in your world, but trust me—he's no threat to what I feel for you."

Alaric's lips twitched but then he ran his nose along my jaw, nuzzling the sensitive skin beneath my ear. "The deed?" he murmured against my skin. The room went fuzzy as his lips moved against my neck. His fingers trailed along the bare skin between my throat and shoulder, making me heated and dizzy.

"I must be mad. What is it that you feel for me, Stella?" His voice was husky with that whiskey-smooth tone. My eyes burned as I erupted with my pent-up secrets.

"I love you, Alaric. As crazy as that seems in such a short time. I love you. I don't know for certain if it's the enchantment because I've never felt like this before. But I can't imagine this feeling ever going away."

"You are too young to know what love is," he whispered against my hair.

"*That's* crazy talk. Love is *more* intense when you're my age. I won't change my mind. What I'm asking you to consider is to wait for me."

He raised his beautiful brown eyes to mine, and it was my turn to look away. He lifted long fingers to my face, holding me immobile for his perusal.

"Stella, be very clear about what you want. What are you suggesting *exactly*?"

"You seem to have lived a long life. Three years can't be so long in comparison. For me, three years without you seems like forever. Time will pass slowly if I don't have you in my life. I can still be married to Murad in name only—and we can still see each other. Discreetly and platonically." I choked on that last word but rushed to get it out, afraid he would stop me at any moment.

"I see the way women look at you, and it makes me want to do bad things, even if I can empathize. I know I don't want to break this curse only to find you've disappeared, moved on to someone else." I was putting my whole self out there, hoping he felt the same.

"Stella...you won't feel this way later. You don't know me that well.

There are things about me I haven't told you..." He drew in a ragged breath.

"I don't care! Nothing you tell me could change how I feel about you. I accept you for whoever you are. Why can't you trust me?" I grabbed his hand, pressing his palm to my cheek.

"This is an infatuation, Stella." His fingers curled into my hair, as if he couldn't help himself. Then he stood abruptly with me in his arms and I realized how much of my coercion he'd merely allowed. He plopped me unceremoniously upon his desk before he leaned forward with fists pressed to the wooden surface on either side of my hips.

He tried to look stern but then his lips were on my face, running across my eyelids in feather light sweeps before trailing down my cheeks and across my sensitive lips.

"Damn it, Stella. I'm not good for you. This...attraction...could get you killed. It's too hard for me not to touch you. I've never struggled like this in my entire, very long life."

It took considerable mental fortitude, but I pushed against his chest until he stood upright, no longer touching me.

"We can be smart. I'm very strong-willed in case you didn't notice—", He chuckled and I slapped his chest playfully, "—we can spend time together and not kiss or touch. I just want to be with you. I don't want to go away and miss you so much my soul feels inside out."

I saw the moment he teetered. So close I could taste it. And then it was gone. He raked hands through his hair and then shoved them into the pockets of his black trousers, rolling his shoulders back. The motion stretched the fabric over his arms and chest in delicious ways yet I kept my word to be discreet and platonic, only glancing quickly. Several times.

"You are beautiful, Stella. Inside and out. You are also still grieving Silvan." He strode to the windows and turned his back to me. I wanted to join him, wrap my arms around him from behind. But I needed to prove to him that I could exercise restraint.

"I think you might be feeling an absence with Silvan's loss," he began. "Perhaps you're trying to fill one love with a different kind. I cannot deny there is an attraction but you don't know the difference yet between lust and real..."

A heavy domed paperweight sailed through the air and collided with his back. He turned and glared at me in surprise. I glared right back.

Springing to my feet, I yelled, "You don't get to psychoanalyze me if it's to turn me away. I *know* what I feel. If you don't share my feelings or are unwilling to give up dating for a few measly years, then that's your choice entirely. But don't try to dismiss what I know I feel." Angry tears pinpricked and I clenched my palms hard, fighting for control. His face shuttered and he turned his back to me once more.

"Stella. This is impossible. It's in your best interests to forget about our time together. You'll have a long and happy life with this arrangement with Murad. You don't know me well enough, nor have you lived long enough, to decide something so important. I'm also not a man to sneak in the shadows. You're an impulsive child with a temper. I don't have time for you."

Each word pierced my soul. I knew he cared about me. I felt it in his kiss. His hands. How could he behave as if he couldn't get enough of me and then just coldly throw me away to someone else?

"I suggest you look forward to your wedding." He concluded flatly. The ice prince was back. He wasn't even giving us a chance. Smoothing my skirt, I dug deep for dignity as I moved towards the door. He spoke quietly as my fingers touched the knob.

"I'm stepping out to torture someone in the basement and will be gone awhile. I'd appreciate it if you behaved yourself for at least one night." There was Alaric. Arrogant and making jokes as if something important hadn't just happened. Tears burned by nose and eyes but I refused to turn around.

"Thank you for allowing me to stay here. I appreciate your hospitality," I said stiffly, to the solid wooden door before me. I left, proud of the mature way I closed the door behind me. It was quiet in the apartment. I considered returning to my room but was afraid of the lure my bed held. I could so easily get sucked back into the black hole of melancholy. I wandered into the kitchen where Grayson was decorating a cake.

"Impressive, Grayson. You should have been a chef," I commented, my voice sounding fragile and unnatural even to my own ears. His pleased smile faded when he glanced up and got his first full look at me.

"Oh, yeah. Clara removed the last of the ugly juice. I look like this now." I circled my head with my middle finger. He closed his mouth and continued his work, apparently willing to go along with my deflection.

"Apologies, Ms. Avery. I didn't mean to stare. It's just that you...look more refreshed today," he finished. I climbed unsteadily onto a stool at the kitchen island.

"Thank you, Grayson. Murad was freaked out a bit."

"I'm sure he'll recover," Grayson assured me.

"One hopes. Hey, is there anything to eat?" I asked. His surprised smile told me the change of subject worked. Grayson dropped his knife and leapt towards the enormous refrigerator. He practically hummed as he began taking out prepared dishes. We discussed the merits of this and that before compromising on a bowl of reheated mac and cheese. I took a tentative bite and gave Grayson a thumbs up. He stopped staring and resumed squeezing a pastry bag filled with royal icing onto the vanilla cake.

"I'm sure it was quite a shock," he said amiably.

"Do you know where Jing San went?" I asked around another bite.

"Wherever she likes, I imagine. She's enjoying her freedom these days after being tied to the West Coast," he said. I shook my head. It hadn't been my choice she'd hung out in Portland. "I've never seen her actually arrive or leave the apartment. Where does she go?" I asked. Grayson frowned and switched from one pasty bag to another.

"Jing San has an adjoining apartment to this one. As she's been friends with Alaric for years, he offered her the property when it was built. There's an entrance in the library but it's a secret. I would not recommend ever looking for it unless you want to be severed in half," he said mildly. Bless this man for understanding I needed a distraction. Challenge received and accepted.

The cake smelled amazing. I watched him carefully craft small roses from icing along the border. "Are there any pictures of her? Lila, I mean."

Grayson rubbed his chin with a gloved hand, squinting over my shoulder. "There used to be several portraits. She was, understandably, a sensitive topic for many years. I believe any portraits remaining would be with His Majesty. Perhaps if you asked, he might show them to you." I deflated. Asking Murad to pick at a wound was not something I could do. It would be like kicking puppies.

"Did you ever meet her?" I asked, curious.

"Unfortunately, that was before my time. I was a captain of the British Empire under Earl Lloyd-George of Dwyfor in 1915, during World War I. We battled the Ottomans, you know. That was how I first met Alaric." I stared at Grayson, trying to wrap my mind around his age. It was hard to imagine Alaric living such a long life. When Grayson seemed distracted, I scooped a finger full of icing. He smacked my hand with a spatula. The man had eyes in the back of his head. While I nursed my fingers, he cut a thick piece of the completed cake and placed it on a fancy dessert plate before sliding it across to me. He waited expectantly. I took a bite, rolling my eyes as it melted on my tongue. I hadn't felt hungry for so long and the sugar was just the right sweetness.

"Amazing, Grayson." I waved my dessert fork for emphasis. He flashed a pleased smile before moving to clean up.

"Would it be rude of me to ask—what you are, Grayson? I mean, you've obviously lived a long time, but you don't eat and I've noticed your interesting way of...getting around." I said delicately.

"Ah. I'm a shade, Ms. Avery," he responded. I glumly licked the back of my spoon, waiting for him to explain what that meant. He leaned against the counter, sponge in hand.

"A shade is someone that has been brought back from the dead. Neither dead, nor alive. This is very different from a wraith. A wraith is a dead, hungry thing that is a slave to whomever holds their enchanted bones. Stay away from wraiths, Ms. Avery." He returned to wiping the black marble counter.

"So—are you a ghost or something? Is that how you're able to move around like a shadow?"

"Not exactly. A shade occurs when a Primati with exceptional power wills their own life into a person at the moment of death. The two become bonded. As long as the Primati being lives, the shadow of the person who should have passed over is tied to them. As you can see, a shade retains their intelligence and delightful personality. We can choose to disagree with the being who keeps us alive. A wraith is a dead person. Devoid of their soul or humanity, they are often used by sorcerers to do dark deeds on their behalf.

"And before you can ask, Alaric created me as I am now. We'd partnered on military missions together, and when he discovered me shot in a ditch by a shared enemy, he asked me if I wanted to live. He offered me a choice and saved me. Here I am, all these years later," Grayson said on a bow, flourishing a dish towel.

"There are others like me in Master Alaric's guard, yet I'm responsible for the others and keep things organized," he said with a humble tilt of his head.

"I'm sure he's very grateful to have you in his life, Grayson," I said with a lump in my throat. I might love-hate the man's ever-loving guts right now, but I was still glad he had Grayson to look after him.

"Well. We look out for each other," he said, removing his apron and tossing his gloves into a bin. "I must be going now. It's my night off and there is a game of darts and a certain pub in Brighton expecting me," he said, rubbing his palms together briskly. He disappeared before my eyes. I blinked, unaccustomed to people doing things like that. The silence of the kitchen was depressing. I longed to return to my bed and sob into my sheets for days. Instead, I slid off my stool and washed and dried my plate and fork. The sun was still up and I set off to find Jing San's secrets.

Chapter 23
The Seeker

Alaric

She had fucking *embraced* him.

The image of Stella in my brother's arms had seared into my mind. My thoughts were interrupted by gurgling cries. I stared with regret at the broken man before me. He sat tied to a chair in my interrogation room; a chamber which would have made the most experienced military operative green with envy. Long silver pins pierced his hands and encircled his wrists to the arms of the chair. A thin wire kept his neck in place and his body from sliding to the floor.

I turned away, haunted by Stella's indelible scent of freesia and sunshine. I could still feel the silk of her skin, the white glow of her aura as she cried out beneath my lips at her throat. I wish there was some way to bind the memory of her touch. The exact sensation of her skin so easily touching mine that I might recall it after she was gone from my reach. I locked my distracted musings away with great effort; there was work to be done.

I'd thought to work off the intense emotions Stella generated by continuing my interrogation of Marcus's follower, but he'd denied me that pleasure. As soon as he shared a name—Marcus—a mind spell exploded as effectively as a cyanide pill crushed beneath a tooth. The man was a shell, and his heart would soon stop beating.

I stepped into the next room and ordered my cadre to fire up the incinerator and dispose of the body. They moved quickly to follow my directions, and I transferred to a place far away from New York City.

The wind was sharp and cold on this high hill outside of Istanbul. The Bosphorus gleamed in the night air below, separating me from the distant hills of Russia. This small island once held an effective military fortress capable of stopping any ship foolish enough to attempt passage. I turned to behold the crumbling remains of the stone fort that had once housed hundreds of my soldiers. Voices rose from a modern military base far down the hill, yet I ignored them, marching toward the ruins.

It was dark and darker still inside the decaying building. Broken stones were covered in bird droppings and disturbed bats flapped overhead as I began to dig in the eastern corner. In time my efforts revealed a smooth stone with a partial seal still legible. I lifted the stone and peered into the dark chamber below. I hesitated, steeling myself to see something I hadn't unearthed for hundreds of years. Taking a breath, I dropped through the hole into a small, reinforced chamber. My vision was acute in the blackness, and relief swept through me to see the medium-sized box unmolested.

Opening the lid, I gazed upon the last memories of my mother.

Her favorite sea silk scarf called to me yet her fragrance was no more. My goal, a large jewelry case, soon weighted my hands. I raised its dusty lid and eyed the contents. Lila had lovingly wrapped each of my mother's favorite pieces in fabric, saving them from the harem's greedy fingers. I'd been a boy, unable to guess how much it would mean to me one day to possess her favorite objects. I unwrapped each cloth sachet, pausing briefly over a pair of dangling gold ear drops I remembered from my childhood. When a velvet bag revealed my mother's gold and sapphire ring, I relaxed. Stella said she had no engagement ring from Murad. I would give him this to present to her. The sapphire would match her eyes.

Placing the ring in my pocket, I focused my attention on the mother-of-pearl box that held her tears. Opening the box, I gazed upon the physical embodiment of my mother's sorrow. No one could explain the magic that had turned her tears to raw diamonds, yet Lila had collected them for me to keep. The box was half full. I did not touch their milky white surface, grief and guilt rising as ghosts to stay my hand. I had only ever parted with one. That one had gone to Lila's brother as a token of gratitude many years ago. I closed the box and returned the items to their hiding place.

I made certain the vault was utterly concealed with large boulders before I was satisfied. I owned this island and leased it privately to the state for the operation of a small Turkish military base below to ensure this historic place remained undisturbed. Such personal things did not belong in a cold bank treasury. I took in the silent hills and decided to visit an old friend. Closing my eyes, I shifted into the beast and transferred to the demon realm.

I found Jon standing over a fresh grave. The sky was red, with a skyline that burned with the ferocity of summer wildfires in all directions. Fine metal rain showered the landscape. It would have melted the flesh of mortals, yet my skin was impervious to it.

"What do you want?" Jon asked flatly.

"Who have you buried, old friend?" Jon's shoulders tightened at the words "old friend." Demons did not bury their dead. They burned them in the only fire strong enough to do so, Lucifer's Pit. This was unusual.

"My wife. A hybrid who was not strong enough for this plane—yet forbidden to the mortal plane you protect so well," Jon said bitterly. His wife must have been unstable. Demons who could pass as human and who demonstrated compassion for humans and self-control were allowed on the mortal realm. Even then, they were watched closely and tasked with specific work on behalf of the Primati. Hybrids, a forbidden mix of demon and human DNA, did not live much longer than humans did. Jon himself was the only exception I knew of. He appeared human, yet had demonstrated the longevity of a demon. Which wasn't that long when you considered most got themselves killed within their first century. Jon was closer to my age, which said a lot for his moderate temper and cleverness.

"I'm sorry for your loss," I told him finally. He rose and faced me. A fresh scar cut across his face, marring the visage of the blonde Bulgarian I remembered. He noticed where my gaze landed and laughed roughly.

"Got this trying to save her from mercury demons. Someone is stirring them up, and they are more aggressive than usual," Jon explained wearily.

"As long as they stay on this plane I cannot interfere. You've exiled yourself, Jon. Three hundred years is a long time. You are welcome—needed—on the mortal plane right now," I told him.

"How's that? Your brother is a real bastard, and I don't see that changing anytime soon," he said, spitting on the ground. I pulled on deep reserves of patience. Jon was a rebel who chaffed at the law and order Murad had implemented.

"One of Lila's daughter's survived. Her last descendant is a seventeen-year-old girl who is in danger. I can't be everywhere at once and need someone I trust at my back."

"How is that possible? The last time I saw Lila your brother had her locked in a box."

"She was. I can share the tale on our return. You'll need acclimating to the age, and I can have a safe house at your disposal while you get up to speed. In the meantime, do you feel up to helping me negotiate for dragon yew? Clara needs it and it will heal your face."

His expression softened at Clara's name. Jon looked at his wife's grave and his shoulders squared. "I make no promises but I'll help you find the dragon yew. For Clara," he clarified gruffly.

I nodded and he held out his arm in silence. I clasped his forearm and transferred us to the rocky cliff where the dragon yew tree grew. We were instantly surrounded by fire leopards. The cats grew upwards of four hundred pounds, their white fur streaked with grey markings. They could withstand extreme temperatures, ate a diet of pure meat, were highly intelligent and absolutely fearless; even I did not relish the sting their razor talons could inflict.

"You know the price," came a voice. I glanced behind us as a short demon approached. His skin could have been leather, his eyes completely black. The Keeper.

I nodded but allowed Jon to negotiate with the demon while I eyed a fire leopard that had crept too close. The females were larger than the males, their talons sharper and this one was pregnant. She came to my waist, and I stilled as she sniffed my clothes, prepared to call up Michael's sword if attacked. Another fire leopard drew near and she snarled at him, flashing her claws in warning. He screamed at her in a bloodcurdling shriek, yet heeded her warning, pacing away. Satisfied her claim was established, she rose on her hind legs and sniffed at my chest. Shocked, I looked over at the two demons discussing price. They'd stopped speaking, the Keeper's jaw unhinged. Fire leopards were only known to touch if you were locked within their jaws. I remained as stone, showing no fear.

The female ran her nose across my throat before licking the area over my carotid artery. I tensed, prepared to rip her in two, but she dropped to the ground and sauntered away. The other leopards followed suit. The demon stared at me in astonishment before holding up two fingers. Two drops of my blood for the dragon yew. It was a bargain.

Chapter 24
The Magician Reversed

Stella

Grayson said the entrance to Jing San's apartment was in the library, so that was the first place I searched. The large room was eerily still; only the steady tick of an antique mantel clock disturbed the quiet. I studied the room. No obvious sign of a door other than the entrance. Channeling Nancy Drew, I examined the wainscoting along each wall, searching for a crack of any kind that would indicate a secret room. I spent the most time on the fireplace. Nothing. I searched the bookshelves, pulling ancient-looking literature and first editions out at random. Amanda would flip over these if she saw them.

This was much harder than the movies, where people tipped over a candelabra and a whole wall swung open to reveal a cobweb draped passage. Frustrated, I slumped on the low red sofa facing the fireplace. I pinched my lips with my fingers, considering the marble mantelpiece. It was modern, without any ornamentation that could be disguised as levers or buttons. My eyes wandered, and I paused at two landscape oil paintings hung one on top of the other on the far wall. They depicted the same farm fields at both sunset and sunrise.

The wall was dark wood, and within a gap between the frames was a small brass knob. I jumped up and hurried over to touch it. Holding my breath, I slowly twisted. Nothing happened. I tugged, and the wall swung forward, becoming a door. *Jackpot.* Modern lights switched on automatically, revealing an elegant hallway with striped wallpaper. I stilled, expecting an alarm to trip, but several long minutes later the hall remained quiet. The last thing I wanted was Alaric to show up after our tense exchange and find me being nosy.

Grabbing a pillow from the sofa, I wedged it into the doorway before I crept down the secret hallway. It led directly to another door and I cautiously turned the handle. An opulent room of red came into view. The walls were lined with bookshelves—another library? I tiptoed across the threshold and spied a low wooden table placed in the center of the room, surrounded by round pillows on the floor. Otherwise the room was empty of furniture. Framed ink drawings of samurai warriors shared space with hooks holding sharp-looking weapons. The swords were a giveaway. This was Jing's place, alright.

With an eye to the far doorway, I ambled over to the shelves to check out her reading material. Lots of history books, particularly on battles, the silk trade and ancient Japan and China. Loads of books on swords. I moved to the next wall and drew up short. *Hello.*

The entire wall was filled with paperback romance novels. I laughed quietly. Wait until Silvan hears...And just like that I remembered there was no Silvan to tell about Jing San's improbable reading material. Taking a deep breath, I inspected the books and finally selected one with a torrid cover of a pirate holding a damsel in an off-the-shoulder dress.

I moved to the coffee table, placing the four plump pillows in a row before lying down on my makeshift bed to read. I woke when a slight sting bit into my throat. I brushed it away, but my hand met cold, hard steel. My eyes flew open. Jing San stood over me, a very long and sharp-looking sword in her hand. She appeared furious; her lips pulled back in a silent snarl.

I yawned. "Nice digs?"

"I should slit your throat. It would save us all so much trouble," she hissed. The cold tip of the sword pressed harder. I put my hands up, wishing I wasn't flat on my back.

"You *could* do that. Except it would make an awfully big mess on this nice wood floor," I pointed out, patting it next to me. The muscle in her jaw jerked. She glowered at me for an uncomfortable minute before pulling the sword from my flesh. I expelled a quiet sigh of relief.

"There is that I suppose. I would need to get the floors refinished, and I hate the mess of a remodel. Contractors and dust everywhere," she said moodily.

I nodded in agreement. She released her tense pose and picked up the book from the floor. Her cheeks reddened and she swung the sword expertly in a flashing arch. I remained motionless.

"So, you've been nosing around. Spying on people. I think I liked you better comatose and depressed."

I flinched, although she was completely right about the spying. I'd been a total creeper. I also couldn't keep my big mouth shut.

"I see you like romance novels. I think I read that whole series of Sweet Valley High over there myself about five years ago," I replied, stifling a smirk. Cold steel rested alongside my neck in a flash and I swallowed hard.

"You will not, under any circumstances, tell anyone about my books. If I even hear a *hint* of a rumor about this, I will cut you into such tiny pieces, only plankton will be able to swallow your bits from the ocean floor. Understood?" she asked coldly. I nodded. *Fully understood.*

"Say it."

"I promise not to tell anyone you like cheesy, mushy romance novels with pirates who rip ladies clothes off." Her lips quivered. I grinned impishly and just like that she decided not to murder me. At least I hoped not today.

"Where is Alaric?" She returned the sword to its place on the wall. Hurt swamped and I waved a hand while shrugging as if to say, *how would I know?* She must have seen something in my eyes because she only nodded and offered her hand. I took it and she brought me easily to my feet. For such a small girl, Jing was very strong.

"So, this is your apartment?" I asked, fascinated.

"While I'm in New York City. And I'm *not* giving you a tour. This is the only room you will ever see, so don't ask," she said.

Darn it. My eyes flickered with longing towards the open doorway leading to the rest of her apartment. "Can I use your bathroom?"

"No. Go back and use your own."

"Please? It's an emergency," I wheedled, hopping a bit. She sighed.

"You can see one bathroom and that is all. You will follow me and you will not wander," she demanded, her tone deadly.

"Of course!" I said with a casual eye roll. Her brows lowered in suspicion, but she escorted me from the room. We entered a hallway and passed through a sparse living room with a Buddhist altar along one wall. I slowed to admire a large bronze statue of a seated Buddha performing the cosmic mudra. Candles burned before it, casting a warm glow upon its compassionate countenance. I stopped in my tracks, drawn to it.

"Keep moving," Jing San gritted out. Among the various items on the altar was an ink drawing of a woman and a photo of Silvan. I could no sooner move away than I could stop breathing. I didn't touch it, but I did bend closer, absorbing the vision of his face as my treacherous eyes burned. It was a snapshot from inside Jing's Manga shop. Ford and

Silvan were grinning, leaning against the counter. I raised my eyes to Jing San. She stared at the photo.

"This is a sacred space for me, Stella. You have no right to intrude," she said quietly. Shame swamped, leaving my limbs cold. Jing had cared about Silvan.

"I'm very sorry, Jing San. Please forgive me." She jerked her chin in acknowledgment. A terrible feeling of imbalance lay between us. Impulsively, I spit out my own secrets.

"I'm in love with Alaric, but he refuses to admit the same for me, even though I know he does. That he is, too. I mean..." I slapped a hand over my mouth as a look of awkward horror flashed across Jing's face.

"So, I guess that makes us even." I finished lamely, rocked back on my heels. She crossed her arms and looked at me from the corner of her eye.

"Well. He usually just has sex with women. You, he seems to care about. Maybe a great deal," she said, continuing to avoid direct eye contact. Trust Jing to be the epitome of sensitivity. Mental note not to engage Jing in girl chat again. Like, ever.

"I really do need to use the bathroom." She shook her head.

"Just like Silvan with all the bathroom breaks." She pointed. "It's over there." I left her for a few minutes and returned, much relieved.

"Thanks," I said to her back as she marched us to the library.

"Hello...Are you home?" a male voice called. I drew up short, the voice familiar. Dawning recognition came as the voice called again, coming closer. Jing glanced away, hands on her hips. No way. Ford entered the library, a big grin on his face. His smile morphed into a look of surprise when he caught sight of me. Why was Jing's store employee all the way in NYC with her? She didn't even like him.

"Stella, is that you? Gosh, you look different. In a good way. Like a million bucks!"

He grabbed me up in a big bear hug and I allowed it. It was surprisingly good to see someone familiar.

"Put her down. Now we won't ever get rid of her. She's like a curious cat, always poking about for cream. Put her down, already," she snapped. Ford laughed in my ear but set me back on my feet. His face grew serious.

"I'm so sorry about Silvan's passing. He was a good friend to me."

I patted his arm, unwilling to allow the floodgates to open. This raw awakening from the dark was still very new.

"What are you doing here?"

"Oh, I'm Jing's blood companion. Didn't she tell you?" he said, looking at his boss.

"A blood whosit whatsit?" I asked. With eyes closed, Jing pinched the bridge of her nose.

"A blood companion. Wait. Didn't you already know that? Oops," he said sheepishly, darting a glance towards Jing.

"Follow me," Jing instructed, her voice resigned. She led the way back through her apartment and the secret hallway back to Alaric's library. Ford took a seat on the sofa and I could tell he was familiar with the room. I perched on a nearby chair, watching Jing San as she paced back and forth in front of the fireplace. She wore all black today, and her hair shone like glass under the lights. The red dye streak I'd always known her to have was gone.

She abruptly stopped before me. "Okay, nosey. Three questions. Go."

This is one of the reasons why I admired her so much. Direct and to the point. I lifted a hand and began ticking off three fingers.

"One, what is a blood companion? Two, *what* are you, and don't you dare skimp on the details. Three, will you teach me to fight like you?"

She shook her head and continued pacing.

"I shall reverse the order of your questions so the answers make better sense. Three, *hell no*. Two, I am a Chishioni. This might also be considered a vampire." She plopped down on the chair opposite me. "My father was an important Shogun in Japan. My mother was Chinese. One night a group of Chishioni vampires broke into our complex and murdered my family in revenge for my father's enforcement of his territory. The leader was a woman who gave me a choice to die with my family or turn." Her voice was emotionless as she shared her tale. She might as well have been reciting a story about a stranger. "I was a coward and chose life.

"The Lion had hunted these monsters and tracked them to my home, where he found me on the road. It was dawn by then. I recall looking up into the purple blooms of our ancient wisteria tree, thinking of my parents' bodies growing cold and already regretting my dishonorable decision." Ford moved to stand behind her chair, touching her shoulder. She blinked and looked at her lap. I tucked my hands beneath my thighs and waited.

"I begged him to kill me, but he said honor is complicated. He promised me revenge if I joined him and so I did. That day, when that Chishioni vampire taunted me with a choice, I chose life over my family and honor. Every single day I regret that choice. That is all you need to know about me." She stood, shaking free of Ford's hand.

"One, a blood companion is someone you choose to provide blood for you. I must drink every day from a vein or I grow weak. Although I have had several blood companions, they tend to die. My enemies hunt me as I hunt them, and anyone close to me becomes a target." She shrugged. Ford beamed as if she had just announced he was the new wide receiver for the Seahawks.

"Before you can ask, I'll give you one for free. The Lion is not

Chishioni. He was once human and angel but now he is vampiric demon and angel. The only one of his kind. His self-control is legendary, and counted upon to keep the balance amongst the different Primati factions. Regrettably, rumors have spread lately that he is killing humans without provocation and locking himself away in his tower." She got up and moved towards the secret door.

"Wait! Can I ask one more question?"

"Stella! Enough," she hissed, turning on me with pupils so large her eyes appeared black. Ford edged away from her. I leaned forward in my seat and asked her anyway.

"Will you help me avenge Silvan?" My fists bunched the fabric at my knees as a slow, wicked smile curved her lips.

"What do you think I've been doing? Just stay out of my way. Oh— and do not ever enter my domain without invitation again. Not unless you want to lose your head." She disappeared and Ford followed with an apologetic smile and wave. Damn it.

Alaric did not return for dinner. I'd been living inside such a bubble I wasn't sure where and when he even ate dinner. Shame stung once again. I'd been so obsessed with my muffled existence that I hadn't noticed his routines outside of the time we spent together. Maybe he was right. I didn't know him as well as I thought.

For the first time since I'd arrived, I felt the urge to explore the streets of Manhattan. The alternative was to slip back into bed and the arms of that hungry half-sleep that would only keep me churning inside with grief and rejection. I had a feeling he would not be checking on my dreams tonight. The memory of his turned back while I begged him for a chance spurred a quick change into jeans and my old sneakers.

When I pressed the elevator button, the doors slid open to reveal an ugly surprise. The back of the elevator car was a wall of writhing black and grey smoke that twisted and curled wildly, but did not dissipate; nor did it leave the confines of the elevator. The scent of moldy straw emanated from its swirling depths. There was a foot of empty space at the front, and when the shifting mass stayed in place without smoke alarms wailing, I studied its erratic patterns.

I slapped my palms together. No reaction. Perhaps it was just a weird magick art installation. Only one way to find out. I held my breath and tried to slip inside the elevator car, planning to stay near the buttons. The sliding shadows flowed forward and solidified into an unyielding wall that refused to allow me entrance. Huh. I reached out a hand. When a pocket of haze pushed forward as if to meet my fingers, I chickened out and drew back at the last second. I flapped my hands, testing whether it would dissipate as smoke or settle as fog. It coiled backwards, only to rush forward, ice cold, when I tried once more to enter.

After several frustrating attempts, I took off my shoes and threw them at the shadows, only to have my sneakers bounce off, tumbling along the polished marble of the foyer floor. The elevator doors slid shut. My safe haven had morphed into a jail and I was the prisoner.

Grayson did not respond when I spoke in the air as Alaric did for him, which may or may not have been related to my choice of language. Alaric's office was empty and I was alone in the apartment. I knocked at Jing San's secret door, but all I got was a whispered apology from Ford. I could call 911 for a rescue, but something told me that would be a very bad idea.

I wandered the empty apartment in a rage, finally making my way to the rooftop garden. I screamed, long and blood curdling, into the humid night air. The barrier around the roof dug into my belly as I stared down at Fifth Avenue, with its endless lines of cars, taxis, and people going *somewhere*. Turning, I spied the large Hemlock Alaric and I had emerged from that first night. The idea came in an instant. I raced back to my room and went straight to the walk-in closet, sighing with relief when I spied the Powell's book tote hanging from a hook. I dumped its contents onto my bed and stared down at a thin book on druids and another on elemental magick.

If I couldn't leave, then I would use my time to research magick. Namely, how to transfer from one place to another. I found a small notebook and pen in my bedside table and set furiously to work.

An hour later and I still knew nothing about transferring. All the advice on magick related to herbs, moon phases, and old wives' tales. No mention of transferring or instructions that were helpful. I tossed the book to the foot of the bed. If only I could speak with Thomas and ask for his guidance. I thought back on that day at the cliff when I'd jumped. More than one person claimed the air carried me down. All I recalled from that jump was visualizing a slow fall. And I remembered Tess explaining how my enchantment was influenced by intention. Could it be that simple? Imagine something hard enough and it would happen?

I assumed a lotus position in the center of the bed and placed my hands loosely on my knees. As I did in meditation, I focused on my breathing for several minutes. Then I began to think about Thomas. I imagined how it would feel to go to him. Find him. I envisioned his face, his eyeglasses, and nervous gestures. My entire focus was on Thomas. If I could locate him, then perhaps we could communicate, or maybe he could even transfer me to him.

Several moments passed. A warm feeling intensified at the base of my skull and sweat pooled, making even my fingertips slippery. Just as I was about to give up, I felt the bed dip violently.

My eyes popped open to find Thomas sprawled sideways across my bed. He wore athletic shorts and a green hoodie, his hair wild and his expression horrorstruck. I screamed, and leapt from the bed. Thomas was making plenty of noises of his own. I clutched my chest and Thomas rolled off the bed, backing away towards the windows.

"Thomas!"

He pulled his hair and frantically glanced around the room. Without thinking, I made the international hand signals for *calm down*.

"It's okay! You're safe. Did I...did I *bring* you here?" Thomas straightened and his heaving breaths gradually slowed, but still he didn't speak.

"Why aren't you saying anything?"

Eyes darting about my bedroom, he approached my bed to pick up the little notebook and pen. His writing was comprised of quick, jagged strokes and when he flipped the pad of paper around for me to see, it read *WTF!*

I shrugged, just as surprised as he was. He scribbled more, showing me the page. *I'm mute.*

Fingers of ice flicked along my spine.

"I don't understand, Thomas." Oh, God. I was going to have to try to contact Clara or Tess for help. Had I damaged him? He paused to cast a stern look at me, as if willing me to understand something. I had nothing. He shook his head and scribbled another word. *Punished.*

"Punished?" The only beings who might use such a word might be Murad...or the druids. The druids...who prized their privacy above all else. Whose existence Thomas confided in us about.

"Did the druids take away your ability to speak?" I asked, aghast at such a barbaric consequence.

He tapped the side of his nose with a finger. Bingo. I rushed to him, flipping the page on the notepad, encouraging him to explain.

"How could they do such a thing—is it magick? They wouldn't take out your tongue..." I snorted. Thomas laid a finger alongside his nose again. I stepped back, stunned. That was some medieval bullshit for sure.

"Oh, Thomas. Is this because you talked to me?" He nodded; lips tight as he wrote something else. *Not your fault.*

I fell back against the edge of the bed. "I'm so sorry," I whispered.

He raked fingers through his hair, his jaw tense. Grabbing the notepad from my slackened fingers, he scrawled a question. *Where am I?* I forced my throat to form sensible words.

"At my friend's apartment in New York City. I don't know if I can send you back! I didn't know I could bring you here in the first place." What had I done? If the druids had removed his tongue for speaking with me, what would they do to him if they found he'd transferred to me against orders? I was a plague on everyone close to me.

With an alarmed expression he raised his arms so they made an X and shook his head emphatically. He wrote more. *No! Don't try. I can return by tree myself if one is nearby.*

"We have one on the rooftop," I said, glad to have something in our favor. He frowned and wrote another message.

"*Are you alone?*" I nodded. His question raised my adrenaline level even further. What would Alaric or Grayson do if they found him here? He showed me a new page.

"*Must be in earth for it to work for me. Not potted*". Oh. I thought for a moment.

"We have a problem, then. Central Park has lots of trees and is a few blocks away—but I can't get out of here. The elevator is...not exactly working."

His brow furrowed in thought. He picked up the notebook again.

It's possible to float down a building using air for resistance. You did it once before. Try?

Was he using drugs? *NO!* I wrote beneath his sentence, underlining it twice for emphasis. He crumpled the page in frustration.

Then he began writing and continued to write for a long time. He finally rested his hand and shoved the notebook towards me. His penmanship was beautiful.

I'm on house arrest. If they find I'm gone then my mom and dad will be killed. I told secrets without permission, and to the Druidic Order that is the worst thing I could do. They took my tongue as a lesson. With time I may get it back with magick. As long as I don't break the rules! Help me get down to the park.

"I will help you. But first, I want...*need* you to answer a question. Did your group have anything to do with killing my mother—or Lila's family? I've been hearing things that don't add up."

Thomas was already writing furiously before I even completed my sentence. He showed me the page.

That is what they want you to believe! Don't be stupid, Stella. Think! My order was there to protect Lila and her daughters. There is something special about you, and someone else wants you dead.

I shook my head. I didn't know what to believe. If Thomas' order caught him off house arrest, he and his family would be killed. That didn't sound like people who protected others. "Wait—there has to be a fire escape! I mean, all buildings have them, right?"

He huffed sharply and jumped up, motioning for me to hurry.

I led the way from my bedroom and through the apartment. The space beneath Alaric's office door was dark, and the penthouse was just as silent as it had been earlier. Yet somehow the apartment felt—on alert. Shaking off a sudden bad feeling, I guided Thomas through the kitchen where I entered the code for the garden door. It clicked and I pushed through.

The evening was still warm but quite a bit windier, and I had to catch the heavy door with my fingertips to keep it from flying. Flowers and shrubs swayed in concert with the heavy breeze. Thomas explored the space, touching the enormous Hemlock and patting it regretfully before he joined me to prowl along each wall in search of a fire escape.

I returned to his side when he slammed his hands down on the stone wall several times to get my attention. I looked where he pointed and my stomach sank. There was a fire escape but it started two floors down. How could Alaric live here without a fire escape? The likely answer was that he didn't need one with magick.

Thomas pointed to me and then to the fire escape. I pretended not to understand.

"You want me to jump down two stories? I'll break my legs."

He rolled his eyes, exasperated. I crossed my arms in mutiny. With a calculated gleam in his eye, he hefted himself up onto the wide stone wall. The wind was stronger up there, and he held his arms out for balance as gusts tore at his clothes.

I inched closer, prepared to grab his feet, but he shuffled farther away. What was the idiot planning to do? He stared at me and made a noise low in his throat.

Anger mixed with fear as I understood he was risking his life in belief that I could help him lower to the fire escape with magick. I scrubbed my face with my hands, furious with his game. He remained standing with his arms outstretched. I licked my lips and drew closer. I eyed the drop to the metal frame and gauged the distance between the wall and the escape stairs.

"I'll try, Thomas. If I can't lift you or lower you—if this doesn't work—we're calling the police to break us out. Deal?"

He watched me intently, neither agreeing nor disagreeing to my plan B. I didn't bring up Plan C, which involved me in handcuffs and the police scraping Thomas off the sidewalk far below.

I closed my eyes. Feeling the caress of the wind across my cheeks and hair, I swung my arms from side to side for no reason other than it felt good to build up the energy. I imagined the wind heeding my call. Doing my bidding. Not a slave but as one sentient being in partnership.

A breeze circled my body and pulled gently at my clothes. I remained in that moment in perfect peace, absorbing the air into my lungs and releasing it as if the wind pulled it from my lips.

My mind was fully present as I imagined the breath in my body as a continuation of the breeze dancing across my skin. I visualized the air as an enormous hand. A hand that gently scooped up Thomas from his place on the wall. It would carry him out slowly and lower him as a feather to the fire escape landing. He would drift down, down, down all the way to the street. Thomas would be safe. The air would enclose and protect him.

My eyes opened and then bugged wide. I scrambled forward, searching the fire escape. It was empty. I prayed frantically, afraid to look down. If he'd plummeted to his death, he'd done so silently. I inhaled raggedly and forced myself to look. I blinked and blinked again, not trusting my eyes. A figure resembling Thomas stood on the sidewalk, waving both arms. I scanned the entire sidewalk to be sure. No bloody bodies anywhere.

Thomas walked backwards towards the park. Street lights illuminated his green hoodie and familiar grin. I offered a weak wave in return and Thomas turned and ran towards the park. I sagged against the wall, mentally giving myself a fist bump. The air died down just as a foreboding sensation crept along my spine. Something was off.

Suspicious, I turned in a circle, seeking out the shadows around me, but I was alone on the rooftop. The breeze rumpled the drowsy roses and box hedges. I still couldn't believe I'd lowered a man down the length of a building.

"Stella," called a booming voice. I jumped in place, startled. Murad stood in the doorway to the kitchen. He marched towards me, scanning the rooftop. His eyes glowed red in the night, and my feet edged backwards. This was a different Murad. Someone physically more dangerous. A table dug into my hips as he stopped before me; the dim light illuminating his face. Its angles were sharper, his voice deeper, scarier.

"Are you hurt? A druid broke Alaric's protection. I need to get you out of here," he growled. Several figures appeared from thin air, weapons glinting within the shadows. They wore all black but for red sashes along their left sleeves.

"A-a druid?"

"Did you see anyone?" he barked.

How could I lie to Murad? On the other hand, if he knew I was friends with a druid, a member of an order he despised enough to go all red-eyed, what would he do to me? Would he force me to tell him about Thomas, who was already a prisoner?

"Absolutely not," I said, unblinking, despite the fact that my heart was galloping a mile a minute. Murad's eyes went vacant while his mouth hardened. He made a gesture to his guard. When he snapped his gaze back to me, he seemed a tad more in control. At least his face had gone back to its normal shape.

"Alaric is on his way. He was in Bulgaria but knows that I am taking you from here to my private sanctuary."

"Are we going to—to Paris?"

"We are going somewhere no one can touch you," he responded tersely. And then he grabbed me.

Chapter 25
The High Priestess

Stella

The windy rooftop disappeared. We stood within a quiet dark space, Murad's hands on my shoulders. The scent in the confined area was sharp and overpowering.

"How are you doing? Okay?" he asked. The resonance of his voice had settled into its regular timber, thank goodness. That deep growl had freaked me the fuck out.

"Yes," I mumbled, uncomfortable to be so close, unable to see.

Light spread as Murad pushed a door open and we stepped into a small room with stone walls. Gasping for fresh air, I turned to see that we'd stepped from a closet with strange shapes carved into earth-caked walls. I wrinkled my nose and shut the door. The pungent, bitter odor still burned my nostrils.

"Sorry about that. I should have warned you. The closets are made of iron and then coated with a special clay mixed with herbs and a few other deterrents. My own version of a home security system," he said apologetically.

The room was pretty empty. One wall featured an enormous fireplace flanked by two green painted doors, one of which we'd emerged from. The walls and floor were rough cut stone, covered by a thick wool rug in muted jewel colors. The only furnishings were a low table and two leather chairs set before the fireplace, a backgammon set between them. A scattering of gas lamps lay across the thick mantle, and a monster's head snarled frozen from above. I jerked backwards at the sight. The creature could have been a cross between a tiger and bear but for the odd human-like eyes—I'd seen nothing like it before.

"Where are we, Murad?" I gasped, my throat dry.

"My estate in upstate New York. It's heavily enchanted for privacy. My Paris home is accessible to too many people and it's known. No one knows of this place. It's where I come to feed." He rubbed the back of his neck, offering a polite smile. I didn't know what he meant by *feed* and wasn't going to ask so soon after seeing him go all red-eyed.

"Do you play?" He gestured to the chessboard.

"Sam taught me but I'm not very good. My friend Amanda is much better."

"Well. We'll see about getting you some practice if you'd like to learn. For now, I'll show you the main house." He opened the roughhewn, wooden door. It was night, with only the muted stars above for illumination. He set out with long strides, forcing me to take twice as many steps. A lurch of homesickness hit at the scent of pine. Birdsong and warning screeches followed our path from above. Odd that birds would be singing at night.

"I had that cottage carried over from Istanbul many years ago— stone by stone. It holds good memories and serves as the only spot to transfer in and out for us in this place," he explained as he led us up a slope. The grass was cool and soft against my bare feet, the trees much shorter than I was used to. The trees thinned, and we approached a wide lawn. Beyond it lay a sprawling Beax-Arts styled mansion made of polished limestone and marble. Weeping willows dotted the landscape. At least there would be electricity.

"There's a stable out back, yet I would ask you not to ride as I don't have enough staff to chaperone you. Do not be put off by my groundskeeper or housekeeper. They're shades that have been with me for years. Do you know what a shade is?"

"Yes. Someone like Grayson."

"Good. Yes. They won't harm you," he assured me.

"I won't have time to ride. I expect you can return me to Alaric or back home to Oregon tomorrow," I said firmly.

"I think not. If the druids found you in that fortress, they can find you anywhere. Better for you to stay here until the Council meeting." I smirked. If he thought to keep me prisoner, he had an extra special something coming. But wasn't this my fault? If I hadn't called up Thomas, my butt would still be in the Penthouse. And Alaric would have to talk to me. At least to take me home again. We neared the house and its doors were thrown wide, revealing a birdlike woman in a red cardigan. Murad raised a hand, his steps unhurried.

"You're free to roam, but please remain to the south of the stone cottage where we came from. The driveway leads to a main road, but there is a boundary you will not be able to pass, so please don't try. My nearest neighbor is far to the north and suffers from Alzheimer's. It's better to leave the neighbor undisturbed. If you need anything, just let Layla or Adem know."

"Wait—are you just leaving me here?"

"I'll see you settled and give directions to the staff before I return tomorrow tonight. I don't know how druids bypassed Alaric's security, but we will track them, have no doubt," he promised darkly in that other, deep timbred voice that raised the tiny hairs along my nape.

He was beyond obsessed about druids. I felt kind of bad about omitting that it was I who'd brought the druid to the apartment. Really bad, considering that the resulting alarm had just gotten me stuck in his secret vampire lair. I bit my cheek, unable to tell the truth and reveal my emerging power over air.

"You aren't wearing shoes!" he commented, glowering down at my bare feet.

I wiggled my toes. "Don't worry, this is normal for me. My shoes are back in the apartment with the rest of my clothes. Also, my toothbrush, my phone..."

"Oh. I wasn't thinking," he said in a non-apology kind of way before continuing, "I'm not used to visitors here. You may have to wear something of mine until I can bring your clothing." I nodded but felt a little strange about wearing his clothes. Which seemed silly considering that he planned to marry me. I should tell him I was having second thoughts, but not tonight. Not with the memory of the look on his face before he'd transferred us here.

He strode up the marble stairs and greeted the housekeeper. She looked ancient, with weathered, honey skin stretched over high cheekbones. The woman offered me a curious smile and began to speak in another language to Murad. They carried on a fast conversation in the same, flowing language that sounded French to my ears.

"Layla says she is very happy to meet you and is looking forward to caring for you. Layla and Adem are fluent in Turkish, yet their English is limited, something I didn't consider. You'll manage, I'm sure." I was beginning to see that Murad was impulsive. Scary impulsive. A trait I often resembled. He'd brought me here on a snap decision because he could. He had rocks in his head if he thought he could drop me off and expect me to stay put.

Murad noticed my expression, misunderstood, and squeezed my

hand. I did not need comforting. Layla smiled and spoke rapidly.

"Layla is very excited to have someone to cook for as I don't often eat here," Murad dutifully translated. Hmm. Something in common with Grayson. I stopped at the entrance, aware of my dirty feet. The dark stained oak floors gleamed with polish, and an enormous silk rug in rich earth tones covered the center of the expansive foyer.

"My feet are dirty." I pointed out when Murad paused to look at me questioningly.

"She says not to worry. She's very glad to have a little dirt to clean up. I'm afraid they don't have much to do here," he explained with a rueful shrug of his shoulders. Murad spoke to Layla in Turkish as we walked up broad stairs to the second floor. She went ahead of us, disappearing from view.

"The language you were speaking sounds beautiful."

"We spoke many languages when I was a child. Turkish did not exist before Ataturk modernized Turkey in the nineteen-twenties. I'll bring you some language course books if you like. It might help you to learn to communicate with the staff." He paused in front of an enormous portrait hung above the landing and studied it with a softened expression.

The painting was life size and depicted a room in blues and greens. An angelic woman stood in its center with a sleepy smile, her entire countenance glowing with light and a sensual contentment that warmed my cheeks. She was a young goddess; long, white blonde hair flowed down her narrow shoulders, her face a heart-shaped beacon of radiance from which everything else faded. Her indigo eyes were laughing, her pink lips curved in a drowsy secret. The details of the room fell away from her beauty, the sweetness of her soul a tangible thing. A thick, silken robe in ocean blue covered all but her fingertips and one pale shoulder. An arched window behind her revealed a sky littered with dancing stars. It was breathtaking.

"Did you do this?" I asked, unable to work my jaw properly to speak.

"Yes."

"Who is she?"

Murad touched the elaborate wood frame with a single finger and then continued walking as if my question had never been asked. But I knew. My eyes were a little different, my face less symmetrical and nose slightly larger but the resemblance was there. I looked up at the young woman, somehow expecting her to speak. I noticed the place on the frame Murad had touched was well worn, the rest of the frame in perfect, polished condition.

"I'll return with more supplies. I should warn you. Layla is agoraphobic and does not leave the house except to tend to a vegetable garden she keeps outside the kitchen door. Shades do not eat, yet all share a fascination with food. She sends her produce to a homeless shelter. Be forewarned—she's already planning what meals to cook for you," he said. Nice for me but it must suck to be a shade. To live forever without chocolate or popcorn sounded like purgatory. We entered a large and airy bedroom to find Layla busily changing the sheets.

"Does she know I don't understand a word she's saying?" I muttered from the corner of my mouth, referring to Layla's chatter as she worked. Murad chuckled.

"She does. But without visitors for so long, I have a feeling she'll be talking your ear off regardless. Understand, they can leave this place but choose not to. Right now, she's telling you all about my exploits as a young man. I told her we are engaged. I hope you don't mind." I did mind but wasn't prepared to make it a thing right now.

"Can you please tell her thank you from me?"

"*Tesekkurediyor,*" Murad dutifully told her. She grinned and fluffed the pillows. I drifted over to a painting, admiring the depth and variation of light.

"These are your paintings," I said, recognizing the colors and brushstrokes.

"You will find this house full of my work, I'm afraid. A very long lifetime and not enough space to house it all. I keep planning to have it all catalogued one day, but that would mean moving it all somewhere else—too much trouble. The West wing will be locked as those are my private quarters. You are welcome to use the studio."

"Thank you." I lingered over the mysteries of a locked room in a forbidden wing of this enormous house.

"My Grandfather will worry about me," I said. I was also missing Sam but refused to share with Murad in case he decided to spirit him here as well to keep me company. Sam would hate that. His jaw tightened.

"Once we complete an investigation into Alaric's security and make certain you are safe there, we can talk about moving you. For now, it's safer for you here." He picked a piece of imaginary lint from his sleeve, careless of the frustration on my face. Why didn't I believe him?

"I must go. Layla will bring you clothing and provide everything you need. Do try to settle in, Stella."

* * *

I woke at dawn after a night twisting and turning in my borrowed bed. Without Alaric, the nightmares had been even more intense. Elegant drapes let in the barest hint of sunrise when I climbed from the bed, Murad's borrowed t-shirt at my thighs. A small pile of neatly folded clothes rested on a chair. I must have slept after all not to have noticed someone coming in my room. The thought was more than a little creepy.

I shook out the fabric and discovered a light peasant skirt that would fall to my shins and a simple white peasant blouse. I put them on and twirled, loving the soft sway against my legs. Approaching a full-length mirror, I studied my image.

With my sleep-wild hair, the full skirt, and the red mala bracelet I wore around my ankle, I resembled an old-fashioned Romany girl. Not the ethereal beauty held by Lila, but something earthier. More real. I was half my father's bloodline and so many others had to have existed first for me to be alive. For the first time, being half Romany wasn't something I resented because of how they treated me. I met the girl in the mirror with a toss of my head. I looked fantastic. Maybe this wasn't such a bad thing.

Hungry, I explored the house until I found the kitchen. A stacked double teapot blew steam from a massive Aga cooker. Layla welcomed me to a table and began putting plates in front of me. Thick slices of tomato, black cured olives, boiled eggs and soft white cheese made an appearance, as did a basket of freshly baked bread and rose jam. I nibbled here and there as Layla placed a cup of hot tea before me. I'd give anything for a cup of coffee but smiled politely around a small sip. Amazed, I took another. The rich brew was heavenly. Layla sat down and encouraged me to try everything until I finally begged off from the sturdy farm table.

"Thank you." I said. She shooed away my efforts to help tidy and I stepped through the kitchen door and onto a wide porch. A lush landscape greeted me; Layla's garden with fenced in fields lay just beyond. Bright green plants and blades of grass glittered with dew in the morning sun. Feeling a tap on my leg, I looked down to see Layla place a pair of wooden clogs next to my feet. I slid my feet into them.

There had to be some way off this property. A road, a neighboring house with a phone, something. I explored the buildings nearest the house first. There were several outhouses, a garage, and an impressive-looking horse stable set far back from the house.

I entered the garage first, surprised to see the four bays empty but for a classic, red Jaguar Roadster with two flat tires. Murad must not do much driving, as it was covered in dust. I noted the key hanging from a nearby hook and filed the information away. The stable was next.

"Hello?" I called out. The air was dry, the scent of hay sharp. The wide planked floor was swept clean, and my attention caught on several dark, reddish-brown stains. It spoke of either serial killers or poor attempts to clean up old paint.

Soft neighs and snuffling snorts drew me to the stalls. I walked through, visiting briefly with a dozen horses. They were all black—most of them over seventeen hands tall with proud necks and glossy coats. They vied for my attention, pushing warm muzzles into my hands in search of treats but for one enormous monster in the end stall. He stomped his enormous hooves, turning in circles. I approached his stall door to see if we could make friends. A soft sound startled me. An elderly man stood ten feet away, a tweed cap held against his chest with a veiny hand.

"Oh! You scared me. You must be Adem. I'm Stella." I extended a hand. The man disappeared. One minute he was there and the next he just sort of faded out, just like Grayson had done. Gooseflesh rose, and I walked backwards, out of the barn and into the sunlight.

Murad had mentioned a neighbor. Something about staying away from them. I found a nice sized branch and let it whistle through the air in broad strokes as I walked north through the forest, watchful of elderly men in caps. The air grew notably cooler once I came to a small creek. The clear water gurgled happily over earth-colored pebbles and rocks. Whereas my side of the creek was dry and sparse, the opposite side was lush and green. The shoreline on the parallel shore was covered in emerald moss and large spiny ferns, reminding me of home.

I kicked off my borrowed shoes and crossed the creek, breathless as the cold water rushed over my ankles and calves. My ears popped as I reached the opposite shore and there was an immediate lightness to the air. Some yards later I came to a clearing and stopped, amazed to see a small cemetery in the middle of nowhere. The headstones were pillar shaped, and the writing displayed vertically in a language I didn't recognize. There were over a dozen graves, covered in carpets of clover and moss. The clearing should have been too shaded for flowers to bloom, yet here they were—a colorful carpet thriving as if they stood in full sunlight.

I breathed deep, paying attention to the air. The magick with Thomas had been accidental. Could I really command air without a need to spur me on? I visualized a breeze lifting my hair and sweeping the treetops. Nothing happened. I imagined my skirt blowing against my legs but when I opened my eyes there was nothing but silence. I scanned the clearing, noting the absolute stillness but for a few drowsy bees. Okay. Practice made perfect, right? I just had to keep trying.

About 400 yards later I came to a white stone wall with an arched gate of black iron that creaked when I pushed it. I froze, feeling watched. Glancing right, I met the angry gaze of a beast-like man, its features, back and haunches far too tall and animalistic to be only human. My heartbeat slowed when I realized it was made of stone. Sharp teeth curled over its lips, a look of avarice upon its face. One giant hand pressed to the wall, its fingers tipped with claws. It reminded me of the gargoyle sculptures of the gothic period. The statue was either an effective trespassing deterrent—I couldn't imagine coming across it at night—or unusual art installation. I tapped its teeth and studied its torn left ear. "Grotesque…" The sculptor was a master of details.

Giddy, I ducked beneath the overgrown vines arching the gate and reappeared into sunshine. Flowers and abundant greenery exploded in every direction. Before me lay a path with irregular-shaped flagstones. I followed it, noting the signs of a very old, well maintained garden sympathetic to its wild surroundings. Creeping thyme bloomed rose pink over boulders, and I ran my fingers lightly over their cool softness. I passed through a pergola heavy with fragrant peach roses and breathed deep. Pink geraniums, purple irises, and white clematis blossoms vied for my attention.

When the house came into view, I held my breath. It was stunning. An English Manor in the Carolean style with ribbed cupola crowns and sash windows. An orangery faced the back of the house. I was trespassing, but so drunk on my senses it was impossible to turn back. Vegetable and herb beds appeared as I continued to explore, and I gazed in wonder at the fat heads of lettuce and collards, pumpkins and tomatoes. A plump, fearless bunny hopped across my path.

A voice rose, singing. A garden came into view, along with two women. One knelt with her back to me, silver hair twisted into a chignon. She was on her hands and knees in a strawberry patch, a wicker basket half-filled at her side. The other was a giant of a woman, her skin deepest ebony while short, wiry tufts of hair sprang above her broad, beautiful face. She spotted me and offered a dazzling smile.

"Look, Lilly—we have a visitor," she called out to her companion, who ignored her. The giantess walked towards me in long strides. The hair at her temples was grey, yet my initial impression that she was elderly seemed an illusion as there was such a vitality to her that she could be any age. She wiped her hands on green capri pants.

"Hi! I'm Ela. One L. What's your name?" she asked with a beaming white smile.

"Stella. Uh—sorry to intrude. I'm visiting a friend across the way and was taking a walk—then I saw your garden. It's the most beautiful thing I've ever seen," I said honestly. Ela's coffee-brown eyes warmed with happy crinkles.

"Well, Stella. We don't get many visitors. Lilly doesn't talk much so you'll have to forgive her manners. She's getting up there in age. Do you like to garden?"

"I like to be outside. I know about gardening from my grandfather, but we don't have anything like this," I said, waving towards the sizable garden.

"Well, I'm always glad to meet another gardener, even a novice."

"Is it just the two of you?"

"Just us. Although it's Lilly who lives here full time. She's a little shy with strangers, the poor dear, but she does love to talk to the plants," she said, nodding down at where Lilly continued to pluck bright red strawberries.

"I know this sounds strange, but would you mind if I sketched some pictures—back by the wall? I'd stay out of your way and I'm happy to help out in exchange." *Please say yes, please say yes...*

"Let me ask Lilly, later. She has certain triggers from time to time that can get her upset. If she's okay with you, then I am as well," she responded with a gentle smile. This garden would be a perfect place to begin drawing subjects again. Maybe even practice magick in that cemetery clearing. It might be worth staying a few more days cooped up in Murad's elegant lair.

"In the meantime," she began, turning to scoop up a pair of worn garden gloves from a nearby gardener's table. "...make yourself at home." She thrust the gloves at me, and I accepted them with a grin. When Ela returned to pruning the trellis, I knelt by Lilly's side. The woman paused and met my eyes for a moment, tilting her head this way and that before ignoring me once more. Eschewing the gloves, I dug my hands into the rich soil, letting it sift through my fingers. Soon I was searching through leaves for strawberries, working opposite Lilly.

"I need to take this inside. Be right back," called Ela.

I found a strawberry so fat and juicy that my mouth watered. The fruit was nearly to my lips when Lilly grabbed my wrist. *Jeeze*. It was just one strawberry. She stood jerkily, looped the basket over one arm and gestured for me to follow her. Curious, I followed. She walked around the side of the house to an old-fashioned water pump. She pumped the handle several times before cold water streamed out and into a small ditch lined with stones. She gestured to my hand and waited until I thrust the strawberry beneath the running water.

After a moment she stopped the flow and waited expectantly. I raised the glistening berry to my mouth and, not giving her a chance to stop me again, took a huge bite of the strawberry, all the way to the stem. Juice dripped from my lips and I wiped it away with the back of my hand. A ghost of a smile appeared on her lips and I grinned around my mouthful. She was lovely, despite, or perhaps because of, her age. She must be the one with Alzheimer's that Murad mentioned. Eye contact was nonexistent with Lilly, but she didn't seem disturbed by my presence.

She took the stem from me and flung it out into the garden. I laughed. Lilly took another strawberry from her basket and handed it to me, doing the same. We stood there, rinsing and chomping on sweet berries in companionable silence until the basket was half empty. Then she handed me the basket and walked away, towards the back of the house.

"There you are." Ela appeared, passing Lilly on her way towards me. I met her halfway.

"I have something for you." She extended a cloth bag bursting with fat lettuce heads.

"Ah. It looks like Lilly gave you a bit of treasure as well," she said, nodding at the basket I held. "It's a good sign. Come back anytime, Stella, and bring your paints or whatnot," she beamed. I sighed in relief, feeling as though I'd passed a terribly important test. The chance to work here, to practice the ability to transfer, were powerful reasons to stay a day or two longer. Maybe Alaric would change his mind and look for me. If not, I'd have to figure out just how far I was willing to go— including breaking off an engagement with a Primati vampire king.

Chapter 26
The Sun

Stella

Murad came to visit daily for one hour, arriving just after dinner. We often played backgammon as we argued. Sometimes I practiced Turkish with him once he brought me language books but he refused to teach me the bad words, which made the entire enterprise seem pointless. We didn't always fight. At first, I couldn't get enough of his stories.

I learned more about the Primati community and the search for Marcus—yet he was always distracted. Not that I made a big attempt to keep him entertained—I was plenty tired from my days with Ela and Lilly. But his constant peeks at the clock would infuriate a saint. I had more important things to do than languish like some moron, waiting for him to pop in and disrupt my day for an hour as if I were a chore.

Our bickering began in earnest when I told him I wanted to go into town and he refused. It went downhill from there. He suggested that Layla teach me how to cook to keep me occupied. It was beyond annoying for him to assume I didn't know how to already. I agreed if he would taste my efforts. After the first meal he agreed to drop the subject of my cooking. My own frustration was growing as I was unable to transfer by myself, no matter how hard I hugged trees or how many trips I made to the stone house and its secret closet.

At least tomorrow was the Witch Council. It coincided with the Autumn Equinox, and Murad was taking me to Tess and Clara in the afternoon. I think we were both looking forward to the break. My borrowed bedroom overflowed with botanical paintings and pencil drawings from Lilly's garden that I dared not show Murad for fear he would find a way to block my visits.

He was still unaware that I spent most of my days in the gardens with Lilly and Ela. I always made sure to be cleaned up and present before he arrived, and he never noticed my tan, nor my torn and dirty fingernails. He just assumed I was a good girl all day, and, to her credit, Layla wasn't a snitch. I think she enjoyed feeding my increased appetite from working in the sun all day. I would miss her as well as Ela and Lilly. A week ago, I'd finally succeeded in my personal mission to get Lilly to talk to me. My back sore and temper short, I'd grumbled about pulling weeds.

"How do these weeds grow in rocks for goodness sakes?"

"Life builds on itself. Adapts to fix the weakness," Lilly said in a bell-like voice.

I'd plopped backwards, surprised to hear her speak.

"Lilly, do you know my name?" She didn't answer.

I hurriedly pointed to enormous bushes laden with heavy blossoms. "Why are those hydrangeas so blue?"

"Roots like diversity. Nutrients help them grow stronger and more colorful," Lilly responded. And that's how I'd learned that Lilly would speak as long as it related to plants or the elements. So, I talked about my life, in particular my frustrations with a young man who refused to accept that he adored me, and made sure to end my tirade with a question about the garden. She liked to talk about seasons and how removing what you didn't want in your garden allowed for something new to take its place. I wasn't sure if she meant that I should give up on Alaric after that one, so I stopped bringing him up.

Now that it was my last full day here, I left earlier in the morning than usual, taking a gift of Layla's shortbread cookies for Ela and Lilly. Wearing old rain boots, I splashed through the creek and wound through the cemetery to the garden wall.

As soon as I crossed through the gate into Lilly's land, rain poured from the darkened sky. A kipping sound drew my attention to the ground, and I saw an arctic tern taking shelter beneath the broad leaves of a fig tree. It had to be Bird and I shook my head in disbelief.

"What are you doing all the way out here? Is Thomas around?" I held out a wet hand, but he nipped my fingers and flew away. "Nice to see you too," I called after him. I hugged the cookie tin to my chest and found shelter in the Orangery at the back of the manor. I rang the bell and waited. The roof and three sides were paneled with glass, and I shivered as the rain fell sideways in violent staccato. The door opened.

"Oh, Stella! Look at you, poor girl. Let me get you some towels," Ela said as she disappeared. She left the door ajar and I peered through the doorway into a mudroom. I'd never been invited inside and was careful now to stay outside with my dripping clothes.

"Here you are," Ela sang, returning with an armful of warm towels. I smiled in thanks, happy to see her. Today she wore a dress with printed autumn leaves and, as she drew closer, I caught her comforting scent of lavender.

"They're still warm from the dryer—I was just running a load."

I gratefully accepted one as she threw another over my head and briskly rubbed my head until I laughed. She drew back with a chuckle.

"My children are all grown, so you'll forgive me if I enjoy the odd maternal nudge now and then. You're so good to us, Stella," she said as she accepted the cookie tin from me. I returned the now damp towel to her.

"Thank you—to be honest I don't take to coddling well, but with you it's kind of nice. I grew up with my grandfather, and he's not exactly the maternal kind. I can't imagine being a mom myself." I stopped, realizing what I'd said. I may not ever have children as long as this curse hung over me. Ela gave me a nudge.

"You have years and years to figure that out. The thing about children is that you have to let them learn their own lessons. Everyone creates their own path and their own story—even if they choose the wrong one with an outcome you think you know about. It's the hardest thing about being a mother. You'll see one day," she assured me.

"Where is Lilly?" I asked, changing the subject. Ela's broad smile faltered.

"Oh, she's having a bad day. She insists on living on this island, but now and again a rainy day will come along, and she stays in her bedroom for days. I told her when she chose this place that Washington has more rainy days than not, but she's a very stubborn woman to say the least," Ela confided. Did she say Washington?

"New York. I think you mean upstate New York?"

"Darling, there are no islands in upstate New York unless plopped into lakes. Who told you that?"

"Murad. The friend I'm staying with," I said, confused.

"Oh. Murad's land *is* in New York. But we are in Washington. These things happen sometimes." My skin flashed cold from more than the cool rain.

"Don't get all bent out of shape. I can see your mind spinning. It's simple as can be. If you don't believe me, follow that path over there—

" she pointed to a gap in the far back wall "—and it will take you to the shoreline. Better take a jacket and hat with you unless you want to catch a chill." I turned to look at the pegs holding garments along one wall, and when I swiveled back, Ela had disappeared into the house, the door shut with a firm click.

Thoroughly confused, I moved to the wall and put on a worn fisherman's jacket with a hood. The rain was easing up, and I trudged towards the back-wall Ela had pointed to. Just when I thought I had something figured out, it moved on me. A month ago, my first thought would have been that Ela had been drinking or senile—but my new experiences with the Primati community kept coming with lessons. Things were not always what they seemed. Don't trust anything or anyone.

Beyond the wall were clumps of tall grass and young trees, a worn dirt path cutting through the middle. The rain pitter-patted softly on leaves as I walked the path. I came to an abrupt halt when the scent of saltwater teased my nose. *No way.* I jumped switchbacks down a steep incline and soon came to an opening in the trail blocked by large mounds of bone-white driftwood. I climbed over these and hurried to a shoreline. Waves lapped at a rocky beach, sea stacks in the distance. Further down, a wooden pier rose from behind a rocky outcropping. This had to be magick—or Murad had lied about being in New York.

"Hey! Hey there! Yea—you girl!" came a loud voice from down the beach. I crept towards the sound, wary. "That's it, lovely. Keep a walkin!" encouraged the voice. I proceeded down the rickety wooden length of the pier until I reached the end. There were no boats or sunbathers as far as I could see.

"Oi!" The voice was loud now. I went to my knees and peered over the side. Shock almost had me tumble into the water. A rotund woman with dirty blonde hair was bobbing in the dark water next to the pier.

She had large sparkling green eyes and, from the white half globes that kept appearing and disappearing with her movements, she appeared topless. It was the dark serpentine tail I saw swishing beneath the surface that made me nearly swallow my tongue.

"Hey, girl. Have you seen a white bird anywhere?" the woman asked, pointing towards the tree line behind me.

"You're...a...you are a...a..."

"Come on, you can say it. I'm the most gorgeous mermaid you ever saw. Is that about right?" *Mermaids don't exist. Mermaids don't exist...* She flipped backwards in the water, her smooth body and tail seamless. My mind blanked. That was a freaking mermaid.

"Er. You would be...the only one I've seen. Like. Ever," I choked out.

"Oof, really? Well put 'er there!" The woman hauled herself up to grab the edge of the pier and offered me a hand. Her skin was dull and plastic looking. I was afraid it might squish like dough if I pressed it, but I did it anyway, not wanting to be rude. Relief hit to find her skin firm if cold and wet. She released me quickly.

"I ought 'a pull you in the water for such a stupid move. What's wrong with you shaking hands with a stranger like that? You don't even know me. I could be a predator, ya know," she scolded. I was too taken aback to defend myself. She was absolutely right. I'd never felt so dumb and that was saying a lot considering the last month.

"Okay. Thanks? My name is Stella. Who are you? I mean—what's your name?" I asked, afraid she would disappear.

"You can't pronounce it," she replied.

"Try me."

She began to emit a loud noise reminiscent of a whale but much shriller and high pitched. She broke off with a laugh. I closed my unhinged jaw.

"Are you pulling my leg?"

"Yeah. I'm yanking on it, baby!" she crowed. "I'm just messing with you. You can call me Hillary," she said before she dove under the water and came up again, smoothing her hair back. Her tail was thick, with the mottled green color of a real fish. No pretty rainbow colors or sparkles to be seen.

"Let me guess—I don't look like you think a mermaid should look? Did you expect a Barbie doll with a tail? That's hardly clever. Did you ever see a dolphin with a twenty-four-inch waist? Idgits! I can go forty kilometers an hour on a good day, and you try diving ten meters down off Alaska without a little padding on you," Hillary huffed. I flushed. I suppose if the Primati included vampires and witches, it might as well include merfolk. What other creatures roamed about I'd never known existed? Alaric and Amanda had left me sorely lacking in Primati knowledge.

"So, have you seen a white bird or not?"

"There are lots of white birds."

"He's an artic tern with a red beak and a black hood over his eyes. I've been following him for days and tracked him here." She barely moved as she somehow tread water enough to keep her torso still. Nice trick. Her description sounded like Bird. "What do you want with him?" I asked, masking a grimace.

"I'm going to season him up and eat him with a nice Jamaican beer—look at your face! Nah, he's my boyfriend. I'm just trying to talk to him. We had a misunderstanding but I'm not giving up on 'im."

"Your think your boyfriend is a bird?" I pinched my thigh hard. It hurt. I'd just met my first mermaid and it turns out she's a stalker.

"Not always. He likes to be a bird, but he's also a hunky blonde Adonis and the future father of my little fish fry," she whooped, slapping the water. I seriously could not tell if she was joking.

"Please tell me you're saying he turns into a person."

"Of course. What did you think I meant? He's the most handsome man on earth but has this thing for his bird form and playing hard to get."

"Maybe no means no," I advised. She rolled her eyes.

"Why are you here anyways? This island is enchanted but I saw you walk right out of it. If you aren't careful, you'll have the Lion's army after you. This place is super-secret. I hear he's on a warpath lately and that beast does *not* play," she shuddered.

"My dad told me once that the Enforcer made sushi out of an entire school of rebel merfolk who were kidnapping tourists off the Kerama Islands. Are you a witch?" For some reason, I could only make sense of half of what she was saying. I grasped the last thing I understood.

"No, I'm just a boring human." Hillary flicked the surface with her tale, which drove a fine mist over me. I glared through wet eyelashes. She grinned, exposing extremely pointed teeth.

"Nice one. I like you. Hold up," she said, disappearing beneath the pier.

"Come on out, Piper. Meet Stella. She's a bit of alright," Hillary coaxed. I held my breath as the water rippled. A smaller shape swam beneath and around Hillary until the crown of a red-haired girl emerged from the water. She rose slowly, only showing her remarkable eyelashes and pert little nose.

"Hi." I waved at her, wishing I had my phone with me. Amanda was *not* going to believe this. The mermaid rose until her shoulders were visible and offered a shy grin.

"Hi," she chirped, and then submerged to her nose once more, her hair fanning into a ruby halo.

"I love your hair," I complimented. Hillary grinned at her friend.

"See, Piper. Humans love red-hair. Not like the creeps back home."

Piper dipped beneath the water and Hillary explained. "I know she seems a little shy, but my pal is just used to being an outcast. Red hair makes you a target. She's also wary of our getting caught so far from where we're supposed to be. Speaking of—you have any bolt cutters?"

"Huh? Oh, wow. Did you get wrapped up in fishing line or plastic?" I'd marched in more than a few protests to stop ocean pollution.

"Nah—my sister slapped me with a tracker. I'm on house arrest and she keeps finding me," Hillary responded, holding up an arm to reveal a blue band with a blinking red light.

I shook my head in disbelief. "I don't have any bolt cutters on me."

"How about a trade? If you're here you must be a witch. I happen to know something that the mighty Lion is afraid of. If you bring me bolt cutters, I'll tell you what I know. It might save your life if he ever catches you breaking a rule..." she trailed off. Piper whispered something in her ear and Hillary held up a hand.

"We also want at a dozen peanut butter chocolate cups. The kind from the orange wrappers. Deal?"

I sat back on my hands, considering. I wasn't sure what Layla had in the pantry, but I was absolutely curious about what the infamous Lion was afraid of, especially as I was meeting him tomorrow. I could check the garage for a flashlight.

"I have to get back, but I'll return later tonight. How about nine-thirty this evening?" Murad was usually gone by eight-thirty.

The mermaids grinned, their razor-sharp teeth on full display.

Chapter 27
The Lovers

Stella

Murad and I were silent this evening, both of us lost to our own thoughts. It was a relief when he stood to leave. I walked him to the front door, something I rarely did, but he seemed to appreciate. The moment the door closed I ran up the stairs to change.

It was growing cooler in the evenings, and I imagined the Washington shore would be even chillier, so I dug around until I found a navy fisherman's sweater, my trusty black jeans, and the jacket I'd borrowed from Ela.

I tiptoed to the kitchen and found Layla talking animatedly to the contestants of a dating show on a flat screen TV. I'd asked Murad for a TV and DVDs and he'd brought the weirdest collection of television programs. She saw me dressed to go outside and stood with a worried frown. I smiled reassuringly and went to the pantry.

I didn't see peanut butter cups, but I did grab a new jar of creamy peanut butter, two spoons, and a bag of chocolate chips. I shoved them into a cloth tote I found on a hook and swung it over my shoulder. I found a flashlight in a drawer. Miming a watch on my wrist, I tried to convey to Layla that I would return in two hours. I left by the backdoor and quickly crossed the lawn, steering clear of the stone cottage in case Murad was still there. When I was no longer visible to anyone looking outside the cottage door, I hurried.

The wind rushed over the drying maple leaves in rising, rustling sounds overhead. The flashlight emitted a dim yellow beam, but it led me through the woods. Crossing the creek was a bit scary in the dark, so I did it as quickly as possible. The white stones in the crude cemetery were radiant beneath moonlight. I had no idea how to get to the shoreline without going through Lilly's garden, so that's what I did. I avoided looking at the stone gargoyle, knowing it would frighten the crap out me. Instead I tiptoed soundlessly through the garden and then onto the beach path.

I slowed as I climbed around and over the large stacks of driftwood, not wanting to trip and twist an ankle. The beach appeared, pale stones glowing in the peachy light of a nearly full, harvest moon. The water lapped noisily as I walked the wooden pier in search of Hillary and Piper.

"Oi! It's Stella." Hillary's called out. Relief coursed sharp and sweet. I hadn't imagined them. I knelt at the end of the pier, put the flashlight down between my knees, and squinted over the side. Hillary and Piper appeared, closer to the wooden top of the pier with the rising tide, and I grinned, opening the tote.

"First thing first, let me see your bracelet." I tried not to flinch as Hillary hoisted herself up until she sat on the wooden platform. Piper followed her.

"Aren't you guys cold?" I was freezing just watching them.

"Not at all," Piper said. "We can tolerate extreme temperatures."

Hillary held her pale arm out to me. As I'd seen earlier, it was a thick rubber bracelet with a flashing light. I took out a pair of scissors.

"Wait! My sister said there was a steel cable inside. Scissors won't cut through."

"Hillary, this is a modified fitness tracker. It's not an electronic tracking device. See here?" I explained, just as I snipped it from her wrist. It fell to the platform and Hillary picked it up, turning it around in her hands.

"What is a fitness tracker?"

"It counts how many steps you take—it tracks your exercise."

"That lousy, fracking cow," Hillary cried, chucking the bracelet into the water.

"Total meddler," agreed Piper.

"I can't believe she got the better of me on that one. My sister Jessie is such a pain! Just because she's the oldest she thinks she can tell me what to do. We'll have to plot our revenge," she said to Piper, who nodded solemnly.

"Sorry, we didn't have peanut butter cups. But I brought you something better." I said, pulling out the peanut butter jar and chocolate chips. They watched warily as I opened the jar and sprinkled some chips inside before handing a spoon each to Hillary and Piper. They accepted the offering, sniffing the mixture with suspicion. I waited as they first licked, then devoured the treat.

"Amazeballs," Hillary said in a dreamy voice. Piper was already handing me her empty spoon, and I handed her the entire jar instead.

"Okay—I freed you. Now tell me what the Lion is afraid of."

Hillary smacked her lips, clearing her palette of peanut butter.

"Dolls. He hates them. Oh, and cats."

"Dolls? As in clowns?" I asked, stunned. The great Enforcer was afraid of kittens and dolls?

"If the clown is a doll, then yes. My old nanny used to know someone who knew his old nanny from many years ago. Apparently, his half-sisters used to torment him with dolls, and he hasn't liked them ever since. Cats have always skeeved him out. So, if you ever need to buy yourself some time—just have a doll on hand. Or a cat," Hillary concluded. I looked at her, staggered.

"This is absolutely terrible advice! How do I even know you're telling me the truth?" I demanded, pissed at being tricked. Hillary grew serious.

"I do not lie. I am not my stinking sister. Take it or leave it."

Dolls. Jeez. I shrugged. We sat in companionable silence as they passed the jar back and forth.

"You know, the Lion is terrifying, but I've heard tales of King Murad being much worse," Hillary shared.

"He drinks people," Piper whispered in a horrified tone.

"Of course, he does! He's a vampire, isn't he? I also heard he drinks from a special herd of wild magickal horses," Hillary responded with scorn.

"I thought he was a demon?" Piper asked.

"He's a demon-*vampire*. Keep up, Piper," Hillary scoffed.

"He's a demon-vampire," Hillary continued. "He took Lila's light from her. That's what made him so powerful. He sucked it right out of her. And now he's going after her great granddaughter," Hillary said.

"What do you mean?" My mind was still blanked at the mention of horses. Did Murad drink from his stable of horses? I shuddered.

"Only that that same nanny said that the King needs to keep replenishing his light to stay powerful. They say he killed Lila's family to make sure she never ran away again. I never met the guy, but he sounds pretty scary," she said, flicking her tail so the tip fluttered.

My head spun. "I thought he was planning to marry her?"

"How can he? I heard that all but the water witches have turned against the girl. They think she's an imposter only pretending so she can snag Murad and be queen," chimed in Piper. I sat back, speechless.

"Yup. He'll probably kill her as soon as the Council meets," agreed Hillary.

I stood and accidentally kicked the flashlight into the water. Piper slid gracefully beneath the dark surface and rescued it for me. I tapped it several times but the battery had died. This was turning out to be a terrible evening. Could I really be wrong about Murad? Granted, the mermaids were talking rumors, yet there was usually a kernel of truth in these things, wasn't there?

"I have to go," I mumbled. The mermaids protested immediately.

"I'll try to be back, but if I don't maybe we'll see each other somewhere else," I said, backing away.

"If you see my boyfriend, will you tell him I'll be around for a few more days?" Hillary asked. I nodded and gave her a thumbs up.

"Bye, Piper and Hillary," I called out as I headed back up the beach. I really had to talk to Bird about what he'd been up to.

The path was a lot creepier without a flashlight. I was glad when I reached Lilly's backyard gardens. The house was still illuminated when I tiptoed along the path and I froze at the sound of voices. Although certain Ela and Lilly wouldn't mind my being here, I preferred not to be caught outside like a creeper. I slinked along the path only to come to a standstill when I spied two figures on an Adirondack bench ahead of me. I recognized the occupants immediately and icy dread filled me.

Murad sat on the wide bench with Lilly in his arms. He cradled her delicate body, and I saw she wore a long white nightgown and robe with a lap blanket for extra warmth. Her bright hair was loose and fell like spun cotton candy over the front of her gown. She looked frail within his strong arms.

"Tomorrow will be the equinox. Can't you feel it? Isn't it beautiful?" Lilly asked in her dulcet voice. She was staring up at the star-littered sky. I followed her gaze and drew in a breath. Silver stars balanced within the velvet nest of night. Murad's head was bent towards Lilly, and I saw his profile as he stared at Lilly's uplifted face.

"Yes. It's the most wonderful thing I've ever seen," he agreed. His voice held a tone I'd never heard from him before. It was tender and low, aching with repressed emotion.

Oh, God. The truth dawned. Lilly was Lila. She had to be. Murad had only loved one woman, and it was clear he loved the one held reverently in his arms now, despite the massive physical age difference.

What had Hillary and Piper said about Murad? That he needed her light? Fear gripped me and I backed away as silently as I could manage. Once I met the garden wall, I followed it all the way around to the side of the property. The gate loomed and my feet picked up into a run as I passed beneath its arch. The white stones in the cemetery came into view just before I collided into a tree and fell backwards. Strong hands gripped me as the tree became Murad, wrapped in shadows. How had he moved so quickly?

I fought him, twisting and turning like a savage animal, even biting his hands where they grasped me. He shook me.

"Stop, Stella! You'll hurt yourself!" he demanded roughly.

I shouted through panting breaths, "How could you! You keep her prisoner here?"

"It's not what you think! Please, Stella. I knew you were there. Listen!"

"Let me go!"

He released me immediately, hands up.

I stepped away from him, feeling the wind kick up around us, circling through the stones. Another thought occurred to me, so painful it knocked the air from my lungs.

"Who are these gravestones for?" I whispered. I couldn't see his face in the dark, but I noticed he put his hands in his pockets. Was my mother buried here?

"I don't know. The land from here to there belongs to Lila. She imagines what she wants. That's how her power works. Through intention. She is no longer sane, and so asking her about it is a useless exercise," he said helplessly.

"She chose this spot and it's on a ley line I had enchanted to connect our land. Only my brother knows she exists in this time and place. She punishes herself by allowing herself to grow old. During the day she is locked away in her mind, but at night she somehow comes back to a shadow of herself. Enough to hold small conversations as long as I stick to the weather and the garden," he admitted and I heard his grief.

"You lied to me. You said you had hope that she was still alive. You knew that she was."

"I said the agony of hope was something I've lived with a long time. That's true. She is physically near, yet forever beyond me. Being near someone you need more than air, yet unable to take a single breath, is a specific torture I wish on no being on earth or in hell.

"I have no idea whether she can will herself to die, but I hold hope she will eventually return to her mind and to me. How were you able to cross her wards? No one can cross over but me. Anyone else is turned to stone," he said in a puzzled voice. I remembered the gargoyle-like statue next to the garden wall.

"I don't know. Ela can as well." I pointed out. He tilted his head.

"Who is Ela?"

"Her companion."

"She has no companion, Stella. She doesn't allow anyone near her.

Not in hundreds of years," he said, concern lacing his words. I didn't know what to say. Should I admit I've been speaking with her in the daytime for days? Tell him more about Ela?

"Why didn't you tell me about her?"

"I couldn't risk you upsetting her. If I told you she was here you would have insisted on seeing her yourself. If she ever learned that Gracie, her daughter, lived—if she learned how they all died—she would never, ever recover. I can't demand it but I do beg you—please don't tell anyone else that she is here."

He was keeping her under wraps for himself. It was wrong, but I could tell he would refuse to see it that way. He had a Lila museum set up right here, and he was the only visitor. If I let him, he would do the same to me in a bid to keep me "safe."

"I won't tell anyone," I whispered brokenly.

"I still want to marry you in name only, Stella. It will protect you. Once the curse is broken, we can annul the marriage, and you can meet Lila formally. Once the curse is broken, I hope she comes back to her own mind again. She will have you to focus on, and you will live a long enough life to coax her into living again," he explained.

It was a dangerous man who loved a woman so deeply. I could see that Murad would do literally anything for Lila, and it made him both pitiful and terrifying. She wasn't worth it. If she were worthy of his love, she would never have left him to begin with. She would have fought for him. It was in that moment that I understood Alaric clearly, and I knew what I had to do.

"You still lied to me. At the museum. You told me that grief was like a fog that would eventually end. You said to walk through it," I reminded him. His face crumbled.

"Dear, Stella. I am still walking." My heart broke for him, despite his deception.

"Murad—go back to Lila and make sure she gets inside okay. I'll see you tomorrow for the witch council, and we can talk afterwards. Don't worry. I promise not to reveal your secret," I said, my voice tight with unshed tears.

He reached for my hand and in the next moment we stood before the mansion. His fingers trailed my cheek so whisper soft and fast I barely registered the movement, and then he disappeared, transferring back to Lila's side.

Chapter 28
The Joker

Alaric

I watched the video again. Stella rushed to her bedroom, leaving her door ajar. The hall was well lit, without motion or shadows. Less than an hour later Stella left her room with a slight young man in tow. The video shifted camera angles as they moved through the kitchen and outside. The angle of the two cameras outside showed the events that played out clearly. The boy lowered down to the street by magick and then Murad arrived.

"You did a fine job of putting this together, Grayson," I noted calmly.

"Thank you, Sir. I also know the identity of the young man from Ms. Amanda. His name is Thomas and he is a friend of the young ladies. He is not Primati and their relationship is platonic, Sir," Grayson shared. I flinched, but he adjusted the neck of his shirt and kept his eyes on the screen. I turned off the monitor.

"Delete all copies immediately. We've seen what we need to, and it is for our eyes only."

"Yes, Sir. Already done but for this one copy," Grayson responded.

Alaric, I'm here. My brother's thought invaded my own.

Enter.

"My brother is here, Grayson," I warned, pushing from the desk to stand. Grayson took my place. We were beneath my building, in our command center, and my brother was about to enter from a secret garage entrance. When he came through the door he was not alone. Daria Demir stood with Murad's hand clasped around her arm. The better to keep her from escaping. My brother wore a dark grey suit, his hair perfectly in place. Even without the dramatic cosmetics she favored, Daria owned a beauty and confidence few possessed. Her long, dark hair framed tawny skin and almond eyes that were nearly black.

"Oh, Alaric. It's been so long since I've seen you in this form. Did you miss me?" Daria asked in an affected, vulnerable voice. She'd switched to Turkish, knowing it a nostalgic language we all shared. Murad looked at me with sympathy.

"The bracelets are ready. Follow me," I said, walking my visitors to an interrogation room. I gestured to the three chairs around a metal table affixed to the floor. The table held a box with bespelled cuffs, and I opened it for Murad's inspection.

"The enchanted bracelets will prevent her from performing magick. If she attempts a spell or tries to hold a Pagatio, the curse will implode her every cell, killing her." I hoped she would try it.

"Kill is such a subjective term," Daria purred. My response was soft and deliberate.

"Allow me to clarify for you then. If you try to use magick, you will be dead before the intention executes your will. Dead as in no coming back, dead. If something were to go wrong and you did manage to survive, I will scrape the pieces together and ensure the job is completed myself." Her smile faded and Murad pulled the box towards him.

"Daria, you've already been sentenced to the ground and this is a reprieve from the remainder of your sentence. You will accept these measures, or you will return to bedrock immediately. It might be preferable for all Witch Queens to attend the Council, yet there is also option B—replacing you."

"Murad! How can you say such a thing? Have I not been amenable so far?" Daria batted her eyelashes at him, a wounded child. I flashed back to Daria the way she'd been before her change. As if she could read my mind, she turned to me and smiled with sadness.

"My love. I'm hurt at how little you both trust me. Don't you recall the old days? When we were all three mortal children in the palace?" she asked. The image she painted was blatantly false as Murad was a grown man when Daria and I had been thrust together by our fathers as a potential alliance.

"Stop your pretty tricks, Daria. You make me weary to be in the same room with you." I took the deadly bracelets from Murad and prepared them to engage.

Without my direction, Daria thrust her hands through the thick gold cuffs. She grasped my wrist quickly with both hands.

"No one will love you as I do. How many women have seen your beast and run screaming? I am not afraid, Alaric. I love you as you are. One day you will tire of these games and find me again," she said confidently. My lips curled as I withdrew from her grasp.

"Tell me about the sorcerer named Marcus."

"There are many with this name. I know who you refer to but have no knowledge of this person. Don't forget I've been absent from my court for the last five years." She rolled eyes towards Murad. His response was bland.

"Marcella awaits you in the garage. We are entrusting you into her care. If you try to run, she will face the same punishment and your covens will vote on their next Queen. By the time you rise from the ground, no one will remember your name. Consider your actions carefully, Daria."

Daria stood abruptly, a petulant flash of temper on her face before she concealed it beneath a practiced smile.

"You both have so many enemies. How many great vampire families were slaughtered because Murad wanted it so? How many have witches on retainer? You may never know who hired this sorcerer you speak of.

"But don't worry, I'll be a good girl and attend the Council," she said, tapping a long nail against her cheek. "I wonder if it will work out the way you hope, though? I hear whispers that Murad's little piece is Lila's descendent. Only a handful remember Lila except through stories. They think the Noble King is a fool, tricked by a calculating mortal teenager. A fragile, nasty Ancilla. How pathetic," Daria taunted in a sweet voice that belied her ugly words.

Murad moved so fast even I barely tracked his movements. Daria was on the ground, bent painfully backwards with her hair trapped in Murad's fist. Despite her predicament, her expression was excited, even triumphant. I shook my head. He'd given her the reaction she wanted.

"Rumors? I wonder who started them. You depend on your gender too much, Daria," my brother ground out. In the next instant, Daria was on her feet by the door while Murad straightened his tie beside her.

"Show yourself out, dear Daria. Give my best to Marcella and pass along my message, please." Murad walked towards me as Daria glared at his back. She left with Grayson close on her heels.

Murad eyed me incredulously and I shrugged. I led us to my private sitting room and pulled out a bottle of Raki from the fridge, pouring the liquid halfway up two glasses before topping them with chilled water. The anise flavored liquor turned cloudy. We each took a glass and silently saluted one another before downing the drinks.

"It's a wonder you haven't killed her already, little brother," Murad said flatly.

"In her sick, twisted head, that would only convince her that I cared. I won't give her the satisfaction unless her actions require it," I responded.

"I am worried about the council. They will not disrespect Stella in my presence, yet I think it a good idea to put out feelers and understand who might be spreading these rumors. Honestly, I think Stella could take her," mused Murad.

"What do you mean?" I did not like how he said her name.

Murad shook his head. "She is unusual, don't you think? Obstinate, defiant, has a mean temper but is also...fun. Do you know that she put salt in my tea? All because I suggested she spend her days learning to cook. Why would she want to remain a terrible cook? Doesn't she want to feed her children one day?"

I stilled at the mention of Stella's children. An image of little girls with wild tangled hair came to mind, needling my chest. "Stella is a fine cook. She prepares meals for herself and her grandfather. Besides, why wouldn't their father cook for them?" I asked with a slight smile, refilling our drinks. My brother was too used to people catering to him. Murad laughed.

"Why am I not surprised she tricked me? I suppose I deserve it. For all her mischief she is still...wonderful. Witty, kind to the servants and just a little bloodthirsty. When I told her that I drink from animals she suggested I drink from people instead because they deserve it. I couldn't tell her what I really drink for sustenance." He sighed.

"Did you find anything else out about how the druids entered your penthouse?"

"No trace of druids. The videos show no sign of another person or creature," I lied easily to my brother for the first time. If Stella hadn't told Murad about Thomas, I was not going to out her. My hand crept to my pocket, tracing the outline of my mother's ring.

"Have you thought about a ring for her, yet?" I asked. Murad appeared taken aback.

"I hadn't thought about it. Do you think she will expect one? She seems such a practical girl. I'll have to ask her what she likes after the council meeting. Thanks for the reminder, *Abi*."

"Actually, I have a suggestion …"

Chapter 29
The Magician

Stella

I paused at the top of the marble steps leading down to the party below. It was a scene from hell. Tons of people in fancy clothes chatting about superficial things and judging one another. Looking down their nose at me. A fraud with no magic. I smoothed down the crisp fabric of my black Victoria Beckham capri pants and jacket. I wore a white cotton shirt beneath it and pointy toe flats. The flats were a concession from Clara when I'd balked at stilettos and threatened to kill someone with them if she tried to make me wear them. Overall, I was pleased with the outfit. It was much more comfortable that the dress Tess had originally asked me to wear.

"I know. Pretty bleak, isn't it?" Amanda grumbled next to me. She wore a beautiful blush-colored dress that suited her dark hair. I reached out impulsively and squeezed her wrist. I'd missed her so much. She smiled and we exchanged a look that said we would always have each other's backs. I wasn't lying to her, but I just couldn't confide in her about Lila yet.

When she snagged a glass of pink liquid from a suited server, I did the same.

"You're going to love these. They're called 'Dirty Snow Whites'—appletinis without alcohol and made from enchanted apples. They give everything a little glow but without the headache," Amanda explained.

I took a sip and promptly gulped the entire glass. It was delicious. Crisp and sweet.

"Slow down! You want to keep your head here. Let me introduce you to some of the nicer people." When Amanda said "nicer people" it wasn't about status. She meant good people. I relaxed a bit, grateful to be navigating this weird new world with my best friend.

I grabbed another Dirty Snow White and didn't protest when Amanda tugged me between groups of people. She stopped in front of two laughing young women.

"Stella, this is Tori, my friend from Novice classes. Tori is a Water Witch, third generation. Also, an aspiring artist, so you have something in common."

Tori was a soft young woman, with wise brown eyes and caramel hair. We said our hellos and I admired the Grecian white dress she wore, trying my best to be sociable.

"And this is Irem, an exchange student, also from my Novice classes. Irem is an Earth Witch." I shook hands and admired their clan tattoos.

I genuinely liked both girls right away. Irem had long golden hair and sharp hazel eyes that missed nothing.

"I like your name. Does it mean star?" asked Irem.

"Yup. Twinkle, twinkle little star…" I trailed off, nervous.

"…how I wonder what you are," the other girls recited as if on autopilot. They met my bemused face with sheepish smiles.

"There you are, Stella!" Clara approached, flanked by two women.

She wore a pleated green dress that made her look like a goddess. Her strawberry curls were held up in emerald clips that sparkled, and her lips were slicked with deep raspberry lipstick. She might as well have been painted by Botticelli...I choked on my drink. Was it possible? She gave me a critical once over as she waved to the girls to relax.

"I'd like to introduce you to Bromely, my Second in the region. My formal Second is missing at the moment and so Bromely is filling in," Clara said. I immediately recognized Bromely as the girl from the bookstore. The one who'd run away in terror at the sight of Alaric. She wore a plum top with a crimson crinoline skirt and boots. Her hair was purple today, coiled in sections all over her head. I nodded and she gave a bob of her head.

"And this is Marcella, First Sister Witch for the Earth Covens. Marcella is Second for Daria Demir, the Queen of Earth Witches."

Tall, with coppery brown skin, Marcella radiated grace and intelligence. Her hair was pulled from her face with gold encrusted braids that transitioned into flowing waves down her back. She wore a golden dress that clasped above one shoulder, the other bared.

"It's a pleasure to meet you both," I said politely.

"Do you have an agenda, Stella?" Clara asked. Amanda quickly pulled one out of her clutch and handed it to me. Clara spoke as I read.

"We'll move to the grand chamber to mingle. Then we'll hear an announcement from King Murad before we adjure ourselves to the Grand Council meeting and vote."

I lost her after the word "mingle" and was relieved when they said their goodbyes soon after. Amanda led us back up the steps, across the enormous veranda, and into the main hall. The room was already filling with men and women, and I noticed a lot of curious looks shot our way. A tall man with thick grey hair approached, giving me the stink eye. He took Irem's elbow and shepherded her away without a word. Irem cast an embarrassed look in our direction as she mouthed goodbye. Amanda's lips pulled down. She turned to me.

"Stella, can you stay here for one moment? I need to talk with Clara about something."

Did she mean stand here alone with all these strangers staring at me?

"Sure. No problem. I have Tori to keep me company." My smile must have been convincing because Amanda slipped into the crowd. A girl resembling Tori tapped her on the shoulder.

"Mom and Dad want to talk to you. Now." Tori introduced me to her sister and apologetically promised to find me later. I thrust my shoulders back and met the hostile glare of a woman in black. Maybe there was credence to what Hillary said about how the witches believed I was a fraud. I walked along the edge of the crowd and found a small nook that allowed me to see the room with my back against a wall.

Marcella walked towards my spot in the alcove and met my tentative smile with a regretful one. Before I could wonder the cause, she stepped aside, revealing a living doll with tanned skin, tawny eyes and jet-black hair. The woman was dressed in a tight red dress that showed every curve and she examined me as if I were covered in bat dung.

"May I introduce Daria Demir, Queen of Earth Witches?" Marcella didn't even wait to announce my name before she glided away. Marcella worked for Daria, yet I had a feeling she didn't like her job very much.

"Er—I'm Stella." I held out my hand. Daria inspected it. I continued to stubbornly hold out my arm until she limply pinched my fingertips with hers. Was she for real?

"So, you're supposed to be Lila's girl." She studied me dispassionately. "It's been a long time, but you might have something about her in that faded blonde hair of yours and pointy chin. You might want to engage a witch with more skills to fix that for you." She waved a small hand in the general area of my head. She wore so many rings I wondered how she could even lift her hands.

"Thank you." I smiled. "You must be ancient to remember her." Daria's eyes tightened.

"It's interesting that you were just—discovered—after all these years. We thought the lot of that little second family of hers perished eons ago. Exterminated. But then you suddenly pop up. What was your mother's name?"

I gritted my teeth behind a banal smile. My cousins had taught me that allowing a predator to scent blood only increased their hunger. I shrugged and her expression turned icy.

"If I wasn't on probation from magick—" she jangled heavy gold bracelets "—I would compel you to tell me her name." The bracelets glowed as she shook them. I recall being told that she'd recently been taken out of punishment to attend the Council. It looks like they didn't trust her very much if they kept her from using magick.

I lowered my chin and stepped closer to the woman who threatened to take my free will. My hands closed into fists, thumbs rubbing.

"If you ever *try* to compel me against my will, I will give you a reason to magick scars from your face before you can blink."

"I have no idea what that means—but I do as I *like*. You don't want me as an enemy, little imposter *Ancilla*." I got the impression that not many people stood up to Daria Demir.

"Before you can blink," I repeated. Daria's brilliant smile revealed overlapping lower teeth. *Finally, a sign of imperfection around here.*

"We'll see. Catch me on a good day, and I'll have you singing like a parrot," she stated with an arrogant shake of her head. Her flashing hands smoothed the ends of her hair.

"Parrot? Do you mean canary? Sing like a canary?"

"Whatever. English is not my favorite language." She waved a hand. "There are many here who believe you are a liar. That you're only taking advantage of a certain similarity of looks—pretending to be Lila's family to gain Murad's interest—and his throne." Her expression grew sly before she continued.

"Then there is the rumor that you cannot do magick. I find it hard to believe the human lineage of the Goddess Danu is just a common Ancilla. This business of claiming you for a coven is a waste of time. No one will support your marriage."

"I doubt Murad would lie," I said, my voice treacherously unsteady, recalling that Ancilla was a derogatory term for human. She smirked and tilted her glossy head, clicking her nails against a gold bracelet. A tattoo of roses and golden vines encircled her thumb and wound up and around her hand.

"Murad has been unstable for centuries in grief over Lila. He is desirable because he holds a heady combination of beauty, power and tragedy. The unattainable heart. Once he finds out you're just a pretender he'll fall into the abyss again. There will come a time when he will truly go off the deep end, and The Lion will become Noble King—making *me* the Noble Queen," she gloated. Her eyes flashed as she tilted her chin smugly. I swallowed past the sudden lump in my throat. Wouldn't her declaration be considered treason in the normal world?

"I didn't know he was engaged. Congratulations?" I was extremely uncomfortable, bordering on claustrophobia.

"Thank you. The Enforcer is a powerful creature. *He* is for women who live on the edge and play with fire. I've allowed him lovers but none know his true form. You do know by now that all witches carry a trace of angelic blood from the time before such things were forbidden? We both hold the blood of angels—even if my father fell from Grace—and so will be a wonderful match. In all things." Her lips curved in a confident sneer. My stomach threatened to barf Dirty Snow-White cocktail all over her handkerchief of a dress.

"I thought The Lion came from a different lineage?"

"Oh, his mother was daughter to the archangel Michael, blahdey, blahdey, blahdey," she said dismissively before she continued.

"This is true, but I refer to the demon bite. The Lion carries the blood of both Michael and Morning Star—but it is the beast that I love the most. We met before all of that—in fact we've been inseparable since we were children," she shared, clearly expecting me to be impressed.

"That sounds like a very long engagement," I replied dully. The arrogant convict scowled, and I was saved from further conversation when a bell clanged three times. Everyone moved to either side of the cavernous room, leaving a path leading from an arched doorway on one side to an impressive raised dais on the other.

"Excuse me," Daria said with glittering eyes. She made her way to the dais where she was joined by Clara, Tess, and a small old man with a large white mustache.

The bell clanged again, three times. The entrance doors were flung wide. I pressed my way through the crowd until I was in the front and able to see the show. Amanda and Tori appeared at my sides just as a man in a velvet suit broadcast the newcomer.

"Announcing the Noble King, Murad!"

Murad strode into the hall, a true Prince of night beneath the glittering chandeliers. His thick hair gleamed chocolate mink. His chiseled features and smoldering eyes were almost too pretty on a man, yet his physique and the set of his jaw was the epitome of all that was masculine. He wore black leather pants, a fitted black shirt and leather vest that molded to his chest and flat stomach. His boots were gleaming

Italian leather.

He wore no crown yet a swath of cloth across his chest appeared embroidered with gold. He was every girl's dream before they knew what to dream for. Just not my dream. He paused, scanning the faces lining the long aisle. They lit up the moment he found me. He crooked two fingers in my direction.

Heads turned to see who he was gesturing to. Their faces reflected curiosity, jealousy, and even disdain once they saw I was his intended target. Whispers rose all around us. Murad remained posed in place, waiting. Amanda sucked in a breath at my side.

"I think you've been summoned. It's okay—go to him," she whispered. Please, please let the floor swallow me. If there was ever a time for me to acquire magick, I prayed it happened now. I could disappear and transfer back into my attic bedroom, content with never knowing this world existed.

I gave a small, not so subtle shake of my head. Heads whipped back and forth between us. He smiled and raised an eyebrow in challenge. The whispers grew louder, a few titters audible behind raised hands.

I turned to Amanda for a way out, but her eyes were glued to Murad. Startled by the dreamy quality of her smile, I made a mental note to tease her about this later. She nudged me gently and I took a tiny step away from the relative safety of the crowd. Murad offered an encouraging twitch of his lips. I kept my eyes trained on his as I slowly walked towards him. It felt like the longest walk of my entire life.

"Pretender," someone hissed. I glanced furtively towards the voice and saw a short, fat man with cold eyes. The man next to him stepped on his foot and I was glad not everyone seemed out to humiliate me. When I reached Murad, he held out his arm and I accepted it gratefully, hoping he might keep my upright if I passed out or fell down.

"You're doing fine," he whispered in my ear. I nodded, tucking and then untucking hair behind my ear. Murad kept a reasonable pace as we walked towards the dais. It was clear people here were fascinated with Murad. Lots of smiles and borderline hysteria when he chanced to return a smile or respond to a blessing. I received obvious stares, but when Murad was distracted elsewhere, I noted contempt on quite a few faces.

As we neared the witch nobility, I saw Tess and Clara frown. Tess caught my eye, and smoothed her features into a placid smile. I was disappointing them for sure. When we reached the platform, Murad turned back to the gathering. A bell clanged and the doors reopened. The crier announced a new arrival.

"Prince Abbas, Noble Enforcer and The Great Lion," the man bellowed.

The Enforcer strode into the room. Men and women alike gasped aloud at the sight of him. He was enormous, easily over eight-feet tall. His skin was darker, his face frightening with its sharp planes and black eyes. His hair was deepest sable and almost touched his shoulders. Horns curled upward from the top of his head. Most remarkable were the black wings that framed his striding figure. They were shaped like a bat's wings with claws that contracted as they stretched. Instead of the thin membrane of a bat's wings, his were covered in fine black down that shivered with the air as he walked. The wings were closed, yet when he passed the archway, he snapped them outward, revealing a huge wingspan. Gasps rang from around the room. Daria purred at my side, and I looked over to see her lick her lips. *Ick.*

Regarding the crowd, I saw her response wasn't singular, although most people just appeared frightened to death. Whereas Murad seemed loved, the Enforcer was obviously feared. The silent room seemed to breath with relief when he took a place at the foot of the dais to my right. Jing San and six others followed him. Funny I hadn't noticed them before but they formed a line to his right. Murad patted my hand. Could he hear my racing heart? I'd tried to imagine what The Lion might appear like, but had not even been close.

Clara, Tess, and Daria took turns welcoming the attendees and yammered on about this year's group of novices, activities for the year, the status of Wiccan protests in Australia and so forth. When Clara finally wound down and turned to Murad, he took my hand in his. He squeezed gently, no doubt feeling the clamminess of my palm.

"Distinguished coven, I greet you and recognize the importance of your numbers in holding peace within the Primati community. As I announced previously, I have decided to take a wife. Allow me to formally introduce you to Mademoiselle Stella Avery, your future Noble Queen." He paused to a scattering of applause. I wanted to die. Perhaps it was my imagination, but the silence felt oppressive and pointed.

Murad released me. Faces blanched and I peeked up at him. His eyes had turned deepest red. He bared his teeth and razor-sharp incisors slid into place. Was this part of the program? I mentally kicked myself for not paying closer attention. The hiss of Jing San's samurai blade being slowly drawn from its metal sheath was like hearing Death whisper.

The Lion shifted the barest inch, and the entire room of occupants froze in place. He whispered something and every witch in the room dropped to their knees, heads bowed. I heard the witch nobility gasp behind me. A sword of blue fire appeared in the Enforcer's hand. Even Murad flinched at the sight of it.

"No—please," Clara whispered in a tight voice. As the Enforcer stalked slowly to the center of the aisle, he passed close by where I stood. I did the only sensible thing I could think of. I screamed. As the winged beast turned towards me, I stumbled and fainted dramatically—falling off the dais.

He caught me, the sword disappearing to wherever it had come from. I was dead weight and felt him swing me higher into his arms.

"Air. I need air," I cried in a panicked voice, my eyelids shut in distress. I felt the Lion swing in Murad's direction and then my fiancé's response.

"Take her, brother. I need to have words with the witches."

Chapter 30
Judgment

Stella

O ne moment we were in the Hall, the next we were outside in the night air. I opened my eyes and shivered to see the dark outline of the Enforcer staring down at me. The harvest moon hung above, concealing his face. His black wings unfolded slowly, rising high above his shoulders to surround us. I shuddered.

"Don't be afraid," he said, his voice guttural. He lowered me gently to the ground. I scanned our surroundings and noted the hedge labyrinth to our right. I began to shake and backed away from him. "Don't run." He raised a claw tipped hand and dropped it. I turned and ran into the labyrinth.

"Stella," I heard him rasp. I'd never been good at outrunning people. As soon as I knew someone was in pursuit, my instincts were to drop low and begin swinging my fists. This time I made sure to run as fast as I could. Small torches illuminated turns within the labyrinth, the sweet scent of grass and honeysuckle rich in the air. I tried to make only right turns and avoid backtracking, but that strategy failed a few times, leaving me scrambling to find a new path. I could hear and sense him close, yet he did not overtake me. Not yet.

When I reached a small clearing, I stopped. There were a few sapling trees and a circular stone mosaic lay in the ground. A round stone ball lay at the mosaic's center and it gave off a pearly glow. Magical torches lit the area and a sturdy bench made of alder wood sat nearby.

I rested on the bench, trying to catch my breath. It didn't take long for my pursuer to step into the clearing. His black eyes were guarded as he remained some distance away. He wore all black, an angel of death in moonlight.

I stepped up onto the bench and beckoned him to come nearer. His expression grew wary. I motioned again for him to come closer and tried not to get distracted by how fearsome he looked. By his obsidian eyes and strangely beautiful face.

He did not do things by halves. One moment he was twelve feet away and the next he was directly in front of me. I did not hesitate, knowing I may not get another chance.

I slapped him as hard as I could. Except my hand never made contact. He held my wrist inches from his darkening expression. I gulped to see his huge hand enclosing mine. That didn't stop me from pulling from his grasp and trying again. Once more, he captured my wrist and hand.

"Why are you attempting to strike me?" he asked with a dangerous glint in his eyes.

"You're such an ass! Do you really believe I am so stupid, Alaric?" I shouted.

His eyes threaded with red fire as he took a step back.

"How did you know?" he grated.

"Know what? That you have more aliases than a superspy? That you are Abbas the Lion, ergo the Great Enforcer, otherwise known as

Alaric? Let me list the ways for you. How about the way you toss people around? How about the scars on your palms from Michael's sword? Or the fact that your elevator doors are etched with gold lions...it's a long list. I've suspected who you are since the night Silvan was killed. Seeing you break people in half kind of made everything click into place."

He continued to stare, dumbfounded. *High five, sister.* For once I was the one with the surprises.

"But you allowed me to take you away that night," he ground out.

"That's right. Because I felt safe with you."

"You came to see me about protecting you from the Lion—you were afraid of him—me—kidnapping you," he said, his gaze heated as it raked my face, looking no doubt for signs of madness.

"That was before I realized *you* were the Lion." Why was he struggling with this?

"Why did you slap me?" he asked darkly.

I crossed my arms and leaned towards him.

"I *tried* to slap you for not telling me you were engaged to Daria Demir! How dare you kiss me when you knew the entire time you already had a fiancé? You lied to me. And how could you turn your back on me after I spilled out my heart to you that day in your office?"

He gaped at me for several seconds before his eyes glittered with something unpleasant. He stepped closer, his face inches from my own. I made sure to breathe as I held my ground. It was hard. Very, very hard. If I didn't know Alaric was in there, I would be terrified.

"Never try to strike me again. Never try to run from me again. Not when I am in this form. I may not be able to control myself with strong emotions or challenges—and I don't want to hurt you."

"Is that what you tell your *fiancé*?" I sneered.

"Damn it, woman!" He snarled. "I am not engaged. I told you there was no one else."

"Then why did she tell me you were?" I argued.

"Because she's a psycho bitch who wants it to be true," he roared in his new voice. "Our fathers talked of a marriage and drew up a contract, yet it was never formally announced. She's been stalking me for centuries." His passionate response drew me up short. Having met her, this had the ring of truth to it.

"You mean—you aren't even dating?" I asked, my tone a trifle less accusatory.

He gnashed his teeth, revealing even larger incisors than Murad displayed earlier. I gulped. The air trembled around us as he obviously struggled with his temper. An electric current hummed, raising the hair on my nape and arms. He took a step back. No. That was not happening. I leapt forward, throwing my arms around his neck. His wings flared but I clasped my elbows, determined not to let go.

His hands rose to span my entire waist, holding my weight. His flesh was much warmer in this form; my body burned where it touched him.

"Stella! Have you no sense? Are you not afraid of me?" he grated, his lips hovering before mine.

"I'm only afraid of your stupidity, Alaric." I inhaled deeply near his new jaw, pleased that he still smelled very much like my Alaric. Frankincense, mint and perhaps more cypress than sandalwood…

"Stop sniffing me for one moment. I can't think. You knew this entire time?"

I nodded. "I wanted you to tell me yourself that day in the office, but you just shut down. "I'm doing this for your own good, Stella," I mocked. His hands tightened on my waist, crushing me close, and I wiggled to make sure I could still breathe. His grip relaxed.

"I was trying to protect you. Maybe I was protecting myself as well. I knew you would find out eventually that I was the Lion you feared—

and hate me."

I ran my palms experimentally to his shoulders and back again before allowing them to drift up to stroke his face. I didn't have the nerve to inspect his horns, though I wanted to. He was different, but I could still see Alaric inside.

He stilled completely at my touch.

"When will you understand that I am absolutely serious about my feelings for you? Nothing will change my mind," I whispered. I witnessed his transformation. Soon I looked not into the eyes of the beast but into Alaric's honey brown gaze. He had shifted for me. I pressed my lips to his and felt his arms encircle my hips.

The night was perfect. He was perfect. The hunger in his lips was the response I craved. The time away from him, working in Lila's garden, trying to avoid thinking about him, seemed like no time at all. His hand dug into my hair, yanking sharply so that my head fell back, but not painfully so. His lips explored my jaw, his nose running gently along the sensitive skin of my throat as he inhaled me. He pressed his teeth to my tender skin, and I moaned, opening my eyes to take in the starry night and full moon above. He went still just before I felt a jolt.

"Remove your hands from my fiancé," Murad said in a low growl.

I followed Alaric's gaze to his right shoulder. The tip of something silver poked from the cloth of his shirt. I peered around Alaric and saw Murad, his appearance fanged and red eyed.

Alaric gently put me down and pushed me behind him. I shrieked to see the large dagger that pierced his left shoulder blade. Had Murad literally stabbed his own brother in the back?

"Stella, would you mind pulling that out for me? I cannot heal if it remains there," Alaric asked me quietly over his shoulder. I felt sick but took a deep breath and gingerly grasped the black leather handle of the knife. I gave a testing tug and it barely moved, embedded in bone as it was. My stomach churned. Alaric kept talking to Murad as I tried again.

"Murad, I would ask you to allow me to explain, but you don't seem open to a conversation right now," Alaric said in a low voice.

"An explanation? I saw you ravage her. You were supposed to be protecting her—not seducing her," Murad ground out, a second blade appearing in his hand.

Anxious, I pulled harder at the dagger in Alaric's shoulder, wincing at his soft grunt. Black liquid dripped and then turned to ash before it could hit the ground. *What the hell?*

"Seducing her? I would hardly call a few juvenile kisses a seduction, brother," Alaric said in a dismissive tone.

Juvenile kisses? The flat of my palm tapped hard against the hilt of the blade, driving it deeper into bone. To his credit, he didn't make a sound. I stepped around Alaric.

"No one seduced me, Murad. Are we living in the dark ages? It was me. *I* kissed *him*." I may as well have been invisible. He continued to glare murderously at his younger brother. Grayson appeared from the shadows, followed by Tess.

"Sir, there is a report that an army of something unknown is assembling nearby," Grayson told Alaric. Tess wrung her hands, wild eyes moving from my mussed hair to Murad's face.

A vibration buzzed in the air until a shimmer was visible around Alaric's outline—and then he once again resembled the fearsome creature from the Hall. He reached behind his shoulder and pulled the dagger out in one yank. Nausea stirred at the wet sound the blade made as it tore free.

He turned quickly, scooped me off my feet, and transferred us back to the Hall. This time we appeared in the doorway of the Grand Council chamber. The others appeared seconds behind us. He put me down immediately and stalked away without a backwards glance.

I turned and watched him join Murad as they walked together towards the main hall. Murad looked back at me once, concern and perhaps a twinge of disappointment etched on his handsome face. Amanda stood at the entrance to the main hall, twisting her hands. I offered her a small smile, hoping to put her at ease.

Tess grabbed my upper arms too tightly, making me wince. I didn't complain, seeing the worry in her eyes.

"Are you alright, Stella?" she asked. I nodded, a bit unbalanced to be in two places within seconds. The gulf between Alaric and me seemed greater than ever. I'd now upset Murad and caused friction between them. This day would be one for the record books.

"Murad really scared the entire community over the actions of a few in the Hall. I'm so sorry if you were upset. We're about to begin the Council meeting. Please come in while I seal the door. Everyone else is present," she said.

From inside, it became clear that the circular chamber was actually a tower. A tower set within the center of the castle. Windowless stone walls curved, opening high above into a night sky without ceiling. Every few yards, water trickled down the stone walls into wood and glass troughs that emptied into others. The center of the room boasted an enormous round table made of iridescent stone. In the center of the table was a small fire pit, its flame crackling. Fire flickered from various torches, making the walls appear alive. Concealed vents blew air that swirled about the tower in a continual breeze.

Beneath our feet were intricately knotted silk carpets in vibrant colors. I looked upward, marveling at the moon framed within the circular hole. Bromely coughed at my side.

"The room holds all of the sacred elements. The stones in the wall honor the year and seasons, but you can see those better during the day. Let me show you where to sit," she offered, and I followed her.

The table held ten seats. Marcella sat to the right of a glowering Daria. Clara next to Bromely, a man introduced to me as Flynn took the seat at Tess's right. Tess took her place and I sank into a chair. Across from me was the wizened old man from the dais. Clara introduced him as Babak, the Spirit Wizard King.

"As we do not need Stella for the entire meeting, I thought we could begin by confirming her membership to my coven," Clara began.

"I'm afraid that's not possible," Daria said. "She's non-magick and therefore excluded from our membership." Clara tilted her head to one side, her lips curling in disgust.

"I knew you were going to pull this. Why do you always have to be such a crotch Nazi, Demir?" asked Clara. Tess put her hands up in a soothing gesture. Babak smiled at me as he settled deeper into his seat. I hadn't heard the guy speak once, and with this crowd I could see why.

"Come now, Daria. It's only a matter of time..." began Tess, but Daria banged both hands against the table, her rings and bracelets striking its surface in sharp jangles.

"Absolutely not—and without a three-quarter majority she cannot be voted in, either." Daria gave Clara a malicious smile that generously broadened to include me.

"Then it is good I am here," said a voice behind us.

Several people emerged near the firelight brightened doorway. My jaw dropped with recognition as they approached. Within a heartbeat, every witch at the table but Daria and myself had a Pagatio in hand. Tess held a black wand that looked like tourmaline. Clara's was a pink quartz with red smoky shadows. Babak held an unusual feather.

"This is impossible. I sealed the tower!" cried Tess.

"The seal keeps out those who don't belong. I belong."

My grandmother Mahari stepped to the table and took the empty seat at my left. My cousins Midora and Mira flanked her chair. I gaped at them, but they studiously avoided my gaze. Stunned, I could think of nothing to say. This was worse than when she showed up on my first day of middle school.

"As heir to the last Fire Queen, I belong at this table as much as you do."

"I would know if that were true," a confused-looking Clara said. "Unfortunately, the last Fire Witch died with her heirs in Auschwitz."

"My mother," replied Mahari calmly. "Records were falsified to allow me an escape to America." Everyone sat back, considering her words, and I was glad when Pagatios were lowered to the table. Daria leaned forward.

"If you lie, you and your cubs here will die a slow and painful death. There are ways to confirm the validity of a Fire Queen. If you fail the test, the consequences will leave you praying for a quick death," Daria said, grinning with excitement. Mahari quirked a thin eyebrow and relaxed further into her chair.

"Give me your test."

Tess made some motions with her hands, and the flame in the center of the table turned bright blue. It crept across the stone table towards us. I was on the verge of tipping my chair back to run when Mahari stretched out her hand. The flame raced into her palm and up her arm. It turned bright red and danced along her bare skin in joyful waves before flowing back to the center of the table, where it once again became a normal flame.

"Plot twist. It looks like she's telling the truth. She and her little slatterns are Fire Witches. Royal heirs to be exact. Otherwise the Council fire would have burned them to ash," Daria explained.

"*Slatterns?* Is that like sluts?" asked Mira suspiciously

"Silence!" shrieked Daria. "This is a formal Council meeting. Visitors are not allowed!"

"I think it's like a seventeenth century term for prostitute," I stage whispered.

"Seventeenth century? How old is this boujee bitch, anyway?" Midora asked.

Daria sprang from the table. Her bracelets glowed and she shook them as if they burned. With a glare that promised retribution, she sank once more in her chair. Mahari cleared her throat.

"You were about to vote on which coven my Granddaughter belongs to?" she prompted.

"No, we were not. She has no magic and therefore is not eligible," Daria grated. The other three leaders looked at one another.

"With a Fire Queen here we can now vote to a majority on which element house Stella belongs to, regardless of whether she can demonstrate magical ability," Clara said. Bromely nodded at her side.

"There is no need to vote. She is claimed by the Fire covens," Mahari said.

"Also—I can prove that Stella has magic," my Romany grandmother declared coolly. All eyes trained on me—yet I was just as stumped by her claim as everyone else.

Midora and Mira were suddenly behind me. They scraped back my chair as I clung with fingertips to the edge of the table. A hot wind pulled me from my seat and sent me skyward. I heard gasps and protests, but it was too late.

My ascent was inelegant. I crashed against the side of the tower, banging my elbow and hip. And then I was above the tower, suspended. My body was flipped and I saw fire. It did not burn or hurt, but fear stole my ability to scream. I blinked and could see the small figures below around the table. All but Daria had risen to their feet with wands raised. I saw Mahari lower her arms and I was suddenly falling.

Gravity was a fierce thing. Within seconds, I dropped yards down the tower. The image of a parachute entered my mind, and I imagined it opening with a whoosh. I still fell—but at a much slower rate. I twisted without thought and landed in a crouch on the table top, red flames from the center fire moving to engulf me before they tapered down and I stood, unscathed.

Wonder replaced the urge to attack my kin for nearly killing me. The faces around the table reflected that same incredulity. Had I really done that? Stopped myself from falling to my death?

"Our own Stella holds magic," Mahari said simply. "You just witnessed her mastery of air and fire. She holds magick."

"Impossible. You helped her. Someone helped her!" Daria screeched. Marcella and Flynn examined me with a great deal of interest. One by one the witches shook their heads at Daria.

Babak held out his hand, but I ignored his aid, jumping down to the floor. Midora and Mira quickly moved back. Smelling smoke, I patted my hips before tearing off my jacket. My lovely suit was scorched, burnt holes visible. I twisted my hair out of the way and met the gaze of each witch in turn. Shit was about to get real.

Chapter 31
The Empress

Stella

"Guess what?" Before I could answer my own question, a cracking boom sounded from above with vibrations that shook the tower. Screams erupted from the Hall.

Chittering noises grew in volume from overhead. Dark shapes with glossy red eyes scurried along the top of the open tower and slithered down the walls towards us. Midora screamed, pointing upwards while Daria eyed the newcomers with an eerie smile. What was *wrong* with her? Tess appeared frozen but Mahari swiftly pulled me aside.

"Mercury demons! Water witches are vulnerable to them. I can transfer no more than two additional people at a time. Survive, and I will return for you," my grandmother thundered, grabbing Midora and Mira's hands with one of hers while reaching towards a torch flame with the other. Mahari's eyes seared into mine, and her voice lingered as all three disappeared into flames. "I did not abandon you as a baby. I gave you a better future."

Babak pointed his large feather at the walls and a white light burst forth, meeting its targets with shrieks of pain. The sharp scent of ozone and sulfur swept through the tower.

Bromely and Flynn tried to pry the door open as they screamed warnings to those outside. One of the creatures landed in the room behind Clara. Her pink Pagatio burst into life with writhing red shadows and, raising her arms, she turned to face the interloper. An invisible force shoved the demon back where it struck the wall. Pinned in place, it screamed when the water trickling down the walls flowed over its writhing shape, swallowing it completely. Encased in water, I could see its mouth gape open, revealing double rows of serrated silver teeth. It wasn't drowning, though. It writhed in fury, attempting to free itself.

A second demon slammed near the first as Clara began to gather more of the grotesque creatures with her power. I pushed out my hands experimentally, trying to make air move, send fireballs—anything that might help. Nothing happened. An odd sense of vertigo made the tower swim around me.

"Mercury demons are only vulnerable in heat. I can't drown them but I can keep them pinned. We could have used your grandmother's fire. Hide, Stella," Clara yelled. She was keeping the creatures clear of me while watching her own back. I was a distraction, making her vulnerable. Clara waved her hand and water from the wall was sent across the room in a fine mist that forced more otherworldly shrieks from the frightening creatures.

"Will you *stop* with the *fucking* water, Clara!" Daria screamed, a murderous rage burning from the single eye visible beneath her dripping hair. She alone of the witches appeared soaked.

Marcella appeared, pointing to her left before she decapitated one of the demons with nothing but her fingernails. I tried not to vomit as red dust burst from its ragged neck. Following where she'd pointed, I shoved beneath the Council table. The space was shallow due to the large pedestal it rested upon, and so I braced my back against it, prepared to kick any threat that came near. An unholy scream pierced the hazy air. Eyes watering, I peered from beneath the table just as the entire tower room spun like a carnival ride.

Daria cursed as she slammed into a line of demons. Bracing my feet against the floor, I pressed myself against the table pedestal as legs flew past my hiding spot. The massive force soon became too much. I flipped out from beneath the table and landed on the rug. In an instant, the room stopped spinning. The tableau awaiting me as I rose to my feet was nightmarish.

The Witch Queens and their Firsts were frozen in place, as were dozens of beasts in various poses of chaos. The creatures appeared partially human, but for their misshapen, muscular builds, red eyes, and strange skin. They ranged in color from smoky grey to a pale cream that matched the stone walls. Chameleons? Mahari had called them mercury demons.

I heard a cry behind me and twisted. Tess swayed on unsteady feet. She held out her hand, palm up. "Come with me, Stella. There is a traitor in this room, and they've broken enchantments protecting this hallowed place." I backed away on wobbly legs.

"We can't just leave everyone!" I howled, staring at an unmoving demon petrified into a crouch at my feet. His glistening ruby eyes slowly blinked. Suspended red dust created an amber haze. Did I hear the scrape of metal?

"Tess, are you holding everyone in place?" She must be incredibly powerful.

"Yes. But I can't keep this up for much longer. Now, Stella! The enchantment is weakening," she called in strained tones.

Growls echoed from the top of the tower. A new wave of dark creatures crept in dripping shadows. High above, a small white shape appeared against the inky night. At first I thought it the moon, but then the moon never dipped and glided like this. More than one creature failed to swipe it from the air with lunging talons. As I stared up in astonishment, white wings soared in looping circles down the tower. Bird's red-orange beak bent towards me and then his bird's form exploded just before landing. The arctic tern was replaced by a Nordic God. The man, clothed in head-to-toe black, straightened, shaking out his limbs. He took in the tower's inhabitants before he locked relieved eyes on me.

"Hello, niece," the tall blonde man said with a nod.

"Hillary wants you to call her," was the only thing I could think to say.

"The scaly stalker?" he queried with a frown.

"She's rather nice," I mumbled, offended for Hillary.

"Taurus! Enough with the family reunion. We have a crisis going on," Tess cried. I gasped, my chest suddenly tight and burning.

"Why are you allowing her to breath this polluting air?" Taurus demanded of Tess. The look she cast him was filthy. The man held his palm in front of my face and pain spasmed from my chest and throat. I turned and retched red liquid.

"Stella! Take my hand. I can't hold them any longer." Tess's lips were white with strain. The taste of ozone met the back of my sore throat. Tess pleaded once more.

"I assure you, Stella—once we are gone, these demons will slink back to their pits. They are only on this plane for you. Once we escape the others will be safe."

"So, if I go with you, the rest of the castle, Amanda, Alaric, King Murad—everyone—will be okay?" I asked. Her nod was firm.

"I can guarantee the demons will leave once you are no longer here to capture." Tess's brow glistened, as did her upper lip. It must be taking an enormous sum of power to keep everyone immobile. The man who'd once been Bird the artic tern, but Tess called Taurus, spoke.

"Something is off here, sister. What have you done?"

The flame in the center of the table popped, the fire rushing forth several feet in the air. Mahari stood on the table, a pouch grasped in one hand. She took in the room and beckoned to me.

I glanced between Tess, Mahari, and Taurus. The best decision was one that kept others safe. Mahari was untrustworthy, her motives questionable. I reached for Tess.

Just as she took my arm, Taurus leapt forward. "The Stone of Mercy, Stella," was the last thing I heard him say.

* * *

We reappeared in a large room with narrow panes of stained-glass windows and an altar. It didn't seem like a house of worship, though. A single sofa in green velvet faced the altar. Tess released her grip and walked towards it, leaving me to trail behind.

"Did that really happen, Tess? Oh, my God, we have to go back and help. We have to warn Alaric and Murad." Dizzy, I swayed and fought back nausea.

On closer inspection, the platform was just a wood table that held an enormous book. Behind the table was a magnificent mural that filled an entire wall. At its center was an enormous golden tree. I approached it slowly, noticing that the image was really a mosaic of tiny squares of gold and painted tile. Spotlights in the ceiling caused the gold to emit an otherworldly glow while the rest of the room lay in shadow.

"What is this place?" I stood at her side, gazing between the golden tree and Tess.

Her lips curved into a soft smile. "I haven't seen my brother in human form for well over a century. I wonder why Taurus chose now to appear? And how is it that he seemed to know you? Have you been keeping secrets, Stella?"

Seriously? Our friends and family were fighting demons back in that tower. I checked my phone and groaned in frustration at the black screen.

"Where is your phone, Tess? We need to call reinforcements and return. What will happen if the mercury demons become unfrozen before our friends do? It was Daria who let them in, wasn't it? How will they protect themselves?" She stared at me blandly for a long moment and then stroked the open book with trailing fingertips.

"We're at my home in Scotland. This is my private chapel, built from druid stone and bespelled so that no one can enter without my permission. Can you guess why?" she prodded. *Really?*

I shrugged, impatient. She contemplated the mural with an inscrutable smile. Eager to humor her so we could move on, I stepped closer to the mural to read the scripted writing it held. Nestled among the tree's branches were names, dates, and locations. When I recognized my own name, three quarters of the way down, comprehension dawned. I stumbled back several paces to view it as a whole.

"It's a genealogical chart," I whispered. My family tree to be precise. There were my mother and father's names. I searched the top and saw Lila's name next to Charles Samuel Avery. Comprehension punched like a fist into my solar plexus. What were the odds that this name matched my grandfather's full name? It hadn't been on Thomas's version.

"Impossible," I murmured.

"Oh, you noticed Sam's name? It *is* the same man, by the way. Lila gives off quite a thump. Her love just lifts the men in her life right up, although I suspect Sam is close to the end of his very long life. Look at what happened to Murad on the field—her desire to save him by giving him her light was enough to make him into an entirely new species—a murderous creature she found abhorrent.

"Somehow, Lila imbued Sam with enough of her life-force during their brief time together to keep him alive over three hundred years," Tess explained bitterly.

My Sam was Lila's American husband? Rapid connections checked off in my mind. Both doctors. Both had resided in Virginia. If this was true, poor Sam had witnessed his entire family die for fifteen generations. Who could live with that kind of suffering?

"You know, just when I think the man will finally die of old age, he seems to grow twenty years younger. He's done remarkably well under the radar so to speak, looking over all of you ducks. Caring about you only to see you all die—oh, so young and tragically," Tess pondered aloud, a sharp bitterness to her sly smile. I've been a complete idiot. And, if true, Sam's life was a version of hell.

"Don't tell me it was all about a curse," I said slowly. "It was *you* who sent the mercury demons to the tower," I accused, fury melting the ice in my veins. The woman who'd pretended to be my friend tilted her head like a curious raven. Tess threw out her palm, and I was thrown upwards, pinned against the wall by a powerful gust of air. My legs were free, and I kicked out into empty space. My hips and outstretched arms were held immobile, but clarity came at last. She would kill me. No one would be left to care for Sam or warn the others.

The wind curled around me and I was flung down across the table, its edge catching my side with such force that sharp pain bloomed beneath my ribs. The book slid to the floor and then I was airborne, thrown from side to side before being slammed back into the wall so hard my head bounced. She stood beneath me, triumphant, then backed away as if to better view her handiwork. She was so strong. I had no control over my power. Or did I? I'd caused Thomas to appear by just thinking about him. I'd survived a fall within the tower. *Focus, Stella.*

I drew in a deep breath, ignoring stabs of pain as I did so, and opened my mind. I imagined Alaric, Murad, Clare, Amanda, and Jing and then pushed a visual of what I was seeing here in the empty chapel. I tried to convey the room, Tess before me, and the word "Scotland." I thought of poor Sam and of Lila, frail and locked within her mind. I would never get to tell her the truth. Never ask Sam the questions I wanted to.

Tess stood in the center of room. Her hair blew in every direction, ebony sheets of it dancing in the magicked wind. Her blue eyes were lit from within as madness emanated from her. It was as if the porcelain perfection of her had imploded, revealing her true form.

"I don't know how you did that little trick in the tower. Your mother held a weak control over air, but your power seems to include an affinity for fire as well. I can't risk you growing any stronger." Her face twisted into a snarl.

"You've forced me to move too quickly. It's sloppy. Why couldn't you just fulfill the enchantment and *die*," she screamed at me.

"You—with your appalling taste in fashion and ungrateful attitude! You are the embodiment of Lila and it is *wasted* on you. All those years I had to watch as he loved *her*. Not *me*!" She thumped her chest with a fist.

"Have you ever heard of an Everwish, Stella? There truly *is* a curse, although I can't deny I haven't helped it along from time to time. Precious Lila with adoration of all that was good—*I* saw him first!" She choked out a gasp that became a crazed wail. I winced at the terrible sound. She stalked closer, her black Pagatio raised as it winked sapphire with power.

"You have no idea. Murad was beautiful and so...alive. He was there, holding Alaric when we arrived to take Isabeau to the sky. The world was new to us, and our human bodies strange. I locked eyes with Murad but then Lila stopped to comfort Alaric. Once Murad laid eyes on Lila, he was lost to me," she cried.

The pressure pressing me against the wall was intense but I was able to lift my knees enough to slide my feet flat against the wall. Was this about some twisted sibling rivalry?

"I hate her! I *loathe* her!" Tess screamed. The table rose to slam against the wall and windows in brutal strikes, sending showers of glass and wood splinters to swirl dangerously inside the room with the powerful force of wind that Tess commanded. A shadow passed beyond a window.

"I would have done anything for him. I would have died for him. She wouldn't even *live* for him! He's been imprisoned in mourning, all caused by her selfishness," she shrieked.

"Were you the one? Did you steal her coffin?" I shouted over the squall's roar. The wind died down infinitesimally as Tess stopped tearing at her hair long enough to fix wild eyes on me. She blinked, distracted from her tirade.

"You're sharper than I thought you might be. I was the one who triggered the earthquakes in Istanbul that distracted Murad. I stole her body from the Tower and hid her coffin deep within Fontainebleau Forest. I couldn't stand watching him cry over her any longer. He *wouldn't* move *on*," she cried, a disbelieving look on her face. The irony of her statement seemed to escape her.

"The Fairy Queen found out. Fontainebleau Forest holds her summer home, so it was partially my mistake. She forced me to marry her insipid son in order to buy her clan's silence. It's too bad he's a mad prince now, locked away in her vaults to keep her kingdom safe," she said, a manic gleam in her eyes to match her cunning smile.

"But then one of her spies were captured and informed Murad that

Lila was in Fontainebleau. He asked Clara and me to help him look. I barely had time to move her off to the wilds of America before he was sniffing all around *fucking* France looking for her."

I hoped she kept talking. The more she vented, the more time it bought me to try to get off this wall. Tess was such a cliché. All this for a man. If Alaric ever fell in love with someone else I would…what? A different pain flooded and I force myself to take slow, deep breathes as she continued to spill her guts.

"Poor Murad. He needed me then. Clara was busy helping Alaric manage the Primati, but Murad knew he could always count on me. Outside his grief, those years were glorious. I knew that one day he would see me as more than a friend," she recounted in a dreamy voice. I couldn't take that delusional smirk one more moment.

"He loves her still, you crazy bat," I shouted. I was thrust forward and then slammed against the wall so hard that my head cracked. Hot, wet liquid seeped down the back of my neck. I heard Amanda's voice. Blood was power. It could fuel magick. Desperate, I focused on the wetness and gave it a try. Alaric's name became a silent chant. Odd, I imagined his voice, saying my name in return.

"Murad cares for me! One day he'll fall in love with me the way I want him to. But that won't be possible with you in the world, reminding him of her and giving him hope. You were supposed to die, along with all the others. It was my secret pleasure—witnessing girl after girl die as the curse took effect." How had I ever thought Tess cared about me? *Because I'd wanted to believe.*

"Of course, once Murad found out that one of Lila's daughters survived with Sam and that *you* existed, things became more complicated. Do you know how sickened I felt to have to act surprised and thrilled to learn that you lived? Clara and Alaric made it impossible to catch you without exposing myself or my associates. I waited for seventeen years, wondering if you might also inherit a thread of Lila's power."

"But you wanted him to marry me." My wrist slid an inch.

"When Murad suggested his solution—to marry you—I wasn't worried. I mean, you could still fall in love with a human out of wedlock, right?" she suggested slyly.

"The enchantment would find a way to kill you off. Murad thought he was being noble, saving the life of his true love's last surviving progeny. He hopes one day you will have enough magick to find Lila. He doesn't believe she's gone, my foolish King." Her face darkened and her lips pulled into a sneer.

"But then you had to make Murad fall for you. Knowing your marriage would be in name only was the only thing that kept you alive, stupid girl!"

"You're crazy! Murad doesn't love me like that!" I panted, barely able to manage my lips around speech as I fought the violent wind that pressed me hard against the unyielding wall.

"Liar! When I came upon you all in the labyrinth tonight and saw Murad stab Alaric, I knew he must have feelings for you. I didn't wait centuries just for some little gypsy trash to take him from me," she shrieked. I gritted my teeth and glared at the unhinged woman.

"That's racist! We are Romany," I shouted. She struck out with her Pagatio and a shard of wood cut my cheek open before impaling itself in my thigh. I screamed. This was not working. Anger did not seem to be sparking or fueling my magick.

My family tree gleamed. It would end with me. All of the names that came before me—their legacy would die. I imagined each one, all the way back to Lila. Women who lived too briefly, yet existed in order for me to be glued to this wall. It was all so wrong.

"Is there even a curse or was this all you?" Tess moved to the mural and caressed my ancestors' names with eerily affectionate strokes. The pressure lessoned on my limbs, and I wiggled my arms experimentally.

"Oh, the enchantment is real. Lila was the most powerful of us, followed by my brother. But he doesn't care about power or responsibility. No, he'd rather remain airborne most of the time. Do you want to know what I think? I think that sensitive Lila cursed *herself* with an Everwish. A wish of sacrifice and so intense it comes true for eternity. Cursed herself with her guilt and pain. She couldn't forgive herself for unleashing Murad on the world as a monster, and she made you all pay. An unintentional side effect of her own self-hatred. Although, I might have helped a few of you along. Your parents, for example. They deserved it with their sickening love-conquers-all attitude."

"You murdered my parents?" I managed. Tess lit up. She touched the tip of her nose and then pointed her finger at me with a wink.

"I sent wraiths to track Vivian down in San Francisco. Different from the ones circling this chapel, waiting for me to let them devour your flesh." I glanced at the darkened windows. Had it become night so soon?

"Your mom was the only one of any of you to show signs of real magick, and I realized what a danger she could become. She evaded my attempts for a while, but it wasn't enough to save her. You see, your parents were vulnerable once you were born."

Sick fury filled every cell in my body as I pushed and gathered energy near my heart.

"Did you know that Alaric saved you? He was too late for Lasho and Vivian, but he tore that car to pieces to extract you before it caught fire. Your mother had created a bubble around you, only able to protect *you* from the impact as they lay broken and bled out next to you. Did he tell you that? Oh. I see by your face that your crush has been holding secrets from you," she said in a sing-song, tsking voice. My stomach flip-flopped. Alaric had been there?

"I know how much you hate secrets. Come now, Stella. See things my way." Her smile was indifferent, her eyes cold. "You come across as so confident, but all you did back in the council tower was to cower beneath that table, allowing everyone else to fight for you. You're nothing but another weak mortal girl, the last one to be exterminated."

How had I ever thought her kind? She was a psychopath. Empathy and mercy were things she could never understand. *Mercy.* Bird-Taurus had shouted "Stone of Mercy" when we transferred. It made no sense. Mercy was an action, an idea. The only stone we shared knowledge of was the crystal he'd given me when in bird form. It was still in my pants pocket. I'd been keeping it close as good luck charm.

My hands were immobile at the wrist, but I could open and close my fingers. I visualized the lump in my right pocket, imagined the stone slipping free and landing against my right palm. The harder I thought about the small rock, the warmer my leg became. I let go of any other thought and envisioned the stone in my grasp. Like a magnet, it slipped from my pocket and into my hand. I felt it there, hot and pulsing. The heat crept up my arm. A new feeling slowly began to take the edge from my rage. I stared at the names on the wall.

All of those young women who never lived to see their daughters grow. All the daughters without mothers. Their lovers came from many countries and backgrounds, all contributing to the genetic melting pot that was me. What had Lila said back in her garden? Nature fixes a weakness by adapting. Was I stronger because of all the women and men who came after Lila and Sam? Mahari was pretty badass. I was the sum of them all, carrying me forward in time to this moment. The truth of it released something hard in my heart, compassion softening the walls of fear.

I was tired of fighting the current of wind that held me against my will. If this was my time then so be it. Nothing would change the past. The moment I replaced resistance with acceptance, the force of the air lessened, allowing my legs to move. My eyes popped open. That was it. My power lay not in fighting the elements but in uniting with them.

Things happened when I set my intentions to be one thing, unseparated. I sensed the air around me, *seeing* it as I never had before. Experimenting, I pulled the wind to me, imagining all the air in the room flowing into me and out the top of my head. I dropped to the floor instantly. *Whoa.*

Inhaling, I gathered energy from the air. Tess turned from the wall and saw me. Her arm began to rise, her Pagatio shining. "Stop," I shouted.

Tess paused mid-step. I blinked but she remained still, panic skittering across her face as her arm remained fixed in place. I'd actually made her stop. But for how long? If there was one lesson I learned from my vicious Romany cousins it was to give no quarter. The second you let someone bigger and stronger land the first punch, you were a goner. The trick was to attack when they least expected it and not let up until they called uncle and meant it. Anger returned, swift and bitter and I rushed her.

Seconds later, I sat astride Tess, using fistfuls of her hair to ram her skull against the stone floor while she scratched at my wrists. Even when she went limp, I couldn't stop. "I told you—*slam*—no—*slam*—more—*slam*—secrets—*slam slam*—" I was panting. How long did it take to knock out an immortal? With a low moan, Tess disappeared, and my knees hit the floor. My palms pressed the cold stones and I shook off thick strands of black silken hair from between my fingers. Blood pooled on the flagstones, but it wasn't mine. I spotted the stone on the floor where it must have rolled in my efforts to bash Tess's head into the floor. I scooped it up, feeling it grow hot.

I searched the chapel and spied Tess crouched upon a wooden beam beneath the arched ceiling. She shook her head as if to clear it. I stalked her, raising my voice.

"All of my ancestors had what you will never know, Tess. They found love. You will *never* know what that's like. All of your whining— my God, no wonder Murad only saw you in the friend zone. You are the most pitiful of creatures. Not only a woman obsessed with a man who will never return her feelings, you betrayed your *sister*. Your family. You deserve forever all alone." Even to my own ears, my words sounded like a curse. She screamed in rage and glanced towards the windows, at the shadows churning beyond the remaining panes of glass.

I couldn't allow her to release her demons. On instinct, my hand with the stone clenched into a fist over my head and I brought it down to my side. Tess toppled as if pushed by invisible hands. The roof also cracked, stone and dust falling to reveal hazy sky. Before she could rise, I gave into a new, prickling instinct, bringing air between my hands, pulling and shaping it into a spherical force. I kept winding the air until the tension was too difficult to hold. She got as far as her knees when I released the energy. Now it was Tess pinned to a wall. She clenched her Pagatio. I walked over and plucked it from her fingers. She glared with hatred, but the wind stole any words her lips tried to shape. Now it was me who smiled. I bared my teeth.

"Stella!" The doors to the chapel had been thrown wide. Murad and Alaric filled the doorway. As if released by an invisible wall, they rushed forward. Alaric appeared at my side in demon form, his wings shielding me from where Tess remained pinned to the wall. I was sweating now with the effort and losing sight of her caused me to release the air holding her in place. Her body hit the floor with a thud as Jing San, Amanda and Clara appeared behind Alaric.

"Are you hurt?" he growled.

"Just my heart," I said, ignoring the pain in my ribs and the dizziness from my head wound. His heated hands ran up and down my arms as he bent down to study my face. The fearsome creature that struck terror in the black hearts of demons with just the utterance of his name ran his nose along the bloody gash on my cheek, growling. His nearness tempted me to grab him and never let go. But this wasn't over.

I pushed gently until he gave in. Tess leaned against the wall before an immovable Murad. She reached out to touch his chest and he hissed in warning. Her hands dropped.

"I can explain, Murad. Stella's a traitor—" She actually pointed a finger in my direction. *No, she didn't.* I flicked my hand and Tess's lips sealed shut as air suctioned them together. *Wow. I could do that?* The others turned to me in unison. I shrugged. *What?*

"How did you do this, Stella?" murmured Jing.

"Tess knew Lila's daughter lived and she's behind the demons tonight. She killed my mom and dad," I responded in a dazed voice, ignoring the question I wasn't ready to answer.

"We heard. She will pay," Alaric responded, his obsidian gaze staking Tess where she remained mute against the wall. Murad's form had shifted, his fangs extended, and Tess dropped her eyes beneath his red glare.

"We could hear everything outside the door but couldn't enter until the enchantments that sealed this room collapsed," Murad explained in a raspy voice. That must have been when I reversed the air. Had I impacted her spells as well? Perhaps my knocking her insensible had caused her to drop them herself.

"We killed the wraiths outside. At least we know who's been commanding them," Clara shared, looking at her sister as if seeing her for the first time.

"We also saw the tail end of you banging the Sky Queen's head against the floor," Jing added.

"Is it true?" Murad asked Tess, his voice quietly murderous. I released the seal on her lips. Tess tried to rally. I saw she tried. The look of disgust on Murad's face undid her. She lowered her head until her thick black hair concealed most of her face. Murad placed a fist next to her head, the stone wall indented with the pressure he applied. He spoke with measured wrath.

"You will be put to death for your betrayals, Tess. I'll remove your head from your shoulders myself. How could you do this?" Murad's voice was guttural.

"Excuse me?" Amanda edged closer to them.

"Before you sentence her, Noble King, perhaps we could ask her about where Marcus might be? He's the sorcerer who killed Stella's cousin." I screamed at Amanda in my head. *Scarlet!* You don't ask a vampire at the end of his rope for favors. Unless you're me. And then you do whatever the heck you want and worry about consequences later. Her question was logical, though. We still didn't know where Marcus was and I wanted him brought to justice. Murad bowed his head, fist still pressed inches from Tess. He amended his threat.

"I can't trust myself in this moment to ask anything of you. But I'll have you tortured if necessary until you tell me everything your traitorous, black heart has done and who has helped you. And know this—I *will* marry Stella and she will rule by my side with no interference from you. The curse will be broken. You have failed."

"No," came a deep, snarling voice. Stunned, I looked up at Alaric. His eyes glowed as a blue flaming sword appeared in his claw-tipped hand.

"She is never going to be your wife. All our lives I have given you the best of me but no longer. Stella is mine." Incredibly, he seemed to grow even larger, moving so that he shielded me from Murad with his wings. Their soft downy feathers drifted across my cheek before he thrust me back even further behind him. Jing moved gracefully to Alaric's side, her sword pointed downward, but ready.

"What are you saying? You want the curse to take her?" Murad's tone was astonished.

"I won't let it. She loves me and—I love her," he said. I staggered towards him. Clara put her arm around my waist and dragged me backwards with iron strength.

"That's the damn problem! That kind of love has led fifteen women and innocents to their deaths! How can you make the same mistakes?" Murad shouted.

Alaric stilled with a fury that made my skin prickle with danger. "You doubt me, brother? I'm also immortal and can keep her safe. You aren't the only marriage option."

Tess used their discussion, and distracted attention, to edge away. Clara moved to block her exit and Jing shadowed her with a raised sword so that Tess was boxed between them.

"Stop," I muttered. No one seemed to hear me, so I pushed past Alaric and stepped between the two brothers. The air was charged with violence, but I repeated myself.

"I won't marry either of you. I'm not even eighteen year's old yet for cripes sake," I yelled. Murad's eyebrows rose into his hairline. Alaric just glared down at me bullishly. I allowed myself a moment to admire just how scary he looked before shaking my head.

"The curse is mine to figure out. No one else. I appreciate the offers, but they aren't necessary," I insisted. A piece of paper was not going to matter when I had true love at my side. Maybe one day that would change, but for now I was done with good intentions and a shielded life. They wanted me to grow old, but I wanted to live. Besides, Alaric's drive to protect me was unfair. I wouldn't be a victim he felt compelled to rescue by tying his life to mine.

I was not a fragile creature and I was not Lila. My life was my own, and I was about to live it on my own terms. No matter how long or short that would be.

Chapter 32
The World

Stella

T he midnight-blue ball gown I wore was hands down the most daring piece of clothing I'd ever worn. The bateau bodice was a tight corset with cream-colored cutouts that gave the illusion of skin. It molded my waist into a tulle and silk skirt that sparkled with tiny crystals I suspected were diamonds. Mira kept trying to touch them, but Clara slapped her hands away. I smirked behind Clara's back at Mira, happy to see there was someone besides Mahari that she feared. She flipped me off. Ah, family.

I wasn't comfortable with the top of my breasts on full display, but everyone else seemed to love it. Amanda smiled through happy tears and Clara circled her finger for me to turn. I sighed and turned, showing them my semi-bare back. I turned once more, swishing the long skirt behind me and she smiled in approval before a frown knit her forehead.

"Stella, are you wearing sneakers?" Clara asked, a chilled warning in her question.

"Yep."

"What happened to the heels I put out for this dress?"

"I have no idea." Probably still under my bed where I'd tossed them.

"I thought we agreed on a compromise, Stella. You would wear heels as long as we kept them under two inches. Those were kitten heels, Stella!"

"This *is* a compromise. If it were up to me, I'd go barefoot," I grumbled.

"I think we need gloves. Long, silk gloves to the elbow," Marion interrupted.

"Hmm. She refused jewelry, so gloves might be the perfect accessory. I have a pair that would work," Clara conceded after a beat. She disappeared and reappeared with a pair of gloves that matched the deep blue of my dress. They were simple and perfect. She winked, handing them to me. We'd both been learning when to pick our battles. She'd won the skirmish over my hair. Tiny braids with more sparkling stones were woven into my wavy hair, pulling it away from my face to fall heavily down my back.

We stood in the Hall of Mirrors of Versailles; the location Murad had rented for the Samhain Ball. Hundreds of creatures supposedly waited for us outside in the gardens, but the two most important were waiting for me just beyond the doors.

"Here, Bird," I called. My uncle swooped down in his arctic tern form and settled on my bare shoulder. He nipped my ear with his beak and I laughed.

"Kidding! I mean Taurus."

Amanda knocked and the triple doors were pulled open by men in black formal wear, exposing us to crowds on the veranda and below in the gardens. Once again, I was standing at the top of a grand party, looking down—but things were different now. I held my head high. Let them whisper about the imposter and look their fill. Murad had announced that we'd reconsidered our engagement but remained committed friends, whatever that meant.

Alaric waited at the bottom of the stairs in his human form. Clara had closed off his aura in a complicated spell. As almost no one remembered him as human, it was his way of being with me on this night without revealing our relationship. He worried over his enemies marking me for retribution. I noted several people eye him curiously. Even in human form, he commanded the attention of everyone near him and my heart skipped a beat or two. Next to him stood Sam, my great, great, great.... well, just great-grandfather. Sam still didn't know that Lila was alive, and we were keeping it that way, despite how guilty in made me feel. Murad had made him a guest tonight in an unprecedented move that no one questioned as Bromely had cast an "inconspicuous spell" on him to prevent the Primati from remembering him.

I kept my chin up as I glided down the steps with my friends and family. The gardens and fountains were magnificent. Lanterns and subtle lighting gave the gathering a fairytale ambiance. Halfway down, Murad appeared. He offered his arm and I accepted it with a smile he returned indulgently.

"You look stunning. No more secreting you away, huh?" he asked, and I could tell by his wistful tone that he would whisk me away to his secret lair again if I but asked for it. I pulled my arm from his and clasped my hands together.

"Nope. I'm not hiding anymore," I said firmly. He chuckled.

"How do you like Versailles? There is a certain irony that it was once the palace of the Sun King."

"Ah. And now the King of Primati?"

"As lovers and enemies, neither dark nor light are complete without the other. Speaking of—there are many creatures here tonight. It's best not to look anyone unknown in the eyes tonight." I'd had similar warnings from Clara and Amanda. They needn't worry. I was only interested in hanging with the monsters I knew.

We walked down the remaining steps, and Alaric immediately moved to intercept Murad, who looked daggers at him jokingly. At least I think he was kidding. Alaric brushed his hand possessively where Murad had touched my arm. I sighed and stepped closer to his side, seeking to calm the snarl I sensed rising in his chest. It worked. Craning my neck, I soaked in his scent and nearness.

Sam struck his walking stick on the step below the Primati King, making Murad pause. I stifled a smirk. My grandfather and Murad had been treating one another with aloof respect, but there was no friendship between them. Murad always seemed to look at the air above Sam's head, while Sam refused to address him directly. Still, Sam had always had the gift of accepting the present moment for what it was. He leaned forward and kissed my cheek, ignoring Alaric, who kept long fingers wrapped around my waist.

"My eyes are failing, Stella—and I'm about ready for bed—but you look wonderful, dear. Happy eighteenth birthday." Love swamped me as I gave Sam a hug. My movement dislodged Taurus, who leapt skyward in graceful flight. Sam's bones seemed more prominent, fragile, and I breathed in his scent of pipe tobacco.

"Did I ever tell you how you got your name? Ms. Mahari named you. When she told me where to find you, she suggested we name you Stella because it means Star, and the Star tarot meant hope," he said. I released him, surprised. He'd never once told me that Mahari told him where to find me. But he'd been forgetful for a number of years now.

"Thank you, Sam. Thank you for telling me that. I'm so glad you came. I know this crowd isn't really your thing." This was an understatement but he'd insisted on not missing my birthday. "Clara is going to transfer you home as soon as you're ready to rest." I said, still reeling from the unexpected revelation about Mahari.

"That's right," Clara chimed in, encircling Sam's arm with both of hers. "It's you and me, Sam." He flushed and muttered beneath his breath while she patted his arm.

Taurus hadn't gone far. He swooped low and circled to land on another woman. Gasps and excited whispers could be heard as those closest to her bowed low.

Ela approached with a brilliant smile, Taurus on her shoulder. She appeared slightly older than I'd last seen her, bright silver fanning from her temples. She was majestic and the air throbbed with a heady energy as she approached. Her dress was something from a dream, the skirt made of green moss studded with tiny purple blossoms. Her waist was wrapped tightly in autumn leaves and shavings of birch bark while her bodice appeared made of rose petals. The scent of lavender heralded her arrival.

"Stella, may I introduce you to the Goddess Danu?" Murad bowed with the introduction. Ela scowled at him.

"I still don't like you, boy." she said, dismissing him. She lifted a hand to caress Taurus's snowy breast. I was undone with the revelation, and Ela stretched a finger beneath my chin to close my jaw. There were so many questions buzzing in my brain, starting with Lila. She smiled knowingly and nodded.

"I don't need an introduction. I know Stella well," she said in an over-loud voice. "It's a shame your magick is so faint, but I came to wish you a very happy birthday, my dear." Whispers swept around us in a river of sound. Her eyes twinkled and I smiled back, understanding she had just publicly acknowledged me while making it clear I was no threat. She was making it known to all the bad and uglies that I was a friend of someone powerful indeed.

"You look lovely, child."

"And you look glorious. How is Lila tonight?" I whispered.

"Oh, she's the same. But I think that might change in the future. I hope you will still come visit us?" She quirked an eyebrow. My nod was sincere. Tess was still not talking and there were discussions of putting her in bedrock "for a hundred years to soften her tongue." She refused to tell us anything about the druids, and Thomas hadn't tried to contact Amanda or me. Murad promised to tell me more about the night Lila's family was attacked and why he was so sure the druids were behind it— one day. I intended to press the issue and make him see reason, if for no other purpose than to save Thomas and Carol from his hounding.

"Look how you shine. Providence may be your savior yet." Ela touched my cheek and walked away, melting into the crowd, and Alaric used the excitement of her passing to tug my hand until I followed him across the lawn.

He led us towards an open black carriage waiting on a gravel path. I spied similar carriages tasked with carrying revelers back and forth to the dance area set deep within the trees. Our driver soothed the horses and opened the carriage door. It gave me more time to look my fill of the man at my side, his tuxedo and snowy cravat in perfect form. I swallowed hard at his perfection. He lifted me into the carriage where we settled against dark leather.

"You're playing with your lips again. Aren't you happy?" he asked, pulling me against his shoulder until I snuggled into his side. I breathed in his scent and never wanted to leave.

"Hmm," I murmured. The driver flicked his reins with a click of his tongue and the horses pulled us down the shadowy lane that meandered through the enormous garden.

"Sam's new apartment is just below Jing San's. I have a helipad and a private plane on standby, so Sam can visit you anytime in New York." Alaric was trying to make this easier for us. Sam and I still hadn't had "the" conversation yet. The one where we talked about magick and his past. We were both a little tender right now and taking our time easing into a new reality. One where people could travel by trees and his true love still lived.

"Remember, I'm only in New York for another month. I promised Sam I would come home to finish out my last year of high school."

"Then I will also be spending the year in Oregon."

"Don't you have work to do? Mayhem to wrangle? Wraiths to squish?" I teased. He tugged a strand of my hair.

"I'm actually handing over some of that work to Murad. It's high time he assumed his fair share of wraith squishing," he said.

"Alaric—I feel guilty. You're giving up something important to follow me. I'm hardly worth ignoring your responsibilities. Or having people whisper about you and the "star girl" you are spending so much time with. No one likes a Yoko," I said quietly, looking up at the shivering cypress treetops. When the carriage moved into the darkest part of the path, he took advantage of the deep shadows to pull me onto his lap.

"You think I look at you as some celestial consolation prize?"

"Albatross," I corrected. He exhaled sharply and pressed his forehead to mine.

"Stella. When I see you, I see rainbows within clouds."

I pulled a face. "Rainbows?" He leaned back; his fathomless eyes locked on mine.

"A story from religious texts. A promise of a future. You are mine. Your existence is improbable proof that the Creator has not forsaken me. Your love is a miracle. It's not just that. You are part of me now. Your voice is sweeter to me than any other. Your touch—." I smothered his husky explanation with my lips. He groaned against me and I wanted to sink beneath his skin. One of the horses neighed and I dragged myself away to marvel at the vow within Alaric's burning gaze.

"Well," I whispered. I'd just wanted to hear him tell me he loved me again.

"Well." With a warm hand at my nape, he pulled me closer. I trembled in anticipation.

"Happy Birthday, darling," he whispered, and then he pressed his lips to mine, giving me my wish. When our carriage stopped before the large clearing, my toes tapped to the music and Alaric swung me to the ground. He led us to the dance floor and people parted before his path without hesitation. I ignored the murmurings around us as Alaric led us to its center. When he took me into his arms, everyone else faded.

"I think blue is your color, *petite etoile.*"

Alaric guided me with elegant mastery into arcs around the floor. I laughed and tipped my head back on a dip and a crescendo of applause followed our movements. It felt greedy that he would be a good dancer on top of his many other attributes. But I wouldn't complain. A long, gilded mirror behind the orchestra captured my attention and I held my breath each time I caught our reflection. My dress shimmered beneath the lights as my skirt swirled around Alaric's legs, and my hair sparkled with its tiny diamonds. We were yin and yang. We were magick.

As we circled the floor, I recognized a few friendly faces, including Amanda's parents, as well as the unsmiling countenance of Murad from the sidelines as he watched. Only the gleaming, spiteful eyes of Daria Demir interrupted my happiness, but when I tried to find her on our next pass, she'd disappeared into the crowd.

* * *

I will forever remember the feel of twirling beneath the moon in a dance with Alaric. Yet long after the ball, our early morning breakfast and quiet whispers alone, it was my dreams that night that stayed with me.

The woman of my past nightmares stood outside on a wooden porch in the night. As I watched, rain began to fall from a black sky. A nearby lantern illuminated the utter darkness enough to see that she wore a simple blouse and long skirt. The sadness etched upon her face was so visceral I felt my heart break. As the rain drummed against the ground, she walked from the shelter of the porch with her face upturned to the downpour. The cabin door opened and a man ran out in the rain after her.

"Lila! Come inside before you catch your death of cold," Sam begged her.

The woman cried; her face crumbled with sadness.

"I can't, Samuel."

"Can't what? Please come inside," Sam pleaded. I blinked at seeing him with an unbowed back and dark hair and I ate up the vision of his beloved face. He leaned over her with concern.

"I can't love you like you need me to. I love you with a cup half full," she cried.

He pulled her to him in an embrace, shushing her.

"It's enough. I will love you enough for us both."

She pulled away roughly and he recoiled in surprise.

"You don't know your own worth husband. I'm broken!"

"Then I will heal you. I am a patient man, Lila," he told her as rain wet his hair and streamed down his pleading countenance. She cupped his face sadly. He turned to kiss her hand and then let her go.

"I'll get you a blanket," he promised, as he ran back up the steps and into the log cabin.

I turned back to find the young Lila look at me with deep anguish.

It was the first time in my dreams that she seemed to notice me.

"I'm not worthy. I killed him. I took away everything he loved. He saved me in every way. Gave me everything and I killed them," she told me.

I took her by the shoulders, surprised when I actually felt substance beneath my hands.

"Listen to me, Lila. Sam forgave you. Gracie and Sam lived—and he forgives you." Her brow crinkled with confusion and then she angrily tore away. She walked backwards as lightning struck a nearby tree. "Beware of the sorcerer. He is not who he seems," she cried.

The cabin door opened to reveal Sam, a dry blanket within his grasp and Lila ran into the night. I woke from the dream sobbing. Not pretty little tears but gut-wrenching sobs that only come from a shattered soul. What had she meant about the sorcerer?

I wasn't sure how we were connected like this, but I knew I couldn't leave her alone in her personal hell. One way or another I would fight to bring her back to the light. Just as I would fight to stay with Alaric.

"Stella," he shushed me, pulling me into his arms. I burrowed beneath his shirt until my arm wrapped around the naked skin of his waist. Only with contact did the dream recede. He stroked my hair as the shudders faded.

"It's okay, Stella. I love you and I'm here."

"I love you, too. Always." And I meant it. I was making up a new rule. *Once you find the people you love, hold on.* I would find a way to make this last, but if it didn't, if the curse took my life, always could live in a single glance. He kissed me tenderly and the nightmare faded.

Chapter 33
The Wish

Alaric

———⟋⟍———

The stone path was cold beneath my bare feet as I paced through the penthouse garden, coming to a stop as I searched the night sky in vain for a single star. The city's electric lights obscured any sign of the heavens. For the first time, I allowed myself to consider the story Murad told me as a child. That my mother was there, taken by the heavens to shine above. An honor, he'd said. It'd always hurt and enraged me to think how unfair it was that she was *there*, unending, and so far from me. I let down my guard and squinted upwards, surprised now to discover the idea of my mother being ever present was...comforting.

The streets below bustled in nighttime splendor, and I dragged in a deep breath. Stella slept soundly inside and there was peace in knowing that the nightmares had left her for the evening. My palm met the bare skin of my chest as I wondered at the sweet ache I felt there, knowing she was physically safe and nearby. I dug the sapphire ring from my jeans pocket. It sparkled, just like Stella's eyes. She was extraordinary, adapting to so many new experiences with backbone and grace. And yet doubt gnawed. I'd lived for centuries while she was still finding herself. Stella was so sure we were meant to be together forever, yet what did someone so young know of forever?

There was only now. I'd waited over 500 years for her. She was mine and I would move heaven and hell to keep her safe—even from me. We would break the enchantment together. Returning the ring to my pocket, I perused the night sky once more, giving a prayer of thanks to have this chance in time to be with her. Wind ruffled my hair and I moved towards the penthouse, already missing her.

Lila   Charles Samuel Avery, 1711, England

Hope Avery 1747 1755

Grace Avery 1745 1762

Waya (Cherokee) Georgia US

John Walker, England   **Mary Avery 1762 1782**

Abraham Hawkins, PA, US   **Rachel Walker 1782 1800**

William O'Reilly, England

Mary Hawkins 1800 1817

George Hansen, Germany   **Jane O'Reilly 1817 1835**

Elizabeth (Betsy) 1835 1853   Aiden Banks, Scotland

Jack LaCroix, France   **Alice Banks 1853 1870**

Emily LaCroix 1870 1980   Michael Westcott, NY, US

Benjamin Clark, CT, US   **Charlotte Westcott 1890 1907**

Magnolia Westcott 1907 1926   Conner McGuire, NY, US

Angel Martinez, Valencia, Spain   **Rose McGuire 1926 1943**

Caroline Campbell 1943 1962   Elijah Schmidt, PA, US

Ethan Johnson, KS, US   **Hyacinth Schmidt 1962 1980**

Vivian Johnson 1980 2000   Lasho Pankova, CA, US

Stella Avery 2000

About the Author

Amelia resides in the Pacific Northwest with her husband, son and fur-baby. She can be found writing about imaginary friends, cheering on the sidelines, reading, taking long walks in the woods, visiting bookstores and consuming as much coffee as humanly possible. She loves rainy days and connecting with other writers and readers. You can connect with Amelia in the following ways:

Twitter: @oz_amelia
Instagram: @oz.amelia
Author Website: ameliaozcom.wordpress.com

If you enjoyed this book, please consider leaving a review on Amazon or wherever you purchased this book. Authors depend upon their readers to help them spread the word. Thank you for reading!

Acknowledgements

This novel would not exist without the love and support of my husband and son, who miraculously believe in me and never complain about take-out meals and conversations about imaginary friends. I'm thankful for my dad, who inspired my love of storytelling, and my mom, who indulged my love of reading. My grandma for making sure we knew our roots and who is my oak tree. My nieces for inspiring me to write a novel they might want to read one day. I'm forever grateful to my writer friends, champions and beta readers, particularly JoAnn the Magnificent, Hillary Hun-Bun, Michelle who lives by a river, K.M. Allan, Julia Blake, Rebecca Carpenter and Becky & James at Platform House Publishing for the amazing cover design and interior formatting, Maria and Sherry. Your support and encouragement mean everything. I feel so blessed.

Special Note:
The painting that Stella and Murad viewed was called The Woods in Twilight by William Carter. This fictitious painting was inspired by my favorite painting, *The Forest in Winter at Sunset*, a mid-19th century oil painting by Théodore Rousseau that currently resides in the Metropolitan Museum of Art in NYC. If you are ever fortunate enough to view it (it does move around) I hope you will see its special magick for yourself.

CPSIA information can be obtained
at www.ICGtesting.com
Printed in the USA
BVHW082340230920
589459BV00006B/720